ALL THE FORGOTTEN THINGS

Chronicles of Lim: Book Two

L.M. Dodds

For Ellie and Yas.
I wish you both had seven lives.

1

TREVESTEN, 7225

The jungle enveloped us like a sodden coat. We couldn't tell where our sweat stopped and the air began. At every stream, we stopped to refill our canteens and dunk ourselves in the cool water. Other than our shoes, there was no point in removing our clothing to bathe or taking Connery up on his offer to dry us afterward.

The languid air, suffocating with the scent of so many flowers, had soaked through everything from the moment we'd stepped into the lush green trees. Giant insects with iridescent wings swirled around our heads, drawn by the smell of our blood.

I'd been to Solbaina several times to retrieve various ingredients and to study the magic. The jungle, which lived in the southwestern tip of Trevesten, had so much power that was yet untapped. It writhed among the vines and flowers, dancing around us. The magic here was not truly wild, it was tied to the plants, animals, the ever-present insects. But it was constantly changing, which was why I believed our best chance to portal to Sverresen lay within.

Brigid and Elwin forged ahead, swords at the ready, their eyes alight with wonder. They'd been with me on a few trips out here, but had never been so deep inside. Connery walked next to me and Solvan hung back, occasionally stopping to place his hand against a tree or rock, light flaring from his fingertips as he left a magical signature for us to follow on our way back home. He casually sang under his breath. Foolish tavern songs we all knew mixed in with some bawdy sea shanties we'd belted out during long days on the water.

He'd just begun the song about the one-eyed dragon named Clyde when Connery and I had to stop briefly to allow a massive yellow snake to meander across the path, its tongue briefly darting out to taste us on the air.

"How can it possibly detect us among the flowers—it's overwhelming," Connery asked, his bright eyes watching the snake's winding body. "Lovely, but overwhelming."

"It's not just tasting us, it's eating us." I grinned at his look of incredulity. "It can detect minuscule variations in scent and flavor, and for those that it likes, it has the power to digest the nutrients from our sweat in the air. And now it could easily pick both of us out of a crowd, should it want another bite." I snapped my teeth playfully at him.

Connery gave me the look he'd given me more and more lately. It was a mixture of interest, almost awe, and something that made my blood heat. He'd been with us for almost three years now and, despite his proper upbringing, seemed to slot into our group like he'd always been there. Of course, I was becoming more biased with every passing day. He'd given his blood and power to the cause, enabling us to finally complete the device to reach Sverresen, while also storing some of his magic in a few of the daranas we had brought.

Some of the magic I'd purchased for the trip I'd sold already, for a hefty profit, of course. Each darana now held a little of all the most useful abilities. If we brought them back full of wild magic to sell, we could retire. Considering that we all had over two hundred years left, that was saying something.

"That's why it can get so big," I said, pretending I hadn't seen his look. "No fangs, so nothing runs away from it. They don't even notice."

He gave me a sly smile while looking pointedly at my neck. "Or maybe some people enjoy giving it a little nibble."

If my skin hadn't already been flushed with heat, he definitely would have seen the blush creeping up my cheeks. As it was, I just rolled my eyes at him. "Don't make me melt you."

We had another eight hours of hiking ahead of us before we'd get to the place we'd make camp. In the morning, there'd be another two to three hours to get to our final destination, a cave I had calculated to be the place best suited to use the device. By this time tomorrow, we would be in Sverresen.

Brigid and Elwin joined in the singing,
"Oh, Clyde, he sat upon his horde
late into the night,
And dreamed of stealing a pretty star,
her glittering so bright.
He had a dream. He hatched a scheme,
And upon first light,
to us it looked like folly, but to him it seemed alright."

We joined in as well and passed the rest of the hike with relative ease, joking and telling stories that distracted us all from the incredible risk we were taking.

We set up camp in a clearing near a sparkling waterfall. The water swirled, bluish-green magic bursting from every drop. I'd tested it repeatedly, but it didn't seem to affect us. Whatever power it possessed must be reserved for the animals and plants here in the jungle. Probably a built-in defense mechanism to keep criminals like myself from storing and selling it. I'd produced a fire to ward off the animals, and we sat now, finishing the remains of our dinner.

"No," Brigid said as she methodically unpacked the contents of her pack. "That merchant from Lilingow was the worst by far."

Elwin 'hmmed' in agreement as he folded his tall body to crawl into their tent. "Grotesque specimen of a man."

"Certainly the least intelligent, if not the worst." Connery shook his head as he stretched his legs out in front of him. "Who brags about beating their assistant?"

"Someone asking to be an easy mark," Brigid replied. She readjusted the thin band of material she used to keep her curly hair off her face. Little strands of it still escaped, sticking to her dewy bronze skin.

"They're all easy," Solvan said, his eyes closed, head tipped back, a lazy smile on his face.

I chuckled under my breath. We'd never stolen from someone who couldn't afford it, but the Lilingow merchant had been a real piece of work. All of us felt a little better at making off with not only his valuables but also relieving him of his assistant, who was now spending a much more enjoyable life not being a blowhard's errand boy.

Connery had been with us for a year at that time. At first, he'd only venture out at night to ensure he had the best chance of keeping his whereabouts secret. By then we'd also figured out why he was using hush. It had taken that long for him to master the correct dose to block Sabine's ability to communicate with him mind-to-mind without making his own thoughts muted as well. I knew he'd packed a significant store of the green dust in his pack.

He assumed she would understand he was blocking her purposefully and respect his decision. I had my doubts. The idea of losing him, even as a friend, was unthinkable. If I had a claim to him as strong as a mating bond, nothing would make me give it up. But other than routine patrols, we'd had no run-ins with Sabine or her people.

I wasn't sure whether it got harder or easier for mates when they were separated, but if it had become harder, Connery hadn't mentioned it, hadn't mentioned her, in over a year. Sometimes, I caught him though. His eyes would frost over, he'd lose track of the conversation, like a memory was forcibly inserting itself in his mind. A sharp cut of pain or a storm of anger would pierce his expression.

Other times, the ones increasingly more painful for me, it was a look of love. His face would relax in a way that was nearly foreign to me, a deep contentment smoothing his features. In those times, I would get up and walk away, pretend that I hadn't seen.

It was late now, but still warm. One by one, everyone had gone to bed except for me. I'd agreed to take first watch. Not that anything had ever attacked me in the jungle, but it seemed wise all the same. My eyes found a sliver of stars through the endless leaves. Were they laughing at us, thinking us all as naïve as Clyde? That wasn't really fair to Clyde, of course, but the question remained, would we be fools or heroes?

Connery had shocked us all when he'd declared he was going with us to Sverresen. While I'd let myself dream a little, I think all of us assumed he'd punish Sabine for a few years but eventually make his way back. Sverresen was a risk, a calculated one, but still a risk. He could lose her forever.

I remembered being dumbfounded when he'd casually asked why we had not included his pack when allocating our supplies. His head had been bent over our lists, our plans, and he hadn't noticed the shared look of confusion.

"You want to go? With us?" I said, holding my breath.

Connery's head snapped up, his sea-blue eyes rounded in surprise. He took a step back upon seeing our raised eyebrows or, in Solvan's case, a deep frown.

"I was under the distinct impression that I had contributed to this job." He crossed his arms over his chest and narrowed his eyes. "Were you planning on stabbing me in the back so soon?"

"No...that's not it." I exhaled. "We didn't realize you'd want to go." I looked around at the others for confirmation.

"What she's too polite to say is that we thought you'd tuck tail and run back to the palace. Or hide out here while we did the real work," Solvan drawled. Beside him, Elwin chuckled. Brigid drummed her sharp nails on the table, examining Connery for weakness.

Elwin, who was closest to him, slapped a hand over his shoulder. "No shame in it. We're not doing a light prison break or something. This is a risky job." Elwin only had two inches on Connery but somehow made it seem as if he was looking down on him in a benevolent but patronizing way. I was almost certain he was goading Connery, testing his resolve. I rolled my eyes. We'd never broken anyone out of prison.

"We'd still give you your cut, of course." I did my own testing. Next to me, Solvan choked, and I elbowed him. "We're not cutting you out, but I think we all honestly thought you wouldn't want to come."

Brigid, who had remained quiet during this exchange, tipped her head to the side thoughtfully. "I don't think you'll find a hush dealer in Sverre-sen. Are you prepared for that?"

The question underneath it hung in the air. Was he really prepared to leave Sabine without the use of his crutch? Part of me wondered whether I was prepared for him to be without it as well. How many more of those moments would I have to pretend not to see?

I startled out of the memory when I heard Connery lay down beside me. He propped himself up on his elbows, stretching out his long legs. My smile faltered when I caught the solemn look on his face.

"Something wrong?" My voice was low, careful not to wake the others as I rolled onto my side to face him.

Connery stared at the fire, his voice contemplative. "Are you nervous?"

"A little. But we've done a lot of risky things for less. You know how the fae get bored as they get old," I joked.

Connery huffed a laugh. "None of you are that old."

"Please, stop, you'll make me blush," I deadpanned. I pushed his shoulder with my hand and he caught it, holding it in his as he rolled to face me. That serious look was back again.

"I need to tell you something. I should have told you a long time ago, but when we first met, I didn't really care and then the years went by and I thought it wouldn't matter." He blew out a breath and his eyes landed on my hand, where his thumbs brushed against my skin. "I," he paused, weighing his words, "I don't think it will matter, but—" He dropped my hand and ran a hand down the side of his face.

He was so close to me. I could smell the cold stream water in his hair. I leaned toward him slightly, apprehension pooling in my stomach even as my heart began beating wildly in my chest. "What is it?"

His eyes dipped to my mouth. When his eyes met mine again, he spoke, "I'm only half royal. My blood is only half royal. My mother met her mate on a trip overseas. That's why my father—stepfather really — got exiled to Eloisha. He tried to attack my mother when he found out about their affair. She was... not impressed by the attempt."

I kept my eyes on him, refusing to let him see any reaction but the one I'd prepared for this moment, knowing that he'd tell me before we left but not knowing when. He'd certainly cut it close, but I still won the bet. The others were all convinced he'd wait until we got there. Every day that went by and he didn't tell me gave me more confidence. Like he was waiting until we definitely couldn't get rid of him... or he couldn't back out.

"I know."

His eyes flew open, and he leaned back. "What? How?"

A small alarm was ringing somewhere in my head and I reminded myself that I'd prepared for this. "I tested your blood. I knew we needed royal blood. We had to be sure we got the real thing."

"Do the others know?" His face had gone hard. It was an expression I hadn't seen in a very long time, not since we first started working together when he trusted none of us and shared next to nothing about himself.

"Yes." I sat up and crossed my arms across my chest. "Of course, they needed to know there was a variable in our plan."

He stood quickly with the speed of a fae readying to fight. "I'm a variable, am I now? Some*thing* you just discuss and deal with?"

Bracelets of fire twisted up my arms, but my tone was sharp and cold. "You're upset that we didn't demand you explain yourself to us before you were ready? Or you're mad I didn't risk this entire job and my crew to save your pride?"

He stared at me for a beat before the fight drained out of him. His face relaxed, and he rubbed his hand down the side of it again, exhaling his frustration. "No, obviously not. I'm so sorry, Asra, that's not about... you did the right thing."

My hands fell to my sides, but my guard was still up. We were all aware that Connery had issues with trust, and I wondered once again how Sabine could have been so careless with their bond. He held out his hand. I hesitated, but took it, and he lifted me up and pulled me close.

I had to tilt my head to look up at him, his eyes full of apology and something that made me wonderfully afraid. It was as if I was about to fall, but instead of backing away, I was standing on the edge and luxuriating in the anticipation of smashing into a thousand pieces. I wanted to freeze this moment in time so there was nothing before or after to ruin it.

"I sometimes wonder if it was more than luck that I ended up in Oderon." His thumb began brushing small circles against my skin.

"Bad luck, considering how well you were doing at cards," I said with a sly smile. My emotions were rapidly repositioning themselves in case the exchange went a different way. We'd worked together so long, and even though I wasn't blind, I knew when a male showed interest, his affection was still complicated. The hush was there, but now barely noticeable in his eyes. Or maybe I'd just stopped noticing it. Only our hands were touching, but every part of me was alight with the feeling of him.

He didn't smile as he leaned down and his lips came within an inch of mine. "I don't think so," He murmured, his breath warm on my face, his other hand sliding up to rest on my hip, leaving a trail of heat in its wake. "I think there was an excellent reason I ended up underneath you, even if you did have a knife to my throat."

My breath caught and I let my fingers run up his chest, pushing up onto my toes just a little. "Well, maybe you can play your cards better this time..."

He smiled and pressed his lips to mine, the fire beside us crackling to new life.

2

LASHIA, 2208 PW, THE NEXT DAY

We found a small but serviceable structure among the ruins to sleep in. The floors had rotted through and it leaned listlessly to the right, but there were four walls and a roof. The villagers had given us woven mats to layer on the floor under our things and a wax candle I lit, cringing at the minor effort it took to do so, and put into a metal cup.

Exhaustion weighed on us all.

After that first little girl, there were more people to heal. Solvan had given the initial bit of healing power to a young mother. We'd divide the rest among the others tomorrow. As we already shared power, it didn't make sense to take it all ourselves, especially if we were planning to leave.

If we could find a way out.

We worked with her all day long while she healed injuries from falls and infections. The villagers drank from a stream, and although they understood the water needed to be boiled before drinking, it wasn't always possible with the constantly changing weather. Laura, our unofficial guide, told us sometimes hurricanes kept them holed up in their homes for weeks.

Everything was damp. A storm came up in the afternoon, and Connery created an air bubble around the settlement. Sheltering us all long enough that I could dry the ground, wood, and clothes before moving things inside.

Most of the villagers lived inside the mountain. They'd selected the location well. There were hundreds of caves, protected from the elements but lacking in light and ventilation. Others lived in ramshackle structures like the one we stood in now.

"Tomorrow, we can go hunting. Maybe we can find some more animals for them to raise," Solvan said from his position on the floor. He sat cross-legged on his sleeping bag, drinking the tea I'd made for us all.

Brigid preferred to stretch in her jaguar form. Her sleek coat gleamed in the firelight. "I'll go fishing."

Elwin was studiously writing everything down. He'd noted everyone's names, the power we'd given out, and managed to get some semblance of a timeline figured out. It sounded like the terrifying storms Laura had told us about happened over two thousand years ago. If what happened this afternoon was normal, I couldn't imagine what it had been like then.

"We can give them some power to dig better cold storage." Solvan tapped Elwin's notebook so he would add it.

"The two of us can dry or smoke whatever we don't eat fresh," I said to Connery, even though my mind was elsewhere. I was itching to take out the kunli and go over my specifications. To look at every ingredient and figure out what went wrong so we could get out of here as quickly as possible. I pulled out my notebooks and motioned for Solvan to hand me the device. The magic had all bled, and now it looked more like a child's toy and not a powerful object that took years to make.

"Want me to walk you through the checklist?" Brigid offered helpfully, referring to the extensive list of magical components I'd used to create it. I sighed in resignation, pulling it out and handing it to her.

"Perhaps this place, because it has no magic, acts as a barrier?" Elwin suggested, writing his theory down.

"Kysalt and Tulo have easily accessible portals to Malan. So we should consider, if it looks easier, trying to get there as well," I mused.

"How are all of you this calm?" Connery said irritably. He was rifling through his bag and I didn't think any of us were in any doubt as to what he was looking for. "Aren't you angry? Upset? Scared?"

"I am upset," I snapped. "That's why I want to focus on fixing this stupid thing." I held up the kunli, which mocked me by losing another piece. I grabbed a bag and shoved the pieces inside, afraid of losing a single sliver.

"Whoa." Elwin held up his hands. "I don't think any of us are happy about this, but we've been in some shitty situations before and done alright. Day one is not the time for panic."

"Oh, and what day shall I schedule for panic?" Connery asked, pulling the packet of hush out and sprinkling it on his tongue. It was a sign of his agitation. We all knew, of course, but he normally never did it in front of us.

"You knew what you signed up for, shippie," Solvan said. His mist-gray eyes narrowed in annoyance. "Now is a little late to tell us you didn't think it through."

"Me? I'm not the one in charge here." Connery rounded on Solvan.

Brigid let out a low growl. Solvan's throwing star instantly appeared in his hand.

"You might want to take a little break, Con. Maybe sleep on it before you say something you'll regret." Elwin's tone was deceptively lazy. But the darkness in his eyes was usually more than enough to convince someone to back off.

Connery turned slowly and his eyes found mine. The same eyes that were filled with heat and tenderness less than twenty-four hours ago.

"Take a walk with me." I stood up and walked through the thin material that served as our door. A few moments later, Connery's footsteps sounded behind me.

We walked for a while, far away from the others. When I reached a copse of trees, I turned to him.

"Spit it out."

The walk seemed to have worked, or maybe it was the hush. He looked calmer.

"I'm sorry. But you know why it didn't work. And unless there are some other royals around here, we are fucked."

"You don't know that." I crossed my arms. "And even if that's the reason it broke, that doesn't mean we can't get home. It's a different journey."

Connery paced. It wasn't frantic. He took measured steps, back and forth, thinking. It was unnerving. Finally, he turned back to me.

"Last night—" he stopped, reconsidering.

"What about it?" My heart sped up, and I had the urge to check my surroundings, an animal sensing danger.

"You said you tested my blood. Was that before or after you started having feelings for me?" His eyes bore into me, like he could see through them into every thought I'd ever had about him.

"Before," I gritted out. "I tested your blood the very first time you gave it to me."

"But you didn't compare it to any other royals? There was no way you could have been completely sure." He'd put his hand against a tree and quickly withdrew it as a skinny brown snake with tiny pointed fangs stuck out its head and hissed angrily.

I threw up my hands and let out an indignant noise. "When I tested it, it worked the way it was supposed to with the other ingredients. But it was always a risk." Bitterness crept into my voice. "And if I had a bevy of royals to compare it with, I wouldn't have picked the one with so much baggage."

"Exactly." Connery's voice was filled with disappointment. "If you were thinking objectively, you wouldn't have picked me. Because of Sabine and because I'm not a full royal."

His words were like a slap. "Wait." I faltered, trying to grasp his meaning. "You're mad at me for choosing you?"

"No." He shook his head slowly. "I'm mad at myself for taking advantage of you." He ran a hand down the back of his neck.

"I'm not a fucking child," I spat, shame filling my cheeks. "I knew what I was doing."

'Lie,' a voice in my head whispered. I'd held back from Connery for so long. Telling myself I wouldn't touch him while he was still on hush. But as he got better with his dosage, I convinced myself it was alright. Never mind that I'd never done hush, nor did I know what kind of effect it had on him. It did the thing I cared about, muted his bond with Sabine. And last night, when he confessed his secret, when his hands roamed over my skin, I told myself he was choosing me. He chose to come with us, to leave her, maybe forever.

A thought rushed through my head. Had I done this somehow because I wanted him to leave her for good? I pushed it away, shutting it out completely. I couldn't have done that. Wouldn't have done that.

"I know that." His eyes softened, and he stepped toward me. "But it doesn't change the fact that I should have done better by you. I should have, at the very least, told you sooner and not let my own feelings get in the way. Maybe then you'd have waited for someone better to come along."

The stillness between us was a yawning chasm. I couldn't bring myself to move and every moment I didn't felt like an admission of my failure.

"I'm sorry, Asra. I told myself that Sabine didn't include me in her plans because she was selfish and controlling. But I'm wondering whether she didn't include me because she knew I wasn't mature enough to make tough calls. A strong leader would have made the hard decision, wouldn't have allowed this to happen."

I stepped back, my eyes wide with hurt.

"No, I didn't mean that." He reached for me, but I pulled away.

"You did mean that. You think I made a poor decision because I had feelings for you. And you're mad at yourself for not noticing sooner that I'm a shit leader and deciding for me. I'm honestly not sure which part of that is the most insulting."

"No—" he hesitated. "Yes, I think you should have found another royal to at least compare it to, but—"

Fire sparked at my fingertips, rushed into my blood, readying for attack.

"Go fuck yourself, Connery. I *will* get us out of this. And I absolutely guarantee my feelings for you won't get in the way anymore."

I stormed off through the trees, wishing I could burn something to the ground, but I wouldn't give him the satisfaction. Of all the pompous, self-absorbed, condescending bullshit! I screamed internally, biting down on my fist. I'd leave his ass here when I found a way out of this shithole.

My chest heaved as I finally stopped walking. I ran my hands through my short hair and pulled. Tears slid down my face as I sank down onto a rock. I crushed the heels of my palms into my eyes until I saw pops of light. Silent sobs wracked my body, and I struggled to get enough air.

It was so weirdly quiet here. I hated hearing only the sounds of my stuttering breaths. There should have been more birds, more insects, more everything. It felt utterly lifeless after Solbaina. Flexing my fingers, I could feel the dampening of my power. Would this place eventually smother it completely? My head fell back, and I looked up into a sky even the stars had abandoned.

He wasn't wrong. I could have waited. The kunli required more to work, but I could have scraped a few drops from another royal, just to compare, to be sure. Servants were easy to bribe, especially ones in the stingier royal households. They wouldn't even have had to try that hard. A discarded bandage would have been enough.

I'd been stupid and careless.

His words from last night came back to me, and I snorted. He probably didn't think it was luck now. A curse maybe. The Allmother punishing him for breaking his bond by saddling him with me in this dying world.

The others had to be disappointed in me, too. I hadn't even apologized to them yet. I tried to remember Elwin's words, but panic clawed up my throat, anyway. We were stuck here, at least for now.

I had to fix the kunli. And then we'd go home. And Connery could find someone else to patronize.

3

LASHIA, 2208 PW

Solvan smacked his arm, leaving a palm-shaped red mark. "These fucking bugs will be the death of me." His eyes searched the air for any more of the tiny predators. "How come they don't bite you?"

"Blood's probably too hot for them." I fanned myself pompously.

The two of us, along with a dozen other humans, were helping in the garden. Solvan overturned a huge plot of land with his borrowed magic, crumbling the soil into something manageable. Now we were raking the earth into rows, staking sticks at regular intervals for beans and other trailing plants.

The soil wasn't great. It was mostly clay and sand. Magic could help the plants grow but couldn't create them from nothing, and there was little variety. We'd been exploring farther out each day, trying to find other varieties to bring back. Sometimes, we brought other humans back too, small bedraggled-looking groups.

I'd just finished staking the end of my row when Alice, a girl around fourteen to whom we'd given healing abilities, came running up to me. She said something I couldn't understand and gestured at me to come with her. I waved to Solvan before following her out of the garden.

I balked when Alice led me to where Connery was staying, but she grabbed my hand and pulled me inside. He was doubled over in pain on the bed. His face was waxy and sweating with exertion.

I sucked in a breath. "What's wrong?"

He said nothing, but retched into a bucket on the floor. Alice motioned at him with her hands, speaking rapidly to me in their language. She mimed getting near him and then being pushed away. I frowned at him as I grasped her meaning.

"Why won't you let her heal you?" I asked, anger unconsciously rising in my voice. Why hadn't she run for Brigid or Elwin? I sure as stars didn't want to be there.

She twisted her hands together nervously, looking back and forth between us.

He spit into the bucket. "Don't want her to." He gritted the words like each one had cost him. "She already tried Brigid." He collapsed back on the bed.

"Why not?" I demanded. He looked like someone going through their rishival. His body shook with tremors. I noted the untouched food and water near his bed.

"Just withdrawal. I'll be fine." His voice was weak as he lunged for the bucket again.

The scowl I'd been wearing every time I looked at Connery in the past few months deepened. "So you're punishing yourself? Is that it? Think you deserve to suffer for your poor choices?" The shame I felt at my enduring need to help him was almost as great as my anger.

He groaned and started to shake. Alice looked at me and I knew she was hoping I'd just allow it, force him to accept her help. She was young, but she'd been one of the first to volunteer. The child they brought to us on our first day here, Sadie, was her sister.

I shook my head at her and motioned toward the door. "You can go. I'll take care of him."

She looked at him once more, like she might argue, before sighing deeply and stepping outside.

Stomping over to the windows, I pulled them open, trying to air out the room. A breeze rushed around us like the wind had missed him. I flinched as the current swept by me, reminding me of how it could touch my skin at his request.

A flick of my fingers cleaned the mess from his body and the bucket. The blanket beneath him was soaked through with sweat. I grabbed a clean one and floated him a few inches so I could put it on and take the other off. Most fae would agree that, like bathing, laundry benefitted from manual effort.

I was probably less gentle than I could have been setting him back down.

With one hand, I reheated the soup while I used the other to move him into a sitting position. Other than the occasional whimper, he'd been quiet while I worked.

But when I moved the spoon toward him, he shook his head. "What's the point?" He eyed the now empty bucket.

Annoyance flooded through me again as I realized Connery had never been sick before. He'd never had to feel a moment of discomfort without being healed. Healing power was as rare as any other ability, and although it was one of the few things you could purchase legally, the fae in Oderon often made do without it for anything minor.

But as a lord, Connery would have done no such thing. I didn't recall him ever being sick before we came to Lashia.

"So you're punishing yourself, feeling all noble by experiencing this discomfort, meanwhile you don't actually know how to take care of yourself so it doesn't get worse? Did you consider that you might end up wasting more resources that way? And what does your absence cost the village?" Fury spiked in my stomach, bringing heat to my skin. "Getting food into you will help, so drink the fucking soup and find some other path to martyrdom."

Connery's eyelids drooped as he took shallow breaths. His eyes searched mine for a beat before he nodded and allowed me to tip the warm liquid into his mouth.

He drank half of it before falling asleep. The minute I released my power, he collapsed softly back onto the bed. After cleaning everything again, I lit the fire and went to Brigid and Elwin's.

"That's some masochistic shit," Brigid breathed. "What's he trying to prove?"

"Who knows?" I muttered, arching my back. "He said Alice tried you first?"

"I was on my way to the river. I told her to heal him if he asked, but otherwise, he was a grown ass male who could make his own choices."

I cocked my head at her.

"Or I said that in my head and just used hand motions to tell her not to worry about it."

"How long do you think it'll last?" Elwin asked from next to the fireplace. He'd been learning to whittle and had created several vague figures from the downed pine trees. If I squinted, one looked kind of like a bat.

"No idea. I've never seen anyone go through it. Can't last longer than a rishival though."

"She might be able to bring us back," Brigid said, her eyes distant.

The three of us sat in silence, contemplating the possibility that Connery could speak to Sabine again and that she could pull us back into

Trevesten. I doubted she would leave him here, but it would be difficult for her to summon us. And we'd probably be arrested the minute we got home. Idly, I wondered what the sentence would be.

We'd played the game before. How long of a sentence was too long? How many years would it have to be for you to choose execution instead? We all varied in our answers. Solvan was short—twenty years. Brigid and Elwin both thought fifty would be their breaking point—shorter if they had to be apart. We could afford to be cavalier, we were all nyssar.

I liked my life. I wasn't sure anything less than the maximum sentence, one hundred years, was worth ending it and having to start over.

Correction, I *used to like* my life. What would happen if we died here? Would we be reborn here or in Trevesten? The fae were normally reborn near the place of their death. Some traveled back to their original birthplace when they got old to make it easier for families to stay together. But I didn't know any fae who'd died in the other worlds. It didn't bode well for us.

"Better go check on the patient then, see if he can get his girlfriend to pick us up," I sighed.

Brigid snorted as I made my way outside and back to Connery's house. He'd cobbled it together from other structures, like all the houses here. Some were in better shape, but each one had a little patchwork. Windows from other houses or rocks stacked to make a fourth wall were the most common. It reminded me a bit of Oderon's walkways. Not particularly safe, but they got the job done.

I opened the door, and the stench of vomit immediately filled my nose. I hastily cleaned the room before going farther in. The windows had fallen shut, and I reopened them. Despite being clean, the smell lingered. I lit a fire and threw some dried juniper and sage on top to help.

Connery was still in the same place, curled on his side. He didn't look better, but at least he didn't look worse. I closed my eyes, hating how much I wanted to comfort him, how much I still wanted to touch him. I was about to reach out my hand to brush the matted hair off his face when I remembered the reason he was punishing himself was because he felt responsible for failing to keep me from making a stupid decision, and I snatched my hand back.

I left one window cracked but closed the others. It wasn't particularly cold, but Solvan wasn't wrong about the insects. They could be vicious. I left and brought back some more food and hot tea. When his eyelids fluttered open, I sat him up and fed it to him. There was no point speaking to him. He barely saw me as he chewed and swallowed.

An hour later, he threw up, and I started all over again.

"Asra?"

I snapped awake and Connery backed away. It had been almost a week. Two days ago, he'd been able to feed himself, as well as keep the food down. But he'd continued to get fevers that came and went and tremors that rocked him so hard I was afraid he'd bite off his tongue. I told him that if that happened, I'd bring Alice back, whether he liked it or not.

Without thinking, I reached out to clean the room, but it was already clean. Connery flexed his fingers.

"Seems like I'm back to normal again." Despite the words, his posture was defeated.

I shrugged, standing and stretching my arms upward. Furious buzzing expanded in my head. I'd barely eaten and stood up too quickly. To keep from swaying, I bent down to tighten the laces of my boots.

"Asra, you shouldn't have helped," he said in a pained voice.

My eyes closed, flames licked up my insides, and heat burned in the corners of my eyes. I turned to him, my voice lethal. "Strange. That didn't sound like a 'thank you.'"

He pushed his hair back, and I noticed it was wet, freshly washed. How long had he been up and about while I was asleep in his room?

"Thank you. It's not that I don't appreciate it. It's that I don't deserve it."

The angry buzzing increased. "Oh, for the Mother's sake, how long are you going to be like this? We get it. You feel terrible and no torment is too much." The words were bitter in my mouth. I hated the way I sounded.

Connery pursed his lips and stood up. "I don't mean because I deserved to feel like shit. I mean, because I don't deserve your affection or your friendship. There is nobody in this world or any world that is worse for you than me. I screwed up the job you'd been planning for years. I slept with you despite being mated to another. And I'd still be an addict if I had access to the hush." He looked like he might grab me but settled for squeezing his fists at his side. "I'm desperately trying to do the right thing by you."

"And what about what I want?" I cursed myself immediately for saying it. I didn't want him. He was a condescending idiot.

"I've given you no room to find what you want. What you deserve is someone who easily chooses you above anything else. My stepfather may have been wrong for attacking my mother, but she should have done the right thing and left him before getting involved with my father. You deserve someone who isn't bound to another. Not someone who,"—he paused as if looking for the best place to dig the knife in deeper—"still loves his mate. Even if I could love you, too, my love is not worth it."

My jaw ached from clenching. He hadn't mentioned Sabine in years and certainly not mentioned still loving her. Was that true, or was he saying it to keep me away?

"I will support you always," Connery continued. "I will help you and the others always. But I think it's best if I keep my distance."

A blanket of sadness smothered my fire. Taking slow, measured breaths so he wouldn't hear it in my voice, I ground out, "I didn't come here looking to reconcile, you narcissistic asshole. I'm here to find out whether you can speak to your amazing mate now that you're not using."

Connery blinked in surprise. His gaze turned inward, searching for his connection with Sabine. We stood in silence for several long minutes while he fought to regain the bridge between them.

"Nothing?" I narrowed my eyes, holding back tears.

He gave a tight shake of his head, and there was unmistakable regret in his eyes.

Every feeling crashed into the other. The hope of getting out of here quickly was crushed, while part of me was pleased, knowing he didn't need the hush to mute the bond with Sabine. My anger reignited while my heart sank with grief for all of us.

Before he could see any of it, I turned and walked out.

4

LASHIA, 2308 PW

We'd been on edge all day. It was the twenty-fifth anniversary of Solvan's passing. I'd made a list of every child who'd been born within three years of his death. I didn't recognize any of those children. None of them looked at me with his eyes.

We'd been disheartened but not surprised to discover that the humans never went through a rishival. If either of their parents had been gifted magic, their powers manifested soon after birth, growing stronger with each year. No new power was gifted to them at twenty-five, nor did they ever remember any past lives.

When the first child was born to parents to whom we'd given magic, I hadn't needed to test her blood to know she'd inherited it.

There had been a lot of screaming.

"In a minute, I'm going to need you to push, Keisha. Are you ready?" Keisha looked exhausted, but her deep brown eyes were strong as she nodded at Orla, the midwife. Her husband, Zachary, looked terrified, but he did his best to hide it. Orla was one of our healers, but she was afraid to do too much before the baby was out.

None of us had ever seen a fae child born, let alone delivered one. And the humans, despite their new magic, seemed so much more fragile. As she readied to bring life into this dangerous world, Keisha gripped Brigid and Zachary's hands.

I stayed out of the way. My job was to keep the water boiling. Elwin's was to keep things clean. On the other side of the room, Connery was cooling the air. I could feel the wind curling around the room. Solvan was distracting the children somewhere. No doubt telling them stories that he wildly embellished despite them already being filled with things the children couldn't even dream of.

"Deep breath, now push!" Orla commanded.

Keisha pushed, and we all held our breath. Six pushes later, Eliza arrived. She seemed extremely upset about it. Cheers went up around the room and I felt a tear slide down my cheek. I wiped it away as I heard the excitement spread outside. People yelled their congratulations to Keisha through the window. Her smile was pure light as she held her child for the first time. Eliza stopped screaming, but still looked adorably disgruntled.

"I know how you feel, kid," I said under my breath.

Later, when Keisha was resting and I was sanitizing the room, Brigid came in with the baby. She'd wrapped her in a blanket and we both stood there, just staring at her, for a long moment. As we did, a metallic shimmer rushed across her skin before fading away.

Both of us gasped.

"That was..." Brigid's voice trailed off.

"She's a shifter." But not just any shifter. That metallic sheen meant that Eliza was a serpent.

"But we didn't have any serpents donate power. We cataloged everything." Brigid's eyes were wide and filled with hope neither of us had felt in decades.

We started crying. Not only were the children able to inherit power. The power mutated and adapted just like it did for fae. They could gain powers other than the ones we'd given them. They'd survive without us.

The memory filled me with happiness. It wasn't all bad here. It was never easy, but there were bright spots. We didn't even need to drain anymore. That had been a relief. We'd seen shifters, healers, and lots of elemental fae.

But not a child with a penchant for quick wit and quicker blades.

We'd still been so sure that we'd go through our rishivals, even if the humans didn't. We were fae, after all.

The war should have been enough to distract us from constantly looking for Solvan. But there are long periods of waiting, healing, strategizing, regrouping, lots of time to feel the pain of every passing second.

As the day wore on, Elwin journaled and updated our maps. Brigid went out hunting. I started making bread just to give myself something to do. Each messenger that didn't alert us to a sudden illness sent us deeper into melancholy.

"There's still time. Maybe we don't recognize him, but we know this place affects our magic. We just need to wait for him to come to us," Brigid said, crossing her arms determinedly, like she could will this to be true by saying it.

"I bet he's just screwing with us," Elwin agreed.

Like all of us, Solvan should have had six more lives. Brigid was probably right. Something about this place suffocated our power, and you needed a lot of power for a rishival. We watched as the sun slowly dipped, as if it was dragging a piece of us below the horizon. For the next two weeks, each sunset had an equally gutting effect.

Nothing.

Here, in this pale imitation of Malan, our friend was truly gone.

We would be truly gone.

5

LASHIA, 2309 PW

Brigid stood with her arms crossed, anger emanating from her in waves. I stood behind her, Elwin at my side.

"These are children." Each word from her mouth had that dangerous quality I associated with her jaguar, ancient and smooth.

"Children who have committed heinous acts!" James shouted from where he stood across the room. "Murderers, vandals, and thieves."

"And you think the greater the offense, the more mature they must be? How is that even remotely logical?" Brigid snapped.

"I agree with Brigid," Henry said, standing from the table where we'd all originally been seated. "There's no need to take any action now anyway, not until we win this war. Fighting amongst ourselves is unproductive." His hair had been brown at the beginning of this war, but watching the death of so many will age you pretty quickly.

Henry had called this meeting. We'd captured over fifty people, half of which were between thirteen and sixteen. Restraining their power was hard for us to watch, but a necessary evil. This war between the Jinns, the more powerful humans, and the Tals, the less powerful, as well as Brigid, Elwin, Connery, and I, had been going on for three years.

James and his supporters wanted to execute everyone we'd captured. "To set an example, to show them we're serious."

Execution, without the promise of another life? That was too much for us already. But executing children? That was unthinkable.

James and his people, and I suspected quite a few others, didn't trust me. Elwin's impervenan power was inoffensive, and he was great in a battle. He could dive into the fray and retrieve anyone injured, bringing them back quickly so the healers could do their work. Brigid's jaguar was a precise weapon. They'd even used her as a mascot to encourage other Tals to fight. She'd been tentatively okay with it at first, especially since the Jinns had targeted animal shifters first, but now the sight of a crudely drawn cat filled her with irritation.

But my power was destructive. It didn't matter that I used it to sanitize water, as a shield, to cook their food. They saw me purely as a weapon. And while they loved to use me, I saw the looks. Several of the more powerful Jinns were fire-wielders. Not as strong as me, but still terrifying. Every time the Jinns burned a home or scorched a field of crops, the suspicious and fearful whispering would get louder.

They blamed me. Not without good reason, but it still hurt. I was out there every day risking my life for them, and they still resented me.

Brigid gave me a look as we filed out. When we were safely out of earshot, I said, "Yes, I heard it too."

"Now?" she grumbled. "No need to take any action *now*. They're actually still considering it. Just biding their time until this is over."

"Henry and the others are reasonable. We have to continue to support him, ensure that James and his ilk don't get too much power."

"They found another obahn yesterday," Brigid said, opening the door to where we were staying and closing it behind her.

"How many does that make?" I asked while cringing internally. When the first children with magic were born, I'd shown the humans how to identify some abilities. The obahn and damari power wasn't very useful for survival. We'd given it to mostly older members of the settlement when we'd arrived in order to empty the daranas. But it had popped up again here and there.

"Four," Elwin said. He went to the small sink to wash his hands.

The three of us were filthy. I longed for the days when we could have cleaned ourselves with a wave of our hands.

"And they're still saying they want to use them to brainwash the Jinns?"

Brigid took her turn at the sink. "Erasing the war. That's the line. They want to erase their memories so they don't know which side they fought for."

"If they want to execute them all, what would be the point of that?" I asked, trying to remove the ever-present mud from under my fingernails.

"Exactly." Brigid nodded solemnly.

"You think the execution is a smoke screen? Maybe they don't really plan on executing anyone? Maybe they just want us all riled up so we'll agree to erase their memories?"

"So our choices are death, loss of memory, or loss of power?" Elwin groaned a little as he sat down, picking up his knife and latest whittling project. It was Apa, the Allmother's elephant. He'd already carved Isa, the raven, poised in flight.

Brigid frowned out the window while I took a seat at the table.

When the more powerful humans began consolidating their power, it was worrisome but not unfamiliar. The royals also attempted the same. But while their power was stronger, they'd never discovered a way to cultivate specific abilities. When they'd begun treating lower-powered humans as second-class citizens, it concerned us enough to act.

At one time, the five of us would have been enough. But not now, not after so much draining. My fire was all I had left. You can't solve every problem with incineration.

Some things take diplomacy, maneuvering. Brigid had become skilled at this. The others came to her with their problems, their worries for their children. When a human with powerful water magic flooded the fields of a farmer who'd offended him, they went to her. When taverns required a certain level of magic for a table, they went to her.

The Tals would need her in a position of leadership after this revolution was complete. When those powerful humans were behind bars and everyone had a good understanding of what would happen if the magic got out of hand again.

Unusually, I thought about Sabine a lot. What it took to run a country, to keep people happy enough, fed enough, safe enough. I tried to remember tactics she'd used, improvements she'd made. Connery and I discussed her more now than we ever had before.

"I miss Oderon. At least people were upfront about wanting to slit your throat." I grabbed an orange off the table. It was on the dry side, but I peeled and ate it, anyway.

Elwin huffed a laugh. Brigid just shook her head before pulling a small packet out of her pocket and tossing it to me. "The latest from Connery."

I opened it, pretending I wasn't eager to read his words.

Dear Brigid,

Things are better here. I could almost imagine a war wasn't going on. Whatever you're doing up north, it's working. We've gone a whole month without an attack. Per your request, I destroyed my two daranas. I agree with you. There's a high chance of improper use in this war, and it's not like we need them.

I'm doing my best to help the people here rebuild. Two days ago, we got the mill working again. And the forge is creating a printing press. I'm hoping to document some of Malan's stories and songs. I'm even planning to leave in Solvan's ridiculous changes and additions.

We had a wedding yesterday. A bright spot in the darkness. That's actually what got me thinking about Solvan's stories. Everyone knows that 'One-Eyed Clyde' is pure propaganda, but very few know the real story. It's a catchy tune, though. I wonder if King Elsiu commissioned it himself. Maybe he even wrote it.

I've enclosed some more seeds and a sample of the bark I mentioned. Seems promising. I'm sure Asra can do something with it.

I opened the packet to find a small piece of blond tree bark. It smelled divine, sweet, and green.

I look forward to your letter telling me this is over, and we'll be back to normal. Are the others still giving you a hard time? Asra refrained from torching anyone for looking at you sideways?

"That guy deserved it," I grumbled, and Brigid snorted.

After the war is over, I want you three to come visit. We'll go to the sea. Maybe we can build a little Oderon here in Lashia.

Give the others my best,

Connery

I folded the letter and put it back in the packet, keeping the bark for myself. Connery had mentioned it before and had done all the usual tests to ensure it wasn't poisonous. But I'd need to do them myself before feeding it to anyone here. One of the hardest things about Lashia was eating the same things day after day. It brought everyone so much joy when they had something new.

There was a quick rap at the door. I opened it, revealing Henry.

"Hello. Figured I'd come and check on you all after that fun conversation." He stooped to enter the room, and I gestured for him to sit down.

"We don't like this, Henry," Brigid said. "They're getting weirdly fanatical. All this talk of execution, erasing memories. It's insane."

He nodded and glanced around at Elwin and me.

"They're just trading one problem for another," Elwin added.

Henry's eyes darted to my hands as I laced them together and stretched out my arms. The movement sent tiny tendrils of flame running under my skin.

'You too?' I muttered under my breath and put my hands down. Even our allies were wary of me.

"We need to work with them, or we won't survive." Henry sighed. "Isn't there some justification for their ideas? Isn't this what obahn and damari power is for?"

"Obahns can be used as healers," Brigid said, coming to stand in front of Henry so he had to look up at her. "Their power can be dangerous. But it can retrieve memories too, recover things repressed by trauma or erase things that cause pain."

"The prison in our world uses damaris, but it's not endless punishment. And it's certainly not used on anyone who hasn't committed a crime." Elwin spun his whittling knife before sticking it into the table. "James is talking about this being a permanent solution."

Henry looked at me again. Was he looking at me to help him? To disagree with Brigid and Elwin? I crossed my arms and clamped my mouth shut as I saw him give my fingers another once over.

"Do you have any alternatives?" Henry rubbed his palms on the top of his thighs, his mouth a thin line.

The three of us were silent.

"It's difficult," Brigid said. "I think we all agree on that. And I know they don't want to hear from us. But that doesn't mean it's impossible." Her voice fell off at the end and a cloud passed over her face.

The people listened to her when they needed something. When they wanted us to solve something. They were all fine with using us for our magic, and theirs, but not when it counted.

"Maybe they don't deserve our help," I muttered. Henry's eyebrows shot up and Elwin frowned. But Brigid's face fell, as if she was hoping I wouldn't say it, but knew I would.

"Maybe," she said to Henry. "But we'll continue to help, anyway. At least to keep the peace." She shook herself and gave him a tight smile as Henry stood.

He gave us a small head bow before leaving.

"Do you really think that? That we should abandon them?" Brigid didn't look at me. She sat down and began unlacing her boots.

I shrugged. "I don't know if we have a lot of options. They don't want to listen to us, so what's the point of beating our heads against the wall?" I glanced at Elwin, but he was looking at his mate, concern etched on his face. Outside, the sounds of battle training continued, the whoosh of fire and sizzle of steam as a jet of water put it out. "Are we going to start another war to get our way?"

Brigid looked up, but not at me. Her gaze was somewhere far away. "Do you remember the fireworks? For Sabine's rishival?"

Nodding, I asked, "What made you think of it now?" A brief image of the children of Lashia watching in delight as the fireworks scattered tiny shapes among the village popped into my head. The picture twisted as the little hearts and stars were squished into the mud.

Elwin came over and sat beside her. He wrapped an arm around her shoulder and pressed his lips to her temple. She leaned in, squeezing her eyes tight. They'd lost so much. In Trevesten, they'd wanted children, but Brigid said she didn't want to bring a child into this world yet. Meddling in this world worked out so well. It might be best for us to let them sort themselves out for once.

"No reason," she sighed.

6

LASHIA, 2310 PW

It was over.

I swallowed the blood pooling in my mouth before sinking into the couch.

I hadn't slept properly in days, weeks probably. The people who'd likely died in the firestorms I caused haunted my dreams.

The Tals had killed or cuffed the last of the really powerful humans. I shuddered. It still hurt to see it done. Watching my magic weaken year after year had been painful. Having it removed completely with no hope of having it returned would be unbearable. I would be half a person.

I shifted my position, pulling up my shirt to reveal a dark black bruise on my side. It was swollen, waves of blue and purple moving outward across my belly. The kid who'd hurled a sea of boulders at me with incredible air power couldn't have been older than fifteen.

Part of me hoped he'd gotten away when the other Tals came to my defense. But he was alone, and I doubted it. The Tals combined their skills and worked together, just like Connery had taught them, to take down bigger threats.

We helped them win.

The door slammed open, dragging me from the memory, and familiar footsteps pounded toward me.

"She's in here!" Elwin called, sinking to the chair next to me and taking a long pull on a bottle of beer. Brigid came running in after him. Her shirt was torn and someone had sliced off a chunk of her hair, but her face was alight.

"Why are you being such a party pooper?" Elwin asked, handing me a bottle. "We've had so little to celebrate. It's finally over!" A long gash that ran from his ear to his collarbone was slowly healing itself. There were other bruises and cuts waiting their turn. Until we'd arrived in Lashia, I'd never even seen Elwin's blood.

Gripping the bottle so they wouldn't see my hands shaking, I grinned, wincing a little. "Just a little bruised for celebrating."

"Tell me about it. Relief is the only thing keeping me on my feet." She rummaged in her bag for the pain medicine I'd concocted. None of us could heal anything more than a paper-cut anymore.

"Hooray." I gave a weak cheer and Brigid nodded in understanding. The end of the war was something to celebrate, but it had come at great cost.

She held out the vial to me, but I shook my head and she put it back in her pack. "The Tals are rounding up the last of the holdouts. Cuffing them for now until we figure out what to do."

"Cuff them and every one of their no-good, dirty bloodline?" I smirked, quoting James. He and his supporters were still overly fixated on punishment. And their numbers had grown. We held out hope that most of the Tals, especially the really low-powered ones, just wanted peace.

Brigid snorted. "Exactly."

As if we'd summoned him, James appeared in the doorway. He entered the room quickly, his people filing around the edges. Brigid and

Elwin rose, and I pushed myself up too, hoping nobody saw the effort it took me to do so.

"What is it? Is something wrong?" Brigid asked.

"Henry is dead. Caught in the final battle."

I sank back into the couch and put my head in my hand. He wasn't my favorite, but he was the voice of reason. Not like James. In front of me, Brigid and Elwin shared a look.

Did Solvan have this haziness at the edges of his vision? He'd gone so quickly. Did he have time to notice the dark tendrils swirling inside, like shadows calling me to sleep?

"Henry asked me to give you this." James approached with one of his men. He was an ice-wielder, but I couldn't remember his name.

It happened so slowly.

The man leaned forward, reaching out with a note for Elwin. I called for my flames, but they died on my fingertips, consumed by the shadows.

"Brigid," I tried to shout, but it was weak. Her head snapped to mine before looking at Elwin in alarm.

The tip of the ice shard protruded from Elwin's back before ripping up through his shoulder. Immediately, two more of James's people stepped forward to separate Elwin's body so he couldn't heal. The moment the ice had formed, Brigid transformed. She leapt at James, but he had been ready.

Black covered half my vision, and I fell to my knees in front of the couch, reaching for my friends. Had they already gotten to Connery?

With all the strength I had left, I pushed inward, trying to find a spark. Elwin's dropped beer rolled toward me. Grabbing it, I hurled it at James, my insides tearing further at the motion. The glass smashed against his head, drenching him.

Beside me, five people restrained Brigid. A snarl ripped from her throat, but I heard the wail beneath it. She was rabid, her golden eyes darting between James and her fallen mate. A woman tried to approach James to heal him, but he pushed her away.

"We will never have peace while the four of you exist." He spat at my feet. "Magic has brought us nothing but bloodshed. It has taken our children, our livelihoods. And it is entirely your fault." His foot came down hard on my hand, breaking my fingers.

No cry, no scream escaped me. The weight and pain in my side was too unbearable. Blood seeped from between my lips as I stared at Elwin.

Brigid broke free and swiped a massive outstretched paw at James. Deep gouges appeared in his neck, the blood pouring freely down his shirt.

With my last drop of power, I sent a spark of flame at him, igniting his shirt and the beer. He screamed. The healers tried to rush toward him, but the flames attacked their hair and clothing. A water-wielder stepped forward and doused them all. The burned remains of James' face reconstructed itself under the touch of the healers. He grimaced down at us with bottomless hatred.

I collapsed on the floor. Brigid made it to her mate's body, covering it with her own. There was no time to warn her, to tell her I loved her. The ice-wielder sent ten knife shards into her body, securing her to Elwin, even in death.

The cold and the dark found me before I felt the first stab of ice.

7

LASHIA, 2706 PW, PRESENT DAY

I arrived back in my attic bedroom in the early afternoon. The jump between worlds was effortless, especially after being in Trevesten, where my power was strongest. Regular visits would be necessary to ensure my abilities didn't wane like before. I'd barely had a moment to note the strange messiness of the room when the door flew open.

"Oh, my stars!" The voice of my mother said before her soft red hair surrounded me. She gripped me with enough force that, had I been human, my bones might have broken. I could hear my father murmuring his greeting beside her. When she stepped aside, I saw the toll this had taken on them both. Their eyes were bright with tears and weak with relief, but it was as if they'd aged a year in the weeks I'd been gone.

"Hey there Calimea." My father moved forward, and I hugged him tightly.

We sat around the kitchen table, empty tea cups and cake plates scattered among us. Keen and Ayla were at school. My parents listened patiently as I gave them an incredibly abridged version of my life until now. Who I was, Aiden, Audre, Indie, and Simon. It still took the better part of an hour, but that was mainly because of my mother's constant questions.

My parents didn't even know I'd been with Aiden that night or that our relationship had taken a turn from friendship into something more.

"So this Sabine woman is holding him hostage?" Her eyes flashed with concern. I hated that I'd given her even more cause to worry.

The memory of an unconscious Connery tied to my bed surfaced, and I almost laughed. "No. A royal is supposed to be returned to their family as soon as they're born. All the tattoos are recorded. Since he hadn't had his rishival yet, she had every right to take him to his family."

"And he just left you?"

My father's eyes bounced between us as he leaned forward on his forearms.

"It's... not like that. He wouldn't have had a choice. And she probably thinks as soon as she gets him back to the palace and removes his cuffs, they'll live happily ever after."

"Will they?" My mother was positively affronted at this turn of events.

I rubbed my head, the tension building behind my eyes. "I don't know. But he should come out of his rishival any day now. At that point, if he chooses to leave, she can't stop him." The thoughts in my head swirled and twisted uncomfortably at the thought of him. I needed to change the subject. "Sorry again for making you worry. I take it things here haven't been good? How is everyone?"

My father got up and started clearing the table. He gave a look to my mother that she should start.

She toyed with her necklace. "Everyone is okay, but there was a warrant out for your arrest."

My eyes flew open. "What? Why?"

"That registrar, Chiwel, he also went missing," my father continued, coming back to the table. "There's a warrant out for him too."

I folded my hands under my chin and grimaced. "They think we're working with him?"

"Well, maybe, maybe not," my mother said, her voice strained.

My eyebrows knitted together. "Wait, you said 'was' a warrant out for our arrest?" I asked, my hand going to hers.

"Your mother," my father said, coming to sit beside her again, "has been impersonating you and Aiden for weeks. When you first went missing, we reported it, but not a whole lot was done until the registrar went missing as well. Then, of course, everyone was very interested in your whereabouts."

My hand went to my open mouth. They must have been subjected to so much, the police, their neighbors, everyone believing they were harboring fugitives. My eyes examined the room, and I noticed what I did not before. Piled-up dishes, papers and toys strewn about haphazardly. None of the clean cheerfulness I associated with this kitchen. The state of my room also made sense. I wondered how many times the police had searched it.

Being harassed by the police was surely traumatizing. But not knowing what had happened to me, the disappearance of their child without a clue or any kind of hope at all seemed to have aged them the most.

My eyes stung, and I had to clear my throat before speaking again. "You removed your cuffs and pretended to be us?" I was impressed. That had to have been extremely difficult. My mother didn't know Aiden that well.

She nodded. "I had to tell Marie so she could make his excuses at work. Indie wrote him a note to say he'd suffered an injury to his arm. That's what we told everyone, that the two of you took a spontaneous romantic hike, you got lost and Aiden got injured. They questioned both of 'you' for hours," —I winced at that— "but they've revoked the warrant and backed off for now."

I blew out a breath. "Thank you. You are amazing." I glanced at my father's weathered face as I squeezed my mother's hand. "Both of you."

"Meanwhile," my mother tacked on, "the Tals are getting more agitated, not less, and there have been several further incidents."

"Oh, really?" I snorted, rolling my eyes. "The census didn't calm them all down and assure them everything was totally fine?"

"Funnily enough, it did not," my father said, giving me a small smile. "But it also doesn't help that there have been two more Jinns arrested for not having cuffs, as well as some fairly obvious uses of magic." My father explained how dozens of previously withered trees in Eudora had burst into bloom overnight. A smaller lake in Chelsea froze over for the first time, and one of the Eudoran council members found his entire office filled with cats. "They're not actually sure that the last one was magic and not just a very dedicated prank, but all the same, it doesn't make us look good."

"Just Jinns? No Tals this time?" I asked.

My parents shook their heads.

"How are Indie and Simon? Audre?"

"Audre is good, helping with the rebuilding of the restaurant. Indie and Simon have had to install some further security at the office, especially on registration days, but otherwise, they're okay. They're all worried about you and Aiden."

Heat boiled in my stomach. If anyone touched my friends, I'd turn them to ash. Fire danced at the tips of my fingers. My parents shared a look of surprise.

Banking the fire, I shook my head, trying to repress the immediate need for vengeance. That wasn't who I was now, and wouldn't serve any

"No." I drew out the word, not understanding. "Anyone. There was never anyone that couldn't receive the magic that I recall." I closed my eyes, trying to drag up the memories that were still swirling around with my time in Trevesten. "We gave out the original power we'd brought with us in the daranas. Then the five of us refilled them. We did it over and over. It drastically shortened our lifespan." I couldn't help glancing at Audre, who shot me a suspicious look.

"Right. But the original population of Lashia was less than ten thousand people. And it hasn't grown much." Simon looked at his wife, who was nodding, her eyes shrewd.

"Yes." I tried to remember the number of people in the original settlement, the ones after, the descriptions in Connery's letters after he left. A wave of fear and doubt threatened to overcome me as I thought of him in the palace. "Yes," I finally said. "That sounds about right."

"But we've always been told that magic only passes via the maternal line," Indie said, emphasizing the words so I would catch on.

I frowned as I remembered that. Blinking slowly, I recalled crying babies and their relieved-looking mothers. Children with weak abilities honed over time.

"And presumably, we also had children, maybe not in that first life," Indie said at the sad shake of my head, "but later?"

I shrugged. That was entirely possible. My memory did not extend after my first brief life in Lashia. If the five of us came back before this life, we must have been cuffed. Simon and Indie both looked like they were doing complex mental calculations. I remembered all the times I'd thought they'd been having a silent conversation. Once we got to Trevesten, and they both got their cuffs off, they'd be able to do that for real.

"Ahem. Would the two of you like to share with the rest of the class?" Audre's hands danced at her sides before she crossed them, annoyed at their failure to explain. My mouth twitched at the memory of all the times she'd spun a utensil in her hand or been unnecessarily creative with her knife skills.

"Assuming all of that is true, it seems highly unlikely that the population is equally split between Tals and Jinns," Indie said. "It sounds like magic is a dominant trait. At the very least, they've lied to us about it only passing through the mothers."

"What?" Audre and I said together.

My mind began piecing it together. Unless something happened along the way, Indie was right. I remembered Chiwel's strange comments, Sydney's flyer. "The registrar," I breathed. "She uncuffed both Jinns and Tals. Because... Tals have magic too."

"Damn it, that was missing from our chart." Simon looked supremely disappointed in himself.

"All the registrars must know, and the accompanists." Indie's fingers drilled against her arm as she thought out loud.

I snapped my fingers, making all of them jump, "The accompanists. That's why they're obahns."

"Oh-whats now?" Audre squinted at me.

I rolled up my sleeves to display my cuffs, changing the color back to red. "We bought magic from an obahn for the daranas. Obahns have the power to mess with your memories. The accompanists are there in case any of the Tals display magic before the registration." I covered my hand with my mouth. The memory of what that idiotic teacher had said to Sasha. "They also maintain the fake population split by periodically telling Jinn women that they've given birth to Tals."

They looked at me with various expressions of shock and revulsion.

I'd done this. I'd brought this all to Lashia. In our attempt to help the humans here, we'd given them power that led directly to the registration, the separation between Jinns and Tals. The government had kept it a secret because, of course, if everyone had power, they would be right back where they started. Stronger Jinns oppressing the weaker ones—and forget about anyone born with no power at all. So they stoked the divide to keep us in line. Using the Tals' fear to keep them from looking deeper.

A phantom pain in my side had me wrapping my arms around my waist and glancing at Simon's chest.

But now the Sun Guardians were protesting their cuffs. Did they understand what would happen? Or did someone plant the idea and allow the others to unknowingly push us all toward a revolution? So far, it sounded like the uncuffed were only a small group. But with Chiwel, and perhaps the other registrar and accompanists from Asheville, there would be more.

"Would we know?" Audre asked. "Would we know if any of us have had our memories erased?" Her eyes flitted about as if she were searching her mind for gaps.

"No." Rubbing my fingers hard against my forehead, I added, "Maybe. Handils are a class of powers that affect others. That includes damaris, obahns, comverdias — that's what Ayla is. There's a catch to using their magic. It leaves a mark."

"The cuffs?"

"Yes, and no. Handils can leave a signature like the cuffs, but they don't have to. It's more like they leave a piece of the power behind. Think of a damari having a bag of handcuffs. It can apply them to you, but if you are strong enough, you could remove them. That's why they use manacles imbued with damari power in Trevesten, so the prisoners can't use the power themselves."

"So, theoretically, we could have removed the cuffs ourselves if we were in Trevesten?" Simon asked.

"Yes, but you'd need to give them to someone else. Only a damari could take them back without having to wear them." The room was silent while they contemplated that issue. "Using the signature so they could track everyone was a stroke of genius. Even if they were assholes," I mused, playing with the color of my cuffs.

"So Chiwel took your memories instead of cutting off your power?" Indie asked. Her gaze was somewhere else as she asked, the knowledge compounding in her head. Simon was diligently taking notes beside her.

"Still don't know why, though."

The three of them were quiet, thinking of every unbelievable thing I'd just told them.

Inhaling, I met each of their eyes. "I want to give everyone back their magic. But I want to ensure the same problems don't happen again. No more Tals, no more Jinns."

Simon raised his eyebrows while Indie's chin tilted up in acceptance. Audre gave me a familiar look, like it was insulting to even question her support.

This was my responsibility, and I needed a plan. The thought didn't fill me with the fear and panic I thought it would. I'd spent years doing the most reckless things. Plans that were nothing more than the vaguest ideas coupled with unbridled confidence, mine and my crew's.

But I felt relieved. I could do this. We could do this.

9

The four of us returned to Trevesten without incident.

Audre was eager to go out. She pressed her face to the window, staring up at the fae strolling through the city on the precarious walkways. Her head craned as far as it would go to take in as much as possible.

I pulled what clothes were still useable out of the closets, tossing her a few things. Natalia had come by with some better coats and hats so we could buy supplies without drawing too much attention. I'd given her money from one of three hiding places I had in this house. Apparently, while she was fine with kidnapping, luckily for me, Sabine drew the line at theft.

"I thought you said people weren't allowed to approach us if we don't have our memories back?" Simon asked as he and Indie inspected the room they'd shared for so many years. Indie grabbed the earrings she'd found in a drawer and held them against her face, the gold and jade glinting in the early morning light.

"That's only if we're twenty-five and under. They'll assume you've gone through your rishival."

"Are you telling me I can't pass for twenty-five?" Indie said, examining her reflection in the mirror. By her expression, my response was clearly irrelevant to what she considered the correct answer.

My lips quirked, "They'll know—it's not a looks thing, not with everyone being able to keep themselves looking young. It's an internal awareness we all have. You'll have it too."

"Anyone can do that? I thought changing your appearance was a specific power?" Indie asked, turning, clearly thinking of the wrinkles lining Natalia's face.

I bit my lip, trying to figure out a way to explain it. "All fae possess a general well of power besides their specific abilities. That power varies in amount from person to person and it's normally only capable of some distinct tasks, including keeping the wrinkles at bay. So unless you have a special gift,"—I nodded at Audre, who had climbed directly onto the windowsill—"keeping yourself pretty will take from that general well. Think of it like money. Your priorities change depending on how much you have to go around. Then again, when anyone can do it, it becomes less of a status symbol. Some don't bother, others consider it beneath them to do so."

"Hmph," Indie muttered, and I could practically see the struggle within her. Whether her intelligence and seriousness would be questioned if she remained beautiful forever. "Whatever." She turned back to the mirror. "I'm smart and hot."

I smirked.

Simon stepped behind her and kissed her neck. "Right as always, my love."

The four of us left the house and stepped out into a gray sky. I was grateful for the bitterly cold weather that touched even the south of Trevesten. It made it very convenient to hide our faces among hats and scarves. The winds whipped leaves through the air and around the bodies of bustling townspeople before pushing them toward the harbor.

Oderon's salty air permeated everything. A few blocks away, the ships' bells rang and brought up a hundred memories of sun-baked wooden decks and roasting fish.

Audre, Indie, and Simon were busy making fresh memories, their eyes glued to everything and everyone. Most fae looked similar to humans, but with some greater variations in size and coloring. We passed a female who was over eight feet tall, stooping to wave to shopkeepers through the frosty windows. A male in front of us had glittering spink skin, and a small boy rushed past us with eyes the color of molten lava.

Simon tripped into me as he craned his neck to watch the child, convinced that at any moment, those eyes would alight with fire. I steadied him as we both watched him run up to a fountain gurgling in an alcove on the wall. The statue inside was of the Allmother. They were all over Trevesten.

She was depicted here as a spring maiden covered in flowers. But sometimes, she was a mother with child, a defiant warrior covered in scars, or an ancient crone with wisdom lining a sly face. She was almost always displayed with her two guardians, Isa, the raven, and Apa, the elephant.

The boy threw a coin into the fountain and it clinked against the stone before sinking into the swirling water. We carried on and I was, despite everything, in a cheerful mood. We were all here together again, except for Connery. I wanted to enjoy our time together before it changed irrevocably.

Light spilled from the shop windows, their bells tinkling each time someone entered. Even the cafes were full, their patrons enjoying spiced warm cider or something stronger to drive away the chill. And although the day was frigid, there was a general feeling of hope in the air—the promise of spring not far off.

The others were thoroughly enjoying themselves. Watching all the ways the fae did and didn't use their magic, like the café owner who used his power to heat his patio but still roasted lamb over a manual spit. Puffy blue taffy stretched itself, over and over, in the candymaker's window, but she wrapped her delightful confections by hand.

We'd given power to the humans in Lashia to help, assuming that it would balance itself the same way. Unfortunately, we'd grossly underestimated the impact it would have on a society that had been so powerless for so long. Like giving a child a dagger instead of a butter knife.

When we stepped into the apothecary, their eyes grew round at the selection of potions and powders lining the walls. Things certainly had come a long way. There was a much wider array of medicines to help with the nausea, the headaches, and even the madness, than I'd ever seen before.

Indie stood next to me, paying rapt attention while I spoke to the shopkeeper in Traelish, Trevesten's common tongue. Her eyes bounced between the two of us while I paid a small fortune for several vials, including the light purple one Natalia had mentioned. The apothecary claimed it was the best for reducing symptoms.

"How much money do we have?" Audre called to me from the other side of the shop, her arms overflowing with products. Simon was unknowingly scrutinizing a display of sexual aids. A tiny female with batlike ears gave him a scathing look, and he backed away in surprise. I stowed my purchases in my bag and pulled him away, giving the female a wink.

"I highly doubt you're going to want to pay me back for this stuff in a few weeks." I pointed to a black box on the top of her pile. "Unless you are very interested in starting a career in amphibian husbandry."

"What?" Audre said, staring at the box in mild disgust.

"This is for a rash you can get from working a lot with frogs and lizards. It's helpful in spellwork, but probably unnecessary for you at the moment." I loved seeing the wonder on all of their faces, but I wasn't about to let them waste their money on things that would soon seem positively mundane.

"Ew," Audre said, putting the box back. I helped relieve her of the rest of her boxes except a small turquoise package of stationery. It was spelled to lessen the amount of magic needed for sending messages. I gave her the money to buy it and she clutched the box like a dragon with a diamond.

On the way back, we stopped at a lively tavern for dinner. It had been our favorite. There was fresh paint, fewer broken chairs, and better-dressed clientele, but it was otherwise unchanged. As we made our way to an empty table, my eyes fell on a group of fae sharing drinks at the table where Connery had his ill-fated card game. One of them glanced up at me and I quickly averted my eyes.

He was surely through his rishival by now. There had been no word left at the house. No message from him at all.

Had he chosen her? Mentally, I was prepared. Our time as Aiden and Lim was a fraction of the years we'd spent in our first lives. Objectively, I knew the chances were not in my favor.

It still stung. The pain was fresh, but I also felt the reemergence of that heartache he'd caused me so long ago, like an old injury susceptible to new infections.

I shook it off and went to the bartender, who, at my request, pointed out a female alone in the corner, nursing a glass of something that sent up tendrils of steam. I slipped him a coin in thanks. After sending her a note, something it thrilled me to do again, I joined the others in a booth. She looked around the room until she found me and tipped her drink in agreement.

A troll appeared, escorting a young female through the tavern to a table at the back. Ten feet tall, three feet wide through the shoulders, and with skin the color of pine needles. He was dressed smartly in a deep indigo coat and slacks. She was a little slip of a thing in violet silk. I coughed at my friends, and they looked away briefly, chastised for only a moment, before returning to their ogling.

I leaned my chin in my hand. "I'd say you'll get used to it, but there probably isn't time."

Simon leaned forward, angling himself so his face wasn't visible to the other patrons. "What kind of fae is that?" He spoke so low out of the corner of his mouth, I barely heard him.

"He's not fae. He's a troll. They have a different sort of magic. Their power is earth based, rocks and plants."

"And he's her bodyguard or something?" Audre asked, spinning her box on the table as she watched them.

I angled my head at the troll. He'd led the female to a chair and now waited patiently for the owner to find him a trollbench so he could sit across from her.

"Nope. Looks like he's her date."

Simon made a choking sound while Indie whispered, "That is not physically possible."

Audre leaned past me, practically lying over the table. Her brow furrowed and her head tipped to the side as she gave the troll and female a blatant once-over.

I huffed a laugh. "Well, magic makes a lot of things possible."

The server arrived and saved me from further explanation. Simon and I ordered the spicy seafood stew, Audre got a lamb sandwich, and Indie, a creamy lentil curry.

"You're going to use my special paper to send him a message, right?" Audre asked in between bites.

I swirled my spoon through the dregs of my stew. "The paper is for us. Lashia dampens our magic and makes things we can normally do, harder."

Audre gave me a look to say she knew I was stalling.

"Not sure there's anything to say. Wow, I did not miss that," I said, seeing their matching looks of disdain. "I just mean, if he wanted to, he would, right?"

"This isn't Leo," Indie said, pushing a tight curl from her face and taking a sip of wine. "You're not baselessly chasing someone who hasn't given you a single reason to think they want a relationship."

"Okay, harsh." My eyes cut to the side, avoiding hers. "I get it. Let's not dredge up my prior stupidity."

Her voice softened. "What I mean is that, Aiden," —she sighed— "do I really have to call him Connery?"

"Yeah, it's kind of the law."

Audre made a rude hand gesture to show how she felt about that, and Indie continued. "Fine. *Connery* really cares about you and has been very clear about his feelings. He's also a genuinely good man who wouldn't abandon you without a word."

Simon, whose mouth was full with the rest of Indie's curry, used his fork to point at her in agreement.

"While that is true, he has his memories back. He'll know how we left things. He'll know his decision won't be a shock to me."

"I don't see him giving up like that." Audre shrugged as if that settled things.

I exhaled a breath that came straight from my bones. "I'm happy to have this discussion again once you get your memories back and you have the complete story. But he's a grown male currently living in a palace with his mate. So right now, I'm going to focus on getting you through your rishivals."

None of them agreed, but at least they were quiet. If I thought about Connery too long, my heart started to hurt. His face swam through my thoughts, the blue eyes mixed with hazel. I could feel the way the air shifted when he was around, the way I was always conscious of what he was doing when he sat at my bar. The way he looked fresh out of the shower.

I distracted us all by ordering dessert.

"I'm so glad I didn't know about coffee," Indie said, taking another long pull on the mug she'd ordered after dinner. "It'd have been a constant source of pain, knowing this existed and not being able to get it in Lashia." The others nodded their agreement. She turned to me. "Are you sure you don't want to stagger us, so you don't have to take care of us all by yourself?"

"I think getting it over with is best. I know what to expect. And I'm well-equipped," I said, holding up the bag of supplies we'd purchased.

"I'm just surprised you want to wipe my ass," Simon said cheerfully.

We all laughed. With barely a thought, I floated a glass of water over to Simon and dumped it on his lap.

"Hey!" he spluttered, jumping up from his seat.

With another wave of my hand, the water was gone. The three of them stared in disbelief.

"I am really going to miss being able to so easily impress you three. But as you can see, I will not be wiping anyone's ass. I can keep you clean just fine without having to get all up close and personal."

"Where does it go?" Indie asked, examining her husband's crotch.

"Ugh, it goes where it normally goes. Honestly, an entire world of magic and this is the thing you want to discuss?"

"You want to go back to talking about troll sex?" Audre asked, grinning.

"Never mind," I grumbled.

Back at the house, we continued our preparations. I put them each in separate rooms, attached the restraints securely, and locked the windows. I stored the medicines in my room except for the purple vial they would take tonight as soon as I'd removed their cuffs. They wore matching looks of apprehension, but there was excitement there, too.

"Thank you for trusting me," I said quietly to all of them when it was time. I handed them each a vial of the lavender liquid and they tossed it back together. "In alia vita."

10

The note arrived a week later.

Audre, Indie, and Simon were still attempting to climb the walls, but at least the worst of the vomiting was over. Indie's eyes flashed gold like her jaguar was struggling to get out while Audre's skin seemed to stretch and pull in extraordinary ways.

Natalia continued to stop by and help. Relieving me for a few hours so I could visit my family and get updates on what was happening in Lashia. I had just come back from such a trip when she came downstairs, her mouth a thin line.

"What is it? Is someone awake?"

She handed me a note with the royal seal. "It arrived about an hour ago."

"Why the look?" I asked, taking it from her hands and schooling my face into indifference. If I was getting dumped by a letter, I didn't want Natalia's pity.

"It arrived with a messenger. They're waiting outside to take you to the palace."

"What?" I tore open the note as I went to the window where an all black carriage was waiting at the end of my narrow street. My eyes scanned the short missive.

Lim,

Please come to the palace as soon as you are able.
Sabine

I wasn't sure whether to be insulted or concerned at the queen's use of my nickname. Considering she had signed so informally herself, I went with concerned.

"Natalia," I started, but the older fae just waved me off.

"I'll be fine. Go."

"Thank you. Hopefully, I'll only be gone a few hours." I gave her a quick squeeze before putting my coat back on and stepping outside.

I halted abruptly in front of the carriage. Why had Sabine sent it? Did she not know what I could do? Was it purely a courtesy? It would take all day to reach the palace by carriage. She could have sent a fae who could fly—although it wasn't much faster or nearly as comfortable as a carriage.

There was no point in hiding it. She would find out eventually.

"I can get there faster on my own," I explained to the expressionless soldier holding the door for me.

The guards outside the palace startled only a little as I appeared before them. I'd never heard of another fae with my power. I'd known ones that could move extremely quickly, but not from place to place like I could. Then again, I'd been gone for a long time. Perhaps it was more common now.

The note gained me immediate entrance, and I walked behind two guards, two others behind me. We entered an inner receiving room where courtiers and staff milled about. Instead of moving toward the grand staircase before us, the guards took me left and down a long hallway with a parquet floor shined to a mirror finish.

The walls were covered in portraits. Long-dead ancestors of Sabine and her sister. There was one of Sabine herself as a child in her first life, her coloring as I remembered it from before. A silver metal that

moved like quicksilver, endlessly changing into new designs before my
eyes, swirled around the windows and doors.

I could feel the magic of the castle poking and prodding me. The wards
and other protections here slid over my skin, assessing me for threats and
gathering information for the queen.

The sunlight dimmed as we entered a narrower hallway. No portraits
now, just a long dark rug covering a stone floor.

The guards opened another door, this one locked, and we traveled
down stone steps. I could feel the earth pressing in around us. It suddenly
occurred to me I could have just walked straight into a trap. We were
heading deep underground. The walls themselves were stone now, too.

But I heard no screaming or idle chatter associated with prison guards.
The lights were still on and the air was pleasantly heated. It also didn't
smell like a prison. There was water and moss, but better, homier smells,
also permeated the air.

At last we came to a row of doors and a guard knocked before each
stood to one side.

"Enter," a voice called from within.

I stepped into a comfortably appointed dungeon. There were rugs
lining the floor of a large room. A bed, nightstand, and armoire stood
to one side. On the other, a dining table and four chairs, a sofa and
armchair. Sabine stood next to the armchair, hands clasped in front of
her.

But my eyes went straight to Aiden, Connery, I corrected myself. He
was crouched on the ground, drawing on large sheets of paper. Charcoal
stained his fingers, and he looked like he hadn't shaved in a week. The
clothes he wore were the same loose pajamas the fae often wore for their
rishivals.

He didn't acknowledge me, not even when I stepped right within his line of sight. His eyes were unfocused and wild.

Suddenly, he jumped up, tearing the paper and rushing to the wall, where he pressed his forehead against it and screamed.

I stepped back, stunned. "His rishival just started? Why did you wait so long to remove his cuffs?" I didn't take my eyes off him as he spoke rapidly to the wall in words I couldn't understand.

"I didn't wait," Sabine said in a small voice. She cleared her throat and spoke louder. "I didn't wait. He's been like this since the sickness subsided."

My head snapped to hers. "What? It's been six weeks! I've never heard of a rishival lasting that long."

"I don't think this is the rishival." Sabine marched over to Connery and laid a hand on his shoulder, gently turning him to face her. His face suddenly cleared. He stood taller as he smiled down at her.

"Would you care for a dance?" Connery held out his hand.

Sabine's eyes were soft as she smiled up at him. "I've brought a guest for you, Connery, perhaps we could sit and talk?" He tucked her arm gallantly in his and led her over to the table, where he pulled out a chair for her.

A cold vice squeezed my heart. Was this because of our cuffs? My mind flashed to Indie, Simon, and Audre. Would this happen to them, too?

He looked up at me then, and it was all Connery. I couldn't sense even a bit of Aiden behind his eyes. His smile faltered for a moment, and it was as if the lights in the room changed color. Gone was the lord, and standing casually before me was my friend.

His eyes twinkled. "I wanted to be the first one here on your big night!" He grinned before pushing his hands into his pockets, a slight blush staining his cheeks.

Rocks dropped into my stomach and heat gathered behind my eyes. I had never seen this, never even heard of this.

"Thank you," I got out finally. "Let me get you a drink." I glanced at Sabine, who barely lifted a finger before a beer appeared before Connery. A pot of tea and two cups for us.

She poured the tea while I studied my former crewmember. I sat down heavily in the chair, trying to think of what to say to him. "Do you remember when Eliza was born?"

Sabine's eyes slid to him, but she said nothing.

He frowned at me. "Of course I do." But his eyes had gone cloudy. He stared at the beer before picking it up and downing it in one gulp.

I opened my mouth, but he abruptly left the table, falling back to the floor, where he began drawing again. He muttered to himself. I heard snippets of conversations we'd had and those we hadn't. He stood and went for the wall again.

"Why can't I get out?" he bellowed before disappearing into wind. He wrapped the room in a mini hurricane. The air swept up the drawings, spreading them across the room. I grabbed his glass before it slammed against the wall. The doors of the armoire rattled. Someone had placed a strap over the front to prevent them from flying off.

Through it all, Sabine was perfectly still, eyes mournful and a hand over her teacup to stop it from blowing away.

The storm stopped, and Connery sagged to the floor. I rushed toward him, putting my arms around his shoulders. He rocked back and forth like I wasn't there. But for a moment, I saw him again. Peeking out from behind those unseeing eyes.

"That's why he's down here," Sabine explained, toying with the edge of her cup. "I was afraid to keep him near any windows."

Connery put his hands to his head and started yelling in agony. "Stop moving! Stay down!"

Sabine stood, pulling a vial from her pocket. She refilled his beer before dumping the contents of the vial into it. He grasped at it like he was dying of thirst. As he finished the glass, he stopped rocking. She lifted him with her magic and placed him on the bed. His eyelids drooped and he fell asleep.

Upstairs, Sabine and I sat near a large window in a sitting room. I think both of us were grateful for the light. She poured me another cup of tea.

A male appeared that I vaguely recognized from the night Sabine had taken Connery.

"This is General Antonio. He's here to listen. Antonio, meet Lim Revin."

"Good afternoon, Ms. Revin."

"Pleasure," I said with some hesitance. I may have been a respectable business owner now, but the four stars on Antonio's lapel meant he was someone that, previously, I would have been loathe to meet.

Sabine ignored it. "Do you know why this is happening to him?"

I heard the accusation in her question.

"I certainly didn't cause it. I would never want him to suffer like this." I crossed my arms. There was a time when a conversation like this would have entertained me. The battle of words. How I would revel in tricking people into saying what they shouldn't, simply by waiting them out. But I was out of practice.

Sabine nodded. "What can you tell me about the cuffs? About the magic of Laloten?"

The name was jarring. It had been a very long time since I'd thought of Lashia as Laloten. But Connery and the others had come to the same conclusion. We hadn't gone far enough to get to Sverresen. It made sense that it was difficult for the people of Malan to get to Laloten. There was no similar magic for us to latch on to. It made even more sense why nobody who went ever came back.

I hesitated.

She let out an unqueenly sigh and raised her eyes skyward. The general stepped forward and handed me a paper with the royal seal.

My eyebrows knitted together as I opened it. It was a pardon for me, Indie, Simon, Audre, and Natalia.

"Thank you." I took a sip of my tea and figured it was best to start at the beginning. Well, not entirely at the beginning. I left out the parts before we went to Lashia.

Antonio interrupted a few times to ask clarifying questions while Sabine remained silent.

When I explained the registration, a deep frown appeared on Antonio's face. "An entire world like Tarkana."

"I wouldn't say that." I bristled. Lashia wasn't a prison. I thought of my parents' farm, The Peregrine, and the amazing things we'd accomplished all without the help of magic. Audre had been right. Humans really were remarkable.

Antonio noticed my tone. "I apologize. That was insensitive. I referred only to the application of your cuffs, not to the nature of the people."

I nodded, accepting his apology. But my eyes narrowed on Sabine. "And then you showed up and brought him here. If it weren't for Natalia, I would have been completely alone for my rishival. My parents, his friends, they all thought something horrible had happened."

"Something horrible did happen." Sabine stood and went to the window, absorbing the anger in my words. She stared down into a small courtyard. "I'm sorry for leaving you. I wasn't thinking clearly. It had been so long. Please express my deepest regrets to your friends and family."

It was some kind of signal. A guard walked over and removed a box from a nearby table. She placed it in front of me before backing away to her post. My eyes flitted between Sabine and Antonio before I flipped open the lid. I expected gold, but found about fifty seed packets instead. Someone had neatly labeled them in precise script.

My opinion of Sabine increased slightly. Some of these plants were familiar to Lashia, but others were native to Trevesten.

"They will withstand most disease and adapt to their environment. My horticulturist also spelled them to include a mark which will turn the entire plant to soil if cut there."

I took out a selection. Tomatoes. Pineapple. Coffee beans. The Peregrine would become very popular indeed. "Clever. And thank you." I shook the packet, thinking. The room was silent but for the sound of the rattling seeds. "You could try hush."

"Excuse me?" Sabine's head whipped around and Antonio's eyebrows shot to the top of his head.

Closing the box softly, I said, "I mean for Connery. He used it to dampen the bond when we were here. It's not a long-term solution, but perhaps it might..." I struggled to find words that wouldn't offend her. "Allow him to compartmentalize. So he can heal."

Antonio wore a look of revelation. Sabine also appeared enlightened, but the pain of finally understanding the lengths to which Connery had gone to shut her out tempered it.

"Here." I wrote down the dosage Connery had been taking when we went to Lashia. "I'll try to find out what's happening. My three friends are going through their rishivals right now. If the same thing happens to them..." Fear stole through me at the thought of it. Audre had told Jake she was visiting family. How could I explain it to him if she too couldn't adapt?

"I truly hope it doesn't," Sabine said, her eyes finding mine. "Thank you," she said, as Antonio rose to escort me out of the room.

I gave her a tight smile. I wasn't sure what to say. 'You're welcome' felt like I was acknowledging something I wasn't quite prepared to accept. Connery wasn't himself. Aiden wasn't himself. It was like his lives refused to mix. And until he was whole, I wouldn't admit that I'd lost him.

"I'll be in touch."

11

"Stars! Indie, you scared the hell out of me!"

She gave me a maniacal smile and hopped up to sit on the kitchen table. "Not my fault you've gotten soft." She pulled out a bladed star and began spinning it in her hand.

I narrowed my eyes. "Indie is going to bite you if she sees you like that."

Audre scoffed. "She could try." But she changed back into herself, now sporting spiky blue hair.

I should have known right away. Indie was upstairs sleeping. She'd been out all night hunting and exploring as her fearsome black cat. Simon was downstairs in my workshop, joyfully labeling the jars and using his magic to float them into alphabetical order.

He and Audre had gone out that morning to reacquaint themselves with the city. Oderon had grown since we'd been here last. It was more cosmopolitan. Wealthy visitors chartered sailboats for the day and not just to escape to Eloisha. Down by the water, there were colorful hotels with window boxes overflowing with flowers.

I was grateful they hadn't done away with the elevated walkaways. Although I did see some attempts to make them safer. And no amount of paint could remove the grittiness. Being in the wrong place at the wrong time in Oderon could still end with you losing more than your money.

Audre and Simon had run into more than a few old friends. They came back bursting with updates and gossip.

Without knowing how many times we'd been born since our time in Lashia, we weren't sure how many lives we had left. Or if the lives in Lashia would count, given how short they were compared to a normal fae lifespan.

We all only had two distinct gifts, which, as fae, would mean we'd only had two lives. But I had no idea how the cuffs would have affected us.

"I would absolutely succeed in biting you," Indie grumbled sleepily as she entered the kitchen. She filled the percolator before holding it out to me expectantly. "Please and thank you."

"You know you can do this yourself now?" I reached over and touched the metal anyway, boiling the contents instantly. The bittersweet smell of coffee filled the kitchen.

The three of us had shared a little of our power again. Along with impervenan, healing, damari, obahn, the power to read by touch, and trading my mother's glamor for Audre's, I was getting dangerously close to topping out. My magic would become unstable with much more.

"But why would I waste it when you're right here?" She took a long pull on her coffee, sighing contentedly.

Simon's steps sounded on the stairs below us. With his long legs, he was taking them two at a time.

"Ready to go?" he said as he stepped into the kitchen.

"Just as soon as your mate finishes her coffee," I said as gathered my things and Indie stared at us all indignantly as she savored her last drops.

I'd already sent word to Sabine that none of the others had any issues with their rishival. We were heading back to the palace so Indie could examine Connery.

I jumped the four of us to the front gates of the palace. Guards wearing midnight blue uniforms with gold accents lined the perimeter. Simon and Audre wanted to stay outside in case anything went wrong. No matter how I tried to explain that this wasn't a job and we would be fine, old habits die hard.

"Good luck. If you need us to storm the palace and rescue you, just give us a signal," Simon said, kissing his wife goodbye.

"What kind of signal?" I asked.

"An enormous fire ought to do it," Audre replied.

Connery was on the floor again. The drawings had increased. I recognized The Peregrine, the firehouse, the faces of fae I assumed were his relatives. Brax's sharp grin stared out at me from a painting near the bed. My face was there too, along with Sabine's.

But all of them were a bit off. One layer over the other. As if he'd started to draw someone and halfway through switched to another person. He'd scribbled through a lot of them, so much so that some drawings were just black swirling circles of charcoal.

"Thank you for coming." Sabine shook Indie's hand. The two fae clearly sizing one another up. "I've had multiple healers in to look at him, but all of them are at a loss. The hush did help, made him calmer, but not more lucid."

I let out a sigh. I'd asked Sabine to wean him off the drug for Indie's examination. He darted from one side of the room to the other, mumbling incoherently.

Indie opened her bag and took out a stethoscope and slowly approached Connery. "Hi," she said gently to Connery. "My name is Dr.

Indie Kyo. I'm going to place this on you in five different places, only for a few seconds each time. It won't hurt at all."

He looked at her. There was recognition in his eyes. He said nothing but let her crouch down next to him, where he sat once again on the floor. Indie moved the stethoscope around his chest, then his back. She used a small flashlight tool to look into his ears, nose, and eyes. We watched as she took his blood pressure and asked him several questions. Some he answered, some he just ignored.

Finally, she held out her hands and held them over his body. Light emanated from her palms as she moved them from his heart to his head and down his spine.

Connery squinted at her. "Aren't you a cat?"

Indie smiled. "I am sometimes. Sometimes you're the wind, and sometimes you're a firefighter. Do you remember me?"

"Yes. You helped Cecilia with the burn on her side. And Devonte with the broken wrist."

"Yes, those were all people you helped escape the fire in Marais. They're much better now." Indie pulled back her hands and stood up.

He suddenly slammed a palm against his head. "He told me to get out. I should have listened to him. I see his body burning in Lim's restaurant. Her feelings are everywhere. They hurt me." His eyes snapped to mine. He stood up, striding toward me. I stumbled backward. "I told you not to come here, didn't I? You make everything so much harder." His face was one of torment, his eyes filled with pain. "Why don't you listen?"

His words punched me in the gut. The air left my lungs. He was talking about before; I knew that. He wasn't talking about us in this life. My heart cracked open, and my skin flushed.

"Why don't we go upstairs and talk? If you're finished with your examination?" Sabine looked close to crumpling, her eyes hollow.

I couldn't escape fast enough.

We were in the same room I'd been in before. A guard was standing just inside the door. His collar had two silver paw prints indicating his rank as Captain.

"This is Erik, one of my personal guards," Sabine said politely.

"You were in Oderon," I blurted. He'd been wearing a hat and changed his appearance, whether by magic or just a good old-fashioned disguise, but he'd been in the tavern. Sitting at that same table. He gave a subtle acknowledgment. He examined me as if he'd missed something the first time. His hair reminded me of smoldering wood.

"Yes, I asked him to let me know when you returned," Sabine said, drawing my attention back. But I only nodded, barely hearing her. It was my turn to walk to the window and stare down at the little courtyard. Connery had looked at me like I was causing him unending anguish once before. Hundreds of skeletons flashed before my eyes, along with the feeling of Connery's skin pressed into mine.

"There's nothing wrong with him physically," Indie started, "but he's obviously suffering a mental break. I can't heal that. There's nothing wrong with his brain function. I don't know a lot about the magic behind the rishival, but I assume you've already had healers in who do?"

In my periphery, I saw Sabine nod.

I pictured Aiden sitting at my bar, Connery sitting in my tent. My mind could barely distinguish the differences in their appearance anymore. The rishival smoothed the edges like that, made it easier to handle the different lifetimes of your friends and loved ones.

Maybe it was the hush or the drinking? Or both? Something could have happened in his life in Lashia before this one—if we had them.

I closed my eyes, remembering an afternoon when I'd showed up to the restaurant to find Emir passed out cold in the backyard. He was barely coherent, babbling about some woman who'd left him, and positively immovable. Leo had been out of town. I could have asked my father or Simon, but I'd sent a runner to Aiden instead.

Aiden whistled, seeing Emir a few feet from several deep puddles. "Wow, that is impressive. It's a miracle he didn't drown."

"His liver will give out long before his lungs," I sighed. "Can you help me get him upstairs?"

Aiden put his arms under Emir's and hoisted him easily while I ran to open the back door.

Emir mumbled happily from over Aiden's shoulder. "Hey Aiden! Get us another round, Calimea!"

Aiden laughed, his eyes crinkling. "I think you need some water, Emir."

"Nonsense!" he hiccupped.

I put a blanket over the top of Emir's bed so he wouldn't get mud on everything, and Aiden set him down. Emir promptly fell back asleep, snores ruffling the hairs of his mustache.

"I'm sorry," I said to Aiden as we got downstairs. "You've got mud all over you now." I grabbed a towel from the kitchen and poured warm water over it. Aiden stood completely still as I wiped the mess off his beard and neck.

When I stopped, he quickly backed away. "Of course, anytime. I better get back to work." He tipped his hat to me and was gone.

I hadn't thought much of it at the time, too wrapped up in dealing with Emir's nonsense. I remembered what Aiden said to me the night Sabine had pulled him to Trevesten. He didn't want me to see him. Connery had pushed me away too, told me to stay away.

The problem was me.

Sabine and Indie had been talking quietly but stopped when I turned around. The guard's eyes were on me, and I was certain they'd never left, readying to jump in and protect his queen if necessary.

"There's something I can try," I said, hating the way Sabine's eyes lit with hope.

Back in Connery's rooms, I sat down in front of him on the floor. He startled when I put my hands over his, his lost eyes searching my face. He grinned, and for a moment, I wasn't sure who was looking at me. Tears stung behind my eyes and I had to take several deep breaths.

Gathering all of my strength, I placed my thumbs into his palms and yanked on that brisk, wintery power. It resisted, hard. But I clawed at it, finding those hazy gaps where Chiwel had stolen my memories. He'd gone really far back. My young fingers entwined in sandy blond fur. A stubby tail.

Closing my eyes, I willed the power to search me out in Connery's mind, my face, my voice, the touch of my skin. It erased every memory of us, removed me from each story in Lashia. Chiwel hadn't given me that much, and it waned quickly. There wasn't enough to smooth away my absence, and there were jagged holes, especially near the end. But hopefully, the general lack of me would be enough. The patchwork of my essence poured into a box in Connery's mind and I snapped it shut. I pulled back before transferring the red cuffs, leaving only enough to flip the box open again if that time came.

Standing, I found Indie looking at me in horror. "What did you do?" she whispered.

But Sabine wasn't watching me. Her eyes were locked on Connery as he stood from the floor and turned to her. His posture spoke of fine schools and dancing lessons, not scaling buildings and picking pockets.

"Sabine?" he shook his head, wrinkles lining his brow. "What am I doing down here?"

Sabine had to put her hand on the table for balance. "I brought you here for your rishival. Just to keep you safe. How do you feel?"

"Fine, I think." He turned, noticing Indie, and she eyed him cautiously. "Indie? What are you doing here?"

Indie moved toward him. "I came to examine you. You were pretty sick." Her eyes ran over him as if she might see what my magic had done to his mind.

He grinned as he walked over and hugged her. "Best doctor in Lashia."

Her eyes squeezed together tightly as she hugged him back. "I'm going to come check on you next week, okay? To see how you're doing." Her voice caught on the last word, but when she pulled back, her face was friendly and professional. She glanced at Sabine, conveying that she would come sooner if needed.

"Thanks, Doc." He released her and stepped back, looking at Sabine. "I guess we have some things to talk about." He gave her a look of concern, but there was no anger in it.

Sabine looked faint. "Yes. Yes, we do," she choked out.

Connery turned and noticed me behind him.

"I'm sorry. Didn't see you there." He held out his hand. "I'm Connery. Do you work with Indie?"

There was nothing but smoke in my blood as I looked at him and he looked at a stranger. His eyes were open, friendly, the same look he gave everyone.

My chest caved in and I was certain that if we didn't get out of there immediately, I would break.

Indie moved to my side. "A friend of mine. We'll leave you two alone." She turned us both and led us out of the stone room, out of the palace, and into the sunshine.

When I made no move to jump us home, Indie steered me toward a quiet pub near the palace. She ordered drinks for us both.

I said nothing, afraid if I opened my mouth, I would cry. Shallow breaths crawled through my stomach. This hollow feeling felt so familiar. The tears came anyway, slipping down my face and onto the table. Indie reached across and took my hand in hers. My face screwed up, and I wiped furiously at the tears.

"I thought for a long time that there was some reason Connery came to us. And when the two of you started your... thing, I assumed that was it." She handed me a handkerchief, and I wiped my eyes. "And maybe there still is some reason, but I'm glad he doesn't remember you."

My head snapped up, hurt flashing in my eyes.

"He can't hurt you if he can't remember you. And if this is what it takes for you to move on, then so be it. You don't belong to each other, Lim. He belongs to Sabine."

"And who do I belong to?" I said, taking a sip of the weak wine and wiping my leaking nose on the damp handkerchief.

"You belong to us. To me, and to Simon, to Audre. You belong to your family. And maybe there will be someone else at some point. But let that be enough, for now. Leave Connery in your first life." Her eyes were soft but determined. "If for no other reason than that, I get very uncomfortable when you cry."

A breathy laugh escaped me. "You're a doctor. Where's your bedside manner?"

She smirked. "If you get pregnant, you'll see a whole new side of me."

I groaned. "Maybe next century." After taking a longer drink, I said, "Do you ever think about what would have happened if you'd been able to lead? After the war?"

"Do you mean if we hadn't been betrayed and brutally murdered?" The anger flared in her eyes and claws shot from her knuckles. I immediately regretted bringing it up. The memory of Indie's shaking body curled around Elwin's as I died was still incredibly vivid.

"Yes, that."

After a beat, she exhaled, the claws retracting. "I don't know if it would have made a difference. We didn't have much time left."

The two of us sat in silence as we finished our drinks. Both of us contemplated all the choices that had been made for us.

12

Audre had done a stellar job. The bottom floor of The Peregrine was in good shape. It was only missing some tables and the big front windows. The second floor had only been framed so far, but it wouldn't be long.

I caressed the shiny new bar like a lover, cursing my ethical decision not to slip anything magical into the drinks until it was all out in the open. Oh well, it would still be just as impressive when I could do it.

A knock on the door startled me. I'd really need to remember not to do weird things like this once the windows weren't boarded.

A man with concrete gray, close-cropped hair stood outside. His back was ramrod straight, and he gave me a tight nod.

"Detective Durand, good to see you again." I'd never actually seen him. But my mother had changed into him so I could see what he looked like. This was the detective who had questioned her for hours while she impersonated me and Aiden. He wasn't from Marais. Eudora had sent him to investigate Chiwel's disappearance and our potential involvement.

"Thank you, you as well." He stepped in as I held the door open for him.

"Tea?" I walked back to the bar, unable to resist giving it another tender pat as I walked to the teapot. "Just boiled."

"Please." He stood instead of taking a seat on the barstool.

"One second." I walked back into the kitchen, where a square glass tank sat with three small fish. We'd tried different ways, but sending notes between anyone but fae in Lashia didn't seem to work. And our ability to send notes to Trevesten was equally ineffective. After many failed experiments, I'd figured out a crude solution. I could send the fish to a tank in the palace, as well as Natalia's house, and they could send them back. The fish couldn't speak, though, so it was merely a signal to me. I sent one to my parents before grabbing some more tea and walking back to Durand.

"Looks like you're almost ready to open." Detective Durand eyed the repairs appreciatively. He seemed like he was taking a friendlier approach than the detective who'd questioned me about Emir's death.

"Almost. Glass is taking its time." I poured a cup of tea and pushed it toward him, along with a small milk jug and honey pot. He added copious amounts of both.

"Have you heard from Mr. Adegbe?"

"You think my answer has changed since the last forty-seven times you asked me?" I cocked my head at him, my mouth a thin line.

"Yes," he said bluntly. "We have reason to believe that he may have contacted you recently."

"And what reason is that?" I blew on my tea, eyeing him.

Durand only hesitated for a minute before responding, "He contacted a friend of his. Told him he'd been kept against his will. Said you might be someone who could help him."

"What friend? Kept by whom? And why me and not the police?" I ticked off the questions on my fingers with a harassed look on my face.

Durand said nothing, but took a slow drink from his cup.

"Hey there, sorry it took so long. Your mom and I were both in the field and didn't see the fish." My father's voice echoed in my head and I forced myself to keep my expression neutral. "What's going on?"

"Detective Durand is here. I mainly wanted Mom on the line, in case he asks me something I should know."

"Sure thing."

A moment later, "Why is that horrible man back?" My mother sounded annoyed.

My father had been working hard. He'd beamed with pride when he first told me how he'd learned he could bring two people together like this.

"He didn't mention his captor's name, out of concern for his friend's safety," Durand said at last. "And as for why he thinks you can help him, that's something I'm hoping you can answer."

"Again, with these cryptic answers. It's infuriating," my mother hissed. "And he speaks so slowly, you just want to shake him and tell him to get to the point."

"I think that may be part of his process, honey," my father responded. "People who are riled up let things slip."

I heard her make a 'hrumph' sound and had to hide my smile.

"I don't know why he would contact me. I have no idea why he thinks I can help him or with what."

"Do you mind if I take a look around?" He took a step toward the kitchen.

"Yes, I do mind. I'm sure you can understand why my patience has run out." I smiled innocently. "He's not here. You might want to ask yourself why he gave all this information to a friend who clearly has loose lips."

"I'll do that." Durand' lips twitched. He put down his teacup. "Thank you for your time. I'll see myself out."

"Good riddance," my mother said, but I could hear the relief in her voice.

"Why would Chiwel contact you, anyway?" my father asked.

"Not sure. I'll ask Indie and Simon to make a chart."

Based on the individual abilities, I guessed that there were ten uncuffed people still at large. Or at least ten who were willing to use their magic publicly. The council had found two of them.

Their executions were again swift, with no trial and little notice. It was both horrifying and amazing how quickly the town got over it. For a week afterward, everyone was shocked, a gray wash over every expression. But after that, it was mostly business as usual. People were not built to feel such extremes for long.

The Sun Guardian insignia seemed to be on every wall I passed. The flyers littered every surface. I was becoming more and more certain that someone who knew Tals had magic was stoking their efforts to have their cuffs removed. But how would they have known?

The market had changed. Several vendors were missing. There was less talking and fewer smiles. People made their purchases and left. Tals and Jinns kept to their own groups. I tried to take a page out of Aiden's book and continued to act as if nothing was wrong, smiling and saying hello to the people I knew—Jinns and Tals alike. But by the time I'd walked the length of the street, I'd given up. Thinking of him hurt, especially as he could easily ease some of the tension here.

I saw a group of kids scuffling as I turned down the road to my parents' house. I recognized Keen's voice and immediately ran over.

"Take it back." Keen was kneeling over a kid while others surrounded them, egging them on.

"Keen, what the stars? Get off him!" I dragged Keen back, and the kid jumped up, wiping his nose. He spat in the dirt at our feet, and I raised my eyebrows at the waves of anger emanating from my usually cheerful brother.

"He started it!" Keen shouted, lunging for the kid again.

"Whatever. You and your Jinn sister are next! All of you freaks." The kid made a rude gesture at us, and I clenched my fist, banking the flames that threatened to ignite at my fingertips. He ran off, taking two of his buddies with him.

At my narrowed look, the rest of the kids scattered.

I let go of my brother and then changed my mind, pulling him into a hug. I hadn't told Keen or Ayla much. They knew we were keeping something from them, but I didn't want to risk it. Something might slip in a situation exactly like this one, when tensions were high and they were desperate to prove themselves.

"Where is Ayla?" I asked, inhaling the scent of his auburn hair. Pencils and sunshine. It was darker now that summer was long over.

"She already went home. Called them all ignorant rock munchers and left."

I laughed. "That's a new one."

Keen gave me a sad smile and shrugged out of my embrace. "I'm thirteen next month."

"Yes," I said, knowing where this was going.

"I want to know what's going on. Where did you really go? And where is Aiden?" He was as tall as me now and he took full advantage of it as he stared me down.

"In Eudora, like I said."

"Sure." Keen frowned and walked away, dust swirling at his feet, grabbing his bag where he'd discarded it on the side of the road.

"Keen." He stopped but didn't turn around. "I promise I'll tell you everything soon. But we're going to be alright. All of us, I promise."

"Yeah, right," he scoffed and stalked off.

"Thirteen indeed," I grumbled. But I saw his point. The kids could tell something was different, that I was different. I'd put them through just as much trauma as my parents when I disappeared. Maybe I could just tell them? They'd kept their cuffs a secret. 'Leaders make hard decisions,' the voice echoed somewhere in my memory.

I turned and walked back to town.

Bastian's office was exactly how I remembered it. Soft leather and old books. That distinctive smell of hearth fires.

His grin was genuine, and our embrace was easy and comforting. I had always been grateful for him, but even more now that I had my memories back. I barely recognized the person I'd become, pining after Leo like a lovesick teenager. At least I'd never gone crawling back to Connery once he'd rejected me. Well, at least there'd been no actual crawling involved. Bastian had made me feel special. Even if, in the end, it wasn't the right choice; it wasn't a bad one.

"Are you going to tell me where you've been for the past few weeks?" Bastian asked, a smile playing on his lips.

I froze halfway to my seat.

"I'm not sure who that was, but the woman I saw at the station being questioned by Durand was not the Lim I know."

Swearing under my breath, I said, "Oh, why do you say that?"

"They intimated that if things didn't work out with Aiden, you might be amenable to reconciling. We haven't known each other long, but I knew you weren't that inconstant."

A blush stained my cheeks as my eyes widened in horror. My mother and I were going to have a serious chat when I got home.

"That was my mother. She likes to keep my options open, apparently."

"I see." He raised his eyebrows expectantly.

"My mother is a shapeshifter. That's her ability." I paused. "I removed her cuffs." Might as well get that part out of the way.

He nodded, but said nothing. I'd had a more elaborate speech prepared before I arrived, but this interference by my mother had thrown me.

"Both Tals and Jinns have magic," I said, deciding to be blunt. "In a past life, I came to Lashia from another world called Malan. I'm fae and we, Aiden and three others who came with me, gave the humans magic. When it got out of control, our theory is the rulers at the time figured the only way to keep everyone from destroying each other was to cuff everyone, convince us that only half of us had it and stoke the divide between the two groups. The registrars and accompanists know."

Bastian's mouth had fallen open after my first sentence. His expression remained stunned as he struggled to keep up with the rapid flow of my words.

"A few weeks ago, Aiden's mate finally figured out where he was and pulled him back to Trevesten—that's in Malan. That's where we were. My mom pretended to be us so that they wouldn't think we'd run off with Chiwel—we don't know where he is by the way—and now I'm back, but Aiden is still there because I erased his memory of me using the accompanists' power that Chiwel gave me when he pretended to verify my cuffs. There's a longer story there, but it's not relevant now."

It was over two minutes before Bastian spoke. I counted.

"Any questions?"

"A few, actually." Almost involuntarily, Bastian pulled a notebook from his desk and started jotting things down. "Let's start with how you know Tals have magic, too?"

"Fae remember their past lives. When we went back to Trevesten, it triggered those memories. So I remembered when we came to Lashia, around five hundred years ago." Bastian paled, but I continued, "We gave magic to thousands of people. Not just women. And back then, a child of a parent with magic always had it. Indie and Simon think that based on the population now, it doesn't make sense for it to be split."

"Nobody would have agreed to that treaty if they all had magic." Bastian's brow furrowed.

"Not knowingly. I don't have any memory after my first life here. But once they started the registration, it would have been easy enough to tell people they were giving birth to children without magic. The accompanists can erase the memory of any magic they don't want to be there."

"Right... right." He blinked. He stood up and pulled down the book he'd shown me with the Treaty law. "Those possessing any magical ability, as determined by a Qualified Registrar, shall receive magically restrictive blue cuffs. Those possessing no magical ability, also as determined by a Qualified Registrar, shall receive yellow cuffs," he read aloud. "Well, lawyers aren't the second oldest profession for nothing."

"What?" I asked, confused.

"They say the blue cuffs are magically restrictive, but they've carefully omitted any description of the yellow cuffs. It doesn't say they're ineffective, so they're not breaking the law by applying anything they want—as long as they're yellow."

"Ah. Nice to know they care about being on the right side of the law they wrote, even while lying to the entire population and murdering anyone who stands in their way."

His jaw tightened, and his eyes glittered with anger. "Executed without trial. And now I finally know why. They wouldn't have wanted to risk anything getting out."

"But why only the Jinns then?"

"I'm not convinced it was only the Jinns. They were just the ones executed publicly. Otherwise, it would have raised too many questions. Very few people" —he gave me a pointed look— "know that Tals were involved."

"Chiwel knew. He mentioned it to me on Halloween."

"Did he now?" Bastian exhaled, thinking. "As far as I know, wherever he went, he went willingly." He sat back down, notebook in hand, and with a much calmer countenance. His eyes had that calculating look, like he was developing a war strategy. Which I suppose we were.

"Is Aiden in danger?" Bastian asked quietly.

"No, he's not." I exhaled. "He was very sick, but he's better now. And he has his mate to take care of him."

Bastian frowned but didn't dig."Next question. What do you want to do and how can I help?"

13

SABINE

Sabine closed her eyes as Connery wrapped his arms around her waist. She leaned back into his warmth. His body felt like home, and yet the knowledge that she was lying to him, again, made it nearly impossible to enjoy.

His chin touched the top of her head. "I think that went well."

She exhaled. The counselor had been Antonio's idea. She and Connery had been separated for centuries and had parted on bad terms. Her general suggested it would be a good idea for them to talk through their issues with a neutral third party.

Cassandra had come highly recommended by Lady Elestra. She'd been a good friend to Sabine after Connery had left. Elestra's husband had lost most of his arm in an accident. It was difficult to regrow limbs at the best of times, but his had been severed by a wyvern. Their venom made it impossible. He'd fallen into a depression and Elestra claimed Cassandra saved him and their marriage.

She and Connery saw her once a week. She gave them homework too. It was helpful, but Sabine knew they couldn't properly repair their relationship while this awful secret ate away at her.

"I think so too. Are we still on for this afternoon?" She had a meeting with her own council and Ambassador Venten. She was careful not to push too much, but she wanted him to have an opinion at these meetings, to feel heard.

Soon they'd travel to Boralta to find out which ancient fae she'd need to put up with for the next two centuries. If nobody assassinated them first. When anyone might ascend to the throne, a Boraltan ruler really had to watch their back.

"Yes, I'll be there." He stepped out and came before her. "It's interesting, isn't it? Cassandra has powerful water magic, but she decided to be a therapist instead."

"A what?" Sabine asked.

"Sorry, that's what she'd be called in Lashia, Laloten."

Sabine gave him a soft smile. "We should use 'Lashia.' After all, that's what they call themselves."

"I think the equivalent would actually be Earth." He slipped his arms around her again, and she tipped her head up to look at him. Those hazel eyes were just as striking as his blue ones. Each day, she found it harder to identify the differences.

Her fingers trailed up his arms. Cassandra had said they should wait a little before consummating their physical relationship again. Sex confused things. Sabine was grateful. She wasn't sure she could make love to him until they figured out how to give back his memories without him becoming sick again.

But when he held her, his breath caressing her skin and she could feel him pressed against her, her resolve weakened.

She settled for pressing a deep kiss to his lips. "I'll see you this afternoon then."

He smiled at her, his eyes crinkling, and a delicious warmth spread through her. She stepped out of his embrace before her willpower crumbled and she dragged him off to her room.

There was a knock on the door behind them.

"Enter," Sabine called.

"Good morning, Your Majesty, Lord Connery." Erik bowed to them both.

Sabine promoted the soldier she'd seen so committed to his disguise in Oderon. Erik had an affable demeanor but, according to Antonio, was deadly in a fight. He was now one of her personal guards. She didn't recognize him right away when he'd first reported for duty, which surprised her, but then again, the first time she'd seen him, she'd been very distracted.

"Good morning, Erik," she replied.

Connery gave the guard a broad smile. "How you doing, man?"

"Good, good. I'm here to escort you to lunch." He tipped his head at her.

She repressed a sigh. She had lunch with her aunt, which she normally enjoyed, but it was just one more thing at the moment.

"Thank you." She turned to Connery, and he gave her a sly look. Like he was thinking of things besides lunch. A shiver ran down her spine before turning to nausea. This guilt would eat her alive. "Enjoy lunch with your family."

"The enjoyment has been slim so far, but I'll do my best." He pretended to steel himself. Connery's family had been overjoyed to have him back. But, other than his mother, their excitement was rooted mainly in his relationship with Sabine and what that meant for their status at court.

Connery gave Erik a friendly bump on the shoulder before walking out.

The carriage floated along the road, its wheels only a backup to the power that allowed them to glide through the air instead of tumbling over the cobblestones.

Sabine rubbed a hand over her neck.

"Something bothering you, Your Majesty?" Erik eyed her neck as if he'd somehow missed a gaping wound.

"Many things." She smiled at him. "How are you enjoying being at court? Bored yet?"

"I'm never bored. I make my own excitement." He gave her a ghost of the lascivious smile he'd given her when he was pretending to be a drunk in Oderon. It was only just inside the line of appropriate, and she pressed her lips together at the kind of fun to which he was probably referring.

It didn't surprise her. Half her ladies had commented on her new guard. He had eyes the color of amber and a body honed from fighting with weapons and magic. His hair was odd. Inside the carriage, one would swear it was dark brown, almost black, but outside, streaks of deep red appeared.

"Be careful there," she said in seriousness. "Courtiers are used to getting exactly what they want. Disentangling yourself may be difficult. Also, don't sleep with anyone mated or married." There was a bite in her voice at the end.

She knew she had no right to begrudge Connery any comfort he'd found after she'd driven him away. She would never blame Lim either, especially after what she'd done for Connery, for her, but she was sure the three of them would agree that such liaisons led to unnecessary complications.

"That's not a problem. I don't like to share." He grinned at her. "Looking forward to the trials?"

Next year, King Sandlin, Boralta's current monarch, would reach the end of his term. Multiple contenders had already volunteered to take part in the brutal contest that would decide Boralta's next ruler.

She gave an unqueenly sniff. "I enjoy the trials, but the endless diplomatic events are tedious. Have you ever been?" She was careful with her question. They had a tacit agreement not to talk too much about his past. He'd been constant in his loyalty, and Antonio's investigation had put any concerns to rest. And, of course, Morgan liked him.

He shook his head. His eyes swept both the windows before going back to her. They had entered a neighborhood filled only with royal households. Outside, gardeners colored the flowers, maids chatted as they walked to the markets, and the occupants stayed safely behind enormous gates and box hedges.

"It's entertaining. The Boraltans are a messy sort of people, but they know how to put on a show."

"Messy." He smirked. "I like that. And they're the ones that want to regulate things in Kysalt?"

"They suggested it, yes. There is mostly agreement. The rules are less of an issue. Getting everyone to actually act is the hard part. Regulating a block of ice is not high on anyone's list of priorities." Several notes appeared in the carriage and she quickly fired off her responses. They passed more fine houses, doors made of glittering metal and turrets flying flags with the families' crest.

"Sounds like the Boraltans don't think it's just a block of ice." There was a hint of a question in his voice, nothing forceful or presumptuous. It was nicely done. Antonio had been training him well.

"The Boraltans are used to the cold. Probably feels like a summer home to them." She stretched her legs out. Her skirt touched his calf, and he politely scooted away.

Erik raised an eyebrow and nodded, but she could tell he didn't believe her answer. Sabine wasn't stupid. If the Boraltans wanted to regulate access to Kysalt and its resources, they must have a reason. And it was a big enough reason that they didn't think they could go in and just take what they wanted.

There was something there they thought they could use or sell. And once it popped up in the market—or wherever it was most useful—others would figure it out. They clearly wanted ground rules now to protect their rights.

A few times, she'd tried to see into Kysalt with her gifts, but something blocked her out. She didn't enjoy spying on the Boraltans, but she didn't trust them. Venten was tolerable, but he served Boralta, and he would do what it took in service to his country.

Sabine closed her eyes and focused on Boralta's capital. Her vision roamed over their markets, the impressive castles of their wealthier inhabitants, and massive greenhouses. She cast her gaze over the fields, the mountains, even the smaller villages.

Erik, who was now used to her 'trips,' as he called them, stayed silent. He, Antonio, Morgan, and Connery were the only ones who knew of this power.

The Boraltan army was practicing maneuvers. Fae with swords sparred, while others fought with magic. A group of fire-wielders left enormous scorch marks on the ground as they practiced their skills. Being in the north, Boralta valued its fire-wielders. Not only did they make things habitable, they were vital to defense. The largest concentration of wyverns lived in the Boraltan mountains.

She watched the fire-wielders condense into a group of ten before expanding and throwing themselves into well-practiced attack formation. Sabine noted their quick feet and precise flames. They did it again, and again. The moves themselves were familiar. She, Connery, and Morgan had all been trained in such tactics. The formation they were using was a common choice for wyverns or bigger animals.

Her eyes back on the interior carriage, Sabine's brow furrowed.

"Everything okay?" Erik asked.

"How big do wyverns get?"

Erik answered immediately. "Four thousand pounds, give or take. Wingspan of up to twenty-five feet."

A group of ten wielders to take down something of that size was overkill. And wyverns would defend themselves, but they weren't aggressive. They came down the mountain for food and preferred goats to fae. Elestra's husband lost his arm, trying to stop a wyvern from taking one of their cows. In the end, the beast got the cow and the arm.

The carriage slowed to a stop, and Erik checked the outside was clear before stepping out. He did another sweep of the surrounding area before reaching out his hand and escorting her down.

"Tell Venten I want to see him when I get back," she murmured to Erik before striding up the heavy stone steps of her aunt's estate.

14

I lit the fire the normal way, careful not to show off too much power in front of my siblings. As they constantly reminded me, they were still cuffed.

The two of them were playing a board game. Ayla steepled her hands under her chin, analyzing the repercussions of Keen's last move. Brax raised his enormous body off the couch with a groan before climbing down and plopping himself in front of the fire. Keen threaded Brax's tail through his fingers as he waited his turn.

My mother and father returned from the kitchen, and I raised my eyebrows in question. My father nodded as they both took their respective seats. The children looked up, feeling the shift.

"What's going on?" Keen asked.

"It's time for me to tell you the truth about where I was, where Aiden is."

"It's about time," Ayla said, tilting her head imperiously. Keen sat up straighter, his attention rapt.

My lips quirked. "Indeed."

My explanation to the two of them took much longer than it did with any of the others. For every question Keen had, Ayla had two follow-ups. It was over an hour after I'd finished, and I'd left out nearly all the complicated romantic bits.

"So we're all getting uncuffed, right?" Ayla said after I'd finished.

My father snorted a laugh. "Told you."

"I think it's the right thing to do. But we need to be smart. The council is going to resist and we already know they won't hesitate to execute anyone without cuffs." At this, my mother's eye twitched, and I quickly added, "Of course, that won't happen to any of us. I can safely move all of us out of here if necessary."

"To the fae world?" Keen's eyes shone with excitement.

"I would prefer that your visit to Malan is a fun trip, not a necessity to avoid execution." But I couldn't help smiling. It would be wonderful to take my family to Oderon, to a lot of different places in Trevesten.

Keen waved a hand at the thought of his potential death. "Sure. Sure. Are we making a plan? Should I get my chalkboard?"

"*My* chalkboard," Ayla said, glaring.

"I have a plan already. But I will need your help." The two of them grinned before scrambling up and holding out their arms expectantly. "Not so fast," I said.

"I knew it," Ayla grumbled, sinking back to the floor.

"My plan will need to work first. And there may be restrictions on your magic. We need to show them this can work and they don't need to use such horrible tactics to keep people safe."

Keen was undeterred. He rubbed his cuffs as he sat back down to the game, his face brimming with hope.

Later, I passed by Ayla's room, where I could see she was still sulking at having to wait at all. Sitting down on the edge of the bed, I asked, "Want me to read to you?"

"I've read all these books." She avoided my eye by playing with her stuffed bear.

I smoothed my hand over the quilt. My mother had bartered a skilled seamstress for it. It had five separate patterns of cloth sewn into an elaborate star shape. At the tips of each point, she had sewn a small hand-painted bead. After five years of use, only two beads remained.

Ayla's room had always been cleaner than Keen's, but it still held all the normal childish debris. A dozen pictures were haphazardly pinned to the walls, an open book lay on the floor, and a stuffed pink tail poked out from under the bed.

"How about a new story, then? A story from the fae world?"

Ayla shrugged, her lips pursed, eyes still avoiding mine. "That would be okay, I guess." But she sat up and straightened her covers and animals in preparation.

I hid a smile as I began. "One of the first fae kings was King Elsiu. He was a brave and effective king. His mate, Coraline, was a powerful water fae. She could shift into any sea creature and spent a lot of her time beneath the water. After trying for centuries, they were blessed with a daughter and they named her Koli."

"Koli? That's not a name," Ayla interrupted.

"It is a name. It was her name. Koli was incredibly strong and clever. Now, during this time, there was a portal between Malan and Mokome, the land of dragons."

"Dragons! You have dragons?"

I shushed her, continuing. "The dragons were fearsome beasts, not just because of their size, deadly fire, and terrible claws, but because they were smart and cunning. One day, King Elsiu brought Koli on a trip to Makome, to meet the Voden—that's like the dragon king."

"What was the Voden's name?" Keen asked from where he'd been listening by the door. He made his way to the bed and sat down next to me.

"His name was Claudius. He had scales of obsidian and was bigger than any of the other dragons. He took one look at Koli and wanted her to be his wife."

Ayla's nose wrinkled. "He wanted to marry her? How can he do that?"

I choked back a laugh, thinking of a similar conversation regarding the troll in the tavern.

"Magic makes a lot of things possible. Now Koli liked Claudius too and was happy to have him court her. But her father was terrified. He didn't want to lose her to the dragon world. So he told Claudius that he would not accept him as his son-in-law unless he could prove he was worthy. He set out what he thought would be an impossible task for Claudius. But it didn't work. Claudius completed it easily. So he set another one. And another one. He set enough challenges that Koli knew he was being dishonest and that her father had no intention of ever letting her and Claudius be together. By this time, she was more than convinced of Claudius' love, and his dedication and kindness had won her over.

"Elsiu knew he was losing, so he created one last challenge: to capture the Rousen, a terrifying creature twice the size of Claudius. But the challenge was a trap. King Elsiu told the Rousen what would happen so Claudius would die during the attempt. Koli discovered her father's plot and tried to warn Claudius by going to the Rousen herself.

"King Elsiu followed her, but when he arrived, the Voden said it was too late. He'd slayed the Rousen, but not before it had eaten Koli.

"Claudius was furious at the King, but his anger was nothing compared to the devastation felt by Elsiu and Coraline. Koli's mother was so heartbroken she went to the sea permanently, never returning to land. Claudius closed the portal between Malan and Makome, and no dragons have been seen since.

"Years later, and the story became twisted. It painted Claudius as an idiot, pining for a woman he could never have. But in the story, she's no longer a woman, she's a star."

"One-eyed Clyde!" the two of them yelled together.

I nodded, grinning.

"But that's so sad," Ayla said.

"Yeah, he lost his girl, and now everybody bullies him in a song? That's not fair." Keen shook his head in disbelief.

"Well, Koli was fae. She had seven lives. She was on her first life when this happened, but she never returned to Malan. That's why her parents were so sad for so long. Some people think she avoided them, to make them pay for their mistake. Other people think she was reborn in Makome, so she could be with Claudius."

"What do you think?" Keen asked.

"Given my history, I think it's unlikely she was reborn in another world. But it's nice to think about."

"Are you really going to take our cuffs off soon?" Ayla asked.

Of all of us, Ayla's power was likely the most threatening. Angry bitterness slid through my veins at the memory of how the Tals had treated us. The coppery taste of my blood filled my mouth as memories swam in my head, the sight of Indie and Simon on the floor, James' disgusted face as he and his supporters betrayed us. Those supporters were the reason we'd all been cuffed.

"Yes. I promise. But it will come with rules, Ayla. For both of you." I looked at Keen. "Power scares people. And scared people do stupid things. The people of Lashia need to know that everyone will take their power seriously and adhere to certain restrictions. And" —I took a deep breath— "one of those restrictions may be an age limit."

"What?" Ayla sat straight up again, her tiny brows knitted together.

Keen, wisely, said nothing.

"Would you like it if some kid at your school could force you to tell your secrets? What about your friends' secrets? Right now, your power might not be strong enough for adults who are consciously resisting it, but I think you could do real damage to someone your own age."

Ayla crossed her arms and slumped back against the bed. "Maybe."

I pushed off the bed, and Keen stood as well. "Goodnight." I blew out the lantern on Ayla's nightstand.

I headed for the door, Keen close behind me.

"Will you tell us some more stories? About Malan?" Ayla said, her voice small in the darkness.

"Of course. If you're good, I'll tell you some of my own stories." I winked. "And prior me is a terrible influence."

15

SABINE

The maid was staring out the window. She heard Sabine approach and hastily curtsied before running off.

Sabine rolled her neck. She'd been sitting for hours. Aldern, her transportation councilor, had droned on until she could barely see straight. New roadways and repairing the old ones were important, but she wished the male would learn to summarize. She didn't need to know that the southeastern road would be made with a slightly different stone than the southwestern one when, according to all the expert reports he'd quoted ad nauseam, they were identical.

She'd made every effort to delegate, to trust certain decisions to those who had greater knowledge. But some, apparently, still wanted her to approve of their every breath. Was this Aldern's sixth life or his seventh? Sabine reprimanded herself for the petty thought. He was a good male and excellent at his job. She just needed to be firm on the limits of her time.

She passed two courtiers who were standing on an external balcony. They curtsied and went back to watching whatever was happening down below.

'Probably dressage practice,' Sabine thought as she repressed a yawn.

But when she saw Morgan and Lady Elestra, also standing enraptured on another balcony, thoughts of dressage flew from her mind. Elestra, maybe, but Morgan couldn't stand anything fussy or ostentatious. Today, Sabine saw as she approached them, her sister was wearing the same pants she'd had on yesterday and a sweater that had a wyvern fighting a troll on the back.

"What are you two gawking at?"

Morgan smirked and Elestra blushed a deep shade of crimson. Sabine came level with the balcony and looked down into the internal courtyard where the knights and guards practiced.

A soft "oh" escaped her.

Connery and Erik were sparring. The two of them danced around one another in a tight circle. Erik shifted into a crow to swoop under Connery's descending blade. Connery twisted into the wind and surrounded the bird, forcing Erik to change back. Their steel clashed together as often as their magic.

Erik leapt onto a nearby wall when Connery lunged once again. He grinned broadly as he ran across the top of it and Connery laughed, hurling a gust strong enough to make him topple off.

Sabine's fingers found her throat as the two males battled, their shirts clinging to them with sweat. Heat pooled in her center as Connery dodged Erik's sword at the last second, a thin line of blood appearing on his muscled forearm.

The sight of the blood reminded her that Connery needed healing power. He'd shared magic with Lim's crew in Lashia. One of them was an impervenan. Immune to nearly all injury and illness. Not being his natural power, it was gone now.

Something twisted inside her at the thought. She and Connery had never shared magic. Except in limited circumstances, it was illegal. 'So was hush,' she thought. She winced, thinking of how, in the beginning, her cavalier attitude pushed him to a place of feeling like a nagging nursemaid when all along, if given the chance, he had a wild side too. Maybe they could be a little wild again together once his memory fully returned.

Erik brought his blade down hard, but Connery blocked it and the metal sang with impact. The muscles in his back rippled with effort. The two of them stood frozen, each pushing hard enough to hold the other off.

All at once, Erik slumped, his sword slipping off to the side. His shoulders collapsed, and he looked absolutely heartbroken.

"What the fuck?" Morgan said, earning a raised eyebrow from Sabine and an amused titter from Elestra.

"It's been a rough day, huh?" Connery said, audible now that the noise of their fight had stopped.

"It really has." Erik's eyes were wide with sincerity as he looked up at him.

"Maybe you want to just clean off? Have a nice warm bath and snack?" Connery held his hand out for Erik's sword.

Erik took a step but acted as if his feet were too heavy. His next words were strained.

"Yeah, maybe." His brows furrowed as his face struggled between melancholy and the refusal to cede victory.

"I think it sounds pretty good. But we could get a drink if you prefer? How about a nice cold beer?"

Sabine's smile grew along with her arousal as she watched Erik attempt to resist Connery's power. His arm shook as it rose, the strain clear on his face as he tried to fight back.

The moment he curled the pommel of Erik's sword into his grip, Connery released his power.

The crowd erupted in cheers as Erik staggered back, shaking his head, his hands coming to rest on his hips. Connery stuck the swords into the ground and the two males shook hands. Erik jokingly hid his head in shame before casting mournful eyes at the assembled maids and courtiers, all of whom swooned in their united desire to help him get over this tragic loss.

Connery looked up and his eyes found hers. He gave her a suggestive grin and winked. Shivers ran up her spine and her clothes seemed suddenly oppressive. She could practically feel the rough pads of his fingertips running down—

"How's that no-sex thing working out for you?" Morgan's voice broke into the thoughts that were quickly turning filthy.

Sabine glared at her. Elestra politely pretended not to hear.

All three females found themselves drawn back to the training grounds as both Connery and Erik removed their shirts, jostling one another good-naturedly about the match. Sabine groaned at the work of art that was Connery's body, his muscled biceps and abs she vividly remembered outlining with her tongue. He was slightly paler than Erik, who also had tightly honed muscles, damp with exertion.

"I think I'll head home," Elestra said before darting away to what would soon be a very grateful husband.

Sabine knew she should have made herself scarce, at least until he showered, but she went straight to their rooms. She didn't even pretend not to be waiting for him.

Connery prowled into the room like he already knew exactly where she was. He said nothing before pulling her against him, crushing his mouth to hers. Her hands found his bare chest, and she luxuriated in the feeling of his powerful muscles. He was overwhelming, the nearness of him, the scent of him. His presence was like a tide dragging her under, made all the more intoxicating by how long she'd gone without it.

His tongue pushed into her mouth while his hand moved over her ass. She cried out in pleasure and pain as his finger dug into her soft flesh.

"I know," he said as his lips trailed along her neck, "that Cassandra is an excellent therapist. And she has good reasons for things." He pushed her back until she was against the wall and she felt the length of him grind against her. It wasn't enough. He moved slowly, deliberately, giving her just enough friction to make her wet with need, but not enough to truly satisfy her. "But we've been good little patients. Don't you think we've earned a reward?"

His voice was gravel and sand. She was being dragged across the shore, tiny pebbles like thousands of searching fingers on her skin. All the very valid reasons she should not be doing this flew out of her head when Connery leaned down and ran his hand under her skirt. Her nails dug into his skin as she pushed her tongue against his.

"Unless you want me to clean up first?" He pushed his thumb against her clit and she bit down on his lip in response. His answering laugh was full of dark promise. "Like that?"

She might have mumbled a response.

A knock sounded at the door.

"Fucking stars," Connery swore. "Exile whoever it is to Tulo."

"The Ambassador from Ursan has been waiting for twenty minutes, Your Majesty. Should I tell her you're indisposed?" Sabine could swear she could hear a smirk in Erik's voice.

"Tell them she's dead and to come back in twenty-five years," Connery yelled through the door.

"I see, and what shall I say is the cause of death?" Erik was actually laughing now.

"Buried in a landslide of my—" Sabine slapped a hand over his mouth. She might have laughed, she might have told Erik to reschedule. But the minute Connery had said 'landslide,' his eyes gave that unfocused look again. The same look he always had when something he couldn't remember needled at the edge of his mind.

"What?" Connery said innocently. "I was going to say 'love.'"

"Be that as it may,"—she rolled her eyes and straightened her clothes—"I should go. I'll be back later. Why don't you have them send dinner up here?"

He warmed at that, pushing a hand into her hair and kissing her deeply. "Fine. I'll shower, you run the country. Then I'll eat." He winked, and her thighs involuntarily clenched.

She was going to regret not finishing this, but she swept out of the room anyway, avoiding the too-innocuous look from Erik.

When Sabine returned to the room, Connery had lit the fire. He handed her a glass of wine before sitting and motioning for her to sit on his lap. Sabine bit the inside of her lip hard enough to draw blood. This new side of him was more playful, relaxed. And she wanted to lean into it so much. She wanted to be relaxed too, to sink into him and tease him for his brawny display this afternoon.

Instead, she placed the glass of wine on the table and sat down beside him. He raised an eyebrow as if she was challenging, not rejecting him.

"You were really sick during your rishival."

His eyebrows flew up. "Not where I thought this conversation was going, but go on?"

"Really sick. It lasted for weeks longer than it should have. The madness especially." She wrung her hands and saw his eyes dart to the movement.

He frowned, but his voice was soothing. "Tell me."

"Your lives wouldn't meld together. Instead of one person, you were two, battling one another. Your memories were all mixed up." Tears formed at the corners of her eyes. "I was terrified."

His large hand reached out and covered hers.

"I had all the best healers in, trying to figure out what was happening, but none of them could help." She had to say it. She'd already reached the point of no return. If she didn't tell him, if she couldn't be honest with him, there was no hope for them. "Finally, I sent for Lim."

"Lim? You mean Indie?"

Steel wrapped around her heart and weighed it down. It sank into her stomach and filled her with all the same fear, shame, and sadness she'd felt when Connery had left the first time.

"No, Lim. She called Indie after she saw how bad it was."

"I don't understand. I only met her that day." His hand still covered hers, but his brow bunched in confusion.

Sabine finally looked up at him, two fat tears spilling down her cheeks. "Lim is an obahn."

Connery reared back in understanding. "What?" he whispered. "What did she do?"

"She told us you used hush to silence the bond between us. That it worked until you went to Lashia and didn't need it anymore."

His jaw tightened, and his eyes clouded over. "I didn't know you or she knew that, but yes. I'm not proud of it."

"We tried that first." At his look of surprise, Sabine added, "I was desperate. But it didn't work. And, because of the things you said, because of our history and your history with her, Lim thought that if she erased herself from your memories, it might help."

She felt like vomiting, but at least she'd said it out loud. Her skin was clammy as she watched the emotions pass over his face. Shock, betrayal, and always the confusion.

He stood up and walked over to the fire, swiping his drink from the table. He took a sip and his eyes darted from side to side, searching inside his mind like he was examining every gap, each Lim-shaped hole.

Finally, he turned back to her. "I don't understand. Why would removing my memory of her help?"

"I don't know all the details." Sabine felt oily jealousy slide through her. "But it seems you two had a relationship in Lashia. Before... and now. The conflict between it and our bond caused difficulty with the merging of your two lives."

He took another drink. "Is that why she won't bring me to Marais?"

"Yes, and no. It would be obvious to the others that something is wrong if you don't... acknowledge her in the same way. But she's not lying about things being difficult. They are executing people with magic."

He closed his eyes. "I was there," he said in a strained voice. "At the first executions." He looked at her. "There's this cloud in certain memories. I've assumed it was because of the hush—that I'd damaged my mind. But those clouds, like the one I see when I think of the execution, I'm guessing those are her?"

Sabine shook her head and gave him a look to show she didn't know. She could take an educated guess, but she didn't feel like walking through every memory he might have with Lim.

She nearly collapsed with relief when, instead of walking out, he sat back down next to her. He rubbed his hands down his face. "I'm a real pain in the ass, aren't I?"

Sabine stuttered a shocked laugh and wiped away another tear. "I think you're worth it."

He laced his fingers with hers. "Is this the real reason you've agreed to Cassandra's ridiculous suggestion?"

"Not the only reason, but the main one." She couldn't believe it. Was he really going to accept this? Without raging at her for being untrustworthy? "I'm sorry," she whispered.

He pulled her into his lap, and Sabine melted against his broad chest. "You don't need to be sorry. You did what you had to do, both of you. And I am grateful. It could not have been an easy decision."

She wrapped her arms around him, feeling a million times lighter than she had this morning. His powerful arms circled her waist.

"Probably not a long-term decision, though, right?" he said, his breath hot against her neck.

"We'll figure something out." She sighed as she felt his hands make lazy strokes on her back. "Together."

16

Audre hopped up to sit on my workbench. She was a young boy today, with brown hair and a deceptively innocent face.

I glanced up. "Gah! Please don't do that one! You know how creepy I find it."

"Sorry," she said as she changed back. Her eyes were downcast. "Jake and I broke up."

"What?" My head snapped to her. "When did that happen?"

"Two days ago. His family is scared and is moving to Morgantown. They've got more Tals there, I guess. Oh yeah, you need a new sous chef," she tacked on as an afterthought.

"I'm sorry, Audre."

She lightly kicked the leg of my workbench. "Ah, whatever. Who needs a perpetually upbeat boyfriend, anyway? It's just stupid because I can't tell him that there's no difference between Tals and Jinns, and soon it won't be a thing at all."

"You could tell him," I said. If Audre trusted Jake, then I could too.

She shook her head. "No, it's better this way. He can come crawling back to me with his puppy dog eyes when you blow everyone's mind."

I chuckled and gave her a hug. "That man better grovel like nobody has ever groveled before."

Upstairs, there was a knock at the door.

We both climbed the stairs out of my workroom, slipping through the false back in the closet and into the living room. Audre reached the door before me and stood on her tiptoes to see through the peephole.

"Well, shit." She turned to me with an amused expression. "That guy who follows us around is here."

I reached for the door, my eyes widening as I came face to face with Connery. He gave me a beaming smile, and out of habit, I returned it and almost offered him a drink.

"Lim! Good to see you again. This is Morgan, Sabine's sister. Mind if we come in?"

His voice rolled over me, searching out all my most tender places, and I struggled to shut out the memories of his fingers on my skin, his breath on my neck.

"Hi. Yes, of course," I said, fumbling to pull the door open wider. A female with glittering black eyes stood behind him. She wore a faded T-shirt and a short sword hung at her side. She'd been there too on the night we'd returned to Oderon.

"Audre, how are you?" Connery gently squeezed Audre's shoulder as he entered.

Audre gave the princess an unimpressed look. Morgan arched a brow, her face a thinly veiled threat.

"What's the matter, shippie?" Audre goaded. "All the gold cutlery giving you a rash or something? What are you doing back in Oderon?"

Connery laughed, and my heart broke wide open. That grin had been a constant presence in my life, and seeing it again made me realize how much I'd missed it. His hazel eyes held something else. A flash of sadness before he hid it away.

"Did something happen?" I asked.

"Sabine told him," Morgan said matter-of-factly. My mouth fell open.

Connery pinched his lips together, eyes skyward. "Thank you, Morgan."

"Sorry." She shrugged as she wandered around, inspecting the place. She had a small hole in the shoulder of her shirt. Her gaze swept the room, pausing to give Audre another once-over. "Just trying to move things along."

"She told you..." Instinctively, my fire raced to my palms, swirled around my heart, readied for his anger, for the words I knew he could wield so well. All at once, I was back in a desolate copse of trees, angry and heartbroken.

"Yes. It's okay. I understand why you did it. Why you both did it." His eyes were soft, and guilt crashed into me at the sight of him. I didn't want his compassion. A part of me wanted him to rage at the discovery, to demand I return his precious memories of us.

Of course, that was ridiculous. He might know they were gone, but he had no precious memories, had no idea what we'd meant to one another. Did I know what we'd meant to each other? We'd barely begun when Sabine called him back. It paled in comparison to our time in Lashia, to his bond with Sabine. But the time in Marais felt different from our first life. It felt so much more solid.

"So Queenie Sabiney learned her lesson about keeping secrets?" Audre mused.

The corner of Morgan's mouth twitched at the nickname, but she said nothing.

The floor righted itself now that I wasn't about to be attacked. I let out a deep breath, banking my flames and calming the beating of my heart.

"Okay," I said slowly. "That's good to hear." It didn't seem possible that he was comfortable with this. Maybe it was a trap. Any minute, he was going to gut me with his true thoughts on the matter. How I had betrayed him and stolen his autonomy.

Connery gave me a soft smile like he knew what I wasn't saying. It reminded me so much of our games at the bar. "I don't think this is a permanent solution, but I understand you have other things on your mind." His face turned serious. "What is happening in Lashia? The executions?"

I seized on the change of topic. "There haven't been any more." As far as I knew. "I want to uncuff everyone," I added awkwardly.

"Great!" He rubbed his hands together, the movement drawing my eyes as I remembered how it felt to have those thumbs digging into the soles of my feet. "I think we should."

"We?" My eyes flew up at him.

"Yes." His voice lowered darkly. "I have to assume you know everything I do about what happened in Lashia the first time. Someone I considered a friend took my head clean off. I won't allow them to hobble and betray us all again."

"Right," I said slowly, my heart thumping uncomfortably. We'd never known what happened to him and now the vision of his headless body would be burned in my brain forever. He was just as angry as we were. I turned to Morgan.

Connery rolled his eyes. "The princess is not my keeper. Nor is her sister. I want to help and I want to see my friends." He held up his palms. "Please."

"I'm not your keeper," Morgan snapped. "But I had to support my sister through hundreds of years of heartbreak the last time you fucked off to Lashia, so I'm coming with." She raised an eyebrow at me, daring me to demand a 'please' from her.

"You don't speak the language," I stuttered, not liking the idea of Morgan being in Lashia. I didn't object to her in particular, but it was just one more element I'd need to deal with.

"I'm a luvit." Morgan looked at me like I was a tiresome child.

I cocked my head to the side, giving her a long, assessing glance. Being able to speak all languages was pretty handy for a royal, not so much for someone who didn't leave their own country. It was one of those things that solidified my belief that the Allmother gave us our powers based on the needs of our lives, past and present.

"Fine. Why not?" I deadpanned. "I'm only trying to navigate an incredibly tense political situation while keeping anyone from looking too closely at Connery's absence and the giant gaps in his memory. But hey, why not? Bring the whole family," I huffed, crossing my arms.

Audre took out a bladed star and spun it as she stared down the princess.

Connery was looking at me, a smile on his face, but something more. His eyes examined me as if he could find his missing memories under my skin. Like he was wondering what he would have done in this situation if we were still together. Did he like what he saw? Did it make sense to him, or was he surprised to know he'd been attracted to me? He shook his head and glanced at Morgan.

"Actually," he started.

The front door opened, and a familiar head of hair the color of embers ducked through the doorway. Amber eyes met mine.

"Hello again." Erik's lips turned up like a secret. "Room for one more?"

"Remember, you need to call him Aiden. Try to avoid talking about yourself at all, but if you have to, tell them the three of you are from Asheville. It's the southernmost borough, and the most rural." I'd jumped us to Connery's house first.

Audre gave Connery, Morgan, and Erik enough power from the darana to apply their own cuffs. Morgan, in a stunning disregard for the laws of Trevesten, also donated her power to Erik so he could communicate in Lashia. She went with blue cuffs, but Erik insisted on yellow.

"I love going undercover," he said, admiring the glowing rings. "Who knows what salacious things people will say if they think I'm a Tal?"

"I'd suggest you keep your sleeves down and try not to call attention to yourself. You're already going to struggle with pretending to be human."

Erik held a hand to his heart. "Being weak and powerless is a stretch for me but I'm incredibly talented."

Morgan was inspecting Connery's things, his drawing, the books. She stopped when she got to the little house. "I can feel it. That drag you mentioned." She held out her hands as if she could see the dampening of her power.

"Yes. Hopefully, it won't be as bad for you as it was for us."

"We drained ourselves a lot," Connery added, motioning to the darana. "That made it worse."

He'd turn to me when I'd said 'us,' but I didn't dare look back. I tried to find something else to focus on, and the couch drew my gaze. Color rose to my cheeks, and my eyes quickly snapped back to the group. Erik was watching me with a knowing smirk.

"I'm surprised Sabine could spare you," I drawled.

"The Queen and General Antonio have business to attend to this week. She suggested I accompany the princess and Con—Aiden as an extra safety precaution. In case anything gets dicey."

I looked from him to Connery and then to Morgan. The three of them were more than capable of handling themselves in any situation.

"Unnecessary. If anything gets dicey, the three of you are going straight back." Finally, I looked at Connery. "I need to get some work done. I assume you're good to give them the tour?"

Connery nodded. "Yup, let's go, children. It's take your fae to work day."

I jumped back to my kitchen, bracing myself on the table. The memories washed over me. Even the ones I'd been ignoring ever since I'd taken Connery's memories. That was the longest we'd been together since the night Sabine had taken him.

The dark heightened your other senses. In the dark, I could hear his heartbeat, the sound of our breath mingling together. In the dark, we forgot all the things we were supposed to do, who we were supposed to be to one another. We hid from each other and ourselves.

In our first life, tension filled my every moment with him. In this one, he was a calming, steady presence. Was that really true? He'd always been kind and supportive. And whether as Connery or Aiden, he'd tried to do right by me, to do what was best for me, regardless of how he felt about it.

Leaders make hard choices. Not just for others, but for themselves, too. I'd stopped being a leader when we came to Lashia, stopped acting in service to the others. I could have done more—for all of them.

I would be better. For them, I would be better. And for him, I would forget too.

17

"Well, that's not a chicken." I eyed the disheveled man in the corner of my currently unused smoking shed.

"Hi." Chiwel squinted at me. Soot covered his clothing and his usual calm demeanor was gone. Tension hugged his shoulders as he rubbed his palms together nervously.

"I wondered if Durand was making this up," I said, crossing my arms and leaning against the door.

Chiwel's eyes flew to the top of his head. "He contacted you?"

"You've got a crappy friend."

"Damn it," Chiwel swore. "He's not my friend, he's my cousin. I was in a bad state when I got to him. It's hard to keep secrets when you're hungry."

As if on cue, Chiwel's stomach rumbled.

"C'mon, you can get cleaned up and spill the rest of your secrets while I make you lunch."

Chiwel gave me a grateful look but peered out of the door suspiciously.

"There's nobody here, I promise."

We made our way across the yard into the restaurant. I walked Chiwel upstairs. The windows were all still boarded up, but the rooms were otherwise in good shape. And most importantly for him, the plumbing was working.

The water gurgled above me while I made Chiwel a sandwich thick with ham and pickles. I sent the little fish to my parents' house, and a moment later, my father chimed in.

"Everything okay?"

"Chiwel is here. Turns out Durand was right about him trying to contact me. I can take care of him, but wanted to let you know in case anything goes awry." I was still over-sharing my every move with my parents, to ease some of the worry they'd held onto ever since I'd gone to Trevesten without a word.

"Okie doke. I'll keep the link open if you need me. Apologies in advance for any swearing. I'm fixing the shelves in the pantry."

"Swearing is reasonable then," I replied as Chiwel's feet sounded on the stairs.

He was wearing the same clothes, but I'd magically removed the dirt.

"Thanks for this," he said, plucking at the front of his shirt. "Impressive."

"Something tells me that might not be the most impressive magic you've seen so far." I put the plate on my newly repaired table, and he fell into the seat gratefully.

"You'd be wrong," he grumbled, putting the napkin on his lap before sinking his teeth into the sandwich.

I busied myself making us tea while he practically inhaled his food. How long had it been since he'd eaten?

Finishing the sandwich, he took a deep pull on his tea, sighing in satisfaction. "Thank you so much. I know helping me is a risk."

"Helping me during the census was a risk." Light fell across the table, illuminating the dark circles under his eyes. "Why did you do it?"

Chiwel leaned back in his chair, hands on his hips. "How did you get your cuffs off?" He frowned, glancing at the lack of glow beneath my sleeves. I'd used the darana to get rid of the red glamor. "Both sets of your cuffs off?" he amended.

I gave him a look that said, 'you first,' and he huffed a laugh.

"Sorry." He took a deep breath. "Tals have magic, too. The yellow cuffs also bind magic."

I pulled my lips into my mouth and widened my eyes in feigned surprise.

Chiwel gave me a stunned look. "You knew?"

"It is something that has come to my attention recently. Among other things. Like how you stole the memory of my first dog." My eyes narrowed on him.

He blew out a breath and gave me an impressed look. "I wasn't sure you'd figure that out. But I needed to apply something or it wouldn't look right." He ran a hand through his wet hair and puffed out his cheeks. "I really am sorry." He grimaced as he rubbed a finger along the edge of the table, avoiding my eyes.

Sighing, I beckoned at him to go on.

"I didn't know Sloane Mailer, but I knew the registrar from Asheville. Him and his accompanists. We were all contacted by a man named Arthur, who said he knew Tals had magic and fed us a bunch of bullshit about liberating the people of Lashia. He also offered us a lot of money." Shame filled his cheeks. "When I saw you at Halloween, I was all hopped up on my sense of self-importance."

"So you all left willingly?"

"At first. When they executed those people, the ones Mailer uncuffed, I lost it. I couldn't believe they would do something so extreme." His voice lowered to a whisper. "The ones they just executed were mine. I'd uncuffed them before the first executions." He squeezed his eyes tight, as if trying to dislodge the memory of their swinging corpses.

The papers hadn't reported any further arrests. "How many did you uncuff?"

"Four. Two Jinns, two Tals. They caught the Jinns." There was bitterness in his voice as he said the words. "I don't think Arthur wants to uncuff Jinns at all. It was just an experiment. To see whether their power was any greater than people labeled as Tals. I think Harris, that's the registrar from Asheville, has uncuffed a dozen more people, and only two of them were Jinns."

"Why only Tals?"

"Payback. I overheard him talking to Harris. He thinks Tals deserve to have their magic back, so Jinns know what it was like for them. That's when I decided it was time to get out of there." The light in his eyes dimmed. Guilt battled with anger in his expression.

Arthur and his ilk could be descended from some of the worst offenders in the war. He was waging a vengeance campaign based on an arbitrarily assigned label.

I pushed my hands into the pockets of my apron, feeling the items I'd shoved inside throughout the day. A pencil, a napkin, a piece of candy. It wouldn't be difficult to hide Chiwel, but it certainly complicated things.

"Was it Arthur? Who requested that you verify my cuffs?"

"No," he said, sucking air through his teeth and giving me a contrite smile, "that was me."

"What?" I said, sticking my hands on my hips. "Why?"

He waved his hand around the kitchen. "For this. I wasn't sure I could escape Arthur. But I knew, after I saw you on Halloween, you'd likely be the only person who could help me."

"So you manufactured a situation to put me in your debt? No matter the trauma caused? And you took my damn dog?" My words were sharp, but my blood didn't heat with anger.

He placed both palms on the table and slowly moved them back and forth, like he was physically smoothing away the tension. "I'm sorry. I was getting desperate." Chiwel toyed with his napkin. His hands were rough and chapped, not the smooth skin he'd had when he'd cuffed me.

He still looked weak, so I put some more food on the table for him. "Durand thinks I'm in cahoots with you, and me handing you over would sort of cement that theory."

Chiwel smiled gratefully, picking up an apple. "I can't go to the council myself. Arthur has people on the inside. I think one of the councilors is in his pocket, but I'm not sure which one. I'd be dead within the day." The apple paused halfway to his mouth as he considered his dangerous situation.

"Is that what happened to Sloane Mailer?" I asked softly.

"I don't have any proof, but I'd put good money on it."

We sat in silence, both of us considering the options. Chiwel grabbed another piece of fruit.

"If you tell the council to look into Arthur, he's going to claim he's never met you. Besides, you know..." I made a sliding motion with my finger across my neck and Chiwel winced. "His people on the inside will claim you're trying to save yourself by incriminating an innocent person. I'm guessing Arthur still has his cuffs on?"

"Yep. He's not that stupid."

"Hey!" I said in mock indignation, holding my palms up. "Who are you calling stupid?"

"Sorry!" He laughed. "I meant he's not stupid enough to do something that could easily get himself arrested when he's got his eye on a bigger prize."

"So his plan is to what, just uncuff Tals one at a time? That can take a while, especially if you've only got one registrar."

Chiwel shrugged. "Probably doesn't want to rush too much. The council has been so accommodating," he sneered. "Maybe he wants to make sure they're on his side."

They were being accommodating, weren't they? Couldn't possibly upset their favorites. They might not be executing them, but they were probably erasing their memories. Order must be maintained and all that.

Pushing off the counter with my hip, I began collecting his dishes. "You got your ability to erase memories and apply colorful bracelets from a darana, correct? Metal disc?"

Chiwel's eyebrows shot up, but he nodded. His eyes were serious, but I could tell how much he enjoyed being able to discuss all of this openly.

"I used a darana too. But you didn't need the darana for the cuffing, did you? That's your natural ability?" No reason for him to know what I'd done for Connery, especially if the registrars and accompanists didn't know how the power could be removed and transferred.

"Yes." He gave a shudder. "They watch us as children. Waiting for us to grow up and work for them."

"Gross." I gave him a sympathetic look. The councils couldn't rely on the donated damari power in the daranas lasting forever. They needed fresh blood. Digging through my memory, I tried to remember which abilities I'd taught the original villagers to identify. Other than our natural abilities, I'm sure I pointed out obahn and damari. Were there others?

My eyes snapped to him as I realized what he'd told me. "You can take power from the darana—more than one ability."

"Yes," Chiwel said slowly, giving me an amused smile. "I think we just established that."

My brows knitted. "But you shouldn't be able to do that. None of the original Lashians could take more than one ability."

"What do you mean? You've got more than one ability." He waved a hand at his clean clothes. "Is this your natural ability?"

The fae in me scoffed at the insult. Mild cleaning was something we could all do. I cleared my throat, ignoring the question. "I'd like to try something."

Indie finished her initial examination and stepped back. I'd brought Chiwel here under the pretense that I wanted to be sure medical attention was close by. In reality, I didn't trust him. Simon and Audre were outside, just in case he betrayed us.

"What do you think is going to happen?" Chiwel looked at me and Indie.

"Maybe nothing. It might work just like when you received your other two powers," I said.

"Were you sick at all when you received power from the darana the first time?" Indie asked.

He considered the question. "I remember feeling a little lightheaded, but put it down to nervous excitement." He shrugged.

"And you're sure you're okay with this?" Indie asked again. She'd already asked when he'd shown up.

The corner of Chiwel's lip rose, and he affected a small swagger. "I help Lim, she helps me. I help her again. Just trading favors over here."

"Might I remind you I only needed your help because you threw me under the bus."

He waved a hand. "Semantics."

Chiwel put his hand on the bottom of the darana. We'd infused it with a small amount of Indie's healing ability.

After he absorbed the power, I handed him a small knife, and he pricked his finger. Chiwel stared at the cut as it seeped blood, concentrating. Sweat beaded on his upper lip, reminding me of Emir. The wound was closing, but slowly.

"That wasn't easy," Chiwel said, swaying a bit on his feet. His eyes became unfocused and Indie quickly helped him into a chair. As soon as his ass hit the seat, he turned and heaved. She shoved a trash can under his mouth as he vomited. The light in his ochre skin dimmed as he gripped the trash can with both hands.

"Take it out," Indie said, but I was already moving toward him with the darana. I placed his hand on the top and waited. Chiwel's breathing slowly returned to normal as I removed the healing power.

Briefly, I considered doing another round, to remove his obahn ability, too. It seemed horrifying that the registrars were all walking around with two of the most feared powers. With a wave of my hand, I cleared the trashcan of its contents.

There was a knock at the door.

"It's us," Connery's voice called. The exam room became quite crowded once Connery, Morgan, and Erik stepped in.

I introduced Chiwel and explained his situation. Chiwel's eyes were wide with alarm at his secrets being spilled to three strangers.

"Don't worry, they're with me," I said. He frowned, unconvinced.

"So what's the plan? How are you going to stop Arthur?" Morgan asked.

"I'm not planning to stop him at all. There's a Sun Guardian meeting tomorrow. I think between Chiwel and I, we could uncuff quite a lot of Tals."

"What? I thought you were different! You're going to help him?" Chiwel stood up, his eyes hard.

Morgan's head cocked. Erik's hands went to his blades, but when he remembered we'd asked him not to carry them, he folded his arms across his chest. Connery arched an eyebrow at me.

"Calm down, Chiwel. I want to uncuff everyone, not just the Tals."

"Then why are you uncuffing the Sun Guardians?" he demanded.

"Because the government has made a point of listening to them, catering to them, allowing them to stoke this divide between us. Uncuffing a bunch of Jinns would just cause another riot and more executions."

Connery's eyes were intent upon me as I spoke, and he nodded slowly in understanding. "But uncuffing the Tals, showing them they have magic too, turns everyone against the council." I squirmed internally as those hazel eyes continued to search my face. "Clever, Lim."

"Once you do it, the council can't unring that bell," Indie said, leaning against the pale blue wall, one delicate finger tapping against her lips. "They'll have to address the lie."

I tipped my head at her. "And that is when you'll be there to explain to them that their best hope is to get ahead of it now. To prepare to keep people safe without manipulating them."

"Okay." There was no hesitation in Indie's voice. She had a score to settle with the council. Even if they weren't the ones who had ambushed us all those years ago, she was not about to give them a single inch.

"You'll meet with the council while I'm liberating the stupid Sun Guardians." I grimaced, thinking of all the terrible things they had done. "You should take Bastian."

"Did they ever arrest anyone for the fire?" Connery asked quietly.

"Four people. Leo did alright. Had several of his buddies who had businesses on that street join him in his efforts to put pressure on them." I said. I took a deep breath, pushing away the memory of the fire and the aftermath.

I looked up at Erik, who'd watched my interaction with Connery like a hawk. "Time to put your money where your mouth is."

He grinned and gave me a sweeping bow. "Well then, let's not keep our audience waiting."

18

Erik didn't bother disguising himself, there was no need. Some borrowed powers, like my ability to read by touch, were just as strong as a natural power when used, but wore off quickly. Other powers, like Audre's and my mother's glamoring ability, were limited by how much you used and for how long. If I changed my appearance completely, it would wear off more quickly than if I only changed it slightly. For the Sun Guardians meeting, I altered myself just enough not to be recognized and applied yellow cuffs.

Audre, reveling in the return of her first ability, was an entirely different person. She became an older woman with a heavily lined face, tight silver curls, and a permanent sneer on her lips. After discussing it, we decided not to bring Chiwel after all.

Connery and Morgan accompanied Indie, Simon, and Bastian to Eudora. Bastian asked the councilors to meet with him under the pretense that his clients had information on Chiwel and Harris. He delicately dropped enough hints of Chiwel's 'outlandish' claims regarding Tals and Jinns that we knew the councilors would attend.

The Sun Guardians met at a community center. As we walked into the large multipurpose room, I spotted pool tables, ping-pong, and shelves of books. The air smelled of tea and cake.

The three of us took our seats. Not too close to the front or the back, but near enough to the exit. The crowd was chatting but fell silent as a man strode to the center of the room.

"Good evening!" he called, his arms outstretched. Despite the greeting, I had the impression of being scolded. He had thick, brown hair but a thin body, ropey with muscle.

Audre gently elbowed me, jutting her chin to our right. I looked across and spotted Emir's brother sitting with a group of men. Tarik's eyes were just as dark and cold as I remembered. His choice to sit directly under a poster that read, "Be Positive!" with a cartoonish bee giving a thumbs up somewhat diminished his menacing effect.

"Good evening," we all parroted back.

"A traitor walks among us." His eyes scanned the room as the attendees responded with whispers and grumbles.

"Chiwel Adegbe, the registrar that so recently came to our cause, to rid us of the chains tying us to the Jinns, has deserted his duty as a Tal." The crowd hissed and spit in response.

Audre caught my eye. Looks like we'd made the right decision.

There was booing and shouting. The speaker held out his hands for silence.

"We have information that he has returned here to Marais. Which means someone is hiding him. He's still one of us, so unless a Jinn agreed to help him, someone here must know something!" At this, the crowd erupted, denials coming from every corner.

Audre and Erik shouted along with them, shaking their heads and expertly playing the part. I kept my eyes open, considering all the ways this could go wrong. We'd been waiting for an opening, and this was as good as any.

I raised my hand.

Beside me, I felt Audre and Erik tense, but their Tal personas didn't falter.

"Yes?" The man squinted at me from the front.

"Chiwel didn't desert us. The council was closing in. He left to draw attention away from the others." I didn't mention Arthur or Harris, not knowing how much this crowd even knew about them. "I believe they may have already executed him."

Their leader looked incredulous. "Executed him? The council doesn't execute Tals." The surrounding people eyed me with suspicion.

I stood up. "The council is not on our side. They are catering to the Jinn-filth." Audre coughed to cover a snort. "Their only desire is to maintain control. Even at the expense of honest, hard-working Tals."

Even I thought that was a bit rich, but the crowd was receptive, murmuring and shifting in their chairs.

"What's your name?"

"My name is Carla. Carla Kelly. And Chiwel was the love of my life. We weren't allowed to be together while he was a registrar, but we fell in love, anyway." I pretended to wipe a tear from my eye. Erik stood, putting an arm around my shoulder. "We dreamed of a life of freedom, *Tal* freedom. And I've come here today to see if you meant all that you told him, that you promised us. Or if you are as cowardly as the council, executing a man without trial purely for fighting for what is right."

The leader frowned, his jaw working. "We are not cowards." The crowd agreed with him. "But I don't think I catch your meaning, young lady."

I turned to Audre, nodding as if I was giving her strength. Her face was determined. She audibly swallowed and was no doubt dying with laughter inside.

"I can help all of us tonight," I said as I laid my hands over Audre's. The entire crowd was hanging on my every word. "It will take all of us."

People behind me stood to watch in rapt attention as I removed Audre's fake yellow cuffs.

Several people in the crowd gasped before a round of thunderous applause sounded. Audre held out her hands, her voice coming out aged and raspy, "Finally. Finally, free."

"They cannot stop all of us! I will not let Chiwel's gift to me be in vain. If all of us stand together, they have to listen. Cuffs are for Jinns, not for Tals! Cuffs are for Jinns, not for Tals!"

The crowd easily picked up the chant, and they herded me, along with an animated Erik and Audre, to the front of the room.

"Will you show them what you're made of?" I demanded of the speaker. He chewed his cheek nervously, trying to hide the quick darting glance he gave to the side of the stage. I didn't have to look at Erik or Audre to know they noticed it, too.

I held out my hands to him. At the crowd's frenzied insistence, he had no choice but to comply.

This wasn't the original power we'd given back to the darana. The female I'd met with in the tavern in Oderon didn't even have to do a full drain for me to handle the thirty people at the meeting who volunteered to be uncuffed. It was lucky Audre's current face was already in a haughty scowl. It was hard for both of us to hide our anger as I released Tarik's power.

Erik slipped out while I worked. After the meeting was over, and I'd asked my father to relay as much to Indie and the others, we waited for him outside, hidden behind a darkened glass shop.

He appeared, gripping the arm of a young man, probably just shy of twenty. This was who the speaker had looked for when we'd approached.

"Are you a Jinn spy?" I asked.

"No! No, of course not. I work for the Tals."

"You work for Arthur?"

He swallowed and nodded. "I'm just supposed to report back on what happens at the meetings. He's got a bunch of us throughout the boroughs."

"When do you give your reports?"

"Normally, I'd write. But..." His eyes darted between us.

"More of a phone call situation," Audre supplied.

He nodded.

The post office opened at nine. It wasn't a lot of time, but it had to be enough.

Erik let him go, and he hurried off into the night. He might have looked back, but I'd already jumped us to Eudora.

As expected, two of the three councilors, along with several members of law enforcement, waited for us in the office Bastian had borrowed for his meeting.

Since I'd never been there, we arrived in the room through the door. It was nothing like his office. Everything was awash in soft pastels and grays. It immediately made me want to nap.

Indie sat in a wingback chair behind a large pine desk. Simon stood to her left and Bastian to her right. My eyes searched the room for Morgan and Connery. I knew, the way I always knew, that he was nearby, but I couldn't sense her.

Erik's warm breath startled me as he leaned in and whispered, "The princess and your brother have something in common." He jerked his head to the corner of the room, where I saw nothing but a potted plant. "Your ex is with her."

My lips thinned, but I didn't look back at the plant.

The councilors sat in two pale blue armchairs in front of the desk, while everyone else took the less comfortable chairs surrounding a long conference table.

"Can we begin, or would the two of you prefer to wait for Ali?" Indie said, referring to the third councilor.

Cox, the only male councilor, a skinny man with sparse black hair, stood up. "You brought us here under the pretense of having vital information about our rogue registrars. Information you said" —he jabbed his finger at Indie, whose face remained impassive— "you would only provide once we were all together. This whole thing is presumptuous and insulting. It's only because Mr. Dale has worked with us so well in the past that we even deigned to take this meeting."

"Is that a yes?" Indie said, her gaze cool.

Cox looked at Varma, the other councilor. A woman with deep blond hair. She gave a small shrug, and he flapped his hands at his sides in exasperation. "By all means," he said, slamming back down in his chair.

Indie nodded to me.

"Tonight, there was a meeting of the Sun Guardians in Marais. During the meeting, a woman claimed that you executed Chiwel for removing the Tals' cuffs. She proceeded to uncuff about thirty Tals at that meeting."

Cox paled and Varma's mouth popped open.

"You... you should be arrested," Cox stuttered, but he stayed seated.

"On what grounds?" Bastian asked.

Cox flailed, looking to the others for support. "Obstruction?"

"We're not obstructing anything. We want to help you. Tomorrow, those Tals are going to wake up and realize they have magic."

Everyone but us froze. Finally, Varma swallowed and said, "What did you say?"

"Secret's out, lady," Audre replied, hopping up to sit on the desk. "They'll know and they'll talk. The rest of the Tals will be clamoring for the removal of their cuffs by noon."

Cox opened and closed his mouth like an anxious fish. The others in the room all looked at one another in confusion.

"I'm sorry. Did you say 'Tals' have magic?" An officer in a dark gray suit stood up, his hand bracing on the table.

Indie stood. "Yes. Tals and Jinns do not exist. About five hundred years ago, five of us came to Lashia from another world. A fae world. We gave our magic to the people of Lashia. In order to achieve 'peace'" —she made air quotes around the word— "an original group of Tals created the lie that only half the population has magic. That lie has been perpetuated by the people in this room, and every council, in every borough, since then. Apparently, the arbitrary oppression of half the population was considered a reasonable price to pay for this peace." Indie's eyes flashed at the two councilors as she folded her arms across her chest.

There were several long minutes while everyone absorbed that information. Out of the corner of my eye, I saw the officer who stood pull back his shirtsleeves to reveal his yellow cuffs. When neither Varma or Cox denied the allegation, the table behind me broke out in rapid questions.

"Did you both know?"

"What kind of magic?"

"Did you say 'fae'?"

"How could you lie to everyone?"

Varma nervously smoothed down the front of her shirt. Cox was furiously chewing his nails.

"So." I clasped my hands loudly, startling people into silence. "Now that we're all on the same page. We will obviously not be having a society of haves and have-nots. You'll need to be prepared to uncuff everyone."

At that, Cox actually drew blood from his ragged thumb.

Varma, however, sat up straighter, and her voice was strong as she spoke. "It will be chaos. You claim to have been there," she said, her voice incredulous, "then you should know exactly what happened before. We did this to keep people safe. Why do you think you can do better?"

"We made a mistake," I said, and Varma's head turned to me. "As the only ones who knew how to live in a society with magic, we should have done more, pushed more, to ensure Lashia knew how to adapt. But that's a mistake we won't repeat." I looked at Indie and Simon as I spoke.

"That's right," Indie said. "We're going to need some laws." She held out a hand and Bastian placed a sheaf of papers in them. They were a pared-down set of laws from Trevesten. "We will also help you enforce those laws and teach people how to use their magic safely. But the punishment for misuse of magic will not be execution. That will *never* be an option." Her eyes flashed golden, and the councilors reared back.

"You're not even elected," he sputtered. "Who are you to be giving orders?"

Indie leaned forward, placing two hands flat on the desk, and relief washed over me. Erik looked at me, a question on his face, but he said nothing.

"I'm someone who should have stood up to you all a long time ago. We don't need to worry about titles right now. But as I'm going to outlive all of you by at least two hundred years, there is definitely no getting rid of me or my husband."

Simon gave a casual salute but an intimidating smile.

"I won't live as long as them, but I am helpful in a crisis," Bastian, ever the mediator, said with a placating smile. "People will feel they're bumbling around in the dark for a little while. Indie and Simon have the knowledge and experience to help them navigate this unfamiliar territory."

Indie flashed me a knowing look. Bastian was definitely going to be helpful at smoothing out the edges.

Around the room, people were standing, murmuring in confusion.

"Can we go back to the fae thing?"

"Why don't you look older?"

"If you're not from here, why do you want to stay?"

"We care about the people of Lashia," Indie said. Her voice became softer, and the room quieted to hear.

"Otherwise, we wouldn't have given you all magic in the first place," Audre added.

"Especially since it came at great expense to ourselves." Connery appeared in the corner and several people gasped and stumbled back.

"We drained our power, our very life, in our attempt to help," I said. "So don't even think about doubting our commitment to your survival. Even though, in the end, you really screwed us over." Again, Erik gave me that same questioning look. Simon stepped closer to Indie. Could he still feel the cold spear driving through his heart? I shuddered.

"When the war started," Indie took up the story, "we didn't even know which side to be on. Magic vs. Magic. We picked the underdogs, taught them to work together. Afterward, instead of listening to us, letting us help them succeed with this power, they betrayed and murdered us." This time, there was no mistaking those golden eyes. The tiniest tip of her claws caught the light, and Varma eyed them warily.

The faces in the room were a mix of horror and incredulity. It was a lot to take in all at once.

"You may not be the Tals who wronged us originally, but you are certainly acting like them," Connery added.

"Yes. You've let the Sun Guardians get away with murder. Is that fair? Is that the Lashia you dreamed of?" I asked.

"We've made arrests," Cox said weakly.

"And the Tals that were uncuffed? Where was their noose?" Audre spat. "I don't want anyone to die. But you have to understand how shitty that is, to once again make this all our fault. To, time and time again, blame one arbitrary half of your society for a problem you created."

"You weren't supposed to know about them," Cox mumbled, sinking farther into his chair in defeat.

"We didn't know how to fix it. Nobody ever has." Varma's voice was just above a whisper. "And now you want to just unleash it all again? I don't know that laws will help."

"Instead of acting out of fear, of creating laws based on what we want to prevent, we're going to picture what we want to create and work backward. There will be problems, a lot of them. But we can help enforce the laws," Indie said. "And if we need more fae to help." She nodded at the plant next to Connery.

Audre stifled a laugh as a man at the table reached out to touch a leaf, like he was shaking its hand.

"She means me." Morgan appeared, frowning at the man fondling the fiddle leaf, who blushed and stepped back.

"And me. I'm not as powerful as her, but as a third life, I'm pretty good." Erik made a gloating little bow.

"A what?" Varma asked.

I held up my hands. "There's no time for that. Just know that we will help and we will do it properly, without having to resort to lies and murder."

The door opened, startling us all. The last councilor, a woman named Ali appeared, and nearly ran right into Erik, who'd immediately raised his hands in anticipation of attack.

"I'm sorry I'm late." Her eyes glanced around in confusion. "What did I miss?"

"I'm not really from here," Erik whispered to her theatrically, "but it seems like things are about to get a lot more fun."

19

It was almost five a.m. when we left Eudora. Ali's arrival sent everything back into a tailspin. We had to explain it all again. Our arrival in Lashia, the daranas, the war, everything.

There was some shouting, especially those in the room who hadn't known about the lie. The councilors weathered the storm. Even Cox met the complaints head on, as he reminded them what horrible things the Jinns had done. But we were there to remind him the Tals had done horrible things too. And then again remind them there was no difference in the first place.

Over the hours, we discussed the laws, the punishments. I told them of the powers they should expect to see and how things were handled in Trevesten. My eyes were drawn to Connery more than once as I remembered our long-ago discussions about Sabine's tactics when ruling.

When the sun broke the next day, burning through the cool mist, newspapers carried news that rocked Lashia.

COUNCIL ADMITS ALL HAVE MAGIC. JINNS AND TALS TO BE UNCUFFED.

That night, for the first time since it had burned down, I opened The Peregrine.

The crowd was in a frenzy. Newspapers lay open on every table. Jinns looked at Tals. Tals looked at Jinns. Some tables were celebratory, others concerned.

But everyone had to eat.

I watched Connery out of the corner of my eye all night. It hurt to discover that it came back so easily, knowing where he was, what he needed. Marie joined him at the bar and they talked while enjoying some simple roasted chicken. After she left, he nursed a single beer while chatting with the other patrons.

There were smiles and back slaps from the other regulars. Several women, young and old, cooed over his return. He didn't flirt, though. Occasionally, he looked up at me and gave me a bracing smile that broke my heart. He was trying to console me, even now.

I wondered what would happen if, after everyone went home, I leaned over the bar and kissed him. Would that be enough? Could he use that tiny spark to wield the power inside him to bring everything back? Or would it make him more confused than ever? If it brought everything back, would he descend back into that terrible madness?

The crowd slowed. Connery was watching the band pack up. Audre was in the back cleaning. I'd made Morgan and Erik help by running food, a task they both seemed annoyingly comfortable with. Now they were playing darts in the corner with the last two remaining bar patrons.

The band left and Audre came up, ducking under the bar and pouring herself a drink. The three of us clinked our glasses.

Connery cleared his throat. "It's odd. I couldn't stop thinking about you." His gaze was guileless and his tone matter-of-fact.

My heart caught in my throat, and I stilled.

Audre paused, glass halfway to her lips. She leaned toward me, speaking out of the corner of her mouth with her eyes still on Connery, "He can see me, right? I haven't unknowingly camouflaged myself?"

I huffed a laugh even though inside it felt like I was falling down a long tunnel. My eyes flicked to Morgan and Erik.

His brows knitted in confusion. "I can see you."

"Are you sure? Because that kind of declaration of your feelings is usually something you say to someone in private." Audre downed the rest of her drink. It clattered on the bar when she set it down and I flinched.

Connery's eyes went wide with horror. "Oh no, that's not what I was doing. It's just interesting because you're not particularly memorable—I'm sorry, that came out wrong." His face turned bright red as he stopped speaking, grasping for the right words.

My eyes shot to the top of my head as Audre whistled. "Wow, you are moments from being barbeque."

"I'm so sorry, please. I just mean we only met for a second and I've got a mate. And I love her, and not you—" He clenched his eyes and rubbed his hands down his face.

When he looked like he might take another stab at it, I held up a hand to stop him. "Please stop, I got it. You're saying that after we met, you thought about me in a completely and totally platonic way, and that is scientifically interesting. Because even though you have no conscious memory of me, you think a part of you still knew there was something off."

For a moment, I saw Connery standing behind the bar, arms crossed as he cajoled me into a date so I would be happy. Even though he had feelings for me.

He exhaled in relief. "Yes. Exactly. Thank you."

It didn't really surprise me. Weak power on a first try never made for good odds. "It would not be the first time you've implied I could have been more thorough in my work."

His mouth fell open. "That's not at all what I meant."

Audre laughed. "It's fun to torture you again. Like old times." She threw a coaster at him and he deflected it easily with a brush of air.

I laughed as he grinned in relief. He was perfectly clean shaven again, not a whisper of the mountain man beard he sported for so long.

"Who's getting tortured?" Morgan walked up and took a seat at the bar. Beside me, Audre tensed. The two of them were circling one another like feral alley cats. Audre was still harboring old prejudices and was the least comfortable with our new royal friends.

"Your fashion sense," Audre shot back. She'd changed her hair from blue to pink tonight.

Morgan's eyes narrowed as Erik took the seat next to her. I offered him a drink.

"Thanks, chef's choice."

I made him the most pretentious drink I had, complete with a big purple flower on a tiny wooden skewer. I couldn't help it. He irritated me. It was one thing to have Morgan, but sending yet another guard dog? What did Sabine think I was going to do?

Erik gave me an appraising look, a smile playing in the corner of his mouth. But he took a long drink, eyebrows lifting in surprise. "That is excellent. Thank you."

"Welcome," I grumbled.

"Everyone ready for tomorrow?" Erik asked the group.

"I think we've waited long enough," Audre replied.

"Name?"

"You know my name, bitch," Sydney gritted out. Marco stood behind her, glaring. The struggle to save face while avoiding anything that might make me deny them their magic was obvious on the faces of Emir's sister and brother-in-law.

I tipped my head back a little, absolutely relishing the experience of Sydney needing something from me. I wanted to bottle it and put it on my shelves so I could take it out and experience it whenever I wanted.

"Oh, Sydney! I didn't recognize you. Did you do something different with your hair? It looks slightly less electrified," Audre said from beside me, where she was removing the cuffs of a young woman wearing a vibrant green headscarf.

I snickered but said only, "Hold out your hands."

Sydney followed my instructions while audibly grinding her jaw. I expected Bastian, who was checking people in, had deliberately put her in my line.

The council assigned several registrars to each borough, even the ones that had not yet been officially recruited. Me, Audre, Indie, Simon, and Connery all sat at a long table, checking people in and removing the cuffs of anyone over eighteen. Indie and I were using our hands. Simon, Connery, and Audre had the three daranas, mine, and the two the council had. I'd sent Morgan home to check in with Sabine.

Anyone who wanted their cuffs off had to be fingerprinted and have their ability documented.

After removing the yellow bands she so despised, I pricked the finger of her left and let her blood drop into the bowl.

"Ice," Audre said to the young woman as she read her blood's behavior. "Try it out." She waved her hand at the glass of water on the table. Water, wood, food. The table looked like a flea market with all the things we'd collected so people could test their power in front of us.

The young woman looked around nervously before concentrating on the glass. The water in it froze before the entire thing cracked.

"I'm so sorry!" she gasped.

"Not a problem at all. Be sure you practice and start small." Audre smiled and waved her hand to float the glass and ice to a large bin in the corner, full of the destroyed remnants of first tries.

The girl rushed away, marveling at her hands as I read Sydney's blood.

"Strangely, it's not people pleasing." I made a tsking sound. "You're a verdia. It means you can tell when someone is lying."

Audre laughed out loud. "You are about to have a rude awakening."

Sydney glowered at her, and I thanked the stars she didn't have something more dangerous.

"It's actually not a very common power," I conceded. "I'm going to say two things. You tell me, which is a lie. I have a friend named Natalia who changes into a bat. Baldrick owes me money."

Sydney's expression opened in surprise. "It's the second one." She raised her chin and tossed her hair proudly.

"Next," I said, nodding and dismissing her, noting down her power and beckoning Marco forward. He turned out to be a journalist, with the power to commit whatever he saw or thought into writing, sometimes from a great distance. It was a bit of a misnomer, since most of the fae I know who had it didn't use it for journalism but for teaching or spying. I shuddered at the thought of Marco leading a classroom.

Erik agreed to spend some time helping track down the Sun Guardians who had been uncuffed at the meeting so the council could make a note of their names and powers. They'd already found Tarik and a few of the others Audre and I recognized.

Occasionally, I got up to check someone else's bowl if the blood was acting unfamiliar. So far, we'd only found two people that didn't seem to have magic at all. We lied and said that sometimes there was a block and to come back tomorrow if nothing had happened yet.

We would give them power from the darana. Nobody would be completely powerless. After that though, my daranas were going back to Oderon.

An hour later, the scent of salt and sand wafted toward me. Leo set a plate of snacks down between me and Audre.

"There you go." He stretched his arms over his head, showing off his biceps. Nothing could convince him they weren't bigger now that he had enhanced strength. "You ladies need any heavy lifting done?" He gazed out into the crowd, hands on his hips, hair stylishly mussed.

I rolled my eyes. "The food was all we wanted. Thanks, Leo."

He wasn't listening. His eyes had already snagged on a group of women in line. One of them had the nerve to giggle.

"You let me know," he said as he practically prowled toward them. Apparently, Stovi Martinez's daughter had called off their engagement, saying she wanted to wait for a genuine relationship.

Somehow, I was sure Leo would get over it. Sydney wasn't the only Martin with bottomless self-assurance.

"I can't believe the Allmother gave him strength. Like she wanted him to be even more insufferable." Audre took a bite of a small sandwich. "At least he brought snacks. I'm starving."

I laughed, taking a sandwich for myself. "Seriously. Sitting on my ass all day is more exhausting than it looks."

As I stretched my arm across my torso, I held up five fingers to my waiting line and headed to the bathroom inside the library. The air was cool indoors, the smell of new paper mingling with old wood.

When I came out, Erik was waiting for me, leaning casually against a bookshelf.

"Any luck?" I asked.

"Yes. My descriptions were excellent, thank you. Officers are tracking them down as we speak. I told them I'd go to the station later to make sure it's who I remembered," he replied.

"Thank you. Let me know if you want to go home at any point." I walked toward the exit and he kept pace with me.

"Aren't you a little mad? I'd be a little mad." He floated a book off the floor and back onto a shelf as we walked past.

"What?" We'd stopped right before the doors out onto the sidewalk, where my line had grown even longer in my absence.

"Because he hasn't asked you to give his memories back." His eyes watched my reaction closely.

Scowling, I crossed my arms across my chest, heat flaring in my blood. "Why would I discuss this with you? I did what I had to do. Your queen is grateful, Connery is grateful. That should be enough for you, Captain." I practically spat the last word.

My anger only seemed to please him. "There it is. Thank goodness. I knew you couldn't be as okay with this as you seemed." Erik moved closer into my space, and I stood my ground, refusing to be cowed. This close, I could smell him. It reminded me of Fall, orchards, and bonfires. "Have you considered breaking the bond? At least then, he could be objective."

"What?" At this, I stepped back. "You can't break a mating bond." My arms fell to my sides, and for one shameful moment, I thought about all the knowledge we'd gained when searching for Sverresen and whether mating bonds had ever come up. I practically kicked myself and shoved those thoughts away hard.

"So you did look into it." His amber eyes flashed.

"No. Everyone already knows that," I said dryly. "Why are you trying to stir up trouble? You're Sabine's personal guard. Her interests are your interests."

"I'm tasked with assessing all potential threats." Erik gave me a sly smile. "And I don't believe you're going to just lay down and take this. You don't seem like the type that gives up."

I scoffed. "You don't know me very well."

"Well, enough to notice you took a backseat at that meeting with your council." He cocked his head to the side, assessing me like he would an opponent. "While Indie definitely seems like a female you don't want to fuck with, so do you. Care to enlighten me?"

Outside, I could see the people in my line getting restless. People were already showing off their power to their friends and family. It reminded me so much of early Lashia, before Audre died, before the war.

A long exhale escaped me as I closed my eyes against the memory of an ice shard covered in blood, the horrible sound Indie made as Simon died.

"Indie wasn't kidding when she said they murdered her and Simon. I was already dying, but I'm certain they helped me along. They forced her to watch as they ripped him in two." My voice shook, and I had to close my eyes and take a deep breath. But my voice was firm when I opened them. "She won't give her back to any of these people again."

"Vengeance isn't the best motivator." His brows knit, those eyes searching my face for something. "Trust me. Revenge may be a dish best served cold, but it's surprisingly unfilling." Something flickered behind his eyes. Embarrassment, perhaps?

Shaking my head, I stepped away from him. "It's not just that." I rubbed my neck and saw Erik track the movement. "I gave up when we got to Lashia. It was my screw-up. The others, they all became leaders, while I took a backseat and spent decades in unproductive self-pity. The humans feared my power, but they had no reason to fear Indie. She was so good to them, and would have been a spectacular leader."

My eyes found my friend outside. She was laughing, sharing a joke with a woman who changed the color of Indie's shirt from blue to red. "I can't be sure. But I think if I had gotten my shit together, this wouldn't have happened. I could have supported her, pushed all of us, to move this in the right direction." I paused, remembering during the war how she'd brought up Sabine's rishival. "She used to give me an idea, and I'd just run with it. I let them all down. But I'm going to do the right thing this time."

Erik just stared at me. He gave me a soft smile, like I was a puzzle he'd just cracked.

"Stop looking at me like that. Do I need to get a verdia so you'll back off?"

His smile widened. The red in his hair was nearly invisible in the library's soft light. "She will be an excellent leader, I can see that."

Pursing my lips, I turned away and pushed out the doors toward all the people waiting. Erik was antagonizing me to see if I had any plans to undermine Sabine. But we knew removing Connery's memories wasn't a long-term solution. We should consider other options. Without turning my head, because I was almost positive Erik was still watching, I looked over at Connery.

He was hugging a firefighter I recognized. The woman had tears of happiness in her eyes. There was no reason to believe the madness wouldn't return if I gave him his memories back.

'Breaking the bond would have the same result, but he'd have his memories. And he could still choose her, if he wanted.' The thought flew unbidden to my mind and I couldn't help turning and glaring at Erik like he'd planted it. But he was gone.

Bonds were unbreakable. And we were all better off like this. Even if my heart was crushed every time he looked at me and there was no history behind it, no knowing winks or soft smiles. Even though I still remembered every moment we'd shared in the dark, at the restaurant, in Oderon. I'd agreed to forget.

We were just... coworkers now.

20

SABINE

Sabine's brain was going to burst out of her skull. She'd be spying for hours and finally had to go lay down in her dark room, a cool mask over her eyes. She'd seen nothing. The Boraltans were still training a disproportionate number of fire-wielders, but other than that, nothing seemed amiss. Their current ruler, Sandlin, was preparing to hand over the crown to whoever won their contest. And the same issues and squabbles that existed in her court existed there too.

She let a hand graze over the empty half of the bed. Morgan had come back to give her an update. Connery was still in Lashia, with Erik, with Lim. She trusted him, knew he was committed to her again. And she trusted Lim because of what she'd done.

They were no closer to figuring out how to give Connery back his memories without also returning the madness. Now that he knew what the gaps in his memory were, he said they were sharper, more obvious. She winced as the pain lanced through her again.

"Enter," she said to the knock at her door.

Elsa opened the door, her face devoid of sympathy. "I told you this would happen. You cannot go for that long without taking a break."

Sabine waved her hand in concession. "I know, but Venten isn't talking and outside of actually interrogating him, I've got nothing to go on. Just a hunch."

The healer tsked before laying her hands on Sabine's forehead, her power flooding Sabine's mind before retreating and taking Sabine's headache with it. Sabine groaned in relief.

"Why don't you just go yourself?"

"A spontaneous royal visit makes everyone antsy. I don't want them to know what I've seen. And I'll be going for the trials once they start, anyway." Sabine sat up on the bed, feeling better than she had before she'd spent so much time trying to see into Boralta and figure out what they were up to with all those fire-wielders.

Elsa floated a glass of water over to Sabine and she took it gratefully.

"Can't you manufacture a reason to go?"

Sabine pursed her lips to the side, contemplating her chief healer. "Boralta is beautiful, cold, and wild, but it's not exactly a vacation spot." Sabine paced a little, examining her options. She snapped her fingers.

"Got an idea?" Elsa asked.

"I'm going to start a fight."

"Thank you for inviting us to dinner, Your Majesty," Ato said. The Eloishan ambassador was cheerful as he took a seat next to her. He wore a dark suit, shot through with gold and crimson thread, and a high-collared shirt with rubies at the corners.

"Yes, much appreciated," Venten said, smoothing down his braided tie and taking his own seat on her other side.

Diana and Sayla, the ambassadors from Penglynis and Ursan, also expressed their thanks. Diana was wearing silk pants and a matching top in vibrant teal, along with an ankle-length, gauzy tunic with slits up the sides.

Sayla wore what she always wore, a black suit, with a black silk shirt, which contrasted with her bubbly personality. The Ursan Ambassador actively encouraged people to use her cheerful attitude as an excuse to underestimate her. Nearly always, to their peril.

Sabine smiled in response. "I thought we should have a nice meal to get through the pain of this conversation."

The room stilled at that.

She chuckled. "I only meant I wish to finalize our proposals to your countries on the rules for Kysalt. I realize it's not the most exciting use of an evening,"—she playfully rolled her eyes at Venten—"but I'd prefer to get it over with, especially with the trials starting soon."

"I suppose we must," Ato said.

"Are you really going to hold a trial in Kysalt?" Sayla asked. "That's the rumor."

A server poured a golden glass of wine for Venten, and he took a sip before answering.

"I don't think so. Perhaps next time."

"Even with our efforts tonight, the regulations might not be in place yet," Sabine said. "Maybe not the best time to have so many Boraltans in Kysalt."

Venten nodded to her. "We're not out to ruffle anyone's feathers."

A clerk, a journalist, brought over a sheaf of papers and sat at the other end of the table. He raised his head and folded his hands in his lap, poised to take notes on their discussion.

"Well, then. Might as well begin." Sabine announced.

Through the first course of oysters and salad, a main of popped couscous and lentils or lamb, followed by chocolate and passionfruit pavlova, Sabine and the four ambassadors talked. And talked. And then talked some more.

Sabine dragged it out, inserting her comments and subtly bringing up old grudges. Encouraging the others to waste their time on nominal issues.

Three hours later, everyone was exhausted, but they had a firm set of proposals for any resources found in Kysalt.

"Of course, if there is an existing presence in Kysalt, these rules become moot. Each country will need to negotiate separately with their governing power."

Sabine's declaration appeared on the paper in front of the clerk as the others murmured their assent.

"Have you ever seen anyone there? We certainly haven't." Ato leaned back in his chair, propping an ankle on his knee. His eyes were on Venten.

"No. Never."

"But you've found something, obviously." Diana leaned forward. Her skin had a metallic sheen, a testament to her power to control certain metals.

Venten smiled a polite smile. A diplomat's smile. "We believe there may be value in the world."

He had no obligation to tell them what Boralta had found. It was up to the rest of them to figure out what it was, based on how he phrased his requests, the type of export regulations he wanted.

Every country had sent scouting parties and while there were resources to be found, mineral deposits, extensive forests, nobody was clamoring to avail themselves of these. Of course, Boralta could be running short on these resources and didn't want anyone to know. Or, more likely, there was something else beneath the ice they planned to exploit.

Venten had ensured they included plenty of wording around mining operations, precious metals, extractions. He also specifically mentioned 'items coming through the portal from Kysalt to Malan.'

The wording stuck with Sabine, tumbling around in her head.

"You know, perhaps having a trial in Kysalt isn't such a bad idea. We'd all be there anyway, and this way, you can kill two birds with one stone," Sabine said. "We'd get a chance to look around while being together, on even ground, and you can challenge the competitors in a whole new environment."

"Forgive me, Your Majesty, but you want us to create a whole new trial in Kysalt, so you can 'take a look around?'" Venten arched an eyebrow at her. "The trials are massive events. They require extensive infrastructure. It's not a small request."

"I'll admit my king has expressed a desire for another scouting trip, and I'd prefer not to make two," Ato said.

"But the regulations won't be final yet." Venten tipped his head at Sabine.

"Are you so worried? That we'll all find things during the trials? You make it sound as if these valuables are just lying around." Diana crossed her arms.

"Or maybe," Sayla mused, "Boralta doesn't want us in Kysalt while they're distracted with the trials."

Sabine's eyes slid to Venten, who was toying with his wineglass, the only evidence that this conversation had turned in a direction he didn't like.

"Sayla," Sabine said, mild reprimand in her voice. "This won't be a repeat of Kildale."

Venten's eye twitched. "That was not our fault. We had no reason to know the land was sacred."

"Well, there weren't any signs, but you probably could have asked," Ato replied. His voice was soft, and Sabine knew he enjoyed baiting Venten.

Diana's face had gone red. "After all this time? Seriously? The Boraltan's defense to looting three of our ancient temples, is that you just didn't know?" She smacked her hand on the table in anger.

"I will not be bullied into having this debate again. It was a century ago!" Venten snarled. "There was no reason for anyone to know about those temples."

"That's why you need regulations, right? So you can loot whatever you find and feel totally secure in whatever happens, right? Even if you uncover something precious to one of us?" Diana demanded.

Sabine gritted her jaw, her eyes bouncing between the two ambassadors, but inside, she was singing.

"I have made it clear we have an interest in the land. Boralta has proposed regulations in good faith, out of fairness to all of you," he said in exasperation.

"But it's not fair, is it? When you can craft whatever pretty words you want to be most advantageous to that which you seek?" Ato leaned back from the table, his voice both melodic and intimidating.

"Boralta will not be punished for its diligence." Venten mirrored Ato's posture. Small, green scales appeared above his collar. He was struggling not to shift.

'And there it is.' Sabine had to fight to repress her grin.

"Do not insult our capabilities, Venten!" Diana's voice was hard.

Ato scowled, but Sayla's eyes slid to Sabine's.

Sabine avoided her gaze as she held up her hands. "Perhaps it was too much to ask for a trial. We have all seen the lengths Boralta goes through to make the contest an event to remember. But I see that there may be a need for something. Something before we agree on the resolutions."

Venten exhaled. "I apologize. My emotions got the better of me." He nodded to both Diana and Ato. "Perhaps I could organize a group scouting trip before the trials? Something more extensive that would satisfy your need for scrutiny."

Sabine stayed silent as the group considered it. There were portals to Kysalt in other countries, but they were smaller. Boralta had the only portal that was big enough to be useful. The countries had long ago determined that other worlds were not the property of any country, unless and until there was such an agreement, regardless of which country contained the portal.

"I think that is a reasonable compromise. I wouldn't want to be distracted during the trials either," Sayla spoke up.

"Thank you, Venten," Sabine nodded solemnly. "I appreciate your willingness to work together. And on that note, I think I will retire." Sabine stood, and the rest of them got to their feet.

As she exited the room, her eyes caught on Sayla's. The Ursan ambassador gave her a tiny nod, and Sabine nodded back, hiding her smirk.

21

"It's impressive," Connery said.

"Truly a work of art." Audre cocked her head to the side.

"If only they put this much effort into everything." I sighed.

A group of people stood off to the side, some snickering, others look-ing horror-struck. The tree was magnificent, towering twenty feet above them and six feet across. The woman had grown it into the unmistakable shape of a hand giving the middle finger.

Two flora wielders stood below it, slowly remolding it into a less offensive presence. The owner of the field paced angrily but did not approach them.

"What'd they give her?" Connery asked. Indie, Simon, and the council had met every day to review incidents just like this. People using their powers nefariously or accidentally. There was a team of people added to each council's security board who were responsible for putting out fires, removing floods, and, apparently, reversing revenge artwork.

"Two weeks," I replied. She would be recuffed for two weeks and fined for the improper use of magic. Repeat offenders would have lengthier bans depending on the severity of the infraction. Indie and Simon were also discussing how, once they got their powers back, they might be required to donate their ability to the development of Lashia.

"What'd he do again? Cheat on her?" Connery nodded toward the still-pacing owner.

"Failed to mention he was already married." Audre gave the owner serious side-eye.

Once they finished, having created a respectable-looking tree, the flora wielders had the owner sign off on it before returning to their carriage and riding off.

Audre and I had walked over from the restaurant when we spotted it at seven in the morning. The tree had appeared overnight. We'd run into Connery on his way back from the firehouse, where he'd gone to officially tender his resignation.

With regular visits to Trevesten, the five of us saw our power restored to pre-Lashian levels. News of our special strength and extra abilities spread, and we quickly became minor celebrities. Although I was still wary, and hid the extent of my power, we were all committed to helping Lashia adapt to its new normal.

It was like flexing an unused muscle. There was no need for me to shy away from the authority. In fact, I was growing to enjoy being listened to and respected. And while I still wasn't an expert at small talk, I practiced listening instead. People who didn't like the powers they received or didn't know how to use them, children who resented having to wait until they were eighteen, couples who struggled with disproportionate power. I heard it all in my unofficial capacity as Indie's right hand. Or left hand, depending on where Simon was standing.

It was strange to see everyone without cuffs. And although there was still an invisible line between those who used to be Jinns and those who used to be Tals, I knew it would vanish in time. Less than one percent of people had no magic, and we provided most of them with healing or impervenan abilities.

"I'm glad I caught you. Sabine was hoping you'd come to lunch. She has something she wants to ask you." Connery smiled and said "Hello," to several people as the three of us walked back to the restaurant.

"Today?" I eyed him.

"She wants more?" Audre's brows knitted. "Hasn't Lim done enough?"

There was an awkward silence. Since our conversation regarding my removal of his memories, the two of us had studiously avoided discussing it.

Connery gave me a half smile/half wince. "I'm sure she wouldn't ask if it wasn't important."

"Fine." I waved away his concern. "You okay to cover today?" I said to Audre.

She nodded as we approached the front doors. I'd hired another sous chef, and someone to work behind the bar, since my new obligations had me running around a lot during the day.

"Fine. I'll pull us both to Trevesten at noon."

"See you then!" Connery bumped Audre on the shoulder before giving me a dazzling smile and walking off.

Adnatia Palace was a testament to fae with long lives and lots of money. Without the depressing energy I'd had during my last visits, I felt more inclined to appreciate its beauty. Previous rulers had done everything they could to make it enthralling. Stained glass, intricately carved statues and gargoyles, there was something to see everywhere you looked. Sabine's own father had built an entirely new wing with no regard to the existing architectural style. Instead of looking odd, it blended right in with the opulence.

The palace boasted twelve different internal courtyards, and it was in one of these that we were taking lunch. An awning of climbing jasmine and honeysuckle sheltered us from the midday sun.

"Thank you for coming, Lim," Sabine said warmly from the other end of the round table. Connery and Morgan sat to her left, and Erik and General Antonio to her right.

"Of course." I smiled at a server who placed a salad of buttery lettuce and fresh tomatoes in front of me.

"How is Lashia doing?"

"Slow, but well. A few mishaps. Unfortunately, several people have already had to be recuffed for some extended periods, but I think it's working." I looked at Connery and he nodded.

"Yes. We've been doing what we can to train everyone. Things are looking promising," he said before taking a mouth full of cornbread.

"Do you think you'll stay in Lashia?" Antonio asked.

It was something that had been swirling in my mind a lot the last few days. For so long, I'd just wanted my restaurant. A place where I could be happy and unnoticed. But now, so much had changed. My life in Lashia before had been about hiding, keeping my head down. Indie belonged at the head of Lashia. But I couldn't deny I wanted more. And a big part of me itched to feel that same sense of adventure I'd felt in Trevesten.

I couldn't go back to being a criminal, of course. My parents would be very disappointed.

"Honestly, I'm not sure."

"You've put in a lot of work. Maybe you need a vacation?" Erik suggested. His eyes danced with amusement.

"A vacation?" My brow furrowed.

Sabine sighed. "More like a mission. In two weeks, Boralta is hosting a group scouting expedition to Kysalt. A show of good faith while we're negotiating import/export regulations. If you're amenable, I'd like you to go. With Erik and Morgan."

"And the obvious question is..." I held up my open palms.

"I'm asking you because you're a fire-wielder and Boralta prizes those above all others. Sandlin is hiding whatever they've found, but I suspect the way they're training their fire-wielders is a clue. And, of course, with your other ability, you make an excellent spy."

"Don't you have the world's best spy right here?" I gestured to Morgan, referring to her invisibility and luvit abilities.

"King Sandlin has a klaris in his employ, like Erik. He'll be looking for invisibility and glamors," Morgan said as she twirled a piece of skinny pasta onto her fork before taking a bite.

I glanced at Erik, and he winked. Rolling my eyes, I said, "Being able to see enchantments is pretty helpful. Have you considered becoming a thief?"

Connery and Antonio chuckled, and Morgan grinned around a mouthful of pasta.

Erik snorted. "Nah, it's not for me. But this should be a good time. Morgan can play princess and distract everyone while the two of us do a little digging."

"Play princess," Morgan grumbled. "'Playing' seems the wrong word for negotiating my own sale."

"What do you mean?" I looked at her, but she straightened as if she regretted her comment.

Sabine pursed her lips but said nothing.

Morgan's gaze turned determined. "It's common to have the new Boraltan ruler marry one of the higher-ups from another country and tradition for that person to be from Trevesten. It gives a legitimacy to their rule and keeps the assassination attempts down. I'm to marry the winner of the contest."

"And you don't want this to happen?" I said the words slowly, my eyes darting between Morgan and Sabine.

"I certainly don't," Sabine said, and my eyes widened in further confusion.

"We've been over this. A marriage to Boralta would be good for our people. Boralta may be small, but they have a ton of money due to all the mines. I'm not overjoyed by the idea of it, but I know my duty as well as Sabine knows hers." She gave her sister a pointed glance. "And if Boralta is going to dominate the market with some shiny new thing, Trevesten needs to be on their good list."

"And you don't have any idea what they've uncovered? Why not just wait for them to sell it?" I changed the subject, sensing the growing tension at the table. Morgan's casual attitude and unconventional dress made me forget she was just as beholden to her position as her sister. Their family hadn't held on to power in Trevesten for millennia for nothing.

"They won't do anything until the regulations are final and they'll write them in a way that's most favorable to them. Besides, it could be valuable. But it could also be dangerous," Sabine answered.

"Or my favorite, both." Erik popped a grape into his mouth.

My flames stirred beneath my skin as the memories of near misses and successful jobs pushed into my mind. I picked up the butter knife and began flipping it between my fingers.

"What kind of payment will I be getting for this job?"

22

Brax ran alongside our floating carriage, cheerfully snapping at birds. A team of four horses pulled it along behind Morgan's. She sat with her own assistants and guards.

Erik eyed me from across the interior, his amber eyes curious. In the carriage's darkness, his hair was black. But occasionally, when the sun spilled in through the window, the rays would catch and ignite the red strands.

"Given any more thought to what I suggested?"

I tipped my head, confused.

"Breaking the bond?"

Taking a deep breath and exhaling through my nose, I said, "That's not a thing. Even if it were, I wouldn't do it."

"Even if he asked you to?" He folded his fingers neatly over his stomach and stretched out his legs. There was more than enough room for the two of us in the carriage, but he insisted on resting one of his legs against mine.

I shuffled away from him. "There's no reason for him to ask. And again, that's not a thing I can do. It's not something anyone can do."

Erik abruptly leaned forward, elbows on his knees, and I startled at the quick movement. "I can see why it was so hard for him. To resist you."

He made a show of giving my body a long, lingering look. Beneath my clothes, my skin flushed angrily.

"Stop trying to bait me. I don't need to ride in a damn carriage. I can spend the next two days in a lovely seaside hotel, and you can let me know when you get there."

"You've never been to Boralta."

I opened my mouth to retort and had to shut it. That was true. I could get pretty far because of my travels around Trevesten, but I'd never set foot in the mountainous country.

Erik's lips twisted, but he pushed back, palms up. "I'm just saying I get it. You seem like the kind of person who could make a male forget his mating bond."

"Sabine is pretty easy on the eyes," I said dryly.

He smirked. "Indeed, she is. She gets more beautiful in each life."

I didn't bother to respond, instead choosing to look out at the countryside. We'd traveled through several large cities and smaller towns. We passed Poldern, the largest troll settlement in Trevesten, the houses all sporting giant doorways and sheltering enormous horses.

The massive spectre of the Gyemain mountain range rose in the distance as we approached the Boraltan border. We were still a day away, but I could already make out the snow-capped peaks that jutted upward like the spikes of a crown. The Boraltans knew every pass through the mountains, but didn't need to do much guarding. The snow, wyverns, bears, and wolves were a sufficient deterrent for most.

The carriage shook as Brax leapt onto the roof. We could both feel him making the requisite circles before plopping down for a late afternoon nap.

I broke the silence a few hours later. "Have you always worked for Sabine?"

Erik drummed his fingers on what I refused to acknowledge was a very well-muscled thigh. "Nope."

Before I could open my mouth to ask more, the carriage rolled to a stop and Erik rose from his seat. He opened the door, just barely missing Brax as he sailed to the ground. His hand was warm and callused as he helped me down.

The house was humming with cheerful activity. Lord and Lady Miller rushed down the steps in excitement to welcome us.

"Here you are at last! Welcome to our home!" The Lord bowed deeply to Morgan before he and his wife began shaking hands with Erik and me.

"We're so happy you have broken your journey here. Please come in." Lady Miller graciously escorted us inside. She wore a black silk dress and a striking golden coat. Her husband, who walked ahead with Morgan, had on a dark navy suit that buttoned to his neck.

A comfortable warmth spread over us as we crossed the threshold and the scent of oranges permeated the air. An impressive greenhouse dominated the center of the house. As we walked through it, I openly admired the endless trees and plants covering every available surface. Each corner had an enormous orange tree, branches twisting up to reach the glass dome above us. In the middle, scores of colorful fish swam in a deep blue pond.

"Here." Lady Miller plucked an orange from a tree and gave it to me. "Please help yourself while you're here. Our home is your home."

"Thank you," I answered while inhaling the fruit's sweet oil. Traveling with a princess certainly had its perks.

"We don't get many visitors, as you can imagine, being way up here. Apologies if we are coming off a little too exuberant." She smiled, revealing deep dimples in each cheek. Up ahead, her husband was explaining something about the architecture to Morgan, who listened with rapt curiosity.

"We're very grateful to you, Lady Miller. Should we expect to see you and your husband at the Boraltan trials?" Erik asked.

"Please, call me Tish. Oh yes. We'll be there. Even though we've had to pay a fortune to hire fire-wielders. Most of the ones born around here know they can make a lot more money in Boralta. My husband had to go down south just to find some to accompany us."

"They can really make that much more there?" I asked.

"Oh no, now you've given her ideas, Tish." Erik jokingly scolded her. "This one has to stay with us." He wrapped his arm around my shoulders, pressing me against his side.

She laughed. "I'm sure that the queen pays you more than enough to keep you. Besides, unless you fancy fighting wyverns all day long, it's not worth it."

When she crossed the threshold in front of us, I elbowed Erik hard in the stomach. He gave a satisfying grunt of pain and removed his arm.

"Our staff will show you to your rooms." Lord Miller motioned up a large, polished staircase. "Dinner is in an hour, but do let us know if that's not convenient and we'll move it."

After Morgan assured the couple that we were only too happy to dine then, the staff led us up the stairs. The four of us were in our own wing. A female with shimmering blue scales on her neck showed me to a beautifully appointed room with wide windows facing the mountains.

"I'll draw you a bath, Miss. While you're bathing, I'll lay out your clothing for dinner." She gave me a cheerful smile before disappearing into the bathroom.

'Well this is weird,' I thought to myself. I wished Audre, Indie, and Simon were here to see me being waited on and given such special treatment. I ran my hands over the fluffy bedspread before going to the window. Darkness was falling fast. There was only a bit of pink, peeking from between the mountains, fading into blue shadows.

There was a reason I'd never been to Boralta, despite having visited most of Malan. My first life parents had been born there. So had my grandfather. But he'd always discouraged any visits. He was a parrot shifter, and I thought it was because he disliked the cold. But as I got older, I discovered it was because he didn't want me running into any other relatives.

Dinner was a lively and relaxed affair. Tish and Harold were possibly two of the nicest fae I'd ever met. And that was saying something considering they were royals. Ten of their children joined us for dinner, the youngest of whom, Nora, was only seven.

I thought of my sister as I watched her shyly studying Morgan. Ayla and Keen had taken the loss of their magic with more maturity than I expected. They were consoled by my promise to remove their cuffs whenever we went to Trevesten.

Brax was allowing two of the older boys to brush his fur while he lazed in front of the fire. Lady Miller had presented him with an entire leg of lamb on a silver platter. His satisfied purr was a constant backdrop to our conversation.

"You must do a lot of trading with Boralta? Do you need to go there often for business?" Morgan asked the Millers.

"We go up for their two big seasonal markets in Summer and Spring. If we wait until the goods trickle down into our markets, the price is double," said Harold.

"Anything I should keep my eye out for?" Morgan smiled at Tish.

"That depends on what you're into," she replied conspiratorially. "They have all the things you'd expect. Wyvern-hide boots, gorgeous furs, and, of course, the Boraltans are unmatched for precious stones. But there are also less common treasures that don't often make it south."

Harold beamed at his wife before taking her hand. "My wife is an accomplished herbalist. She can do things with tree bark you wouldn't believe."

I laughed along with the others. "Now that I am interested in. What are some of your favorite concoctions?"

Tish answered with obvious excitement. "I make a pretty good rishival elixir."

"Psh, pretty good," Harold scoffed. "It's ten times better than the stuff they sell in the apothecary."

One of the older children piped up. "It really is amazing. She's perfected a way to make the memories slow down and organize themselves, so it doesn't hurt so much."

Morgan and I shared a look.

"That sounds amazing. Would it be possible to get a bottle?" I asked. "Please?"

Tish waved her hand, her cheeks pinking. "Of course, I'd be happy to give you some to take with you."

Later, as I sat by the fire in my room, regretting my third helping of spicy chicken, a knock sounded at my door.

"Come in," I called, too full to get up.

Erik strode through the door and planted himself in the chair beside me. He'd taken off his uniform and was now wearing comfortable black pants and a sweater. He set a bottle of wine on the table with two glasses.

"Make yourself at home," I deadpanned.

"Don't mind if I do," he said as he poured us both a glass of wine. He floated mine over to me and I plucked it from the air.

He remained silent as I continued to stare into the fire and sip my wine.

"Go on. I know you're just itching to give me all your thoughts."

His face contorted with an internal argument before he spoke. "I was just thinking how ecstatic you must be. Connery can get his memories back without losing his mind. You get to be dumped all over again. It's a win-win."

I closed my eyes and tipped my head back, despising that he'd spoken my feelings aloud. "You're an asshole, you know that?" For one moment, I'd been genuinely happy when Tish had described her elixir. Connery would get back all we'd shared in Lashia. He'd remember wanting me as Lim, being a part of my life without all the baggage we had when we first got there. But it was true. I was likely setting myself up to be cast aside all over again.

"I'm a realist. How do you think he'll do it? In person? Or something pathetic, like a letter?" Erik's voice had become soft but not mocking. His eyes were razor sharp, though, as if he was analyzing my every heartbeat.

The table rattled as I slammed my glass down and stood up. "What is wrong with you? Do you delight in everyone's misery or just mine?"

Erik sprung from the chair as if he'd been waiting for me. "I told you. I work for Sabine and I need to know you're not going to go off the deep end and do something drastic in some misguided attempt to win him back."

"You're full of shit. I've given Sabine no reason to think that."

Erik stepped closer to me, his face inches from mine. "Not yet. But I think you're a pretty patient person. Perhaps you're just biding your time."

Flames danced at my fingertips as I struggled to control the rage that bubbled up inside me. Anger at Erik for hounding me and at this situation. I could picture Connery's face, filled with concern, as he let me down easy, and my cheeks burned in embarrassment.

"Maybe you like it," he continued, his voice goading. "You're not brokenhearted. You like toying with unavailable men. Maybe it's just a fun game for you."

"How dare you?" I shoved him hard, and he stumbled. "I dragged his unconscious ass off a floor and let him live in my house. We taught him how to survive in Oderon, included him in jobs where we had no business bringing an inexperienced, stuck-up royal. And then he fucked me and dumped me in the span of twenty-four hours. But even that wasn't enough humiliation. I had to take care of him when hush was violently exiting every orifice of his body, just so he could tell me *again* that he didn't want me."

Erik moved back into my space, ignoring that my arms and torso were entirely ringed with fire. Tears tried to fall from my eyes, but quickly evaporated. My fingers clenched as words that had been stuck inside me for centuries poured out.

"And after all that, we still ended up together in Marais! I still know where he is at all times, cannot for the life of me shut that off. Why? For what? So I could deliver him in a tidy, well-adjusted package to someone else? Is that what I'm good for?"

He stared at me, his eyes no longer shrewd but contemplative. My breathing slowed, the fire dying as shame took over. Why had I just told him all of that? Swallowing, I said, "Well done. You can run back and report like a good little soldier."

"You didn't say whether you're still in love with him."

Closing my eyes, I shook my head. "How I feel is irrelevant."

"Because of the mating bond."

The words tripped over themselves in my throat because I knew the truth of them. "The mating bond is also irrelevant. Whatever else love is, it's a choice, a choice you make every day." I sank a little deeper into myself, my voice hoarse. "And because I know him, I know the choice for him, between her and anything else, is easy."

For a moment, Erik's expression was so unguarded. He'd looked at me that way once before, like he'd missed something important. Suddenly, he cleared his throat and that signature lazy smile slid back into place. "Pretty words. But you didn't answer the question." Before I could rail at him again, he dropped his voice. "You could try to convince me you're truly over him in another way." Erik's fingers slid around my waist, pulling me closer until my chest pressed against his.

The fire in me spluttered, having missed an obvious threat. I couldn't help the nervous energy that raced up my spine, the alarm bells ringing in my head.

Erik placed his other hand on my face, tipping it up to look at him. "If Sabine had no reason to worry about you, I wouldn't have to keep bringing up these uncomfortable topics." His breath caressed my mouth, and I inhaled. Honey and warm spices.

Something stronger stirred inside me. My voice became a soft purr. "I have been meaning to get back out there."

He raised his eyebrows, desire flickering on his face.

"But you first," I whispered before sending him a mile outside the Miller's property.

In the morning, we gathered in the courtyard, readying ourselves for the last leg of the journey to Boralta.

"I'm almost tempted to withhold the rishival elixir, so you have to come back," Tish teased as she pressed a parcel of her concoction into my hands.

Clasping her forearms, I shook my head. "No extortion necessary. We'll see you in two weeks."

"Sooner, if I'm forced to spend the time looking at different types of snow," Morgan added, burrowing farther into her furs.

Erik, who'd been glaring at me since breakfast, mustered some genuine cheer to say goodbye to our gracious hosts before opening the door to the carriage for me.

As I ascended the steps, Brax leapt onto the roof again, a chicken clenched in his massive jaw. A pink ribbon trailed from the fur on his head. Presumably Nora's doing.

"You know, it was rather cold last night," Erik grumbled once we had set off. "Not all of us have fire at the tips of our fingers."

"Should have thought of that before pissing me off." I opened a book and ignored him for the rest of the journey.

23

The Boraltans began escorting us long before we even caught sight of the entrance through the mountains. As soon as we began our ascent, before the green grass gave way to hard-packed dirt, and then to powdery snow, guards appeared from between the trees. They trailed the carriage and wove in front and behind us, swords and bows at the ready for any animals that might get brave.

Brax growled at them from the roof of the carriage where he was on high alert, and I saw several of them stare in awe. There would be no blending in for him here. His deep red fur was a stark contrast to the white blanketing the ground, the gray boulders, and thick evergreens.

Erik rode beside us instead of staying inside with me. The two of us returned to our usual state of tentative truce.

We turned a corner, and the gates came into view. My mouth popped open at the two thirty-foot-high stone pillars flanking the pass. A well-oiled gate with bars as thick as Brax's neck stood open between them, allowing us to join the other riders and carriages flowing through the entrance. After Erik provided the gate guard with our paperwork, several guards peeled off to escort us.

It was another two hours before we reached Aloundale, Boralta's capital city. The city's shops and markets covered the bottom of a valley, lit with glass globes filled with flickering orange fire. Beyond the city center, there were some farms, but the bulk of the inhabitants lived in houses carved directly into the mountain face. Colorful awnings covered intricately engraved metal doors. People chatted and ate on the innumerable balconies jutting out into the air.

Fire, the Boraltans' most precious resource, was everywhere. Symbols carved into the stone, contained within square plinths that decorated the streets, and flowing from the fingers from the fingers of many of its citizens.

"Welcome!" A male in traditional Boraltan dress stood at the entrance to Aloundale castle. Groomsmen stepped forward to care for the horses while others took down the luggage. "I'm so glad you could make it."

"Thank you for inviting us," Morgan said. "It's been a long time since I saw your humble caves."

The male laughed. I understood the joke as we entered the foyer of the castle. Glittering jewels littered the ceiling, arranged into artful designs. It felt as if I was seeing the constellations up close.

"This is amazing," I breathed.

"Thank you. Queen Sabine mentioned she was sending a fire-wielder. Ambassador Venten, at your service." He gave me a polite bow.

"This is Lim Revin. And you know the Captain, of course," Morgan said.

Venten nodded to both of us. "Good to see you again, Captain. I will show you to your rooms. King Sandlin would love for you to dine with him this evening, along with the representatives from Eloisha and Ursan, who arrived yesterday."

I barely heard Venten as I stumbled down the hall after the others, my eyes everywhere but my feet. Even the floors sparkled, white marble flecked with diamonds. The stone walls of the entryway gave way to warm wood and plaster adorned with colorful tapestries and plush rugs.

We passed a drawing room where courtiers were reading or playing cards. A gigantic fireplace dominated one end, large enough for several people to stand inside.

My room was similarly beautiful, but with a smaller fireplace. After I'd once again faced the awkwardness of being waited on by a maid, I stared down into the valley. The fire in the room crackled with my excitement.

My door opened without a knock and I audibly cursed as Erik strode in.

"Well damn, you're dressed." He winked.

I gave him a look that had stopped many a rowdy bar patron in their tracks.

"Oh, don't give me that look. I've come to take you into the city. Unless you'd rather sit here and sulk?" He gave me what I'm sure he thought was a charming smile.

But even my irritation with the captain couldn't stop me from grabbing my bag and hurrying after him.

The two of us wandered through the streets, perusing shop windows and picking up snippets of conversation.

I had to restrain myself from buying more than one present for my friends and family. An incredibly soft, stuffed polar bear for Priya, a complicated board game that folded into a metal box the size of my hand for Ayla, a book of illustrated stories for Keen. A new set of diamond-edged throwing stars for Audre, a beautiful blue coat for my mother, an orange one for Indie, and wyvern-hide gloves for my father. Simon got the complete, unabridged history of Boralta, a book so heavy

I made Erik carry it. I also bought a ton of sweets and Boraltan delicacies to take back.

By the time we settled into our seats at one of the many getrals, Boralta's version of a bar, I had nearly forgotten this visit wasn't purely for pleasure.

Erik piled the rest of my parcels in the empty chair at our table. A hawk-faced female approached the table. She didn't bother with the Boraltan dialect and spoke to us in Traelish.

"I'm guessing we stick out?" I asked Erik after she'd taken our order and bustled away.

"They're probably just used to the same people in here. Can you not tell when tourists visit your restaurant?"

"Considering Marais is not really a big tourist destination, yes, I could tell." I shrugged as hawk-face set down two steaming cups of mulled wine. It wasn't sweet like the mulled wine I was used to, but spicy with a definite kick. It slid into my belly, warming me from the inside out.

The doors opened and a group of six people walked in, all of them in the Boraltan military uniform. Two of them peeled off to the bar while the others installed themselves at a table near the window.

"Ugh, why do they have to be everywhere?" a blond female to the left of me muttered. She was sitting with a dark-haired friend who snickered into her drink.

"If you'd stop sleeping with members of the wyvestri, it wouldn't be so embarrassing to run into them."

"I can't help it. They're always swaggering around like they're Mother's gift and it's like catnip to me." The blond's eyes had already started roving over the group, her gaze on a stocky male with long hair who puffed out his chest in response.

I leaned back in my chair, affecting a voice I heard from some of the younger women at The Peregrine.

"Sorry. I really didn't mean to eavesdrop." I pushed a strand of hair behind my ear. "Did you say they're the wyvestri? They actually fight wyverns?"

The corner of Erik's mouth twitched before he hid it with a sip of his wine.

The females leaned toward me. "Yes, that's just some of them. There have been a ton of new recruits lately, so more than enough to go around." The dark-haired one grinned. "But it doesn't seem like you are lacking for good company, unless this is your... brother?" she said hopefully, eyeing Erik.

Internally, I rolled my eyes. "He's just a friend. Are the wyverns getting worse?" Although I widened my eyes mostly for effect, I wasn't terribly comfortable with the idea of wyverns. I'd never even seen one and the thought that they were as common as bats around here was a little concerning. Black leathery wings and a body as big as Brax did not sound like an animal I wanted to run into anytime soon.

"Oh, I don't know." The blond tipped her head as if it was the first time she'd considered it. "Unless you're hanging out in the forest a lot, it's not something we usually need to worry about."

"I hope you ladies aren't hanging out in the forest. You look like a delicious meal for any beast." Erik leaned forward and pushed a hand through his hair, flexing his well-corded forearms.

They laughed and blushed. The revulsion I'd expected to feel at that comment didn't come. Instead, the low timbre of his voice made a small shiver run up my back. But then I remembered how much of an antagonizing ass he was and stomped the feeling out.

Two of the wyvestri approached the ladies' table and asked them to play darts. I gave them an encouraging smile as they walked off with their conquests.

A note appeared on the table in front of us. Erik picked it up.

"We need to return to the castle. Morgan said we'd better bring her a braid," Erik said, referring to one of the pastries I'd picked up. "She's apparently not impressed with her spousal options."

I nodded, gathering up my bags. "How are we going to find out why they need all those new recruits?"

Erik's eyes slid to me. "Looks like we need to take a little trip to the forest. Know any fire-wielders who'd be willing to keep me warm?"

"Bat those pretty amber eyes at one of the wyvestri. I'm sure one of them can help you out," I said, giving him a saccharine smile.

Erik reached across and grabbed the rest of my purchases. "Tell me what other features of mine you find attractive, Lim." His eyes roamed blatantly over my features. "When it comes to you, I have an extensive list."

At dinner, I sat as far away from him as possible.

The next day, Venten was only too happy to take us into the forest with several more seasoned wyvestri. He suggested we take a sled to one of the mountain peaks, where there was a lodge with excellent views.

Morgan bundled up next to me while Erik rode one of the Boraltan's shaggy draft horses.

"Ah, thank you," Morgan said as I let my fire warm the two of us. "Are you having a good time? I wish I could have gone into town with you two instead of listening to people drone on about trade embargoes."

"This place is pretty amazing. I've never seen anything like it." We were on a well-used path up the mountain, wide enough for the sled and two horses on each side. Up ahead, Brax was darting in and out of the trees, playfully snapping at the guards. "I've never seen Brax so animated."

"And when we get back? Do you plan to give Connery Tish's elixir?"

"I—Uh." I faltered, thrown by the abrupt change in subject. "Of course. If that's what he wants."

"Sorry. Didn't mean to spring it on you, but there's a reason Sabine is queen. I've no talent for tact or diplomacy."

"It's fine. But yes, we can try it. And then perhaps Sabine can call off her dog." I tipped my head at Erik in front of us. He wore a thick wool coat edged with fur. I didn't appreciate how well it fit him or how his very unpretty eyes kept flashing to me.

"I don't know what you mean?" Morgan said, confused.

"According to him, he's been ordered to annoy the shit out of me to see if I break and do something insane to get Connery back."

Morgan said nothing, but gave a small nod and grimace. Her silence a confirmation that such a thing was exactly something her sister would do. A second later, we crested the summit and arrived in front of a long, one-story lodge, surrounded on all four sides by a deep porch. Several fae and other creatures sat in chairs outside, playing board games or reading.

As I stepped down from the carriage, I saw the view Venten had extolled. It was magnificent. The sun gilded the snow, the treetops, even the city down below looked bathed in gold. As I took another few steps, I heard snow crunch behind me, and I sighed in resignation.

"One day, all of this will be ours." Erik's voice was full of humor as he swept an arm out to encompass the expanse. His breath made little clouds in the air as he stepped closer to me.

"You sure you want to torment me now that I've been here? I'm happy to give you a one-way ticket back in the middle of the night."

Erik's retort died in his mouth when I abruptly stepped back and slammed into his chest. He grabbed my arms as the two of us stared in awe at the wyvern hovering fifty feet in front of us. The enormous beast wasn't paying us any attention, all its focus on whatever was beneath it in the trees. It was the size of an elephant. Thick, leathery wings protruded from the back of its arms, extending out over the treeline. It hovered for a moment before tucking its wings and diving out of sight.

"Magnificent, aren't they?" Venten came up beside us. "Come, the lodge has a restaurant with a wall of glass windows. We can eat our lunch and watch them play." Shrugging out of Erik's grasp, I followed Venten to the lodge.

We took our seats among the other guests. Servers appeared with warm bread and mint water for our table.

"Do they ever just,"—I made a grabbing motion with my hand—"people off the mountain?" Another wyvern swooped across the panoramic windows while we sat finishing our meal.

"They're like all wild animals. If they're hungry and you're available, it can happen. But they rarely attack unprovoked. It's when we work in the less populated areas, or travel to the mines, that we need the wyvestri's help. Without them, if you stumble across a nesting site, say goodbye to your arms."

"And if the wyverns don't get you, the bears and wolves will," a wyvestri to Morgan's left said. He grinned, pointing to a long scar on his arm. His nametag said "Tindal."

"Do you have to use fire? Or do other weapons work as well?" Morgan asked.

"Arrows are useless. Swords work, but only if you get them in the joints where their legs or wings meet their bodies. If you're that close, you better hope you've got a fire-wielder."

"Have you ever taken one down on your own?" The princess eyed the thick scar on his arm, her eyes alight with interest but not fear.

Tindal laughed. "No, thank the Mother. We always have at least two wielders."

Out of the corner of my eye, Venten shifted in his seat.

"This food is amazing. How do you plan on feeding us in Kysalt? I don't suppose you've built a lodge like this yet?" I took a bite of the rich cheesecake they'd given us for dessert.

"Not yet." Venten laughed. "We will need to rough it, but we'll definitely have enough to go around."

24

Five parties, not including our Boraltan guides, stood assembled before the portal. Even the Visarian priestesses, usually so unwilling to leave their tiny island nation, had sent representatives. King Sandlin stood before the assembled party, his midnight skin sharp against his silver fur cape.

"Welcome, everyone. I'm happy to see such a wonderful turnout." His voice carried over the brisk wind. "I have provided a contingent of Boraltan guards for your safety. Ellis,"—he pointed to a tall female with blue braids—"will be your camp manager. She will oversee the tents, food, and healers. If you have any questions, please don't hesitate to ask her."

Ellis waved. "You are, of course, permitted to explore on your own, but try not to wander off in groups less than three, so someone is available to get help and someone is available to stay with any injured."

"One would think," the Ambassador to Boralta from Penglynis muttered next to me, "we were children on a field trip."

While she may have considered this a mundane voyage and the instructions not worth her bother, I was anxious. The last time I'd been to an unknown world, things hadn't gone so well. Although logically, I knew that everyone who'd been to Kysalt had returned, the butterflies in my stomach fluttered with wings of lead.

The portal stood before us, twenty feet wide and with two plinths on either side placed by Boralta to mark the entrance. Portals were not difficult to identify if you knew what to look for. This one had an obvious glimmer, like gauze floating in the air. I idly rubbed my forearms, counting all the red things I could see and taking slow, calming breaths.

"Nervous?" Morgan whispered beside me. "Given your history, I'm not surprised. I promise this will be underwhelming." She pulled at her collar, uncomfortable in the finery she rarely sported at home.

"That's what I keep telling myself."

On my other side, Erik leaned in. "The Boraltans have installed those lighted plinths on both sides. We should be able to see the portal back from miles away." His typical smirk was gone, and if I didn't know better, I'd say he looked almost sympathetic.

Someone standing beyond Erik caught my eye, and I saw a male with a deeply tanned face and a maroon coat watching our group. He gave me a polite smile and turned back to the portal.

"Who is that, in the red coat?" I asked, while staring straight ahead. I hadn't seen him at dinner last night.

Erik leaned in, unnecessarily close to me. "He's the frontrunner to win the trials and succeed Sandlin. His name is Halorn."

"I met him yesterday. Seems fine, if a little boring. He's Sandlin's favorite, so I can't count him out. But he's also only a third life, so he'll probably lose."

"I'm deeply offended," Erik whispered.

Morgan spoke with a yawn. "That was my intention."

I still wasn't sure what life I was on. What any of us were on. Indie, Simon, Audre, and Connery—none of us remembered anything after our first life in Lashia. We each only had one new ability, which made me think we were only on our second life, but there was no way to be certain. The thought made me careful. If I had a bunch of short human lives under my belt, I couldn't afford the nonchalance most fae had about their early deaths.

A bell sounded, and two fae stepped forward. There was no need for a kunli, but for this many people, a little boost to the power needed to open it was helpful. The two fae sprinkled powdered erlaub root on the ground before holding their hands over it and murmuring quietly. The dust rose in the air before splitting like a curtain, removing that gauzy layer and revealing the snowy fields of Kysalt. They stepped back and a contingent of Boraltan guards entered first. They would stay at the gate on the Kysalt side while the rest of us explored the first world.

We traveled for several hours, stopping occasionally so people could take soil samples or catalog wildlife. Erik's eyes were peeled, and I tried to do the same. But we saw nothing that revealed Boralta's interest in the land. There were healthy trees, beautiful frozen lakes, and enormous birds, but nothing terribly unique.

As the sun dipped behind the mountains, the temperature dropped considerably. Ellis announced a halt and instructed her people to set up camp. Several guards erected a massive tent, fire-wielders filled it with heat, while others laid out rugs and cushions for us to sit on and await our dinner.

After a filling bowl of rich stew, and stopping to compliment the camp chef, I retired to my own sectioned-off area of the Trevesten tent. I was toeing off my boots when Erik walked in. Brax snored on a large pillow someone had thoughtfully provided for him.

"Don't you ever knock?" I said, in irritation.

He grinned, the candlelight catching his eyes as they lit with amusement. "I did knock." He mimed knocking against the thick fabric. "Is it my fault you didn't hear me?" He didn't wait for a response before placing a map down on my cot. "Here are all the places Trevesten has already explored in Kysalt. And this"—he pointed to a red squiggly line—"is the route we've taken on this trip."

Staring at the map, I let out a long exhale. "If they're hiding something, presumably they would lead us away from it."

Erik drummed his fingers. "I expect they plan to take us all over the place, tire us out until we give up. We're not staying more than a night in each place. I was thinking, tomorrow night, we come back here and take a look around without prying eyes. Unless you've developed the ability to jump places you haven't been?" He looked at me hopefully.

I shook my head. "Nope."

The next evening, after the camp was quiet, I jumped us back to the place we'd spent the night before. Erik and I trudged through the snow in all directions.

"Does it snow in Marais?" He asked, examining a towering pile of boulders.

"No. Only swamps and sand. You need to go farther north for snow."

"Do you like it?" He held out a hand and hauled me up onto the boulders. They were everywhere, a carpet of sand for a giant. But other than a few sparse trees, I saw nothing interesting.

"Yes. It's quiet there. And warm. I have a small boat I use to fish, to collect crabs." I paused, turning back when I realized he wasn't following me. "What?"

Erik grinned. "I've never seen that smile. Many smirks, yes, but not smiles."

"Yeah, well, stop irritating me so much and I might do it more," I said, flustered at the thought of him cataloguing my expressions.

That night, we found nothing.

It was the same the next night.

And the next.

And the next.

On the fifth night in Kysalt, Erik's prediction appeared to be coming true. The travelers were restless, tired of looking at the same snow drifts. There had been a bit of excitement when the Eloishans had discovered a rare plant, long extinct in Malan, but now even they looked ready to go home.

It was two a.m. and I cut off a piece of the endangered plant, storing it in my pack. It smelled of mint and chocolate. Erik was circling a nearby lake while Brax pawed at the ice, frustrated with his inability to get to the fish swimming below. The full moon illuminated everything for miles. I squinted across the fields at a wide fissure between the mountains.

"What about there?"

There was no reply, and I turned to look for Erik. Brax sat up, his ears twitching.

"Erik?"

A breeze ruffled my hair, but there was no snarky reply from the captain.

"I swear on my life, if you are fucking with me, I will stab you."

When I still heard nothing, I marched off in the direction I'd seen him last. Brax followed behind me, his tail twitching. There was a crack, and my head whipped to the left as I unsheathed a dagger from my belt. The muscle memory had helped, but I was still out of practice. The hilt was warm in my hand as I let my fire flow to my wrists, wreathing my skin in preparation.

Another large crack sounded from the ice, and I looked down. Fear stabbed through me. Erik was under the ice, fighting with something that looked like an octopus, but with more legs and a mouth full of terrifying teeth. He struggled as the aquatic beast wrapped a tentacle around his neck, squeezing. Erik's eyes closed in pain before he lashed out with his knife, slicing off the limb.

Without thinking, I pulled Erik to the shore but brought the animal along too. The two of them slammed into the snow, and I ran over, aiming my fire at the animal's eyes while Brax darted back and forth, waiting for an opening.

The thing shrieked in pain. One of its tentacles shot out and seized me around the ankle. It pulled, and I fell backward, sliding toward its open maw. Erik aimed his knife again, slicing straight through the creature's neck, purple-black blood spurting everywhere. The two of us disentangled ourselves, and before the thing could make a last stand, I sent it back into the depths of the lake.

Erik dropped to his knees, his face an alarming shade of blue. Tipping him back onto the ground, I climbed on top of him, wrapping my arms around his chest and warming him through. I pressed my hands to his neck, willing Indie's shared power through my hands to heal the nasty suction marks on his neck. Several minutes went by and my breath finally slowed as I saw his skin return to its normal color.

"If I'd known this is what it would take to get you on top of me, I would have fallen in sooner," he said, his voice hoarse.

I made to climb off of him, but he held fast to my waist, flipping me until I was locked beneath him. My breath caught, and for a second, I hesitated. Just a tiny moment where I contemplated how nice it felt to have him on top of me, his lips hovering above my mouth.

Erik saw it but instead of a rude comment, he said, "Thank you. You saved my life, truly." His eyelids fell, his gaze going to my mouth.

Uncomfortable with his sudden sincerity, I said, "I just didn't want to have to explain how that thing killed you while we were supposedly safe at camp."

He sighed, and his breath skittered along my collarbone. "Of course." He climbed up and held out a hand, helping me to my feet.

"How are you not dead? You were under the water for a good five minutes."

"Third life, remember? I can breathe underwater. Well, I could until that thing started choking me." He waved a hand, cleaning the blood from our clothes. "What about your healing power?" He cocked an eyebrow.

"Indie, Simon, Audre, and I shared our power. You going to turn me in?"

Instead of addressing my jibe, he frowned. "You've taken on magic from three other people? Isn't that dangerous?"

Shrugging my shoulders, I shook my head. "Actually, it's more than that. I also have damari and a bit of obahn power left, and reading by touch." The technical name for the last power was sparsalitu, but it was too much of a mouthful. Listing it like that, it occurred to me how much it really was.

While the damari power I'd received for uncuffing the people of Lashia was strong enough, the obahn power had only been a slice. It wouldn't have been possible for me to give Connery a new memory or touch the memories without me. Indie's healing allowed me to patch small wounds like Erik's. I'd forgone flying for Simon's impervenan power, and I went with glamoring abilities instead of using Audre's command of the rain.

"And you don't feel like you're losing your grip on them? On yours?" Erik's eyes swept along my body, as if he was searching for a sign of magical imbalance. His perusal made small tingles sweep up my back, reminding me of how it felt to have him on top of me.

It was unusual. Once, when the guard had nearly caught him buying, Simon had to absorb a full darana worth of power. It had the abilities of four different fae in it. By the time he'd made it back and I could draw the power out of him with an empty darana, he was nearly manic and extremely ill. No healing ability could save you from a power overdose.

I shrugged again. "I feel fine." Changing the subject, I gestured to the lake. "Do you think the Boraltans have any interest in that? Maybe its flesh is a delicacy or its blood is powerful or something?" There was no sign of the murderous cephalopod under the ice.

"Hmm, maybe?" Erik took out a rag and wiped the blood off his knife before folding it and putting it in his pack. "We can get it tested." He cocked his head at me. "We need some new ideas. You were stuck in a strange world. What were some of the valuable things you found in Lashia?"

Thinking, I called Brax back to us from where he'd been prowling at the edge of the lake, looking for the remains of the beast. "I can't think of anything that isn't readily available in Boralta. Food. Water. Healers. The thing I wanted most, we didn't find until now."

"What was that?" Erik's brows furrowed.

"A way home."

We both paused before slowly turning toward the portal to Boralta. The two beams of light from the plinths reached high into the sky.

I blinked as comprehension dawned.

Erik's lips parted. "That's it, isn't it?"

I shook my head slowly. "The Boraltans didn't find some plants or stones. They found a portal."

"It doesn't take ten wielders to bring down a wyvern," he said, his voice almost reverent.

"It takes ten wielders to bring down... a dragon."

25

Indie popped a piece of candy into her mouth. "These aren't bad." She licked the sour sugar from her fingers before throwing back another one of the Boraltan candies.

"I brought you some more puzzles for the family room, too." Fire crackled in the hearth. The four of us were in Oderon for dinner and a magical top up. "You should join me next time."

Books and journals covered the small table in front of the fireplace. Each of them now tabbed at every mention of Makome or dragons. It wasn't a lot. Our research was never focused on the fifth world. We had a few songs, some folktales. There were no fae living who still remembered when the direct portal between Malan and Makome existed.

"I'm game," Audre said, admiring her new throwing stars.

Indie dusted off her hands before drinking some water. "So are we. Once things die down a little in Lashia."

"I definitely want to see all the things. Especially the dragons," Simon said.

"We still need to find the portal."

"Why don't you just come out and tell them you know? What are they going to do?" Indie asked.

"Sabine and Morgan are considering it. But they won't do anything until they're sure. They don't know what Boralta plans to do with the dragons."

"Does she think they mean to use them as weapons? For war?" Simon began rummaging around in the bag of sweets again. He'd already started the book I got for him. It had little tabs sticking out of the pages.

"Maybe. Maybe not. But Boralta's leadership is about to change again. So whatever Sandlin says is going to happen is only as good as long as he rules."

"How long has he got?" Audre threw a star, and it embedded itself in the wall.

"A year. The trials will start in a few months." I got up and pulled the star out before backing up and throwing it myself. It bounced flat against the wall and Audre wheezed.

"Nice job," she said, nearly choking on her candy.

"Shut up." I flexed my fingers before trying again. This time the star made a satisfying thunk as it sunk into the wood.

"And Connery?" Indie said quietly.

I puffed out my cheeks as I exhaled. "Tomorrow."

Sabine, Connery, Erik, and I stood in the stone room where Sabine had kept Connery throughout his rishival. Her hands only shook a little as she tied the restraints to his arms and legs. He placed a hand on her cheek and their eyes met. I looked away as they kissed, only too aware of Erik watching me from the corner.

A wave of sadness came over me. Decades of memories and hurt lay heavy on my bones. This would either work or it wouldn't, but either way, he still wouldn't be mine. My life would not change either way. What fate had allowed this? Why had the Allmother inserted Connery into my life, to be dangled in front of me, before being snatched away over and over again?

She popped open the deep purple vial and handed it to him.

"In alia vita," Sabine said, a small smile on her lips.

"Bottoms up." Connery gave her and me a bracing smile before tossing back the contents. It was strong. He fell back on the bed almost immediately.

Before I lost my nerve, I marched up to him and placed my hands around his. The last drops of that wintery power moved into my hands, and I willed it to open the box in his mind where I'd stored all our memories. The contents rushed out, seeking their places. His eyelids fluttered as all the time we shared blossomed inside him.

When I stepped back, he was still calm. Sleeping peacefully except for his eyes, which darted around under his closed lids.

"I'd better go. Will you write to me with any updates?" I asked Sabine.

"Of course, Lim. Thank you." She smiled at me.

Erik escorted me to the palace gates.

"No quips today?"

"Careful. I'll start to think you like my quips." There was no playfulness in his voice. He seemed distracted.

"Did Sandlin agree to the flyers?" Sabine had written to Sandlin, letting him know she was willing to agree to the regulations, but wanted her flying fae to scout the area one last time. To ensure they had an accurate map to include with the laws.

"Yes. Too quickly. Which tells me that portal is hidden from the sky. But we're still going."

"I know a guy," I said, thinking of Simon.

"I'll let you know." Erik gave me a terse nod. He opened his mouth but closed it.

"Something else you want to say?" My nerves were on edge and there was no good reason to subject myself to more of Erik's needling, but I asked anyway.

"What will you do if he chooses you?"

Something squeezed hard inside me. What would I do? Erik gave a tense smile to a group of courtiers who passed in through the palace gates. One of them held the hand of a small girl who dragged her feet as she looked longingly back at the excitement of the city. Her mother gently chided her.

"You can't leave your signature on every toy you want in the shop."

When they were gone, I exhaled. "He won't."

He didn't listen to my words, but watched my face, searching it for everything I didn't say. Whatever he saw made him shake his head and march back into the palace.

That night, The Peregrine was packed. The band was popular, and the crowd sang along with every other song. I made drink after drink, ignoring the stool at the end of the bar and trying not to think about whether Connery had woken up yet. It was unlikely that it would be that short, but since he'd technically already had his rishival, I couldn't help checking the back to see if the fish I'd spelled for Sabine appeared in the tank.

Leo sat in a corner booth with a leggy brunette. Elias heard her mention that her ability was size manipulation, and he'd already made several crude jokes about why Leo was going out with her. Elias was an impervenan, like Simon.

"Without being super obvious about it, tell me if that guy in the blue shirt is checking me out," Elias said as he stood at the till, making change.

I picked up a few empties and wiped down the bar, scanning the crowd for Elias' blue shirt. Sure enough, a man with a thick head of black wavy hair and huge biceps was giving Elias appreciative looks.

"I think you've hooked one. But please do not disappear while we're so busy," I said. Audre handed me three plates that I quickly deposited in front of a couple at the bar.

"I'm not that easy. That bear needs to buy me dinner first." Elias swung around and gave the man a knowing smile before turning to me again. "Will Morgan and Erik be paying us another visit?"

Although my ability to teleport was now common knowledge, nobody but my family and the crew knew of my ability to jump between worlds. But Elias still gave me a look to let me know he didn't buy the 'friends from out of town' line.

"You need more novelty? The return of magic not enough for you?" I arched an eyebrow.

"I just like new friends. I think you could use some new friends. Maybe even at the same time."

I spit out the iced tea I'd just tipped into my mouth and he laughed. "I'm just messing with you." He patted me condescendingly on the shoulder before heading back out to the dining room.

"If anyone is getting a shot with the princess, it's going to be me," Audre said from the pass-through, twirling her spatula thoughtfully.

"What? I thought the two of you didn't like one another? You've barely spoken!"

"Who said anything about liking one another? Or talking, for that matter? That's not a requirement and can actually be a deterrent. Besides, with your run of 'nice guys,' maybe things would work out better if you picked someone you didn't like next time."

"Your logical gymnastics are astounding," I said, taking two more plates from her and handing them to other customers at the bar.

"I know a certain roguish captain who seems like he'd be willing to take your mind off things."

For a brief, embarrassing moment, my imagination betrayed me with an image of Erik without his uniform on. I waved my hands, willing the image away and thought of the things I was supposed to be keeping my mind off of, pinching the bridge of my nose in irritation.

"Sorry." Audre grimaced, but I just shook my head. "Lim—"

"It's alright, Audre."

"No. Look." She pointed behind her to the fish tank, where a pink fish with black stripes now swam with the others.

"I wanted to meet with you alone." Connery stood up from where he'd been sitting on the balcony when I entered.

I'd never been in this room before. It was on the smaller side, but had an excellent view of the city. A cool breeze wafted in, alleviating the warmth of the midday sun. The smell of citrus came from the gardens below, reminding me of the Millers' greenhouse.

"It worked then?" My voice was weak, and I cleared my throat.

Connery crossed the floor and took both my hands in his. His hazel eyes didn't hold any pity. Instead, he frowned, looking almost angry.

"It worked. And now, once again, I'm spending an inordinate amount of time contemplating how much better your life would have been if you'd never met me." He sighed deeply. "Lim, what you did for me, for Sabine, giving us time to know one another again... I can't thank you enough."

I pulled my hands from his so he wouldn't feel them shaking. Wrapping them around my waist, I said, "I'm glad it worked. Truly."

Connery ran a hand down the side of his face, his fingers grazing his scars. "I watched you in that bar for so long, Lim. You were magic to me long before you lost your cuffs. Like a starsdamn magnet." He smiled sadly and tears pricked at the corner of my eyes. "Some part of me knew I shouldn't take it further. The first time you looked at me, really looked at me, was at the dinner party where you removed our cuffs. That night, I seriously contemplated moving back to Eudora."

My eyes widened in surprise. "Why?"

He blew out a breath and put his hands on his hips. "That's the thing. I didn't know. I didn't know why I suddenly wanted to run. Just this overwhelming fear that you would see right through me and hate me. Now I know why." His voice softened as his eyes met mine, searching.

"I don't hate you." My voice broke. "Not now, and not then." Memories flashed in my mind of all the moments Connery and I had spent together, not enemies or lovers, just as friends.

A tear slipped from my eye, and Connery brushed it away before wrapping his arms around me. I breathed him in, certain this would be the last time we'd be so close.

He rested his chin on the top of my head. "I cannot wait until you meet your mate. Not just because it will greatly alleviate my guilt,"—I huffed a laugh into his broad chest—"but because it's my greatest desire to see you happy."

Pulling back, I gave him a bracing smile. "I will be happy, even without a mate. I promise."

26

"I thought I was coming to your house?" I smiled at my assembled family. Their faces were alight with excitement. Keen and Ayla bounced up and down.

"We couldn't wait. Let's go!" Ayla held out her arms expectantly.

"Gosh, I haven't even had my coffee. I figured I'd make us a leisurely breakfast, maybe chat a bit about what you want to see."

My parents laughed while Ayla and Keen shouted with impatience.

"They've been up since five," my father said.

I laughed. "Alright then." I moved over to Ayla while she held out her arms. One by one, I uncuffed each of my family members before jumping us to Oderon.

It was Sunday. Audre was covering the restaurant while I took my family to Trevesten. I wanted to wait until the next time the kids were off during the week so I wouldn't miss a dinner service, but my siblings were persistent. Audre also wanted to make it up to me for letting her off early the last three nights so she could visit Trevesten.

The week before had been brutal. A dozen more people had lost access to their power for improper use of magic. Most of it wasn't too bad, but we'd had our first murder. The victim's family, the prosecution, and the perpetrator agreed on an interesting sentence. The man, a snake shifter, had bitten and killed his wife's lover. His sentence was ten years, but in his snake form. We were all morbidly curious about how that would work out.

Indie, Simon, and the Lashian council had visited every borough, attending town halls and listening to the complaints from citizens. Despite some whispers about unequal magic and some protests by the under-eighteen crowd, public sentiment was still very much in Indie's favor. The council, originally so suspicious of all of us, now wanted Indie to run for president. They believed it would be good to have a single person around whom to rally.

"What they mean is they want a single person to blame if it all goes wrong," she'd grumbled. But she'd agreed to it. It made the most sense, especially now that we knew we'd outlive everyone in this generation.

Natalia was watering the flowers outside my house when the five of us stepped out onto the street.

"Such a pleasure to meet you. Lim's told us so much," my mother said, shaking Natalia's hand. Natalia smiled, not understanding my mother but gathering the sentiment. I asked Natalia to show her abilities to the kids, and she obliged by turning into a bat, a snake, and an elephant. Shifter blood ran strong in her. She'd experienced this city from every height and angle.

"What do you plan to do with your day?" she asked, still as an elephant. That seemed to be the major difference between the fae shifters and the humans. The humans could change form just as well, but couldn't speak while in their animal form.

Keen and Ayla grinned, mesmerized.

"Just around town today. I think that should be enough to entertain them."

Natalia waved goodbye to us as she shifted into a snake and slithered back into her house.

"It's so weird to hear you speaking a different language," Keen said.

"I'm sure you all could pick it up soon enough if we practiced." I led them out of the skinny side street and into the heart of Oderon, where I pointed out different things and gave them the words in Traelish.

We took the precariously elevated walkways, my parents gripping the sides nervously while Keen and Ayla ran ahead fearlessly. My family was endlessly curious and made sounds of appreciation at everything we saw. They threw coins into the Allmother's fountains, spent hours looking through shops, and marveled at the way the fae used a combination of magic and technology for all their daily needs.

By the time we sat down for lunch, I was exhausted and starving.

We found a small restaurant I'd never been to before and gorged ourselves on bowls of thick noodles, crispy shrimp, and stuffed dumplings. I'd just pushed my plate away when a note appeared on the table in front of me. Upon reading it, I let out a noise of agitation.

"What is that?" My mother said.

"An imposition." I had previously explained the abilities all fae had as part of their base magic. But my family had never seen it used. I wrote a reply and sent it back, sighing in resignation.

A few minutes later, a familiar voice spoke from behind me.

"Room for one more?" Erik stood next to the table, giving me a smile that said he knew very well that I wasn't happy about the addition. But my family greeted him enthusiastically, excited to have someone else to speak to in their own language. Erik grabbed a chair from another table and sat himself down. "Sorry to crash your lunch." He reached out and picked a dumpling off my plate, popping it into his mouth.

"Not at all," my mother said, giving him a smile I associated with her particular brand of meddling.

"Did you send Lim that note?" Ayla asked.

Erik blinked and appeared to be struggling. "Yes," he said, amused. "Comverdia. That's a terrifying ability."

Ayla smiled smugly.

"As a member of the queen's private guard, I'm going to have to ask you not to use that on me. State secrets and all that." He tapped his nose at Alya and nodded conspiratorially.

Ayla blew a breath out of her mouth. "Nobody ever wants me to use my power. Keen gets to use his here."

"She can't take from the darana?" Erik asked me. "Get something more fun?"

Looking around, I lowered my voice. "Getting a little cavalier about that, aren't we? Besides, they could never absorb more than one ability," I said, distracted as Keen ordered another family-sized entrée for himself.

"But that was when you were giving it to them—starting from zero. This is their natural magic now. You haven't tried it?"

"I want to fly!" Keen said as Ayla shouted, "Can you give me Mom's power?"

Chiwel flashed in my mind. He had two powers. They'd given him the obahn power on top of his natural ability as a damari. I'd taken the daranas back, as well as removed the registrars' extra obahn ability. We didn't need anyone absorbing new powers, while the ones they had were so new. I shuddered as I realized how much the thought sounded like something Sabine would say.

"I'll think about it." My siblings bounced in their chairs in response, discussing other additional powers. "Thanks for that." I pursed my lips at Erik. "Is there a reason you're here, or is it just the usual purpose of irritating me?"

He grinned, and I saw my parents exchange a look of surprise. Maybe I was being a little rude.

"I told you I'd let you know when we were ready to go back to Kysalt with the flyers. If you want to bring Simon, that would be fine, too."

"I told Indie and Audre they could come."

"The more the merrier, I suppose," Erik said, stealing another dumpling from me. Even though I was finished, I had the urge to grab his hand and hold it so he'd stop taking my food.

"I'm sure your queen is paying Lim a fair wage? For all this work she's doing?" my father asked, folding his arms across his chest and leaning forward on the table.

Erik sat up straighter. "She is being paid. Tell your father you're being paid." Erik elbowed me.

"She is paying me, Dad, it's okay. But I'm going to want a hazard bonus if I see a single you-know-what."

"What?" Keen and Ayla said together. Their eyes clouded as my father reminded them of what we suspected was hiding behind a portal in Kysalt.

"When? And how long? I'm going to have to hire someone else at the restaurant," I grumbled.

"Don't worry about that. You've got that new chef, and your dad and I can help out while you're gone," my mother said distractedly, as she watched Keen practically inhale the new plate of food.

Erik stood up. "A week from now. And hopefully, only a few days. Thank you." He looked at my family. "Queen Sabine is truly grateful for all the help the Revins have given."

My eyebrows rose in surprise at his sincerity and his acknowledgment of the burden my absence put on my family.

"And," Erik continued, "it would be my honor to give you a tour of the palace grounds if you're interested."

"A palace? A real one?" Ayla said, shooting up in her chair and making the tiny metal lantern on our table wobble precariously.

"Yes, a real one." He grinned at her, righting the lantern before it ignited the table. "The queen and Connery are visiting her uncle at the moment, so we'd have the place to ourselves. Except for the courtiers, ambassadors, maids, grooms, soldiers, and everyone else, of course."

Erik and I didn't look at one another, but I felt something pass between us. He knew somehow what had gone down between me and Connery the last time we'd met.

"Sounds lovely. Lim?" My mother eyed me, searching for my feelings about the subject.

But I only smiled. "Yes. It does sound lovely. Let's go."

Erik was the consummate tour guide. He answered all of Ayla's many questions, which, even without her power, were hard to refuse. My parents listened attentively as he explained the long history of the palace, the many rulers, and interesting landmarks. When we walked past the guards' training grounds, he introduced us to his friends and colleagues. His popularity didn't surprise me. Nor did the many admiring glances he got from other guards, servers, and courtiers who were out walking.

A courtier with long, flowing white hair and a pert little nose smiled suggestively at him as she passed. "Captain, where have you been? We've missed you around here." She barely glanced at me and I bristled. My parents were some ways behind us, admiring a fountain. A troll carved from obsidian dominated the center. He held a scroll, which magically changed language depending on the reader, detailing his heroic exploits.

Before I could stop myself, I blurted, "He's finally come back to us after all these years. The children have missed him terribly." My siblings rose to the occasion, immediately catching on and giving Erik overzealous, adoring looks.

"Remember Father, you promised to teach me to sword fight," Keen said hopefully.

The female's face paled in horror. "You're married? Mated?" Her voice became higher pitched with each word.

Erik, whose mouth had dropped open, calmly collected himself. "I'd appreciate your discretion, Marguerite, especially as I atone for my mistakes and work on becoming a better male."

The courtier shared a look with her companion before murmuring their goodbyes and slinking off down the path.

The children laughed and took off toward a rack holding numerous practice swords.

I smirked. "Is it weird how I'm not even a little bit sorry for that?"

"Sorry?" Erik said, a lupine grin growing on his face. "You just made me even more desirable." At my confused look, he continued, "Every courtier here will be encouraging my path to righteousness while simultaneously vying to be the one who makes me slip." He said the last word in a voice filled with gravel, his tone low. Erik glanced at my family members, ensuring they were otherwise distracted, before closing the gap between us. "But perhaps I could be persuaded to be a faithful lover, with the right,"—his eyes slid down to my mouth—"motivation."

Some extremely insensible part of me sucked my bottom lip into my mouth, and Erik's eyes flared as he tracked the movement.

"I was serious about sword fighting, you know!" Keen called from where he and Ayla were trying to hit each other with the wooden swords.

Ayla smacked him hard in the shin and he dropped his sword, hopping around on one foot while holding his other leg in pain.

Erik stepped back, a look on his face like he knew all about the heat pooling in my stomach. Part of me wanted to light his hair on fire and the other part of me wanted to prove that I was, in fact, extremely motivating. And why shouldn't I? With all that I'd been through lately, didn't I deserve some fun?

My parents arrived, dousing all thoughts of impropriety. We watched as Erik took Ayla and Keen through the basic motions of sword-fighting, the embers in his hair revealing themselves in the bright sunlight.

A groom walked out from behind a hedge, holding the reins of a horse with gray and brown spots. A courtier sat astride the horse, petting its mane and scratching it behind the ears.

"Where would you like to go today, Gertie?" she cooed to the animal.

The horse snorted, and the groom paused before turning his head up to the rider. "She says it's warm and would prefer the forest to the lake today, my lady."

"Of course, as you wish, pretty girl." The courtier beamed before thanking the groom for his translation.

I eyed the young male as he walked back to the stables.

"Give me one second. I need to grab something from the house," I said to my parents.

27

When I walked through the doors of The Peregrine that night, the bar was still lively. My family was exhausted and, since my parents were usually up by five, had gone home at nine. After checking upstairs to find Brax was out hunting, I went to work at the bar. Elias gave my shoulder a squeeze as he went back out to the dining room. Audre and the new sous chef, a burly older gentleman named Horace, were talking animatedly about a soccer league that was starting within the boroughs. A no-magic-on-the-field rule had already been established.

I quickly got back into the swing of things, making drinks and moving in the rhythm that was second nature to me now. As I filled beers and cleared empties, a strange feeling of finality struck me. My eyes danced over the restaurant patrons, some of them openly displaying their powers, others relaxing at the same table they always used. Their conversations floated over to me: misused power, interesting abilities, repairs that would have previously taken months, now taking only the snap of someone's fingers. But there were more mundane things as well. Several people were also discussing the new sports league, a movie coming to Marais, the birth of children.

My mind wandered idly to Boralta, the dragons, Erik. Instead of helping me picture a dragon, seeing a wyvern in the flesh only made the image more impossible. How could they be even bigger and stronger?

I felt Connery's absence from 'his stool,' but the pain wasn't as sharp. There was a dull ache, but my regret for what once was had to be stored away. I shoved it into the same place I'd put all the debilitating insecurity I'd gained when we first came to Lashia.

When I heard a familiar thump above my head, it was after eleven. Only two people remained in the bar, friends of Elias. I waved to him as he left with the pair, finished cleaning up the bar, and then jerked my chin at Audre to ask her to meet me upstairs.

Horace was singing a song about pie as he closed down the kitchen, carefully wrapping his knives in their case before closing the backdoor behind him.

Audre met me in the sitting room where Brax lounged on the sofa, cleaning himself.

"How do you feel about a little extra power?" I held out the darana to her. "You feel okay—not getting edgy from the other abilities?" Audre, Indie, and Simon couldn't jump worlds, but could make a lot of small jumps around Marais or a big one if they needed to go to say, Eudora.

"I only have three extras. Should be good to go," she said as she placed her hand on the darana. She pulled her hand away. "Hmm. Feels... fluffy?"

"Eat anything good tonight?" I said, turning to Brax.

Brax's brow rose. "I say, that's novel." His voice sounded in my head. It reminded me, weirdly enough, of Natalia. Slow and sweet, with an underlying smile.

Audre laughed. "Amazing!"

"I have always considered myself amazing, but I am pleased to know you recognize it as well, tiny one." Brax smiled his toothy smile at us.

Audre dropped to her knees while I sat on the couch beside Brax, both of us scratching and petting him in the way we knew he liked.

"Oh yes, that's the spot right there. My claws, magnificent as they are, can't always reach it." He purred contentedly. "And to answer your query, I enjoyed an excellent turkey dinner."

"I am going to need to know your thoughts on everyone in this restaurant, Brax," Audre said.

"I am sorry to disappoint you, but I have a difficult time telling all you two-legs apart, to be perfectly honest. By smell, I can differentiate, but the names confuse me. Other than you two, I like those little ones, the man and lady who often smell like my dinner, the handsome man who gives me bones, and I enjoyed beating the furry gentleman at staring contests. All the others sort of blend together."

Only a little pain accompanied Brax's comments about Connery as I focused on someone else's trauma. "Brax, I've always wanted to know. Were you okay about killing that guy who broke in?"

Long crimson lashes blinked at me in confusion. "Who?"

"The two-leg. You ripped out his throat," Audre said cheerfully, and I rolled my eyes. I'd never been sure if doing something like that affected Brax.

"Oh. It's true, he tasted terrible. I appreciate your concern for my digestion." He head-butted me affectionately.

"No... I meant, did it bother you?"

Brax rolled onto his side, his eyelids drooping. "I'm afraid I don't really understand the question." He nuzzled into the cushions before closing his eyes completely.

"Gonna assume that means he couldn't care less," Audre said, standing up. "I'm also going to assume you gave me this power in case we need to talk to dragons?"

"Yep. I'll offer it to Indie and Simon too, since they want to come to Kysalt. I'm glad Simon gave Indie his resistance to injury instead of flight."

"Indie," Brax said, sitting up to reconfigure himself on the couch, "the one with the good nails."

Audre huffed. "My nails are good." She examined her short nails and scrunched her face in disappointment.

Brax ignored her. "I'm glad she has some extra protection for the baby."

"I'm sorry," I said as we both gaped at Brax, "did you say, 'baby?'"

"What are you two doing here? I thought you didn't get out of bed before noon, Audre?" Indie said, opening the door to her house wide as Audre and I trooped inside.

"I'm willing to let that gross misrepresentation slide in light of your—" She winced as I elbowed her in the side.

"Where's Simon?" I interrupted.

"He's in the shower," Indie crossed her arms, frowning at both of us. "What is going on?"

"Nothing. What's going on with you?" I strolled into the kitchen, setting down a basket of muffins I'd made that morning.

We turned as Simon walked into the living room, eyeing all of us as he dried his hair with a towel. "Good morning. Is there news?"

"You tell us." Audre sat down at the table, pulling out a muffin and biting the top off.

Indie threw her hands up. "Both of you are being supremely weird. Tell us what the stars you're talking about or I'm going to start slicing." She held up a hand as five sharp claws protruded from her fingertips.

I folded my arms, smiling. "Tell you? How about you tell us? Anything you want to share? Some interesting developments you forgot to mention to your closest friends."

Simon and Indie shared a look like they were concerned about our mental health.

"We really have no idea what you're talking about," Simon said, holding the towel around his neck and frowning at us in confusion.

Audre and I looked at each other. "Is it possible?" she started before trailing off.

"Yeah, I think so," I mused.

Indie gripped the dining room chair so hard her claws dug into the wood. "Tell us," she gritted out.

I grimaced. "This is awkward. I brought the darana back with the ability to talk to animals. So the four of us could use it in Kysalt. And Audre and I spoke to Brax."

"Really? What's he like?" Simon asked excitedly, but Indie held up a clawed finger and he snapped his mouth shut. "Right, stay on topic, Lim." He pretended to look stern.

"Brax smelled something about you, Indie. We thought maybe you just hadn't told us yet. But, uh, you're pregnant."

"Surprise!" Audre said, her mouth full of muffin.

Indie was not a person who shocked easily. In all our years together, I'd rarely seen her caught off guard. But now, her lips parted, and she swayed a little on her feet.

"What?" she whispered.

"Are you serious?" Simon grinned as he wrapped his arms around his mate and lifted her off the floor. "We're gonna have a baby!" he yelled as he spun her around. Indie put her arms around his neck and laughed as tears rolled down her cheeks. Simon kissed her repeatedly as he set her down.

She wiped her tears away and swallowed. "We've been trying for a really long time."

My face fell a little. "I didn't know that."

"At first, we weren't being very intentional. We just stopped using protection. But it's been three years, and I was starting to think it would never happen."

"I'm so sorry." I stood up and hugged her. Behind me, Audre hugged Simon. "That must have been really hard to go through."

Indie shrugged. "We're still young. I figured we'd just keep trying. But something happened when the cuffs came off, when we went to Trevesten. I think they blocked more than our magic."

Audre's eyes widened in horror. "You think the cuffs made you sterile? Those nasty—"

"No." Indie waved her hands and shook her head. "Not like that."

"Indie and I are mates. So our child would be nyssar."

"You think the cuffs affected your ability to create new fae life?" I said, catching on.

"That's our theory," Simon said, pulling out two muffins and buttering one for him and one for his mate.

Lashia had never had a president before. But with Indie as the face of everyone's liberation from cuffs, the call for her to assume a more official position of power happened fairly quickly. There was nobody running against her. Instead, the voters chose whether to (a) have her as president, (b) have nobody as president and continue with the head council, or (c)

have a president but wait a year to see if any viable opposing candidates presented themselves.

She won in a landslide.

People were understandably upset with the council. , Ali, and Cox stepped down and three more councilors were elected to replace them to serve Eudora only. Similar shakeups took place all over Lashia.

Indie beamed, her elation showing through her every pore as she addressed the crowd once they totaled the votes and announced her as the winner. Simon stood at her side, looking like none of this surprised him, while Audre, Connery, and I showed our support from the front row.

"How's the crowd?" I whispered to him.

"Happy, hopeful, mostly," he said as he scanned the assembled people.

"Mostly?" Flames sprang to my fingertips, and I glanced around, expecting to see pockets of whatever new version of Sun Guardians had popped up.

"There's some uneasiness, but it's small. And a bit of..." he trailed off, making a face like I would when trying to determine the ingredients in someone else's dish. "Confusion? Like things are moving quickly?"

"That's to be expected." I blew out a breath, my fire receding. "Things have changed a lot in a short amount of time."

"They'll get over it," Audre said. She had little tolerance for bullshit. It was one of her best qualities. But I wasn't so sure the humans would adapt as quickly. She squinted into the crowd and then nudged me in the side. She jutted out her chin. "Look."

I turned to see Tarik standing with the same group of men he'd been with at the Sun Guardian meeting. "Is the uneasiness coming from over there?"

Connery's eyes swept over Tarik's group. "No," he said in surprise, chuckling under his breath. "He's feeling proud, like family pride."

Audre made a disgusted face while I laughed. "She'll be so pleased."

Tarik was a cat shifter. Not a big cat shifter, but a tabby cat. He was actually pretty adorable. I recognized one of the other men he was with as another shifter. Perhaps they all were. I supposed it was the nature of all animals, fae included, to assign ourselves to groups.

Indie made some announcements, including one about the new Olympics. This was Simon's idea and people loved it. Every three years, a series of events and competitions where people could show off their abilities. It reminded me of Boralta's contests, but hopefully with less bloodshed.

When Indie finished her speech, we lept to our feet, cheering and clapping along with the rest of the crowd. She smiled down at the three of us, her eyes bright and those fluffy lashes damp with tears.

As I wandered home, thoughts of wyverns and dragons and, annoyingly, a pair of eyes like warm whiskey dominated my thoughts. Erik's allusions to him being popular at court felt like a warning bell. But as much as I tried to convince myself he was like Leo, with a girl in every court, my skin still pebbled at the thought of 'motivating' him. At what point would Sabine decide she didn't need Erik to keep an eye on me anymore? Would he just disappear after that?

28

A week later, I once again stood before the glowing plinths marking the entrance to Kysalt in Boralta. Indie, Simon, Audre, and Erik stood with me, along with five of Sabine's guards. Venten and the other countries' representatives were not attending this time. But Halorn, Sandlin's favored successor, had come, along with his own flyers.

The male again wore a maroon cloak over his shoulders. He smiled at us all, his brown eyes crinkling. "Welcome back. You must love the snow as much as we do."

"What can we say? We're gluttons for crystalized water," Audre said. She spoke casually, glancing around the area and looking bored. It was all for show. I knew she was cataloguing details just the same as Indie and Simon. Playing a game of subterfuge once again, the three of them sank easily back into their first life attitudes and personalities.

"These are our mapmakers." Erik gestured to two of the guards. "And these are our flyers." He pointed to the other three. All of them looked like they spent a lot of time outside. The mapmakers could translate what they saw with their eyes directly onto paper. But unlike journalists, they could do pictures as well as words. It was a unique ability in that it took quite some training to perfect it. The mapmakers studied for years to translate their vision into the specifications of whomever hired them.

Two of the flyers were for the mapmakers. The third one was for me. A dark-haired male named Jayce, who sported full sleeve tattoos. His hair was long and tied in a knot on the top of his head. He flexed his fingers and smiled at me cheerfully.

Erik would fly in his crow form and Simon would carry Audre, as a small child, and Indie. Simon and I had created a modified harness for the two of them so he could keep his arms free.

"Are you our babysitter?" Indie asked Halorn.

He chuckled. "We'll try not to cramp your style. But until we establish rules, King Sandlin would be remiss in not ensuring everything is above board and safe."

"I'll try not to steal any icicles," Audre drawled.

The two fae that had prepared the portal for us last time scattered the erlaub powder. With fewer people, we didn't really need it, but it was nice of them to help us conserve power.

Once we'd entered the other side, those of us who couldn't fly stepped into our harnesses. The flyers secured us before taking flight.

We were only just above the treeline, but the air was already cooler. On my right, Indie, covered in a thick wool cape, held on to Simon's back while Audre was wrapped in a warm fur papoose on his front. To my left, Erik flapped his iridescent black wings.

He spoke to the rest of us. "Follow my lead and stay together."

A deep voice sounded in my head. "I'm connecting the ten of us. If you need to speak to us, use this connection."

I startled, not realizing that Jayce was a mind-speaker, like my father. My father could only connect two people, and not for long. Jayce's power was considerable.

"What life are you?" I asked internally.

"Sixth," Jayce responded. "Flying and mind-speaking are by far my most useful talents." I could hear him smiling even in my head.

"Could you stop flirting? I'm right here." The new voice in my head was feminine and my eyes snapped to the female flyer just ahead of me. She had a shaved head and her tattoos crawled up her neck, like they were cradling her skull. She winked at me. "I'm Nova."

Jayce chuckled. "Apologies, my love."

I grinned. "Is this your first time in Kysalt?" Instead of making the journey with Erik and the other guards, I'd jumped my crew to the Millers before doing the last leg in the carriage. I gave Tish an abridged version of what had happened to Connery so I could commend her on her elixir skills.

"Nope," said Nova. "We've been here three times. Once with the map-makers, but that was two years ago. We're all very curious why there's all this sudden interest again in Kysalt."

I wasn't sure what to say. True to their promise, Halorn and the Boraltan guards kept their distance. They were mostly black dots on the horizon. The same icy lakes and evergreens Erik and I had explored on foot stretched out below us.

"Sabine is suspicious of Boralta's renewed interest in it. She wants to be thorough before agreeing to any regulations," Erik said.

"Did you have this kind of escort the last time you came?" Indie asked.

"Not really," Jayce said. "There were guards stationed at the portal back to Boralta, and they sent one of their flyers with us. That was it."

"So they *are* concerned about us finding something," Simon mused.

Erik turned east, away from the Boraltan contingent. The rest of us followed. A mountain loomed ahead of us, bursting out of an otherwise flat landscape. I watched Halorn, but none of his party seemed inclined to follow us.

We dove closer, speeding through the trees and valleys, slowing only occasionally if a mapmaker requested it. We passed over a waterfall spilling from a gaping cave. The waterfall froze at the edges, but the center continued to flow downward into a beautiful, clear green lake. A herd of bison navigated around the icy edges.

"He's still not doing much," Audre said.

"Nope. Definitely seems unconcerned with us being over here. Let's try south," Erik said. We changed direction again. This time, Halorn and his group followed, but only barely. They were at least a mile away.

We continued the dance all day. Based on Erik's cave theory, we concentrated on mountains, looking for caves. But nothing we did seemed to interest Halorn's group. Except for lunch. They joined us only when we landed to eat the sandwiches I'd packed.

When the sun dipped behind the mountains and the temperature dropped, we returned to the hospitality of the Boraltan castle.

Indie and Simon held hands as they trailed along behind me and Audre, all of us gazing at the bejeweled walls.

Halorn swept us into a smaller dining room than I'd been in during my last visit. A wall of windows dominated one side, and, on the far end, a long buffet sagged under the weight of an array of delicious food. I'd done barely anything physical all day and yet my arms and legs felt like jelly. My mouth watered at the piles of bread, roasted vegetables, and tureens of steaming soup.

We weren't the only ones in the room. Several courtiers were dining at various tables. Their dress was far more casual than I'd seen in Adnatia. It felt more like a casual restaurant or canteen than a castle dining room.

"Did you get what you needed today?" Halorn asked. His smile was friendly, but something pricked at me. For such a powerful presence, they'd been remarkably relaxed about our expedition.

"It's very beautiful," Indie said from beside me.

"Yes. I'm surprised more people don't go for relaxation. Hunting, fishing, etc.," Simon added.

"Epic snowball battles," Audre added, popping a piece of cheesy bread into her mouth and practically moaning in satisfaction. Not finding any on my own plate, I snagged her other piece and she glared at me.

"Perhaps once there are reliable maps, more people will make the journey." Halorn nodded at them.

I spared a glance for the poor mapmakers who looked exhausted. Their eyes were unfocused as they clutched mugs of hot tea. Jayce, Nova, and Kiki, the other flyer, didn't look tired at all. The three of them were reviewing a piece of paper Jayce had pulled from his pocket.

Nova cleared her throat. "So, Halorn. You're a third life. How do you expect to beat the older fae during the trials?"

"I've been training a long time. It also helps that I've done my home-work on the other entrants." He used his fork to point out a tiny female in the corner, sipping a glass of red wine. "She's the one to beat. A seventh life with considerable elemental power." He swiveled his head, looking for someone. "And him,"—he indicated a gaunt-looking fae with muddy green skin—"if a trial is near water, he'll be extremely dangerous."

I saw Jayce write something on the paper he held. Audre, who was sitting next to Kiki, glanced at it and her eyes lit with interest.

"If you're looking to make some coin," Halorn said, eyeing the paper, "you'd likely make the most by betting on the long shot. And I aim to win." His eyes crinkled at the edges.

Nova picked up the paper and folded it, putting it into her vest. "We'll see." She grinned. "But we wish you luck."

I didn't even flinch when Erik walked into my room without knocking later that night. His eyes widened as he found me not in front of the fire, but reading in bed.

"Finally come to your senses? Ready to move things along?" He kicked off the fur-lined slippers he was wearing and crawled across the covers toward me.

King Sandlin had given me the same room as before. The four-poster bed had carvings of animals and flowers, just like the mantle above the fireplace. I rested my book on the green and gold coverlet and let out a sigh.

"Unfortunately for you, I was too tired to even sit in a chair. I can't understand how so much of me is sore when I wasn't the one flying."

He rolled over, scooting up, so we were both leaning against the headboard. "Bracing yourself takes work. If you'd hung like a limp noodle the whole time, it wouldn't hurt so bad now."

I couldn't help but smile. "I'll consider it for next time. Any thoughts on today?"

"We were either nowhere near the portal or..." He trailed off.

"Or?" I prodded.

"Or something else. I don't know. Something feels off. He's too friendly."

I sat up. "That's what I was thinking. He's all polite and smiley, like he doesn't even consider us a threat."

Erik made a show of checking out the book I was reading, pressing his shoulder to mine. His skin was smooth and his hair damp at the edges. He'd just showered and smelled of honey and spices. He turned to me and I hastily looked back down at my book.

He leaned closer. "I think you're right. We're on the right track with the portal. Instead of expecting him to lead us to it, we need a better way to find it."

If I looked up and turned my head, our faces would be nearly touching. The words in my book blurred as I tried to avoid his very pointed stare and the warmth spreading inside me.

"No fae has the power to find portals. We've always just stumbled upon them," I said, annoyed at how breathless I sounded. Erik's thigh pushed against mine. Part of me was running at a full sprint into this while the other part watched, certain a long drop lay ahead.

"I thought you were a master at devices and potions?" The bastard was grinning at me. He knew exactly what he was doing. His fingers inched toward mine. He had attractive hands, with well-muscled forearms.

Clearing my throat, I wore a look of cool dispassion as I faced him. Stars, he'd moved even closer. Our noses were practically touching. "I could work on it."

"Lim, why so nervous?" His hand slid slowly up my arm until it was cupping my face, leaving a trail of lightning in its wake. Internally, I cursed myself for letting my breath catch. "You don't like me, remember? Although I can't imagine why not." His voice was languid and irritatingly nonchalant. As if we were talking about the weather.

At that moment, I couldn't remember why I didn't like him either. He was always goading me. That was it. And Sabine had sent him to watch me. And his job was just to keep me away from Connery, right? But I said nothing as his fingers continued to caress my skin with featherlight touches.

"Unless you've changed your mind?" The timbre of his voice dropped as he ran a thumb across my lips. "And you'd like to take advantage of me? Use me for your own sordid purposes?"

My smirk was wholly involuntary, and his eyes widened in success. Erik leaned closer, his breath hot against my neck as he whispered, "Don't throw me out in the cold again. I want to be where it's warm."

Like he'd called to them, my flames shot to the surface of my skin, begging to play. My heart beat faster in my chest as Erik trailed a finger down my neck, following it with the lightest press of his lips.

I sucked in a breath, and my head tipped back. Was he just doing this for Sabine? Had she instructed him to keep my mind off Connery by any means necessary? It was working. In this moment, with his rough hand moving to my waist and his tongue darting out to taste my skin, I couldn't think of anything else.

When his lips finally captured mine, it felt like sinking, like jumping into a river with all your clothes on. Erik sucked my bottom lip into his mouth, biting down gently. I gripped his sweater, drawing him closer. He reached around, gathering me tight against him before pulling me down beneath his strong body.

His kisses were slow and deliberate, as if he already knew what would please me, and refused to rush it. Erik's tongue pushed into my mouth and my brain lost the ability to form words. It was an avalanche of pleasurable sensations as I tasted him. The pads of his fingers were coarse against me as he pushed his hand beneath my nightshirt. My back arched with tiny rolling tremors as he explored my breasts, my skin. But instead of pushing my clothes all the way up, he bent his head and placed his mouth over my nipple, sucking me hard through my thin shirt.

"Fuck," I bit out.

I dragged my nails through his hair, pulling him closer and relishing the friction. His attention moved to the other nipple while his other hand drifted lower. My nerves ignited with the sensation, sparking at every part of me he touched. There was a growing ache between my thighs and I moved against him, trying to achieve the friction I desired.

"So impatient," he growled into my chest as he slid down, taking the coverlet and my pajama bottoms with him. His fingers pressed into my hips as he pushed his face between my thighs, his lips crushed against the thin piece of fabric covering me. "I'm going to devour you," he said, pulling the lace to the side as he dragged his tongue through my center. "I'm going to torture you like you've been torturing me."

A mumbled "Oh stars" was all I could get out, my core tightening as lights danced on the edge of my vision. He pushed his tongue inside me, making good on his promise, and I cried out. Ripples that would soon become waves started inside me.

Erik flicked his tongue against my clit as he pushed two fingers inside me. "You are such a liar. If you don't like me, Lim, why are you so wet?" His voice was so fucking arrogant, and I burned to tell him he was a terrible lover and this wasn't doing anything to me. But the way I strained against him, wanting him closer, deeper, it would have been a pathetic attempt.

"I don't like you," I gritted out, my words strained and my brain very close to being mush. "But I'm willing to overlook it as long as you keep doing that."

"So callous," he cooed, pushing his fingers farther and faster inside me. "I should stop right now to punish you for that."

"I take it back." The words were out of my mouth before I could stop them. The waves grew, mercilessly crashing against me.

Erik chuckled darkly. "I could never deny you."

He sucked my clit, and I exploded, clamping a hand over my mouth to keep from yelling his name as my body writhed against his mouth.

"Oh no, you don't." He climbed on top of me, pushing my hand away while he slid himself along my wet skin. When his cock was pressed against my entrance, he grabbed my wrists and held them above my head. "I want to hear you, baby. I want to know how much you want this."

I wasn't sure which way was up or down, but I knew I wanted this, wanted him.

"Yes, please."

"Please, what?" He nudged closer, dragging himself slowly along my wet center.

"I want you, Erik." The words tumbled out of me as my need became almost painful.

With that, he pushed all the way inside me, and I cried out at the fullness.

"Fuck, you feel so good. I knew you'd feel amazing, but this is... this is..." The haughty attitude vanished and his face contorted in pleasure. Erik interlaced his fingers with mine, still holding me down as he made long, tortuous strokes inside me.

Rivulets of heat raced over my body. That familiar tightness rose again. A full storm broke out inside me as his pace increased. I arched up to meet him and he uttered a curse.

"Come with me, Erik, please." I leaned up to kiss him, and his tongue slid into my mouth. With a last roll of his hips, we fell together, his forehead against mine and my nails digging into the back of his hands as we wrung out our pleasure. He collapsed next to me, exhaling, before wrapping his arm firmly around my waist.

29

The bread was burning. Shoving my notebook away in frustration, I hopped off the stool in the kitchen and pulled it out of the oven. I'd been up since five.

My notebook was filled with crossed-off theories. When Erik suggested it, it seemed promising. Some fae purportedly specialized in finding portals, but there was no actual ability behind it. All the ones I'd met had been charlatans. But erlaub root wasn't the only thing used to thin the veil, and I'd been confident I could find something to help us.

Pages of crumbled-up paper filled with many terrible ideas later, and I'd lost confidence.

"Does this mean I can go back to bed?" Audre stopped after walking through the door and glanced around the kitchen in surprise. I'd done most of the prep for lunch already.

"This means you can help me." I tapped a pen against my head in frustration.

Audre picked up one of the crumpled papers and opened it, frowning. "You've built tons of daranas and a kunli, you can do this."

"I built a deficient kunli," I said, tossing another crumpled paper on the floor.

"Nah, that was the shippie's fault." She pulled on an apron before pouring herself a cup of coffee, chewing her lip in thought. "We need to go to a portal in Trevesten. Something we can study."

"Excellent plan." I hopped off the stool and began gathering the paper while Audre grabbed her favorite paring knife.

"When you were dating Bastian," Audre started in an overly casual voice, "did you ever feel weird? Because he was kinda rich and dressed fancy?" She started peeling potatoes.

My eyes stayed firmly on the growing pile of trash in my arms as I answered. "I did. He didn't make me feel that way, though. It was all me, just being insecure." Dumping the papers in a basket on the back stairs, I turned to her. "Is someone making you feel insecure?"

"No," she scoffed. "I was just making conversation."

I pointedly rolled my eyes at her, but let it drop.

A decorative iron gate marked the portal to Tulo. The silken divide shimmered in the early morning light.

"Watch it," Audre said as a carriage rolled by, splashing our shoes with last night's rainwater. Unlike Boralta's gate to Kysalt, the portal to Tulo was in town. Two large buildings bordered the heavy gate. Fae and other creatures traveled through the portal as casually as they might visit the printer next door.

Two wraiths floated through, whispering in that ethereal way of theirs. Erik stepped aside, giving them a wide berth. Every country but Visaria had a settlement on Tulo, but it was most popular with wraiths, sprites, or fae like Connery who could become the wind. The atmosphere was heavy. It felt like carrying boulders on your back when you walked through the permanent twilight of the seventh world.

But we didn't need to go inside. I was more interested in what was outside the gate. Even on this busy street, plants clung to it, birds made their homes among the curling iron, the magic resisted domestication. Erik and I pulled samples of all the plants, took scrapings of the iron, and even grabbed discarded bird feathers from the nests. Audre was across the street, speaking to anyone who walked out of Tulo about their experience using the portal.

Erik reached over me to pull a leaf from a vine, wrapping his hand firmly around my waist. "Excuse me, just need to grab this." He pulled me against him, digging his fingers into my hips.

Hiding my smile, I stepped away. "Focus, Captain."

He smirked at me before dropping the leaf into a bag and labeling it. "How can I focus? It's the first time we've seen one another in over a week. If I didn't know any better, I'd say you used me for my body."

I pushed my lips to the side and exhaled a laugh. "Was there something else I should use you for?"

Erik used both hands to push me back from the gate as another party went through. I hit the wall, and he leaned into my space. "You can use me for whatever your heart,"—he dragged a finger down my throat to my chest—"desires. But I was hoping for a little more communication."

Sparks sizzled under my skin in the wake of his touch. His eyes were predatory as they focused on my mouth.

"How come I have to make all the effort?"

"I would communicate with you, but you haven't even given me my own fish." He stepped back, his arms crossed against his chest. There was a small trio of freckles on that chest. The memory of how I knew that was threatening to overwhelm my senses.

"I don't know," I said, pushing off the wall and going back to my collection. "Giving a male his own fish is a big step. Not sure I'm ready for that." It really was too fast. And whatever this was, it was built on some shaky ground.

Erik put a hand on his heart and sighed dramatically. "I see. I'm just a toy to you. A large, fully capable, very attractive, and deeply satisfying sex toy." He shook his head mournfully and turned back to the gate.

I snickered. "Maybe," I said, smiling politely as another group passed between us, "you haven't made a good enough argument for getting a fish. Perhaps I need more convincing." Even though my eyes were firmly on the blue flower I was plucking from the ground, my skin heated as I felt his eyes swivel to me. The intent in them was clear. If we'd been anywhere, even semi-private, my skirt would already be around my waist.

Erik circled behind me as I stood up. His voice was a soft purr. "I want you to know that I could make any manner of terrible innuendos right now about getting into your wet tank"—an embarrassing giggle died on my lips as he pushed my hair out of the way to kiss my neck— "but I'm not going to. Instead, let me come to the restaurant tonight. I'll make *you* dinner. I think that should tip the *scales* in my favor."

My snort of laughter startled the birds next to me as he stepped back to continue his collection efforts. Erik had told me his job was to provoke me, distract me. And while I enjoyed the distraction, letting him make me dinner was too much like blindly ignoring that truth. "I don't think I'm ready for that. But if you promise not to abuse it, I'll get you a fish."

His face clouded, but he quickly adopted a lazy smile. "If you wanna be *koi*, that's fine by me."

"That was pathetic," I said. But I couldn't help my grin as I collected the last of our specimens.

After we finished at the portal, we made our way to the University of Kilgard.

A bored-looking wolf shifter at the information desk directed us to the office of Professor Gossif.

"Welcome!" The professor smiled widely as we entered the office. She was at least eight feet tall with spiraling blond hair. Like Natalia, she'd chosen to spend her power elsewhere and if she'd been human, would have looked about fifty. The curls twisted and stretched of their own accord, and I had the impression they all had individual brains, like octopus tentacles.

"Thank you so much for seeing us," Erik said as we all shook hands.

"Of course. I've been communicating with the queen for centuries. She knows I'm always happy to help."

There was a crashing sound, and we turned to see Audre jump back from a pile of shattered crystal.

"I didn't even touch it, I swear!" Her eyes were round with apology and panic.

"Stop it, Boris," Gossif said with a stern shake of her head. The crystal reassembled itself into a vase again before turning into a small chalk-board. The word 'sorry' appeared on the slate.

"I used to have a ladanka," Erik said in delight as he held out his hand. Boris converted into a wooden hand and gave Erik a high-five. "Good boy." He searched his pockets and pulled out a metal clip, dropping it into Boris's waiting hand. The clip melted into the wood before reap-pearing as a ring around the hand's middle finger.

Audre's eyes widened, and she excitedly searched her pockets for something to feed the ladanka.

"He's very useful, if a bit of an attention hog."

I smiled at Boris as I turned back to the Professor. "As Sabine mentioned, we're researching ways to find portals."

Gossif nodded. "It has been studied. But most of the portals in Malan were discovered by accident. We think we've found all of them, but without an accurate divining method, we can't be sure."

"So there's nothing that works?" I asked, disappointed.

Gossif looked at Boris and he turned into a much larger chalkboard. "Here's what we know: A combination of erlaub, black seaweed, and pearl will crystalize if within fifty miles of a portal. However, it will disintegrate any closer than that." She wrote the ingredients on the board. "The soil around portals often contains a higher concentration of copper. And, unless the veil is particularly thick, such as the portal in Visaria to Harena, birds can travel through the portals without assistance."

Boris promptly organized her untidy writing into three legible lines.

The three of us stared at the board. It wasn't a huge help, but it was something.

"What about negatives? Are there things that don't like the land around portals?" I asked.

Gossif nodded, "Excellent question." She turned back to the board.

"Teacher's pet," Erik whispered at the same time Audre said, "Brown noser."

Gossif only chuckled. "There's no obvious pattern of anything being resistant to the portal. They exist in all different climates, but the portals themselves react negatively to velvetleaf. Prolonged or excessive exposure will cause the veil to harden."

"I knew that!" Audre said. Finding nothing in her pockets, she ripped a button off her jacket to give to Boris. He melted into a wooden puppet, her button transformed into an eye. "No, no, not that. Something else, please."

He changed again, her button an innocuous addition to a square wooden puzzle.

"Good boy." She beamed, and the puzzle vibrated.

"That's right," I said, watching Boris solve himself. "I used sunflower in the elixir for the kunli because it inhibits the growth of velvetleaf."

There was a weighted pause when I realized what I'd just confessed. Slowly our eyes rose from Boris to Gossif, who was staring at me, her eyes comically wide and her curls sticking out in every direction.

"You've made a kunli? Did it work?" she breathed. Boris became a party hat.

"Uh, not really," I said honestly. "We tried to go to Sverresen. Unsuccessfully."

"I see." She lowered her voice and leaned toward me. "I'm an academic, Ms. Revin. Some things should be overlooked, in the interest of science. For research purposes only, of course." She nodded at Erik.

Erik grinned before saying. "You should see her daranas."

"Erik!" I said, exasperated.

"Yeah, zip it." Audre crossed her arms, and I knew only the presence of Gossif kept her from reaching for her stars.

He held up his hands, a smile playing on his lips. "Professor, the queen is already aware of Lim's talent for daranas and kunlis and has given her and her associates"—he gestured to Audre—"full immunity. Perhaps the two of you might find time to discuss your mutual interest in science at a later date."

A pair of clasped wooden hands appeared where the party hat had been.

"Oh right, I forgot that." Audre's posture relaxed.

Exhaling, I nodded at the professor, whose curls shook with excitement. "I'd really like that."

Gossif sent us on our way with a small round container. It would expand upon our request and contained fifty of the most extensive texts on portals. It was a good thing I'd turned Erik's dinner down. While I could use my power to read the books, Indie and Simon were going to want a lengthy explanation.

30

Tossing a book aside, I picked up another one from the pile in my parents' living room. Twenty-seven books and I was no better off than when we'd left Gossif. I found lots of information in the books about various ways to thin an existing veil, the effects of different portals on those who used them, and even an extensive treatise on the theory that all the portals were connected. But no more help on how to find a portal if you didn't already know where one was.

My mind kept coming back to the erlaub, seaweed, and pearly concoction. If I could somehow stabilize it, that might work. Of course, I was not the first fae to attempt it, and so far, nobody had been successful.

Keen and Ayla looked at the books, flipping through the pages for the pictures. My mother was knitting on the couch.

"Here we are," my father said as he came in from the kitchen with a tray. Keen and Ayla jumped up, and I hastily shoved some books back into their small container so they wouldn't get trampled. Gossif seemed nice, but I bet Boris could change into something sharp if I wrecked her books.

"Thank you," I said as he handed me a plate of pie and ice cream. The warm buttery shell was perfect with the melting strawberry ice cream.

"No luck yet?" He eyed the stack of books before placing a plate of pie in front of Brax, who grabbed the entire slice with one swipe of his tongue, murmuring a 'thank you' only I could hear. Ayla and Keen immediately guarded their plates as he eyed them hungrily.

"None."

"Don't you think the dragons will be mad if Boralta uses the portal?" Keen asked. "I thought they didn't like fae."

I puffed out my cheeks. "I don't know. It's been a long time. They might be open to it. It's possible that not every dragon agreed with Claudius's decision."

"How long do dragons live?" Ayla asked.

"As long as fae, I should think. Maybe longer." Dragon lore was not something I studied growing up in Trevesten. It was a non-issue. Wyverns could live twenty-thirty years, but despite looking similar, Dragons were a different breed. Bigger, tougher, and smarter.

"Okay, well, if they agree to talk, what's so dangerous about that?" Keen finished his pie and set it down on the floor where Brax inched toward it, licking up the remnants.

"It would give Boralta an advantage. If they're the only ones that can speak to them and trade with them. If they could convince the dragons to fight for Boralta, they could take over Trevesten." I paused, considering the destruction. "They could take over a lot of places," I said in a quieter voice.

An image of a dragon igniting the buildings of Marais flashed through my head. I shook it off. There was no reason to think like that. I was still the only person who could get out of Lashia at will. There were no portals here.

"Why do you need to find their portal, anyway? Why not just make one of your own?" My mother asked, a tiny Priya-sized sweater taking shape under her knitting needles.

"That didn't go so well for me last time. I couldn't ask anyone else to risk themselves. Especially since we know Makome is dangerous. The dragons could incinerate us on the spot if we just show up."

My mother tipped her head to the side, the firelight catching her hair. She pursed her lips and frowned. "You could take some of Keen's power. They'd never know you were there at all until you were ready to see them."

"You remember the woman who didn't even want me to have magic, because it was too dangerous? Where'd she go? Who is this person who wants to load me up like a pack-balara, potential magical overdose be damned?"

She dropped her knitting. "I don't want you to overdose! But I also know you did it once and now you're better equipped. We would worry about you,"—she shared a look with my father—"we always worry about all of you. But we also believe you can do whatever you set your mind to."

"Mom!" Ayla groaned.

"You sound like one of those posters at school," said Keen.

But I smiled. "Thank you."

I'd never known my parents in my first life. My grandfather took care of me. The only memories I have from my first childhood are in that house in Oderon, just the two of us. Except when Natalia came over, and the two of them would drink tea and gossip at the table while I played in the garden.

My family here was so different from that. All five of us in this house, constantly on top of one another. Baby toys and mess, farm animals and birthday celebrations. I adored my grandfather. But he was a typical fae, always thinking there was another tomorrow, another chance to say what he wanted to say.

After gathering my books and helping with the dishes, I hugged both my parents. "Thank you, again."

On Tuesday morning, I left Horace and Audre in charge of prep while I went to Trevesten. First, I made a stop to see Gossif. The two of us, aided by Boris as a chalkboard, went over the details of my original kunli. I explained the issue with Connery's blood.

"Hmmm, do you think that was it? None of your tests indicate his blood was unsatisfactory," Gossif said, staring at my notes.

"What else do you think it could be?" I replied. Gossif had an impressive amount of research on kunlis, but without the ability to get the necessary but illegal ingredients, she couldn't do more than hypothesize.

"I wonder if Solbaina was the wrong access point. Although I admit that's where I would have chosen."

There was no portal in Solbaina. The magic there acted like a boost to our own, to create a portal where there was none.

"Perhaps. This time, I have access to some better resources."

"Oh?" Gossif looked up at me.

"Boris, what time is it?" Boris immediately changed into a clock. "Let's hope they're ready," I said as I pulled Morgan and Erik to me from the palace.

Erik gave me a look like he was disappointed in me. I hadn't sent him a fish last night. I ignored his look but couldn't say I hated the proprietary way he stood next to me.

"Morgan has agreed to donate her blood and, with Sabine's blessing, given us consent to use the Seer's Courtyard in Adnatia.

The Seer's Courtyard was really more of a field on the castle grounds. The royals of Trevesten had attempted to install pretty walkways and illustrious statues, but to no avail. Other than a low stone wall that bordered the field, the plants consumed all decorative touches. It was also a misnomer, as there were no fae with the power to see the future. But like Solbaina, there was magic in the air, the insects, anything that made its home in the Seer's Courtyard.

Seeing the future was a common joke in Trevesten. When anyone attempted something stupidly risky or dangerous, they were called a 'seer.' As in, 'Seer here, thought it was a good idea to challenge a troll to arm wrestle.'

"Who are you going to take?" Morgan asked. "Besides me and Erik, of course."

"You want to go?" I cocked my head at her.

"Where my blood goes, I go." She pulled a curly dark hair from where it had gotten tangled in one of her many thin necklaces. "Audre?" She said, her dark eyes glittering. She didn't even attempt to hide her interest in my answer.

"Yes. Simon and Indie will stay in Lashia. I will give back the cuffing power so I can also take some of your invisibility if that works." Erik held up a finger to indicate he would also need it and Morgan nodded. I tucked my lips in a smile at how casually criminal Morgan was. And how strangely unsurprising I found it that Erik was just as willing.

"All of us already have some healing power, and you and Audre can talk to animals, anything else?" Erik mused as he studied the specifications Gossif and I had put together.

"You need a gift," Gossif said. "For the Voden."

Morgan blew out a breath. "What do you get a Voden to tell them you're sorry your ancestors were assholes?"

"A fruit basket seems insufficient," Erik joked.

Boris transformed into a wooden cow.

"Not sure I want to show up smelling like dinner." I gave Boris a pat on his cow head. "What did we give to them before?"

"Food, mainly," Gossif answered. "But also protective enchantments. Their eggs are very fragile. In order to accommodate the dragon's growth, they're made from a flexible material which is enough while they're being cared for by the parents, but can't stand up to an attack by other dragons."

"Would you let a stranger give you something to keep in your baby's crib? No questions asked?" Erik looked at me.

I laughed. "Good point."

"I've got it," Morgan said. "We'll give them a star. To make up for the one Claudius lost."

"You know it was—" Erik started, but Morgan interrupted him.

"I know it wasn't really a star. It's symbolic," she snapped. The way the two of them bickered reminded me of Keen and Ayla.

Boris transformed into a crystal star, glowing with embers of light. Inside was the image of a sleeping dragon, a beautiful fae female curled up on his tail.

Gossif wiped away a tear. "Yes, I think that will be acceptable. Good boy, Boris."

31

"This feels familiar," Audre said, looking out at the Seer's courtyard. The air was certainly less humid than Solbaina, but that same feeling permeated the air. Even though I jumped easily between worlds now, pushing back the curtain on a new place would likely always fill me with apprehension.

"Feels like potential." Erik's words were joking, but his face was serious. I'd watched as he'd checked and rechecked all our packs. The sword across his back was gleaming and freshly sharpened.

"If I didn't know any better, I'd say you were nervous." I arched an eyebrow at him. We hadn't been alone together since the night in the Boraltan palace. I'd given him his fish, but there was too much to do. Gossif and I had created the kunli together. She'd fine tuned a few things until I felt confident about our chances.

Sabine had given us unrestricted access to all the contraband the palace had confiscated. Audre's eyes had nearly fallen out of her head when she saw the shelves filled with all manner of illicit items and substances. As a result, it took only a month, and not years, to get everything we needed. My ability to travel quickly to other cities throughout Trevesten also helped.

"Do you know better?" He cocked his head at me, a deeper question in his eyes I didn't want to address.

"Everyone ready to do something ill-advised?" Morgan's voice called. We all turned as she, Sabine, and Connery approached us.

Connery's eyes found mine, and he smiled. "You come back safe, okay?"

Next to him, Sabine nodded. "Yes, please. I have already crossed so many lines with this experiment. Please don't die." She gave me a bracing look before wrapping her arms around Morgan. Sabine gripped her sister so tightly, Morgan looked like she might pop.

Sabine stepped back. Erik saluted her, but she shook her head, taking his hands in hers. "I don't doubt you,"—she looked at each of us—"any of you, in the slightest. But please be careful. Take care of one another." She squeezed Erik's hands before coming to me. "And if anything goes wrong, just come back." I thought that would be it, but she reached out and hugged me, too.

"What are you wearing?" Audre asked Morgan with obvious disdain. Her hair was a pink pixie cut today, her eyes a vivid blue.

"Armor," Morgan said. Thin golden plates surrounded her chest, legs, and arms. "I'm trained as a soldier too, remember?"

Audre kept her eyes on Morgan but jutted her chin in Erik's direction. "He's not wearing that." Erik coughed and looked away. "Do you think the dragons have learned to use swords? Because I don't think that will save you from a fire blast. Or maybe it will. Lim, give it a go." She beckoned at me with her hand, still examining Morgan's outfit with contempt.

I pulled my lips to the side and refused to laugh. Slowly, Morgan turned to her older sister.

"See?" Her eyes were like ice. "I told you this was stupid."

"Forgive me for wanting to protect you!" Sabine exhaled. Connery put an arm around Sabine and squeezed her shoulder. The gesture didn't hurt me like I thought it would.

Morgan called for a page and undressed right there on the field. While the rest of us, including the red-faced page, averted our eyes, Audre watched Morgan with idle curiosity. Like you might watch a chick being born. The princess pulled out a pair of pants from her pack and put them on, leaving on the undershirt she'd been wearing under the armor.

"There. Ready," she announced. The page took off back to the palace, no doubt to shine the armor until it blinded onlookers.

Sabine and Connery stepped back while the four of us climbed over the stone wall and headed for the center of the courtyard. For a moment, I desperately wanted to turn back to look at him, to remember that feeling of starting an adventure with him at my side. But I kept my eyes fixed on the destination and focused on the job.

It was strangely underwhelming.

We held hands so Morgan could extend her power to us. No sense in wasting the slice of invisibility we had. The kunli remained intact. The little red stone at the center still beamed at me, practically insulting.

Makome had a stark beauty. It reminded me a little of the swamps, but without the water. A carpet of blonde sand blanketed our landing site. In front of us, a chalky mountain range. We moved out of the open and backed into a forest of pale gray trees, releasing Morgan's hand. A woodpecker worked somewhere above us.

Behind us, something large moved through the forest. We disappeared, weapons out, waiting for the thing to get closer. I smelled it before I saw it. Embers and peat. The dragon's dark blue head broke through the trees, its wings tucked in tight around its body. Something about its movements was furtive.

"Good, good," it said. The voice was young, and I couldn't tell whether it was male or female. "This is good." It settled down in the undergrowth and started covering itself with tree branches. Suddenly it froze. Above us, a reddish brown dragon soared overhead. Its voice carried, but at that height, I couldn't hear what it was saying.

I was concentrating so hard I didn't realize the other three were staring at me expectantly. Right, this was my job.

"Excuse me. I don't mean to frighten you." The dragon's long neck snapped forward, searching for the source of my voice. "I mean you no harm. I'll come out of hiding, if you promise not to hurt me." We really had no idea how the dragons would receive us. They could still be furious. Either way, a little kindness and humility never hurt anyone.

"Who are you? What are you?" Its voice was frightened. I was speaking to a child.

I let go of the invisibility while the others remained hidden. "Hello. My name is Lim. And I'm not here to cause any trouble. What's your name?"

Instead of attacking, the dragon dipped its head, looking at me like I would a cockroach. "What are you?"

"I'm fae. I came here, hoping to speak to the Voden."

There were several tense moments where I was sure, at any moment it, would roast me. Instead, it stood up, its head reaching twenty feet above mine.

"If you wanted to speak to her, why are you all the way out here? And I'm Oyo." The voice was clearer in my head now, and deeper. Male then.

"It's a pleasure to meet you, Oyo. I brought three friends with me. Would it be okay if they came out to see you, too?"

Oyo nodded, searching the trees for the others. When they stepped out in front of him, he reared back. "How did you do that?"

"It's something some fae can do," Audre answered. She gave Oyo a little bow, and he tipped his head in a gesture reminiscent of Brax.

"If I could do that, Dana would never find me." A little puff of smoke came from his nostrils.

"Who is Dana?" I asked.

"She's my sister. You probably saw her flying."

"I'm happy to see if I can make you invisible, too. Would you be able to tell us how to get to the Voden? And if you've seen anybody else like us around?"

Oyo surged forward and the four of us leapt back in surprise. "Yes, try, go ahead. What do I do?" He asked in an eager voice.

Audre translated for Morgan, but the princess seemed to have gotten the gist.

"This may not work. I've only done it with other fae. I just need to touch you," Morgan said.

"Sure, sure," Oyo said, excited.

I stuttered. "You can understand her?"

"Dragons can communicate with any creature." He puffed out his chest.

"Huh. Well, that was unnecessary, then," Audre murmured. "But I do enjoy talking to Brax."

I looked at Erik, and he just shrugged, confirming that he, too, could understand Oyo perfectly. We'd never discussed communication with Gossif or any of the palace advisors, because Audre and I had planned to lean on the power we'd received from the groom. Now I know why nobody brought it up.

Morgan approached Oyo cautiously while the rest of us held our breath. She reached out a hand and touched his front arm. He didn't turn invisible, but his body took on the color of the trees and shrubs around him. I could still see his outline, but if he stood still, it would be difficult to see him. Especially if you were a sibling flying fifty feet up.

"Unbelievable!" Oyo cried. "This is great."

Morgan smiled and kept her hand on him. "Can you help us, then?"

Oyo continued to admire himself, swinging his impressive tail around to take it in and knocking over several trees. "Sure. I haven't seen anyone like you. But, like I said, you're a long way from the Voden. It would take me until lunch to fly there. My mom or dad would be faster."

"Only I can fly, Oyo. And unfortunately, I'm a little small to carry them. Could you give us directions on how to walk there?" said Erik.

"Walk?" Oyo said the word like he'd never heard it before. "Why would you walk? I can take you. If my mom says it's okay."

"We thought it would be rude to ask," Erik replied.

I took a long drink from my canteen as we waited on the edge of the forest for Oyo to get permission from his parents. After twenty minutes, we saw him soaring back to us, a bright orange dragon, three times his size, flying on his right. On his left was the reddish-brown dragon we'd seen above us earlier. Dana, I presumed.

They landed surprisingly gracefully. The ground barely shook, but their wings kicked up torrents of sand, forcing us to shield our eyes and mouths.

"Hello," Morgan said politely. "I'm Morgan, this is Lim, Audre, and Erik. We are fae from Trevesten and we were hoping to see the Voden. Oyo offered to take us."

The orange dragon said nothing. Dana shifted on her feet and ruffled her wings. The air was tense, and I took measured breaths. Now would not be a good time to panic.

"We don't want to be presumptuous. We can walk, if that's what you prefer," she offered.

Again, there was silence. Morgan looked at me like she suddenly might not be understanding their responses, and I surreptitiously shook my head. The orange dragon craned its neck down until it was eye-level with us and I could feel the heat on my face. She swiveled, sniffing each one of us.

"You know the flames," she spoke finally to me. "I smell the cinders on you."

I let out a breath, but made my voice strong. "Yes. I have fire in me, too." The dragons watched as flames circled my wrists and fingers.

"I am not in the habit of sending my child off with strangers. But if you wait here, I will take you myself. Tomorrow."

"Of course, that's very kind of you," I said, resisting the impulse to bow and scrape in front of this creature that could snap off my head in an instant.

She let out a huff and launched into the sky. Oyo and Dana followed her without a word to us.

"Mother," Erik breathed. "I've never come so close to pissing myself."

We stayed in the forest, but at first light, we went back to the edge and waited. I'd heated coffee and the four of us sat drinking it while we ate a breakfast of apples and cheese.

Oyo's mother approached from the north about an hour later. Her massive form was as terrifying as I remembered it.

Without ceremony, she landed and hugged the ground, stretching out her front leg for us. "Good morning," I said.

"We didn't catch your name last night," Audre added.

"It is unnecessary for you to know my name. We won't see one another after today."

"That sounds ominous," Erik said, hesitating at the edge of her leg.

She made a sound that could have been a laugh. "I meant nothing dire by it. I have no interest in court." We clambered onto her back, gripping the horns that protruded down her spine. She made another little huff, thinking. "My name is Athena."

"Thank you for this, Athena." The words caught in my throat as she rose through the air. My stomach dropped, and I felt the contents of my breakfast come up. She evened out, and I risked a glance behind me to see the others were similarly affected. Morgan was especially green.

Athena's answers to our questions were short, but polite. Yes, she knew the Voden. Her name was Chiara, and she'd been the Voden for fifty years. Yes, she knew the story of Claudius and Koli, but gave no further detail. No, she had seen no one else like us.

We fell into silence as we sailed over the arid landscape of Makome. Occasionally, other dragons passed us, but barely spared us a passing glance. Here and there, cows, sheep, and goats roamed, herded by smaller figures. The dragons made their homes in caves. Everything else must have been like a buffet.

"The animals seem unconcerned that you'll suddenly swoop one of them up," Erik yelled over the wind.

"Why is the taller one shouting at me?" Athena asked.

"Stop yelling. She can hear you just fine." I made a face at him and he grimaced apologetically. It was a long way down for some of us if Athena's patience ran out.

"They do not fear us because we do not swoop. Hunting has been outlawed for thousands of years in order to stem food shortages. We retrieve our share when it is our turn. The livestock flourish again, and none are hungry."

"Are you sad? That you can't hunt anymore?" Erik asked in a quieter voice.

"I would be sadder to starve," Athena replied.

32

Three hours later, Athena descended into the mountains. She swooped lower, tucking her wings tighter as she sailed through a deep ravine. We saw more dragons. Brown, green, orange, with sharp spikes or thick clubs at their tales. Several dragons sat at the mouths of dark caves, watching us with their giant serpent eyes.

Athena aimed for the gaping mouth of a cave, larger than any I'd seen yet. Two yellow dragons sat outside, sentries. They watched as Athena approached and landed gently on the stone.

"I am delivering these visitors to the Voden."

The sentries said nothing, but swung their heads toward us. Morgan approached them, again explaining who we were, what we wanted, and that we meant no harm.

One sentry chuckled at the last part, and I didn't doubt why. The dragons didn't fear us in the slightest. We were like a group of mice promising Brax they wouldn't hurt him.

I turned to say goodbye to Athena, but she was already launching into the sky.

"Thank you, Athena," I said, my voice at its normal volume. Athena's head bounced once at me, and she was gone.

"You may enter," the yellow dragon to our right said.

We entered the cave and expected to be met with darkness, but a short walk led us to a spacious open-air amphitheater carved from rock. Dragons milled around, talking or eating. The smell of freshly killed beef and blood filled my nostrils.

Audre nearly tripped over a pile of clean bones before a brown dragon swept them aside for her with a flick of its tail.

"Thanks," Audre stammered.

"No problem," a young female voice responded.

A smaller blue dragon zipped toward us, blocking our way.

"Hello, hello. Please state your name, so I may announce you." The dragon looked eager, its scales incandescent in the sunlight.

We gave our names, and the dragon turned quickly, nearly knocking us over with its tail.

"Her Royal Highness, Morgan, the Princess of Trevesten in Malan, and her three guards."

Audre side-eyed the lack of introduction, but Erik was unfazed. His eyes were everywhere, and it occurred to me that if anything happened to Morgan, Sabine would blame him.

The blue dragon flitted away to sit beside the biggest animal I'd ever seen. The Voden was twice the size of Athena with glittering green scales. She looked like she could easily crush any building in Lashia. The thought didn't fill me with comfort as we approached her.

No throne, no piles of jewels. Her dais was merely a slightly elevated stone jutting from the edge of the cliff face. There was nothing she needed to look more impressive.

"Welcome, Princess." Her voice was heavy and ancient, as if it came from somewhere deep within the mountain.

"Thank you for seeing us, Voden. A long time ago, my people offended yours. I apologize on behalf of my home, and hope that you will accept this gift, a small token in memoriam of Claudius and Koli's story." Morgan produced the star from her bag. It was multi-faceted and exquisite. Fearful of getting their likeness wrong, she didn't include the image of the thwarted lovers.

She put it down on the ground and stepped back. I called the fire to my palms and blasted it with heat. The star erupted before pulsing with internal fire. It would remain alight for months before the dragons would need to relight it.

The blue dragon swooped down to retrieve it, handing it over to Chiara, who grasped it between two enormous curved claws. The Voden looked at it for a long time.

"I have thought about them more recently these days."

Was that a hint? Was she thinking about them because, for the first time in thousands of years, the Boraltan fae had shown up on her doorstep offering food or magical protections?

"Thank you." Chiara handed off the stone to the blue dragon, who flew away with it.

We'd talked a lot about how Morgan should play this. Whether she should come right out and ask or try to wheedle it out in the conversation. In the end, Gossif said the dragons would not appreciate nuance or subtlety. They would consider either an attempt to be dishonest.

"We believe another nation in Malan has found a portal from Kysalt into your world."

Chiara's head swiveled before she stretched it out, coming eye level with us. Even the heat from her breath was dangerous. While my flames reached toward it, the others looked deeply uncomfortable. Sharp spikes protruded from the top of her head, while fangs nearly as tall as me plunged downward out of her mouth. All of us resisted showing any weakness by stepping back.

"And you've come here to warn us or to complain?" The green scales shimmered and hummed, evidence of the power she held, both as a dragon and as Voden.

"Yes," Morgan said with a small smile. Chiara made the same huffing noise Athena had, which I interpreted as a laugh. "We aren't really complaining. The dragons closed the portal into Malan, and we have respected that. We only come now because this nation, Boralta, has not disclosed how or why they seek contact with the dragons."

"And if they're hiding it, they're probably up to some shady shit," Audre said under her breath.

Chiara's mouth widened into a terrifying smile. Several of the surrounding dragons made huffing noises. I wondered whether they had exceptional hearing or if it was more to do with their power of communication.

Morgan pressed her lips together, but nodded. Audre's off-the-cuff comment seemed to appeal to the dragon's blunt nature. "Have any of the Boraltans contacted you, Voden? Have you seen any others that look like us?"

"No, but Makome is vast. They could be many places," Chiara answered, but she was inspecting the four of us in turn, sniffing and moving her head like a venomous snake. Her eyes were yellow, struck through with bolts of green.

"They've been here," Erik said. "I saw evidence of fae signatures as we flew overhead."

The rest of us looked at him. He shrugged apologetically. It's not like we had time to discuss anything after we landed.

"And we cannot see such things?" Chiara asked. Her giant eyes, so recently fixed on examining Audre, narrowed on him.

"My guard," Morgan said, wrangling control back over this conversation, "can see enchantments. It's one of his magical skills. Even a normal
fae may not see it, but he can. I'm sure he would be happy to show you
where these marks are and we would like your permission to track them.
In order to find the portal."

"It would be faster if we found it for you."

"How can you do that?" I blurted. Morgan's shoulders heaved and fell
as if she'd given up trying to exert authority here.

Chiara withdrew her head, and I felt Audre sigh in relief next to me.
"Because dragons created the portals. We can always find the paths we
made."

Chiara dismissed us after promising to assign one of her trackers to help
us find the portal. The twittering blue dragon, Albie was his name, took
us to a room to wait. By dragon standards, it was probably considered
cozy. Our voices echoed off the ancient walls, and I had to raise a ball of
fire to even see the ceiling.

There was no furniture, of course. But we found some smoother rocks
to sit on. Albie flew back in, leaving a tray overflowing with fruit and
vegetables, a dead goat, and several dead chickens.

"Thank you, Albie. This is very generous. It's more food than the four
of us could eat in a week." She gave him a gracious smile. "Would you like
any?"

"Oh? Really? Don't mind if I do." Albie scooped up the goat in his
sizeable jaws and swallowed it whole. "Thank you. Your tracker will be
here soon."

When he'd gone, Audre shuddered. "There was an entire leg sticking between his teeth. I'm really starting to wonder about Koli's taste in lovers."

We laughed. "It was a long time ago. Even the fae were different. More connected with the magic, less civilized." Morgan grabbed an orange and peeled it as she spoke.

"Is this one of those things where, if we don't make a dent in this food, Chiara will be offended?" Erik held up a chicken, sizing it up and steeling himself.

"I doubt anything goes to waste here, but just in case." I grabbed the chicken while Audre grabbed another. To the impressed looks of the others, we quickly plucked their feathers and quartered them before I roasted them over the stone. The four of us were picking the last of the meat off their bones when a long red neck peered into the room.

"What is that awful stench?" The dragon wrinkled its nose in disgust.

"We cooked the chicken. The fae can't eat them raw."

"Disgusting. No wonder we didn't want any contact with you." His voice was conversational though, and we laughed.

"I'm Egan. I'll be tracking your portal. Climb on and stay very close to my body."

Audre gave me a confused look while Erik said, "Shouldn't we wait to get outside?"

Egan didn't bother responding, just looked at us as we climbed on awkwardly. The four of us followed his instructions and gathered close to him. Erik covered my body with his, his thighs pressing against the backs of mine.

"I don't think that's necessary," I whispered.

"This is for me. This entire visit is terrifying." He dipped his nose into my neck and inhaled. "Thinking of how you looked with your legs wrapped around me is all that's getting me through."

My thighs clenched around Egan, visualizing what it felt like. Erik's hands through my hair, his lips on my skin, dragging his fingers through my—

"What in the Mother?" Audre yelled as Egan's head dove straight through the rock above us. The stone parted like butter as his red scales disappeared into the stone. The opening became wider, stretching to accommodate all of Egan's body, before he pushed through.

I shoved my face against the dragon's scales so hard their outline was surely imprinted on my skin. The breath left my lungs as Erik crushed himself against me.

The stone was inches from us as we moved through the dragon-made tunnel. Audre clenched her eyes while using one hand to grip Morgan's leg. The princess stared at the moving rock walls in horror.

There was no counting, or breathing, or anything that would make this experience tolerable. The four of us collectively exhaled, shaking with relief as Egan exited the mountain, the tunnel closing behind him.

"We could have used a warning about that," Morgan said, her chest heaving.

"Why?" Egan said, unbothered. "I still would have left that way."

Once we were in the open air, I sat up and let myself fall back against Erik's chest. He wrapped one arm around me and the other around the back spike protruding in front of us.

"Now we know how they made the portals," Erik murmured in my ear.

Egan heard him. "Yes. We can travel through many walls, including those between worlds, as well as open and close them as we see fit."

That part had always been missing from the story, how Claudius had closed the portal. Which made sense, since there were no fae on the dragon side to explain it. Sudden panic seized me. Audre turned around, wide-eyed as the same thought occurred to her. If the dragons could open other portals, they could get to Lashia. Erik's arm tightened as he sensed my unease.

"How do you decide which worlds to enter?" Morgan asked, glancing at Audre.

"That is at the discretion of the Voden. But we usually only leave for food, and only for a short time. Makome is our home. This is where we must be."

I'd never heard of anyone seeing a dragon in Lashia. We'd brought songs like One-Eyed Clyde with us; before that, the stories were all myth and legend.

"There." Erik pointed below us. "There's the trail."

I saw nothing but more sand and some trees, but Erik could see whatever hidden magic the Boraltans had used to mark their paths.

A half-hour later, in a valley filled with sagebrush and a smattering of tiny white flowers, Egan dipped and landed. The four of us slid off, grateful to be on solid ground. Travel by dragon was not my favorite.

No gates, no plinths. There was nothing to mark the location of the portal, but we saw it all the same. The gossamer veil floated before a crystal blue lake. It hovered above the ground, fixed in place.

"The dragons made this too? Recently?" Morgan asked Egan.

"It looks recent. Which world is on the other side?" Egan shifted closer to the portal, sniffing the entrance.

"You can't tell? You push through without knowing what awaits you?" Morgan's neck craned back to look at the dragon.

Egan extended his chest in a stretching motion. "We can smell life and food. Otherwise, it matters not. The portals close eventually without regular use. If that happens, we track another that smells promising."

"Why not just reopen it in the same place? If you know there's food there?" Audre jumped in.

"In Makome, our magic is very strong. When we exited the mountain just now, I knew exactly where we would come out. This is not the case for other worlds. We cannot always know where we will end up. Even if we start in the same place."

"Hence the sniff test." Audre nodded in understanding.

"It took us an hour to get here from the Voden's seat. I'm guessing your flight speed is around four hundred miles an hour. It would take them about three weeks to a month to walk and half of that to fly," Erik said as he examined the portal. "If we assume the Voden is telling us the truth, they haven't made it that far. They don't want to alert the dragons to their presence yet."

"Is 400 miles per hour fast? I am extremely fast. And the Voden would not lie unless necessary. I doubt she finds you fae concerning."

Part of me wanted to be offended that we didn't intimidate the dragons, but remembering Chiara's massive form forced my pride to recede.

"Egan," Morgan started, "if dragons created the portals, does that mean one of you created the portal into Boralta from Kysalt?"

The sight of a dragon in Boralta would have spread quickly, and not just through Boralta. But if what Chiara said was true, they had to have used it at least once.

"I have to assume so," he said, but offered no further detail. "Will you need a ride back?"

"No, thank you," Morgan said. "We'll use this portal to get home. Thank you and please extend our sincere gratitude to the Voden."

Egan nodded before disappearing over the mountain.

"Weapons out?" Audre pulled her bladed stars from her belt while Erik and Morgan drew their swords. I ignited my fire. We turned invisible before I spread the erlaub powder and we moved through the portal as one.

As we stepped into Kysalt, the four of us let out similar expressions of anger and disbelief. Morgan slammed her sword into the ground. "Those sneaky bastards!"

33

We were standing only a few dozen feet from the portal into Boralta from Kysalt. No wonder the Boraltans didn't track us, why they were totally unconcerned about where we went in this frigid place. None of the information I'd learned from all of those books would have been useful, because it all would have led me to this area. I would have spun in circles, convinced it was just pointing me to the opening into Boralta. While the other portal hid in plain sight, surrounded by a cluster of towering evergreens.

The entrance into Makome from Kysalt wasn't that big, wide enough for a carriage or wagons but stuck between two bent trees. Of course, for the dragons it would be no trouble to widen it. The image of the mountain closing up behind us as we passed through with Egan flashed in my mind.

"Let's go home," said Morgan. "I don't want to take the chance of anyone from Boralta discovering us here."

I jumped us to Adnatia.

Back in the palace, Morgan went off to explain everything to Sabine while the three of us rested in a drawing room. A server brought tea and cakes. Audre and I held the cups to our noses, inhaling in unison before we took our first sip while Erik looked on in amusement.

"Where's the bathroom in this place?" Audre asked. Erik directed her, and she disappeared.

He stood and circled the couch until he was standing behind me. His hands fell on my shoulders, gently kneading them as he leaned down to nuzzle my neck. The pool of tension I'd been carrying since we'd left the Seer's courtyard melted into a puddle as his lips trailed across my skin.

The teacup and saucer in my hand rattled as his hand moved lower, dipping into my shirt. Audre could come back. Morgan or Sabine—stars, even Connery, could walk in right now and see us. My thoughts jumbled and my breath caught as his fingers searched my skin. His breathing wasn't steady either as he pulled his hand back up and cupped my face, turning me toward him. He opened his mouth to speak when the door opened.

Erik turned and casually leaned against the back of the couch while I took a sip of tea. Sabine entered, with Morgan and Audre trailing behind her. I collected myself, trying to remember the part where Sabine is his boss and Erik's entire purpose in wooing me could be—is—to ensure I don't bother Connery. Surely Connery would have told Sabine, and therefore Erik, that we'd said goodbye?

"I'm so glad you all made it back safe. I've been pacing since you left." She smiled as she sat down in the chair opposite and floated herself a cup of tea.

Sabine couldn't see into any other worlds. She believed she could only see into Lashia once we were there because of her connection with Connery. But Makome was still sealed to her. Knowing the dragons' power over the portals, it made sense. They controlled the pathways by sight or foot.

"If Boralta thinks they can take down all the dragons with fire-wielders, they're delusional," I said. "The dragons aren't scared of us at all, for good reason."

"Morgan said her magic worked, on the young one at least," Sabine said.

"Yes, but it didn't work as well as it does on us. I suspect if she'd tried it on one of the older ones, it might not have worked at all."

"You can burn, right?" Erik said from above me. I glanced up at him, my brows furrowed. "Dragons aren't immune to fire, just like you aren't, even though you both control it. They must fight amongst themselves with fire and claws."

"And giant teeth," added Audre.

"Their hides are tough but not impenetrable. It's not unthinkable that the Boraltans could kill one," Erik said.

"Maybe a kid," I said, my gut twisting at the thought of the fae targeting Oyo and Dana. "But what would be the point? I also don't see Chiara taking orders from anyone in Boralta. What incentive could they even offer her?"

The door opened, interrupting Sabine's reply. Connery strode in, his eyes filled with relief. He gave Audre and Morgan a one-armed hug before crossing to me. I automatically stood, and he wrapped his arms around me. As the familiar scent of rosemary and spring water surrounded me, I stepped out of his embrace.

Behind me, Erik crossed his arms over his chest. I didn't dare look at Sabine.

"Glad you made it back. We've been worried." He sat down on the sofa next to me, but closer to Sabine, who sat in the nearby armchair.

Exhaling, I smiled. "Yep. Met some dragons, the Boraltans are shifty, all in a day's work." I waved my hand and took a sip of my tea. The awkwardness had more to do with my concern about everyone else than it did about me and Connery. He meant his goodbye and so did I. But I sensed the tension, like everyone was waiting for us both to start crying or something.

I stood up. "Morgan can fill you in. I need to get back to the restaurant. You coming?" I asked Audre. "Or do you want me to get you later?"

"I think I'll stick around for a bit. If you don't mind. Haven't had a night out in Adnatia in a while."

"You're welcome to stay here, if you like," Sabine said.

Audre nodded her thanks, and now I was avoiding looking at Morgan. I needed to get out of there before my eye muscles collapsed from the strain.

"Okay, send a fish when you're ready." I said goodbye to the others and left the room. Erik was behind me in an instant, grabbing my arm to turn me around and pulling me into his arms.

"Do you really need to get back? Why don't you stay? We could all enjoy a night out in Adnatia."

Part of me, a very southernly part, really wanted to. But I saw him tense up as I hugged Connery. Did he rush out here because he knew his queen didn't think he was doing a good job of distracting me? I wanted not to care, to say the hell with it, and just enjoy him. But having three—two and a half—failed relationships in the past year was enough to drive anyone to introspection. I needed to slow way down.

"I really should." I smiled at him. "Walk me out?"

His lips twisted down a little. He knew I wasn't being completely honest. "Fine. But Morgan and Audre are definitely not going to let me hang out with them tonight, so I'll just be sad and alone in my room."

"My condolences," I said, my lips twisting, as we exited the castle and walked toward the gate where I could jump home.

Just as we passed the gate, he wrapped his hands around my waist again and pulled me forward. "Do you want to tell me what's going on? I would take this as a comment on my performance, but that can't possibly be true."

I laughed and allowed myself to enjoy the feeling of his strong chest under my hands. "I'm trying this whole actually listen-to-what-peo-ple-say-and-don't-just-read-whatever-I-want-into-it." Leo, Connery, Bastian, they'd each told me what they were about. My ability to momentarily distract them into my way of thinking, or my bed, didn't get me anywhere in the end. "Does Sabine still consider me a threat to her relationship?"

Erik pursed his lips. "I don't think she would phrase it like that." His eyes narrowed and his grip tightened ever so slightly.

"Does it concern her that Connery and I are still friends?"

He frowned. "I'm not privy to everything the queen thinks."

"You just do what you're told?"

Erik released me, shaking his head. "That goes with the territory, yes."

I stepped away and gave him a tight smile. "Enjoy your night in."

Audre wandered back into the restaurant three days later. I was in the kitchen with my father and Horace, who were standing at the stove, cooking and debating crop rotation techniques.

Grinning, I said, "I feel the need to make some kind of innuendo, but I'll refrain because I'm happy for you." Morgan, unlike Jake, would not run away at the first sign of danger. Then again, she wasn't completely without complications.

"I appreciate that. Especially as I wouldn't resist if I was in your position," Audre said, tying her apron around her waist.

"Don't I know it," I said. The two of us completed morning prep in record time, passing over whatever needed pre-cooking to my father and Horace. Except to listen to my instructions, the two of them didn't stop jabbering.

I'd asked my father to come while Audre enjoyed her time away, but he didn't seem inclined to step away now she was back. Finally, I shoved him out the door with some lunch for my mother, and I went to tend bar while Audre and Horace stayed in the kitchen.

Indie and Simon came in around seven, a look of fierce determination on my friend's face.

"Please tell me you have bacon." She'd wrapped her copper curls in a scarf, pulling them away from her glowing skin, the child's power already showing through.

"Hello to you too," I chortled. She gave me an impatient look.

"Give the woman some ham, Lim, before someone gets hurt," Simon said, hopping up onto a barstool.

"Of course. What do you want? A sandwich, pasta?" I looked between the two of them, bemused.

"A plate of bacon. And sure, add some pasta on the side." Indie sat down next to Simon and craned her neck to wave to Audre through the pass-through.

"How you doing, Madame President?" Audre yelled.

"Hungry, is how I'm doing." Indie practically growled. Her eyes turned brighter, like she was about to shift.

"Mother save me, okay, okay!" I held up my hands and told Audre to fire a plate of bacon and a side of pasta.

Simon just hummed as he perused the menu, ordering himself a bowl of soup and grilled cheese.

"I take it the baby has an appetite?" I smirked at Indie as I wiped down the bar. She mustered some smiles and waves for people as they came in, but was clearly focused on her meal.

"Oh yeah. And it changes every day. At first, it was fruit, then pickles, and now it's pig."

"Are you feeling sick at all?" I asked.

"Not really. Mostly, I just get tired a little quicker. But that could also be because I have two jobs now." Indie took a drink of the iced tea I'd poured for her.

"Order up for the scary lady," Audre said. Indie didn't even bother with a retort as she fell onto her plate of food. A few minutes later, I handed Simon his meal.

"Yeah, how is that going to work?" Four more people sat down at the bar, and I started making their drinks.

"It's working. We hired two healers so they can handle most stuff. The births we're still doing without magic, except to help with the pain and any complications."

It hadn't occurred to me, but both she and the other doctor wouldn't be in as much demand now that there were healers walking around. The humans' power was strong, but it wouldn't be enough for everything. There were some things even fae healers couldn't help, like a magical overdose or certain diseases specific to the fae.

"I saw Sasha and Celeste last night. Did they talk to you about baby stuff?" The couple had promised to lend Indie their infant clothes and toys once she gave birth. Sasha had declared they were a one-and-done family, but Celeste gave her a wistful look that made me think the conversation wasn't over.

Indie nodded, finally relaxing as she chewed her fifth piece of bacon. "I think we should be alright. But I need a crib and a stroller."

"I'll get those for you." I cleared some more empties and ran a few more plates from the pass-through. "Maybe I'll get you a Trevesten special." I winked.

She nodded. "Just the necessities, though." Indie glanced to the side and lowered her voice. "We don't need to bring everything here."

The fae enchanted their baby stuff with all kinds of protection measures. You could buy a crib that did all the normal stuff, rocking the baby, singing to the baby, but it could also repel anyone from touching the baby or change its appearance based on what the baby liked. There were strollers with anti-kidnapping protection and temperature control. And that was just for starters. A fae child's power was weaker than an adult's, but it wasn't non-existent. Some things needed to be fireproof, waterproof, covered for the flyers, and able to change size at a whim.

"Understood. Maybe just a little spoiling?" I said with a pleading look. Indie and Simon chuckled before agreeing I could spring for a few more magical bells and whistles.

An hour and three deserts later, Indie and Simon made their way home. The rest of the night flew by and I collapsed into bed next to a sleeping Brax.

"It's kind of awkward to share a bed with you now that we can talk," I mumbled to him as my eyelids drooped.

He yawned, his needle-sharp teeth reminding me of the Voden. "The couch is available if you're uncomfortable."

I barely got out a laugh before sleep pulled me under.

34

On Saturday, before I'd even had breakfast, both Sabine and Erik's fish appeared in my tank. Despite my decision, my skin shivered at the thought of seeing the captain again.

Nobody looked cheerful as a guard escorted me into the breakfast room. Sabine's face was drawn, Morgan looked depressed but resigned, and Erik gave me a tight smile. Connery was closest, and he pulled out a chair for me before looking at Sabine to begin.

Figuring bad news was easier on a full stomach, I floated coffee, eggs, and toast over to my plate. Sabine waited until I'd had a few bites before speaking.

"King Sandlin has invited us back to Boralta to finalize Morgan's marriage contracts and the regulations for Kysalt."

"Oh." There was no suitable response to this news. "You okay?" I asked the princess.

"I'm fine. Traditionally, the marriage contract is only for one hundred years. After that, I have the option to leave with some nice parting gifts if I so choose." She dunked a piece of buttered bread into her coffee and took a bite. The breeze from a nearby window rustled her dark curls.

"And you have to be... faithful?" I grimaced, trying to put it delicately.

Morgan snorted. "Unfortunately, that is expected."

Sabine said nothing, but Connery reached out and clasped her hand. In all things, there were tradeoffs. Money and power on one hand, but a lack of control on the other. Morgan didn't have to go through with this arrangement. Nobody would force her. She was doing it because it benefited Trevesten, and for her, and Sabine, Trevesten came first. Connery had begrudged Sabine for not treating him as an equal, but when it really came down to it, they weren't equals. She had responsibilities he didn't.

"That's not all," Erik said, and I let my eyes wander over to him. Shade fell across him, turning his hair almost black. His eyes dipped to mine, and I remembered leaning against him on top of Egan, his arm like a steel band around me.

Swallowing, I said, "Go on."

"Sandlin knows about your power," Sabine said, and my eyes shot to hers.

"How?"

"He *says* someone saw you outside the palace. Put two and two together." She scoffed. "But I expect he had someone follow you after your first appearance in Boralta."

My brow furrowed. "Well, that's kind of annoying, but I suppose it would come out, eventually."

Sabine sighed and leaned back in her chair. "It won't be long until they learn about your visit to Makome, too." She took a sip of her coffee and her eyes suddenly went glassy. "They're still training those fucking fire-wielders."

I pulled my head back, my lips twisting at Sabine's language. "Tell me how you really feel."

"Sorry." She shook her head.

"We're concerned for your safety." Connery leaned toward me. "That he knows about your power and has expressly invited you back to Boralta seems intentional."

"Yes." Erik cleared his throat, and I turned my head to him. I was getting whiplash in this conversation. Morgan gave a cough that sounded suspiciously like a snicker. "We're worried they might try to kidnap you."

"What?" I scoffed. "C'mon. They wouldn't do that. It would cause some kind of incident." I looked at Morgan and Sabine. "Right?"

"We're not worried about Sandlin, it's the other contenders that might try to use you for their advantage. They're allowed to have a team in the trial and you'd be a valuable addition, willingly or not. And typically, one citizen of a country doing something to another country's citizen wouldn't require the crown's personal involvement." Erik leaned back in his chair and put his hands behind his head. I tried not to look at the muscles in his arms or the way it flattened out his already taut stomach.

"So, I shouldn't go, right?" I played with a piece of bread. I already knew the answer. If Sabine intended to decline on my behalf, she would have already done so.

"Of course, I cannot and would not make you. However, if you don't go, I suspect that will only increase the fervor of their pursuit. It may be best if you come with us so I can show the Boraltans that you aren't just any citizen, but an important member of my inner court and under my personal protection. And that if anything happens to you, the consequences would be severe."

Meeting Sabine's hardened stare, I kind of understood what Connery saw in her, aside from the good looks. Neither she nor Morgan played the simpering royal. Sabine had a reputation of being a just ruler, but also a ruthless one. The fae were powerful people, and they expected their leader to be strong.

"Thank you. I'll go. I like Boralta. But you have to promise we'll stop at the Millers."

"I'd already planned on it," Sabine said with a small smile. "Definitely want to thank Lady Miller in person." She gave Connery's hand a squeeze.

Erik walked me out again. "Did I see a flicker of desire in your eyes back there? Were you turned on by the queen's willingness to draw blood for you? Because I'm happy to play the part of brutal defender."

I rolled my eyes at him. "I was not turned on, but I appreciated her willingness to protect me."

"You mean even though you stole her mate away to another world for hundreds of years?" His usual teasing smile didn't reach his eyes.

Frowning, I walked out of the gate. "Still baiting me, I see."

He crossed his arms. "Was that a fish pun?"

"Nope." I gave him a mocking salute before disappearing.

The tension in the air was thick and, for once, had nothing to do with me. Audre had insisted on coming with me to Boralta. "Like I'd trust a bunch of fancy-ass royals to protect you? They don't know how to fight."

But now I was trapped in a carriage with her, Morgan, and Erik, I understood that her insistence had not been purely altruistic. She sat next to me, smiling and waving goodbye to the Millers as we pulled away from their citrus-scented house, ignoring Morgan's furtive glances.

Erik caught my eye across the carriage as we silently acknowledged the awkwardness. His toe pressed against mine and I turned my head away so I wouldn't smile as he widened his eyes in exaggerated horror at our predicament.

Despite Sandlin's knowledge, I didn't jump us to Boralta. It would have been weird for me to show up on my own, and we didn't want to alert him if he didn't yet know I could move more than myself.

After some excruciatingly long moments of silence, Morgan snapped, "Are you going to talk to me at all?"

"We did talk," Audre barked. "Just because I understand doesn't mean I have to pretend I like it."

"This is my role, my duty!" Morgan looked incredulous at Audre's continued refusal to play nice.

But Audre gave as good as she got and glared at the princess. "You know what?"

"And that's our cue," I said as I jumped us out of the carriage. A flyer gave up his horse for us and we got on. The saddle magically expanded to accommodate us both.

"Like Egan, but more comfortable, and far less likely to kill us," he murmured in my ear.

It wasn't as smooth as a floating carriage, but he was right. "Also, you aren't trying to give me the Heimlich out of fear." I tried to sound casual, like I wasn't putting myself in exactly the kind of compromising position I'd been trying to avoid with him.

"The what?" he asked, brow furrowed.

"Nothing. I just meant you don't have to grip me so hard."

Both Erik's hands were on the reins, but at this he dropped one of them to my leg. His palm curved as he ran it up my pants, letting his fingers drag along my inner thigh. "I can be much gentler this time." His words were a low growl and the sound shot straight between my legs. A warm glow spread from where his breath hit my ear to my chest, and I had to stop myself from leaning back against him, exposing my neck to his lips.

I knew he could feel it, could see my skin pebbling for him. He took the fur cape tied to the horse and wrapped it around me. I frowned in confusion. It was chivalrous, but I didn't need a fur to keep warm.

Then I felt his hand, hidden by the cape, move up my thigh. We'd fallen behind both carriages. Sabine assigned Erik to be my personal guard, a decision I tried not to think too hard about. Since the queen and the princess were with us this time, we had a fifty-soldier escort. They surrounded us on all sides.

One hand loosely held the reins while the other made languorous strokes on my leg. My back pressed against his front, and I could feel him hardening against me. I sucked in a breath as his hand moved to my stomach, pushing up under my shirt and jacket.

Was it really so bad that it was basically his job to do this? It seemed like he enjoyed it. Stars, my principles were really crumbling here. Especially as I felt his rough skin move under the waistband of my pants. He unbuttoned the top button. Then the second one. He had full access to me by the third. I really should have stopped him, but my hands remained firmly on the pommel between my legs.

A redheaded guard passed by us just as Erik slipped a hand over me, reaching down to caress my most sensitive part. Swallowing a gasp, I arched my back, knowing he could feel how much I already wanted him.

"Haven't seen you in a while, Captain. How you been getting on?" The redhead smiled at Erik before nodding to me, "Miss."

"Pretty good, ups and downs." On the word 'down,' he slid a finger inside me and only control of my fire kept my face from blushing furiously as he and the guard kept talking.

"Personal guard to the queen, that's impressive. You need to give me some tips."

"All about dedication to the job." Erik squinted ahead as if looking for threats while sinking another finger inside me and moving them in a slow, excruciating rhythm. My nipples tightened painfully, and I wished on every star and Lashia that we'd get to Boralta soon and I'd be able to feel his mouth on them.

Was I the job? Was this his idea of dedication? The questions died as the pressure between my legs built with every push of his fingers. Ribbons of heat pulsed up my skin and I squirmed in my seat.

"You think we'll be back here for a wedding soon?" Morgan's carriage had gotten even farther ahead of us, otherwise the guard wouldn't have been so bold with his quest for gossip.

"Probably be back for the trials before anything." His voice was still calm, but with a slight edge. He was rock hard against my back and I could feel the rapid beat of his heart.

"Looking forward to that. I saw Sandlin's, he was brutal."

Sweet Mother, how much longer was this guard going to talk?

Erik ground the heel of his hand against my clit and pressed down while making slow circles. Fuck. It was too much. He moved faster inside me and I bit my lip and turned my head away from the guard to keep from crying out. His cock jerked behind me as my thighs clenched around his fingers and I silently came.

"Oh, don't worry, Miss. They can get kind of bloody, but you don't have to watch if you don't want to." The guard gave me a sympathetic look as my breath returned to normal.

I gave him a look of gratitude because I didn't trust myself to speak, and he beamed.

A whistle sounded from up ahead as the giant pillars came into view. Boraltan guards began popping out of the trees to escort us.

With a wave of my hand, I cleaned the both of us up before buttoning my pants.

"The absolute *second* you're alone in your room." His voice was a threat, for my ears only, dripping with need.

My bones felt like jelly. I couldn't have rebuffed him if I tried. Instead, I closed my eyes and leaned back. Erik's arm once again banded around my waist as we trotted into Boralta.

There were no chairs at either end of the rectangular table. Servers appeared from hidden doorways and set dishes at the end, which magically moved down and around the table. I reached for a dish, and it stopped in front of me, allowing me to take a serving of creamed spinach before moving to the next person.

King Sandlin and his wife, Mina, sat across from Sabine and Connery. Sabine had technically arranged their marriage. Mina was Sabine's second cousin, but she'd known Sandlin for hundreds of years before Sabine was even born. They had discussed Morgan's marriage contract in private, and were now talking of more mundane matters.

Across from me, Audre piled her plate high with four different types of meat. Morgan sat to her left and, based on the looks they gave one another, seemed to have worked on at least one of their issues in the carriage. Halorn sat on my right and Erik on my other side.

The female contender Halorn pointed out last time was also at the high table, sitting across from Erik. She had short blond hair cut into a severe bob at her chin. Her name was Isabelle. She leaned forward to speak to him, showing off her ample cleavage. I disliked her immediately.

"You'll be coming back for the trials, I hope?" Isabelle swirled the wine in her glass. Her lipstick was so red it was black.

"If the queen commands it," Erik said safely.

"I plan to put on a good show." Isabelle lowered her lashes at him. It was exactly the seductive look Sydney had tried to master and failed.

"For your future bride?" Halorn said. He arched an eyebrow at her, frowning at her flirtatious behavior. I got the impression Halorn was a strictly by-the-book kind of guy. He'd cut all of his food into bite-sized chunks before taking a single bite and he drank only water.

"My future bride will get more than a good show as my queen," Isabelle said smoothly, raising her eyebrow at me.

I glanced over at Morgan, but she either didn't hear or was choosing to ignore Isabelle's comment in favor of her conversation with Mina. But Audre was agitated. She played with her rice, and her fingers twitched, no doubt wishing for a star to spin.

Taking in the other tables in the vast dining room, I spotted the other muddy-skinned contestant Halorn had mentioned. Was his exclusion a sign there would be no water events in the trials?

"Have the events of the contest been decided, then?" Erik asked Halorn. "Do you know what you'll have to do?"

From the other end of the table, Sandlin answered instead, "Where would be the fun in that? The contestants don't find out the trial until that day."

"Really? Not even a hint?" Morgan used a polite and formal voice I'd never heard from her, but Sandlin pursed his lips and shook his head.

"How many people have entered?" I asked.

"We have six this year. Quite a turnout." Sandlin's smile was wide and eager. I liked him. He'd been twenty-five when he'd won his trials. After a two-hundred-year term in his seventh life, he had the attitude of a child about to get out of school for the summer.

"And you're the only non-seventh life?" Connery asked Halorn.

He shook his head. "No. There is a sixth life, but yes, all the others are seventh." He waved a fork at Isabelle.

"What are all your powers?" Audre addressed the two of them. They both smiled politely but said nothing. Audre made a disgruntled noise. "Oh, it's like that, is it?"

"Both of us have fire and flight. And Isabelle has air as well. But otherwise, the attempt to learn your fellow contestants' abilities is as much a trial as anything else." Halorn floated a pitcher of wine over and refilled mine and Audre's glasses as he spoke.

Isabelle dotted her mouth with her napkin. My irritation with her grew as I saw not a single smudge of lipstick on it.

"Is that why you thought it was appropriate to stalk one of my people?" Sabine asked Sandlin. Her tone was conversational, but her eyes narrowed.

Mina chuckled, and Sandlin grimaced and put a hand over his heart. "I didn't stalk her. Venten saw her outside the castle. It's a power we've never seen before. Of course, he thought it was worth mentioning."

"Yes." Isabelle leaned forward, and I saw Audre, Erik, and Connery studiously look anywhere but at her chest. "How far can you go?"

I smiled politely. They laughed, and we turned to other topics.

35

The walk back to my room was excruciating. After dinner, there had been drinks and games. When I could finally pull myself away, every nerve was firing in anticipation of being alone with Erik. He hadn't touched me once all evening. It was definitely on purpose. When he handed me a drink or leaned across me to speak to Halorn, he left the smallest gap between us. He didn't even ask me to dance. If someone told me before that not being touched all night could be a turn on, I'd have said they ate a bad mushroom.

But when I pushed open my bedroom door, it wasn't to find a naked amber-eyed soldier, but a red-eyed Audre. She was slumped in a chair by the fire, clutching a bottle of beer. In all my years with her, I'd never seen her cry.

"Audre, what's wrong?" I sank down on the floor in front of her, putting my hands on her knees.

She wiped her nose with the back of her hand, sniffling. "Nothing is wrong. Except I'm an idiot."

"I should have been clearer. What's a new thing that's wrong?" I gave her a lopsided smile, and she responded with a snotty laugh.

"She's gonna marry one of them," she said with a long exhale. "And I knew that going in. She told me that the first time we really spoke. She was going to end up in a political marriage, and that was it. And like a complete moron, I fell for her anyway."

My heart sank for her. Behind me, the fire dimmed.

"Stupid honor and duty," Audre muttered into her beer. "I hate her for it and I'm proud of her." She shuddered at her inconsistent feelings.

The door opened. Erik took one step in, bearing two glasses, a bottle of wine, and a face full of wicked ideas. But at one look from me, his eyes darted to Audre, and he backed out, silent as a ghost.

"Who was that?" Audre said, turning.

"Just the maid." I got up and sat in the other chair. Blowing out a breath, I rubbed the bridge of my nose. "When we were in Oderon, things were very clear. We knew just how many miles there were between us and the royals. Do you remember when we met Connery? His differences were so stark. But now, mixing with them like we do, we've forgotten. They're a different breed, with different rules."

"Are you telling me to give up?" Her face held another expression she'd never used with me, anger.

I gave her a 'don't be stupid' look, and she relaxed. "I'm telling you that we can't expect to solve a royal problem without a royal solution. If you want Morgan to avoid this, you need to figure out how she can fulfill her stupid duty without marrying a Boraltan."

"The Boraltans always pick a royal from one of the other countries. Historically, though, because they share a border, it's always been someone from Trevesten. There are two other fae from Eloisha and Ursan, who also want to make the alliance. Sabine said she would support whatever Morgan chose."

"But Morgan doesn't believe her?"

"No, she believes her. That's why she's doing it. Morgan knows it would weaken Trevesten if one of the other countries gets the marriage contract. She said this is the first proper test of her duty. She has to make the right decision, regardless of what Sabine says."

"Right." I rubbed my eyes. I shared Audre's feelings of respect and irritation.

Audre fell asleep soon afterward. I floated her to my bed and laid down beside her. But I was awake for a long time, wondering how faithful Morgan really had to be.

To her credit, Morgan's hand didn't shake when she signed the agreement promising to marry Sandlin's successor. Halorn, Isabelle, the muddy-skinned fae whose name was Ian, and the other contestants were also in the room. Morgan shook hands with each of them, and they promised to honor her faithfully if they won the crown.

Sabine negotiated a reduced marriage time, seventy-five years instead of one hundred. That was something. Audre didn't attend the signing, and when Morgan departed shortly after, it was obvious where she was headed.

Connery looked at me from across the room. People were drinking and chatting, the atmosphere was celebratory for the Boraltans. But he had seen Audre, he knew. He said something to Sabine before walking over.

"Is it bad?" His voice was barely audible.

"Never seen her like this. Morgan?"

"Same." He took a sip from his champagne. "Do you think it would make her feel better if I let her throw one of those stars at me?" His shoulder brushed mine and it made me think of when he'd held me at the execution. But there was no flush of heat or embarrassment, just a reminder that he was still one of us.

I gave a weak laugh. "Probably. But you'd need to let her throw three or four to really be sure."

He chuckled and gave me a bracing smile. His eyes were so clear now, no drunken haze, no green fog. A moment passed between us. An acknowledgment that everything that had ever passed between us was a good thing and that we would be okay.

Suddenly, Erik appeared beside me. "The betting on the contestants' powers is getting serious. Either of you want in on that action?"

Something pulled inside me at his sudden arrival. Did Sabine send him running over here the minute she saw Connery and me alone together?

Connery grinned. "Yes, I'll take that bet. I'm positive Isabelle can change her appearance."

"Oh? And why do you say that?" Erik asked.

"Yeah," I said slowly, frowning. "Why would you say that?" Had they all been staring at her?

He grinned into his glass. "Because Sabine may have made a slightly derogatory comment about her pale skin last night, which is why I noticed that today she's clearly got a tan." Isabelle looked over and gave Erik an obvious appreciative glance. "Probably trying to match you, Captain," Connery added.

I ignored the jealousy I felt in response while Erik and I slowly and surreptitiously glanced at Isabelle. She was laughing with a courtier and she did indeed look like she'd caught the sun overnight. Flame shot to my palms when she caught us looking and gave Erik a little wink.

When we turned away, I caught Sabine's eye across the room and she raised her eyebrows as if to say, 'see?' I covered my laugh by grabbing an appetizer off the tray of a passing server.

"Okay, yeah, I'm betting on that then." Erik put down his glass as Connery wandered back over to join his mate. "Do you want to dance?" His hand was already moving around my waist.

I stepped back. "Did you come over here just because I was speaking to Connery?"

He gave me a bemused look. "I can assure you, out of the two of you, it's not Connery I'm interested in."

"You know what I mean." I crossed my arms. There was no joy in feeling like an obligation.

Erik's mouth fell open to speak, but nothing came out. He closed it and shook his head. "I'm not going to deny that's *a* reason, but not *the* reason."

He wasn't royal, but Erik was just like them. Doing things out of duty, regardless of how he really felt. Or how others might feel. Did I have feelings for him? I certainly enjoyed his company, in and out of the bedroom, but was it more than that?

No. I was not doing this. Not again.

"If you'll excuse me." I left him there and crossed the room, intending to speak to Queen Mina. I wanted to ask about some finer points of Boraltan history for Simon. While I was debating whether it would be rude to ask about a particularly bloody war they'd lost, Halorn intercepted me.

"Enjoying the party?" He had a too calm, non-threatening demeanor. Something about it irked me. It reminded me of one of Natalia's cats. She acted sweet, eyes begging for pets, until you put your hand down, and then she attacked with the ferocity of a mountain lion.

"The food is good."

"Yes, it always is." He paused for a beat. "Sabine has been quite protective of you. I can assure you, Sandlin meant no threat by asking about your ability. You're quite the fire-wielder as well, though? I saw that on our scouting trip." He gave me a kind smile, and I had to admit I saw no claws behind it.

I caught Erik staring at us from the other side of the room and turned so my back was to him. Taking a glass of champagne from a nearby table, I nodded. "Yes, that's right."

"Are you a third-life too?"

"No, second," I said. That was going to have to be the official answer, I'd decided, seeing as I only had two natural powers. Part of me really wanted to turn around to see if Erik was still watching. "What will you do if you become King?" I asked to change the subject.

Halorn inhaled, pushing out his lips in thought. "I'd like to modernize Boralta. We love to hide up here with our jewels and our creatures,"—he gave a small smile—"but there's more to life."

"Such as?" Creating an army of dragons?

"I'm fascinated with the intersection between science and magic. Just because someone has a magical ability doesn't mean everyone does. The world should be accessible to everyone, regardless of their power."

Well, that was irritating. He sounded very reasonable. It reminded me of my discussion with Audre, about the lack of necessity making people lazy. But thinking of my friend made me remember why she wasn't here.

"I'm sorry. Have I upset you?" Halorn's brows knitted in concern.

"No, sorry. Just intrusive thoughts. What will you do if you lose? Surely you can further your scientific endeavors without the crown?"

"If I am not the king, another ruler may frown upon such endeavors." His eyes flicked to Isabelle. Fire leapt under my skin when I saw her. She was talking to Erik, her hand on his shoulder, her breasts pressed into his arm. He tilted his head toward her as she spoke into his ear. Daggers of heat threatened to slide into my palms, but I fisted my hands, suffocating them.

"Then I wish you good luck." I forced a cheerful attitude into my voice. "I think I'll head to my room. It's been a long day."

Hopefully, the soundproofing was good in this castle. I slammed my door and stomped around, preparing for bed. Erik had basically held up a big sign: 'I'm only doing you out of obligation. Otherwise, I clearly have better options!'

"Ugh!" I threw myself back onto the bed, pulling a pillow over my face. Like Adnatia, this castle was spelled against summoning, so I couldn't even bring Indie here so we could hash this out together. It definitely wasn't the time to burden Audre with my problems. I released the pillow, sighing. I hoped Morgan had found her. Seeing the signing made it so real and my heart broke for both of them.

Even if I could go home, I wouldn't dream of leaving Audre here to deal with this alone. Sending off a note to tell her where I was going if she wanted to come, I quietly escaped from the castle without running into anyone from our party.

The getral was still doing a booming business. Boraltans seemed to stay up later than the people in Trevesten, and certainly later than those in Lashia. I saw a dozen wyvestri scattered about and figured this trip didn't need to be a total loss. Sidling up next to one of them at the long stone bar, I put on my best confused traveler look, pouting a bit for effect.

I was still wearing the outfit I'd worn in the castle. It was a dark plum dress with long, fitted sleeves. A gold pattern of leaves and flowers covered the material, and it hugged my figure down to my hips, before flaring out to hang loosely around my ankles. Pretty enough, and expensive since it was Morgan's, but I missed the pockets of my apron dresses.

"Can I help you with the menu? Maybe buy you a drink?" The wyvestri was on the sinewy side, toned but without the bulging muscles of some others. His hair was so blond it was white, and his blue eyes stood out against his pale skin.

"Thank you, I appreciate that. Whatever you think is good." I smiled up at him.

He ordered the drink and stuck out his hand, "I'm Peter." Shaking his hand, I gave him my name and said I was from Trevesten. "Oh, we know. A Boraltan can spot Trevies from a mile away."

"Trevies?" I scrunched my nose in distaste.

"Sorry," he laughed. "It's not derogatory. Trevesten's just too long." The bartender handed over our drinks and Peter motioned to a table where a few more of the wyvestri were hanging out, among others.

As we sat down, and I smiled at the assembled group, I asked, "What makes us so easy to spot, then?"

"Mostly, it's the clothes," a wyvestri to my left said. She had eyes like Peter's, but her hair was a deep mauve. She gestured to her sleeveless shirt. "Layers, so you can move from the bitter cold to a warm getral and still be comfortable. I'm Circe," she said, and I gave my name.

The castle was big, and I hadn't noticed, but now, in the packed getral with its many fireplaces, I absolutely understood her point. My sleeves were already annoying me.

Three notes flew into the air. The fae to my right grabbed one. After reading it, he winced and slid down low in his seat.

"Ignore Steven," Peter said. "He likes to play games in his many relationships. He screwed around with three sisters and is about to find out why that's a bad idea."

"Especially when those sisters have seven brothers." Circe snickered. Four more notes appeared in rapid succession. Steven read one and blanched. He swept the rest to the floor and weakly ordered another drink. He reminded me of Leo, and I gave him a rueful smile.

We chatted about the trials. The contestants—the wyvestri were honor-bound to protect anyone who took the crown, so they didn't openly show support for any of the contenders. But they shared their speculations about the challenges and who they thought might have the upper hand during each one. They had no qualms about joining the betting on what each contestant's powers might be. Three of the contenders hadn't bothered to hide their abilities at all. It was only Halorn, Isabelle, Ian, and the sixth life, Amelia, who'd kept one or more of their powers a secret.

"Why is Halorn the favorite? If he's only a third life?" He'd admitted he had fire and flight, but neither of those powers on their own was intimidating.

"Mostly because he's Sandlin's nephew—from Halorn's first life. The two of them are tight," Circe said. "Sandlin's been grooming him from day one."

"Do people think Sandlin's told him what the trials are?"

"Sandlin doesn't know," Peter said. "An independent committee creates the trials and the current ruler is never allowed to know. To keep them from doing exactly that, giving the throne to their kid or a sibling."

"Any of you thought of entering?" I finished my drink and Circe motioned to the bartender, who brought me another.

The group laughed. "Mother, no," Circe said. "You can die in the trials. And if you lose, you get exiled from Boralta. None of us could live with the shame it would bring on our families."

"I probably could," Peter said jokingly, "but you have to be Boraltan to enter, and I was born in Penglynis."

I shook my head. "So what is it? What do you all think he can do?"

"My money's on wyvern control," Peter said. "He has to have something big if he thinks he can compete, let alone win, as a third life."

The floor dropped out from under me. If I hadn't already been sitting, I'd have had to sit down. "I've never heard of a power like that."

"No, that's why Peter is going to lose the bet." Circe shook her head at him. "Nobody has had mind control for centuries. Other than what obahns can do."

"It doesn't have to be mind control. I never said that. I just said 'control,'" Peter said defensively, throwing a handful of Steven's discarded notes at her.

I'd never heard of mind control, of animals or people. But if the Allmother could give me a power no other fae had, why not Halorn? I chewed on my lip as I considered the possibilities.

"Uh, I think your dad is here," Circe whispered.

I whipped my head around, prepared for the inexplicable sight of Tobias Revin, but met the deep frown of an ember-haired captain. Erik's eyes were like shards and I didn't need Connery's power to know he was absolutely livid.

36

"What do the words 'personal guard' mean to you?" His arms were crossed across his chest and his voice was lethal. "Because an intelligent person might assume it meant keeping that guard informed of your movements."

"Somebody's in trouble," Circe sang drunkenly beside me. Only the look on Erik's face kept me from laughing.

"I just wanted a drink. No big deal." Sudden anger swooped up inside me. Who was he to be scolding me like a child? I was a starsdamn adult and could go wherever I pleased.

Erik crouched down next to me so quickly I flinched. "Do you recall the conversation we had when the queen invited you to Boralta?" Regarding your safety?"

The anger died. Shit. I'd forgotten all about Sabine's concerns. Swallowing, I stood up. "Thanks for the drinks and company, but I should get back." Booze makes fast friends of everyone, so I hugged Peter and Circe, something Erik watched with noticeable irritation.

We walked out of the getral, and I jumped us to the front of the castle. He practically frog-marched me down the hall. I could tell he was itching to grab me by the arm. By the time we'd made it all the way to my room, I thought he might have cooled down, but he seemed even more mad.

I'd started to apologize when he slammed his mouth into mine, pushing me against the closed door. A gasp left me when he bit down on my lip, his fingers gripping the sides of my face and making every one of my nerves stand at attention.

He pulled back. "I searched this entire damn castle for you. We didn't know if you'd been kidnapped or left the country. Sabine was about to wake up Sandlin and demand your return."

"I'm sorry," I stammered. "I told Audre." My entire body was flush with his. The anger was there certainly, but was he really afraid for me?

"You told Audre? Audre, who has been locked in a room, fighting with or fucking Morgan since the signing? I practically had to break down the door to ask them."

Trying to regain some of my dignity at being treated like a disobedient teenager, I pushed him away and scoffed in indignation. "Why not just send me a note?"

He gained on me again, pushing his face an inch from mine. "I did send you notes, a lot of them!"

Damn. Warm shame crept up my cheeks. All the notes piled on our table. I'd assumed they were all from relatives of Steven's wronged lovers.

My chest fell, but I raised my chin. "I said I was sorry and I am. I'll apologize to Sabine in the morning."

The two of us stood, our chests nearly touching. His eyes were molten and with the way they were looking at me, I could almost forget all about his cozy conversation with Isabelle. I wanted him to kiss me again, to show me just how angry he was. A knock on the door saved me from having to exercise any willpower.

Erik stepped closer. When I turned to look at the door, his hand shot out and pulled my chin toward him, tipping it up so I was looking into his eyes again. Our lips were a breath apart. His voice was guttural. "Who is knocking on your door at one in the morning?"

"It's probably just Audre, checking on me." My voice hitched. Erik dropped his hand and walked to the door.

"Who is it?" He barked.

There was a pause. "It's Mina. I was looking for Lim."

Erik swung the door open to reveal a tired-looking queen, and I approached his side. "Queen Mina, what's wrong?"

She wrung her hands. "I didn't mean to intrude. I was hoping to have a private conversation with you."

"Please, come in." I beckoned and Erik opened the door wider. Mina was in a long silk dressing gown. It trailed on the floor as she stepped inside.

Erik made to close the door behind her, but I cleared my throat. "I believe the queen said she wanted a private conversation."

He gave me a look of outraged incredulity.

"Mina is Sabine's cousin. You can wait outside. I'll be fine." I shoved him lightly toward the door.

The Boraltan queen held up a hand. "I swear on the Mother, I just want to talk."

Erik closed his eyes as he tipped his head to the ceiling. His eyes snapped back to mine. "I will be right outside." He nodded to Mina before stepping out.

"Is everything alright?" I sat down in the chair by the fire and Mina took the other.

She gave me a look of serious contemplation. "I knew your grandfather."

At my look of surprise, she laughed.

"He worked for my uncle. Baiting wyverns."

Ugh. Boraltans used to use bird shifters like my grandfather to bait wyverns into following them into traps. The practice was outlawed after my grandfather moved to Oderon. I remember thinking it was barbaric, but he'd been put out by the news. Said it was a shame to take away honest work. Considering a third of the wyvern baiters ended up dead or maimed, I disagreed, but kept my mouth shut.

"How did you know it was me?" As far as I knew, Mina and I had never met.

"He showed me once." She tapped her head.

I nodded in understanding. Mina was an obahn. A powerful royal like her would have incredible control over the ability. She could see into someone's memories as clearly as watching a movie.

"Did you... did he ever show you my parents?" They didn't deserve to be called my parents, according to my grandfather, but I wasn't sure what other term to use.

"I saw them. You're better off." She gave me a warning look. There was nothing good at the end of that road. They'd been neglectful to the point of abusive. My grandfather found me when I was five and told them if he ever saw them again, he'd kill them eight times just to be sure.

A tear slid down my cheek, remembering the warm but gruff male who raised me in my first life. He'd died for the last time thirteen years later. I wiped the tear away. "Sorry, I don't think you came just to discuss my grandfather."

She shook her head sadly and inhaled, but then stopped, considering her words. "I love my husband. He loves me. We could not have asked for better luck in an arranged partner." She smoothed the pale green silk of her robe. "Neither of us ever found a mate, either, so nothing to worry about on that account."

That wasn't surprising. Despite me knowing two mated couples, it wasn't very common.

"That is not, however, how all arranged marriages go. Even the ones between Boralta and Trevesten have sometimes been problematic."

Nodding, I said, "Okay." But I didn't really know. My knowledge of the royal families was sparse. Was she trying to warn Morgan?

"Are you concerned for the princess? You think she doesn't know what she's getting into?"

"Oh no. Morgan knows exactly what she's doing. She's been educated on the finer points of court diplomacy and royal history since the day she was first born." She took a breath. "No, I came to speak to you."

"Me?" My brows knitted. "Why?"

"Because you should know what you might be getting into. And since Sabine and Morgan have never been in an arranged marriage, I thought it was my duty to provide my perspective. I don't want Sandy to know I'm here. He's so excited about our life after court. He doesn't deserve to have a single doubt about my feelings for him. But someone needed to tell you."

The thoughts in my head were moving at a glacial speed as I tried to make sense of what she was saying. Also, that she'd just called the powerful Boraltan king, 'Sandy,' was throwing me off a little.

"I... I don't understand. I'm not getting married."

"Oh." Her eyes brightened. "Then you've already decided? Morgan is going to do it?"

Rubbing a hand down my face, I stuttered an exhale. "Mina, I'm going to need you to start at the beginning and tell me why you think I am even considering an arranged marriage."

The queen's face paled, and she put a hand over her mouth. "They didn't tell you. Of course, they didn't. Oh, my stars. Sabine is going to kill me." She actually looked a little terrified of her younger cousin.

My eyes widened. "Too late now!" My fingers curled in a go-on gesture. "Spill."

"Sandy offered Sabine the option of choosing between you and Morgan to be Boralta's next queen. Sabine has made it clear that you're a valued member of her court. Based on that, and your unique ability, Halorn suggested, and the other contenders agreed, that it was an acceptable marriage alliance."

It felt like I'd been calmly walking along the shore and didn't notice the wave until it was too late. Sabine had been trying to protect me from the Boraltans, but she'd inadvertently given me royal status. Shock struck me silent for several long moments before I blurted, "I've never been with a woman." Why that was the first ludicrous thought to enter my head was anyone's guess.

Mina cocked her head at me and gave me a kind, but pitying look. "The Boraltans don't care about heirs. The gender of the parties to the marriage alliance is irrelevant. It certainly helps if they are amenable to other benefits. But it's not a deal-breaker." She gave me a conciliatory smile.

My flames were as confused as I was. Half of them were poised for attack, while the other shrank back in horror.

"I guess," Mina said in a small voice, "Morgan didn't want them to tell you. She's very proud. She would see it as shirking her duty to let you take her place." The queen pushed her thumb into the palm of her hands in agitation.

I slumped back against the chair. Morgan was proud. She'd forsake Audre for this marriage because it was the right thing to do for her people. Sabine and Connery had kept it from me, too. Because they were afraid I'd do it or because they were afraid I wouldn't? No. The three of them didn't even want me to consider it.

Leaders make hard decisions, and Morgan was a leader.

My eyes fell closed, and I saw a muddy field. An embroidered pink flower. Audre running out of the kitchen, a knife in one hand and a spatula in the other. I'd given Connery what he needed, supported Indie and Simon. Was this what I was meant to do for Audre?

"I'm so sorry." Mina rubbed her hands again, reminding me of Natalia.

"No," I whispered. "I'm glad you told me."

Erik knocked on the door, his voice still filled with impatience. "Everything okay in there?"

"Fine," I said weakly. "You can stop hovering." I choked on the last word. If I was married, Sabine could have no further reason to order Erik to distract me. "What did you want to tell me? About arranged marriages?" My head swung back to Mina.

Her face was full of guilt. "It was more that I wanted you to know that while it can be beautiful, it can also be horrible. The contenders are power-hungry fae and that can come with the need for control over their spouse. If you choose this path, you'll need friends, inside and outside of this castle. Don't allow yourself to become isolated and always have an escape plan. You'll also want to make sure the contract is clear on what behavior will release you from it."

Right. I wondered if Bastian had any experience negotiating arranged fae marriages. Laughter bubbled out of me and Mina raised her eyebrows.

"Sorry, if I don't laugh at all this, I'll go crazy."

"That's an admirable attitude for a future queen." Mina gave me a warm smile.

Future queen. I nearly threw up.

Mina stood, and I followed, like a puppet on strings. She gave me a sympathetic look before embracing me.

"I'm here if you want to talk, whatever you decide."

Erik tried to barge in when she left, but I just shook my head. I didn't need to be any more confused right now.

Despite the many competing thoughts in my head, I'd fallen asleep almost immediately. It was late morning when I felt a slim finger poke me in the side.

"Go away," I grumbled, pulling the pillow over my face.

"Heard you went out drinking and sent everyone into a panic. A finger jab is the least you deserve." A bright morning light came streaming in through the window as Audre tossed the curtains open.

"You're certainly chipper." I tossed the pillow aside, squinting my eyes open until I could handle the light.

Audre floated a cup of coffee over to me. A maid must have brought in the tray when I'd been sleeping. How embarrassing. I never slept late.

"Yes. I've decided to live in denial until absolutely forced to admit the reality of my circumstances." She sniffed at a pot of brothy rice I'd requested again after my last visit.

Sipping the coffee so she couldn't see my eyes, I said, "That sounds completely reasonable and not at all likely to end in disaster."

"Yes, I agree." Ignoring the rice, she took my pastry and chewed slowly, her eyes distant, before shaking herself. "Right, get dressed. We're leaving today, and I want to bring Morgan to Lashia."

"Lim's taxi co. at your service." I saluted her with my free hand. "But I need to go apologize to Sabine first." I downed the last of the coffee and threw the covers off me before walking to the bathroom.

"Don't grovel too much." Audre dusted crumbs off her hands before walking out.

I stayed in the shower for a long time, letting the water mist and spit as my fire leapt and darted around me. This was too much, surely. Seventy-five years, less time than Audre had spent in early Lashia. Indie and Simon's decision to join up with us had felt like that, a decision. But Audre's never had. She always treated her loyalty to me, our friendship, like it was a foregone conclusion. An inevitability.

Leaning my head against the slippery stone, I closed my eyes, my mind racing over the contenders and trying to picture myself with each one of them. None of it seemed remotely appealing. Then another image pushed its way in: Morgan's wedding day, Audre sitting on a wall somewhere in Adnatia, refusing to attend but unable to stop herself from watching. Would I bring her back to Lashia, watch as she poured her sadness into every dish she made?

I didn't have a 'Morgan,' but I had someone. Erik's smirking face filled my vision. The feeling of his fingers painting caresses down my back made me shiver even under the scalding water. He might have only been with me because of some fanciful notion Sabine had about me stealing back her mate, but he didn't hide his enjoyment. I was pretty sure you couldn't fake anything that much. Almost from the first moment, he'd given me the impression that he was holding back, that only time and decorum kept him from doing all the things he wanted to do.

It didn't matter. I turned off the water. This wasn't about me, or what I might or might not have. I said I wanted to make amends, and this was the way to do it.

"You can't be serious," Connery said, his arms crossed as he looked at me like I'd grown a third head.

"I am. It's the obvious choice. It's a win-win for everyone." I injected false cheer into my voice as I looked between my friend and his mate.

Sabine had been speechless since I'd entered their room and announced I'd be taking Morgan's place. She'd sunk into a chair and now stared at me open-mouthed.

"You don't need to do this," she breathed. "Why?"

"For Audre," Connery said. "Because she's got some bullshit masochistic instinct to make it up to us—because we got stuck in Lashia." My eyes shot to him. "I didn't take enough hush to make me stupid, Lim. Still more than a pretty face." His words were angry, but underneath, I could sense the fear.

I couldn't help it. The corners of my lips twisted into a smile, but tears pricked the edges of my eyes. "It's not bullshit. I'm doing something nice for my friend." I turned to Sabine. "For all my friends. And it's only seventy-five years."

"You don't even know what life we're on!" Connery threw up his hands.

"True. Which is why it's more important that I do the right thing when I have the chance." When he looked like he would argue more, I held up a hand. "Don't insult me by saying I haven't thought it through. I have, and it's the right choice." I hadn't told them who had told me, but Sabine could likely figure it out.

She stood and threw her arms around me. "Thank you." The queen exhaled, her breath blowing the strands of my hair. "I don't know much about your life before this. But for the brief time we've known one another, that we've become friends, you've always tried to do the right thing at every opportunity. I'm not sure I've ever met anyone like you."

Surprised, I hugged her back. "If you want to repay me, you could call off your guard dog."

Sabine chuckled, releasing me. "He was worried about you, that was all."

"That's not what I mean," I mumbled.

She shook her head, confused.

"You can tell him to stop,"—I lowered my voice even more and turned so Connery couldn't see my mouth—"paying me so much *attention*. Baiting me, trying to see if I'm going to suddenly go crazy and try to kidnap your mate."

"What?" Connery asked, stepping toward us, clearly having heard every word.

"What are you talking about?" Sabine said. "I would never tell Erik to do that."

"You didn't?" I crossed my arms.

Connery came to stand next to Sabine. He frowned down at me.

Sabine cocked her head and thought for a moment. "He's very good at his job. So antagonizing you to see where you stand on things is typical of the proactive behavior I'd expect from him. But I certainly never told him to,"—she motioned awkwardly with her hand at my body—"do anything like that. And I haven't been worried about you or Connery. Trust is an integral part of our therapy."

Connery nodded, wrapping an arm around her. His touch had such an effect on Sabine, like he'd lit her up from inside. It made me... happy.

"Right. Okay. Forget I said anything." I pushed my lips to the side and gnawed on my lip.

Sabine cleared her throat, and a look passed between her and Connery.

"Morgan's going to fight you on this," she said, saving me from having to further discuss her guard's sex life.

Looking up, I sighed. "She can try. But I fight dirty."

37

Ayla and I walked along the road from our parents' house, the sun warming my face through the canopy of leaves. Wild turkeys gobbled somewhere in the brush.

Ayla and Keen might live long enough to see me through the end of my marriage. And my family could visit. It wouldn't be so bad. Then the thought of a loveless, potentially sexless marriage popped into my head and reminded me it could indeed be very bad. Halorn was attractive. Isabelle even more so. Of course, 'looks aren't everything,' I thought, remembering the precise bites of his dinner.

A bus went by, blowing up dust from the sunbaked road. A child shouted hello to Ayla, and she waved back.

"Are the kids in your school okay? With the magic and everything?" I asked when the bus' clunking engine was far enough away for me to hear her reply.

"Yeah. Even the biggest bullies have backed off, too afraid of what the other kids might do once they get their power back." She swung her canvas bag in a high arc and watched it fall down again.

"That's nice," I said with amusement.

"When will you take us to see the dragons?" She picked up a rock, examined it, and tossed it back on the side of the road.

"I'm not sure that's entirely safe." I looked around for eavesdroppers, but we were the only people on the road.

"You said they were nice."

"Yes, but I only met a few. And I don't know how they'd feel about me showing up whenever I want with whomever I want."

"What's the big deal? They can't be too mad at you. Claudius and Koli got to be together."

"What?" I said, frowning at her as she examined another rock. This one earned a place in the bag.

"You said the dragons created all the portals. So wouldn't Claudius just have opened another one for her? That way, he didn't have to deal with her dad or any of the other fae." She gave me a look to show her disappointment that I'd not already realized this.

Blinking, I tipped my head up, squinting at the sun as I thought. "That would make sense. Claudius was the one who claimed she died. That could have been a lie. Maybe they did just elope back to Makome." But if Koli and Claudius had children, wouldn't there have been some fae in Makome? Or would the dragon genes have been too strong? I shook my head. I foresaw more charts in my future. "We'll go to Boralta first. You'll like it. They have lots of jewels, and at night, ribbons of light dance in the sky. It's gorgeous."

"When?" she demanded. We'd reached her friend's long driveway. I'd keep walking on to the restaurant.

"Soon." I grinned at her. She rolled her eyes, but smiled at me before skipping off down the road, her friend already racing to meet her halfway. Frowning, I tried to clear my head. Something Ayla had said needled me. Maybe it was because my life would soon belong to someone else, to an entire country. I wanted to move about without asking permission while

I still could. So I didn't even think about telling anyone as I jumped to Makome.

I wandered out into the sand, searching for any sign of Oyo, Dana, or Athena. Finally, after an hour of standing around like an idiot, Athena's scaly form flew toward me. I waved my arms and tried not to shout as I called her name.

She landed beside me, graceful as always. Fluffing her wings and sending up great clouds of sand.

"I did not expect to see you again," she said without preamble.

"Yes, sorry." Why was I apologizing? "I was hoping I could ask you about Koli and Claudius. She came back, didn't she? They lived happily ever after or something?"

There were several long moments of silence.

"No. Their relationship was not happy. It was tragic and short." She sniffed the air as if she found this conversation tedious already.

"Could you elaborate on that? Please?"

Athena ruffled her wings impatiently. "Koli always had another portal to use. She came back after Claudius closed the main one. They had a child, but it was defective."

"Defective?" I put a hand to my heart. "It was a child. How could it be defective?"

"Their child was weak. The pregnancy greatly weakened Koli, and the birth did not go well. She died a few months after the boy was born. Claudius disposed of the child. It did not live long."

"Oh, my stars." My hand flew to my mouth. I felt sick.

"Yes. Claudius was beside himself with shame and grief. He should have had hundreds of years left but lasted only another fifty."

At that, I sunk into the sand. One tragedy after another. And since she died here in Makome, there were no fae births to bring her back. "Is that why her father didn't want them to be together? Did he know that would happen?"

"He knew what she was. What Claudius was."

Grains of sand poured through the gaps between my fingers. The woodpecker was back. Apart from the wind, the bird's endless work was the only sound.

"Before she died, she swore this land would not flourish until their heir was on the Voden's seat. It is why we have food shortages, why the once verdant hills are now only sand."

"And they never got the chance to have another child." I'd assumed the dragons liked Makome for its desert-like climate. It was hard to picture the stone mountains filled with lush trees or wildflowers covering the ground. "I apologize for having to ask this, but why not just go to another world?"

"Our power is bound to this land. If we leave, we become mere animals." Athena's long neck curved skyward, hearing things I could not hear.

Just like the fae in Lashia. Our power weakening until we became almost human. Blinking against the sun, I looked up at her, a thought forming in my mind. "Athena, are the wyverns, dragons? The dragons that left Makome?"

"Yes. They are our brethren. Simple-minded, but still family."

"And still pretty scary." Halorn would be a formidable opponent indeed if he could control them. "Athena, have you ever heard of a fae who could control wyverns? Like, by mind control?"

Her orange head dipped to the side. Even with the serpent eyes and giant head spikes, she looked just like Ayla had earlier. I was getting a little tired of people, dragons, whoever, looking at me like I was dense.

"What? I've never heard of it." I sat back on my heels, crossing my arms over my chest.

She swept down until her head was level with mine. The movement was so fast I lurched backward. The breath from her nostrils made the strings of my apron dance. "That is what we've been speaking of this whole time. A fae who can control the minds of dragons. How else do you think that horrible creature convinced Claudius to marry her?"

"Athena said that Claudius had been working against her control. During and after the birth, while she was still sick, he taught the others how to do it. The dragons seem confident they can fight it off, but how can they be sure? It's been thousands of years since they've had to try." I was back in the palace. Sabine and General Antonio sat across from me in Sabine's office, their expressions rapt.

"Her father did all of that to stop her," Sabine breathed. "They must have known she'd be able to get back. Can you imagine? Waiting each day to see if your daughter was going to bring the dragons down upon your world?"

"Do you think they knew she died?" I asked.

The queen and general were silent in response, shaking their heads as they thought through the awful story.

"We all know she didn't come back," Sabine replied. "And the dragons believe this curse? They really think Koli did this, and it wasn't some natural phenomenon in their world?"

"Yes. They do. But they're clearly not out there looking for Koli's descendant." The dragons were truly between a rock and a hard place. Open themselves up to fae control in order to save their land or live freely in a withering world. They'd made it work, certainly, but for how long?

"If Halorn can control the wyverns, he could probably control the dragons," Antonio said.

"And if he can control them, it's possible he's her descendant. They had no other children." Powers didn't predictably flow through family lines, but two people with such a unique power was a big coincidence. I toyed with my empty teacup. They were all empty, the teapot cold and forgotten during our conversation.

Sabine stood and walked to a map on the wall. She'd updated it with the information we had on Kysalt and Makome. It didn't include Lashia. I felt a rush of gratitude for the efforts she made to keep her new knowledge a secret.

"We need to get them to close the portal," Sabine said.

"They don't want to." I shook my head. "They're confident they can fend off any threat. Also, they need the portals open for food runs, and in case any wyverns decide to come back."

"I hate to say it, but this may be up to you." Antonio gave me a piercing stare. He'd been looking at me a lot since I walked in, like he was sizing me up and examining my potential as a future queen.

"Not to be indelicate, but why the fuck would Halorn listen to me? Married or not?" I leaned back and crossed my legs at the ankles.

"Like all things, diplomacy is a skill. And you'll have other abilities at your disposal. As his wife, you have a certain influence."

Sabine and I shared a bemused look, and I laughed. "General, exactly how good a lay do you think I am?"

"That's not what I mean," he chuckled. "While I don't doubt your many skills, what I meant is that the marriage alliance could allow you to prevent such a thing. He can't harm your home country. Normally, that would only include Trevesten because Sabine claimed you as part of her court, but Sandlin has agreed to include Lashia as well."

"And what about the rest of Malan?" If Halorn had any intention of using the dragons to conquer other countries, he'd never agree to my terms. From the look on Antonio and Sabine's faces, they were thinking the same thing.

38

A cool afternoon breeze blew into The Peregrine as the door opened. Leo, escorting a pretty brown-skinned woman, and what looked to be her parents, stepped inside. He waved to me before following Elias into the dining room. My eyes nearly popped out of my head when he pulled a chair out for both women.

The young woman's eyes flashed to me, and I gave her a warm smile. Anyone who could make Leo sit up that straight was a ten in my book. She leaned over and said something to him. He jumped up and approached the bar.

"Hey Lim, would you mind coming over to us when you have a chance? Nikki wants to meet you."

"And I definitely want to meet Nikki." I nearly cackled at the nervous look he gave me. I followed him back to the table, saying hello to friends and regulars.

Leo introduced me to Nikki and her parents. Her father was tall and thin with graceful fingers built for music or painting. His mother smiled politely before grilling me on the menu and ingredients. When she'd finished, Nikki jumped in,

"I didn't believe Leo when he said he knew you." She assessed me from under her lashes. "I'm an air-wielder. I swear I used to feel it under my skin, even with the cuffs."

I nodded in understanding. I'd heard that from many people in Marais. The sensation of something hiding just below the surface, but never identifying it until you got your power.

"How did you two meet?" I asked, as Elias dropped bread and water on the table.

"He delivered a package to the house. Then he wouldn't leave," her father said, his voice a deep baritone.

"Like a stray puppy," her mother added. But she patted Leo's hand affectionately. He didn't look the slightest bit embarrassed.

"I see," I said, biting back a laugh. "It's wonderful to meet you all. And please, order whatever you want. Lunch is on me."

Leo threw me a grateful look as Nikki and her family murmured their appreciation. 'A very well-trained puppy,' I thought affectionately. He was looking at Nikki like she hung the moon. If only Emir could have seen them. Another laugh escaped me as I pictured Emir trying to flirt with Nikki's mom and the derisive look she'd have given him.

I'd just ducked back under the bar when ice-cold fear stabbed through my heart. The customers, staff, everyone in the restaurant turned in unison at the sound tearing through the sleepy midafternoon sunshine.

Moving before I even realized it, I ran to the front doors and flung them open. A green dragon, bigger than Oyo but smaller than Athena, roared, its eyes bulging above its gaping maw. People were screaming, abandoning their possessions as they took cover in buildings. The dragon twisted and turned as it flew over Marais. Its voice rattled the windows.

Running toward it, I forgot myself and yelled, "Why are you here?"

The dragon roared again, but I couldn't make out any words. It seemed to curl in on itself before releasing a blast of flame into the air. The plume was thirty feet long and just missed the top of the library. Even at this distance, I could feel the heat.

I barreled back through the restaurant doors. Some people had their faces pressed up against the glass while others hid under tables.

"Nikki," I said, my voice carrying above the frightened chatter. She turned toward me. "Is anyone else in here a wind-wielder?" Two hands shot up. "The three of you over here." I quickly herded them to the center of the restaurant, demonstrating how they needed to work together to shield the others from any danger above. "Together, the three of you can block the fire." I wasn't sure that was true, but they all nodded in agreement.

The chandeliers weren't lit, but Elias lowered them to the tables, ensuring they couldn't fall on anyone. My father's eyes glazed over as he sent messages to people all over the city. The screaming outside was getting louder. A blast of fire lit up the windows, casting the entire restaurant in a sharp orange light.

"Water or Ice-wielders?" I called out. Two people raised trembling hands. "You two stay here." I assigned one of them to be ready if fire broke through and the other to be prepared to help. I didn't bother asking the ice-wielder I'd assigned to the restaurant to form ice spears. They definitely wouldn't be strong enough for a dragon.

Elias and I shared a bracing look. As an impervenan, he'd be the one to throw himself in front of others. But I had no idea if he was strong enough to withstand dragon fire. My eyes bounced between him and Leo. "Keep them safe." They nodded, Leo already moving to hoist tables against the windows and ordering others to do the same.

Jumping outside, I shielded my eyes and whirled around, searching the sky. The dragon was still spouting fire and refusing my attempts at communication. It flew erratically, not like the smooth movements I'd seen Athena and Egan use. Throughout the streets, there were water and air wielders, terrified looks on their faces, but their hands raised to help.

A man froze in awe, mesmerized by the dragon. The woman next to him smacked him hard in the head and he shook himself, pointing his hands up and shooting water at the small fires that were sprouting up in the street where sparks had fallen.

"Stop!" The dragon roared, the first word I understood.

"We're not doing anything," I yelled. "What do you want?"

It was getting farther and farther away, flying east. I jumped over and over again, trying to get close enough. I needed to get it away from the buildings.

Another jet of fire shot out and incinerated the top of a building. From the street below, water and ice poured from the hands of three people. Flyers were hovering in the air, but I couldn't tell if Simon was among them. They kept their distance, unsure of whether they should attract the dragon or not.

The library, the museum, the market. I jumped, frantically trying to follow the dragon. I swept two air-wielders up with me and then another as I hit the theater. After their initial shock, they quickly rallied, readying for instructions.

"On my signal, push the dragon out to the fields. I can bring it down, but I need to get it away from the people." I didn't wait for them to agree before we jumped again.

"There," the woman with me shouted. Another rush of fire flew past us as the dragon veered toward a field of new wheat. I got them as close as I could before I took off in a sprint to the center. I'd never been here before. Before I got too far, I waved to the air-wielders.

The attempt was clumsy, like children keeping a balloon afloat with straws, but they got the hang of it soon enough. They hurled the dragon sideways, and it clawed the air, looking for purchase. Froth dripped from its mouth, a look of pure rage on its face.

As soon as it blew close enough, I pulled it toward me. The dragon didn't move like a person. It didn't appear instantly by my side, instead it hurtled toward me at speed, only disappearing and reappearing in front of me when it was fifty feet away. Based on that, I assumed I'd need to touch it to jump.

It left a deep grove in the mud as it slid in my direction, crushing swathes of wheat beneath its scaled body.

"A little more. Come on." I tried not to think as I lept for it. I missed and its tail thrashed wildly, the sharp spike coming down inches from my face. Without thinking, I lunged, just barely touching the scales of its foot before launching both of us to Makome.

The stone of the amphitheater crashed into my back as I slid across it, the green dragon nearly on top of me. All around me, the other dragons exclaimed in surprise.

"Please stop him. He attacked my city." Before I could get another word out, a great stone boulder halted my movement when I smashed headfirst into it. Searing pain sliced through me and I was vaguely aware of Chiara's booming roar and other dragons fighting the green one.

Blood coated my hand when I touched my head. I didn't even have time to try healing myself before I blacked out.

The air smelled like horseshit. That was my first thought upon waking up. Opening my eyes, I could see the outline of cave walls. Under my hands was a prickly substance covered by something smoother. Two round eyes and a furry face shoved themselves into my line of sight.

"It's up!" The voice was high and squeaky, like a small, yappy dog.

I sat up, slowly, but there was no pain. Just the mild discomfort of sleeping somewhere unusual. A bed of straw was piled beneath me, covered by a thin fur.

The voice spoke again. "Not dead, then?"

"No. Not yet. Thankfully." I stood up, and the creature scrambled away on all fours. It had a bulbous nose and grayish brown fur covering its entire body.

"Did the Voden stop it? The green dragon," the memory came back to me in a rush.

"Yes. She stopped Rakesh. He was quite angry." The creature laughed indulgently, like Rakesh was a naughty child instead of a terrifying beast capable of swallowing him whole.

"Thank goodness." I let out a long breath. It handed me a wooden bowl of water and I tossed it back. Sputtering, I spit it back in the container. My throat burned. It wasn't water, it was straight alcohol. "Mother, save me. How can you drink that?"

"Cheerfully!" The creature took a long drink out of its own cup. "I'm Morag. The dragons brought you to me to heal."

"Lim. And thank you." I touched the top of my head and came away with a thick, yellow mush. "What in the...? Is this what you used to heal me?" My head didn't hurt anymore, so whatever it was, it worked.

"Yup." He took another drink. "My sheep make the best bile for ointment."

My stomach heaved. "Bile?" Morag nodded. "Oh stars. Can I clean it off now?" He nodded again, scratching his ear with his back foot.

Waving my fingers, I removed the mush and dried blood from my hair and clothes. Wait, Morag said sheep. "You're the helper? You raise livestock for the dragons?"

"Yes, we have done so for thousands of years." He climbed the walls of the cave as nimbly as a spider, disappearing into the darkness before returning with something. "Here." He shoved a bag at me.

Inside was a dripping pile of offal, including two hearts. As a chef, this shouldn't have concerned me. But as a parting gift, it seemed odd.

"Um. Thank you?"

Morag beamed. "The dragons said you need blood."

"Did they now?" My eyes widened. "Did they say what for?"

He shrugged.

"Okay. Well, thank you Morag. But I need to get back to the Voden and find out why Rakesh decided to go rogue."

Morag scrambled out of the cave and I followed him into the sun. We were only a little way away from the Voden's seat, just at the bottom of the mountain instead of the top. Not being sure whether it was appropriate to pet him, I held out my hand.

Morag licked it.

Back in the amphitheater, Chiara was holding court with seven other dragons. All eight enormous heads swung toward me upon my arrival.

"Thank you. Morag was very helpful." I gestured with the bloody bag. "He said you wanted me to have blood? To eat?" I asked in confusion.

A gray dragon lowered his head to the bag, sniffing. "He misunderstood." The gray dragon's voice was scratchy from a thousand years of fire. He unfurled an impossibly long tongue and used it to lift the bag out of my hands before tossing it down his throat.

"You lost a lot of blood," Chiara said, addressing me at last.

"Head wounds tend to do that. So you know to take it seriously." Indie told me that once, so I assumed it was true. It certainly had been for Emir. When several long moments passed and none of them seemed inclined to offer me more information, I spoke again, "Where is Rakesh? Why did he attack my world?"

"He is contained," Chiara said.

"And?" I said angrily, putting my hands on my hips.

"We will close the portal to your world as soon as you go back."

"Close it now!" I shouted. "I don't need it to get back. You still haven't explained what he was doing there."

"The fae were always so loud," muttered the gray dragon.

Chiara tipped her head at a smaller gold dragon who flew off. "It will be done. You may go home now. We will deal with Rakesh."

I didn't move. From where I was standing, I could see the stone where I'd smashed my head. The moss between the cracks soaked up my blood like a sponge. My fingers itched to check my hair, but I resisted.

"Halorn has been here, hasn't he? That's why Rakesh couldn't speak. Except to say 'stop.' Because someone was controlling him." Halorn had used Lashia as a test run. To see how well he could control the dragon. Did he know what was in Lashia? Could he see through the dragon's eyes?

"It won't happen again," Chiara growled, and the stone shook. I stumbled back as small rocks tumbled down the mountain walls around us. "Go home."

39

I jumped to Trevesten, fired off a note to Sabine, and jumped home. My family, Indie, and Simon swarmed me with hugs.

"I'm okay. Morag gave me some bile and a bag of blood."

"What?" Indie said while my mother made a disgusted face.

I explained about the strange furry creature, Rakesh, and Chiara.

"So you think Halorn was controlling him?" Simon asked.

Before answering, I pulled Sabine, Antonio, Morgan, Erik, Audre, and Connery into the restaurant. Sabine looked around in befuddled amazement before composing herself. Morgan placed her hands on her sister and the general, allowing her luvit power to flow toward them. They tested out the unfamiliar shapes in their mouths.

"Cannot believe I missed a dragon," Audre complained, hopping up to sit on the bar.

"It was awesome!" Keen said, but at a look from our parents, he added, "But very scary. I was terrified." Out of the corner of my eye, I saw Connery surreptitiously fist bump him.

I introduced my family to the queen of Trevesten and her general, both of whom shook hands with my parents and asked me if I was okay. My mother was exceedingly short with Sabine and I rolled my eyes at her behavior. No matter how many times I told her we were only friends now, she still held a grudge against Sabine for 'stealing' Connery from me.

"His control sounds poor, but it will get better," Erik said. He tried to catch my eye, but like a coward, I kept my gaze planted firmly elsewhere. "Unless the dragons get better at throwing him off."

"How can we prevent this from happening again?" Indie asked.

"We need to find a way to close off Lashia from Makome. Was anybody hurt?" I asked.

She shook her head. "No, just some property damage, thank goodness. But I met with a lot of angry citizens, all of whom were concerned about my ability to keep Lashia safe. I'll need to issue a statement. So whatever ideas you've got, we want in." She jabbed a thumb at Simon, who crossed his arms and nodded seriously.

My sister turned to Sabine. "Why don't you just... you know?" Ayla drew a hand across her throat, made a gagging sound and closed her eyes. Audre snickered.

Sabine half frowned and half smiled like she wasn't sure if it was a joke. "I'm not in the habit of assassinating people. Especially as we can't be sure it was him at all. The dragons didn't come out and say that, did they?" She looked at me.

"No," I answered begrudgingly. Chiara had avoided the question altogether.

"Oh, my gosh! I can help! I can use my power!" Ayla leapt from her seat, doing a happy dance.

"She's a comverdia," I said in response to Sabine's raised eyebrows. "But our magic doesn't work as well on the dragons."

"Works on fae pretty well, though," Erik said, sizing Ayla up. My sister puffed out her chest, importantly.

"I am not sending my youngest child to interrogate someone who can control dragons," my mother's voice came out high and tight. "Get someone else," she snapped at Sabine.

"It's irrelevant. Halorn will see an interrogation a mile away. All the other contestants are digging for information, too." Morgan blew out a breath. "Don't you remember dinner? He wouldn't even tell us."

Keen opened his mouth, but before he could speak, my father cut him off. "No. Neither of you are going to Boralta. Not until all of this is over."

"What if we had him come here instead? It would throw him off a little," Antonio suggested. "We could have all the contestants come. Like an engagement party. Under the guise of meeting your family before your wedding."

My eyes froze open as a weighted silence descended on the room.

"Oh noooo," Connery breathed, the sound like air escaping from a leaky balloon. His eyes flashed to mine in alarm.

As one, my family, Indie, Simon, Morgan, Audre, and Erik, looked at Antonio, and then at me. Indie's claws crept out, her gaze accusatory.

Audre slid off the bar like a shadow. "The fuck did you just say?"

Morgan was furious. Audre wavered between relief, rage, and guilt. Keen and Ayla found the whole thing very exciting. Indie and Simon looked at me with utter disbelief. My father frowned but said nothing. My mother blamed Sabine.

Erik walked out.

I sent Morgan, Audre, an exceedingly apologetic General Antonio, Sabine, and Connery, to Trevesten.

"I, for one, am looking forward to eating a wyvern. It will be nice to have something challenging to hunt," said Brax as he lounged on the sofa, giving an inappropriate amount of attention to his privates.

"Anything for you," I joked, but my heart wasn't in it.

It was very late, or very early, depending on how you looked at it, when Erik stepped into my sitting room. Brax was out hunting something too easy and I sat in an armchair, pretending to read.

"Mina?" he said in a voice laced with anger. He crossed his arms and stood across the room.

I forced myself to meet his eyes. "Yes. She wanted to offer me some advice. Thought they'd told me. That they'd asked me."

"And you've actually agreed to this?" If he stood any straighter, he'd have been a statue.

"Just the basics. That I'll take Morgan's place. Still need to work out the finer details." I motioned to the desk where the documents from King Sandlin sat, untouched.

Erik's sneer dropped from his face as his head fell forward. "Please don't do this." No bravado, or flirting, or jokes. His voice was soft, his eyes dim. He looked broken, like *I'd* broken him.

"I don't expect you to understand, but I want to do this. It's important to me. I think there's a reason we get seven lives. Seven chances to do the right thing, to make up for past mistakes." I leaned forward, trying to show him my sincerity.

"I do understand. That's the worst part," Erik said in exasperation. He sank to the sofa, resting his elbows on his knees. He ran one hand through his hair and drummed his fingers on his thigh. "My mother, in my first life, gave me up right after I was born."

My brow furrowed, and I tossed the book aside. "I'm sorry. I didn't know that. Why?"

"My adoptive parents said she wasn't all there. Didn't even seem too upset by it." He slowly rubbed his palms together in front of him. "I pictured a person incapable of taking care of herself, let alone a child. Imagine my surprise when I finally tracked her down and found her taking good care of a dozen other children."

Stars, that must have hurt. To see her stepping up for other people's kids, but not her own. Instinctively, I moved to the couch, sitting beside him.

"I was furious. And hurt. But as much as I wanted to get back at her, my adoptive parents were right, she wasn't all there. I spent an hour with her, under the guise of hiring her as a nanny. She never recognized me. I'm still not sure she even remembers giving me up. Unfortunately, a lifetime of feeling rejected wasn't so easy to get over and I still felt like she owed me *something*."

Erik rubbed the back of his neck, embarrassed at the memory. I couldn't help reaching out and running a hand down his arm. He caught it and held it between his own.

He let out a breath. "Then she gave birth to the princess of Trevesten."

My eyes popped open, but I didn't pull my hand away. "You and Morgan are siblings?" Erik nodded. He let go of my hand and stood up, wandering around the room. "I was two hundred and seventy-eight years old when Lucy, my mother, had Morgan. We didn't have time to establish any sibling rivalry then, but we're a bit closer now." Erik smiled sadly and my heart twisted.

Connery told us about Morgan's second birth. She'd been kidnapped, and Sabine's decisions regarding her rescue had been the last straw for him. My mouth fell open as I realized who Erik was.

Erik grimaced. "Yep. That was me. The idiot who tried to extort the queen of Trevesten out of two thousand measly gold pieces."

I put a hand to my chest. "I read about your trial. Your mother testified in your defense."

He smiled ruefully. "Not knowingly. Her testimony of the facts absolved me of the kidnapping charge. Not that it mattered in the end."

"She executed you," I breathed. Trevesten did not execute people publicly like Lashia had. They also had a choice between a death and a lengthy sentence in Tarkana.

Erik held up his hands. "At my request. I was too old for prison." He sat back down beside me. "I put my mother and Sabine through something they didn't deserve. Lucy may have the mind of a child, but I don't, and I should have done better by her. By the time I reached my next rishival, she was gone. I never got to apologize. So I signed up as a guard for Adnatia. At least I can be of service to Sabine and Morgan."

"Does Sabine know?"

"Oh, yeah." Erik laughed darkly. "When she tapped me to be part of the private guard, Antonio put me through an extensive interrogation. Sabine, proving more mature than I ever was, has never brought it up. Hopefully, the years of service I've given her have proved my loyalty."

He gave me a searing look, like he could see straight through to all the thoughts bouncing around in my head, before pulling me onto his lap. He ran a hand along the outside of my thigh and frowned, thinking.

"So you understand. And you're not going to try and talk me out of it?" My hands cupped his face, and I ran a thumb along his jawline. If there was no future for us, maybe he'd be satisfied with the present.

His head tipped into the curve of my neck and I shuddered as his lips moved along my skin. He ran his fingers down my back, while his other hand slipped under my dress.

"I said I understood. Not that I wouldn't do everything in my power to find a solution that doesn't involve you or Morgan marrying someone as horrible as Halorn or as... unsuitable as Isabelle."

"You didn't find her so unsuitable the other night," I huffed.

"So that did work," he said with a wolfish smirk. "I was simply trying to prove that you couldn't be mad at me for getting jealous if you'd react the same way."

Erik's hand reached the apex of my thighs and I found it difficult to form a coherent response. "You've never been jealous."

"Excuse me?" He pulled back to face me. "Wasn't that what we were fighting about? You got mad because my possessive streak came out when you were speaking to Connery? I admit it was immature."

He'd stopped his ministrations long enough that I could focus on the conversation we'd had at the party. "I wasn't mad about you being jealous. I thought you were only coming on to me in your consistent quest to keep me away from Connery, for Sabine."

"Hmmm." His fingers splayed delicately over me, only a thin layer of fabric between him and my growing heat. He whispered into my ear, in between nibbling my neck, "While I would have greatly enjoyed executing such an order, my desire to keep you moaning beneath me has always been of my own volition. It has been from the moment I first saw you, walking into that tavern like you owned it."

I gasped as he pushed the material aside, and I jumped us into my bedroom without thinking. Erik wasted no time, quickly undoing the ties of my dress and pulling off the rest of my clothing. His tongue pushed into my mouth as I grabbed him by the hair. I fumbled with his shirt and belt; his swords clattered noisily to the floor.

We were aggressive and impatient. When his fingers dug into my ass as he pulled me on top of him, I could tell he was still angry with the situation. He bit down on my nipple and I dragged my nails down his shoulders, venting my own frustration. My skin flushed as he gripped my thighs harder, pulling me toward him until I was directly over his mouth.

"I'm going to make you forget about anyone else," Erik murmured, reaching up to drive his tongue inside me. I cried out and grabbed the metal bars of my bedframe for balance. As he slid his tongue along my clit, I shook, sparks running up and down my body. I felt so exposed and part of me wanted to move, to hide, but Erik held me in place, driving me to the edge with each push of his tongue. My thoughts frayed at the edges, strangled by the feeling of him. But they were there all the same, warning me not to give him so much when it would be over soon.

The delicious contrast between the cool air of the room and the intense heat of his mouth drove away any further introspection. My hips moved of their own accord as I rode his face, ignoring everything but the feeling of him worshiping me. He groaned, and the sound vibrated against me.

"Oh stars, I'm going to come. Don't stop." I was weak, my arms shaking, and Erik moved faster as I gripped his face with my thighs. The waves of pleasure rolled over me and through me, pushing me to the edge and past it until I hung my head in relief. I slid down until I was beside him.

Erik kissed me, and I could taste myself on him. He rolled over, his muscles taut as he held himself above me. "Lie to me. Tell me you're mine," he demanded as he sank into me with one long movement.

"I'm yours." I arched off the bed, sucking in a breath, meeting him each time he slammed deep inside me. "Make me yours."

He pushed faster, rolling over me to create the delicious friction I needed. Energy coiled tightly inside me as red and orange streaked beneath my skin.

"Let go, Lim," he whispered. He pushed into me hard. "Fuck!"

I pressed up and exploded around him as he came deep inside me. As we lay together afterward, I drew small circles across his chest and wondered what a verdia would think of my lies. He was arrogant and pushy. But he was also kind to my siblings and respectful to my parents. And there was no denying his other talents were very enjoyable. But there was no future with him. No world in which we went home together at the end of the night.

He seemed to sense my thoughts, and his fingers tightened around me in his sleep. Cursing the tiny tear that slid down my face and onto his chest, I fell into a fitful sleep. My dreams were filled with giant halls, bedecked in gems, but empty of people.

40

Eudora was hot. Everywhere else in the city, people lounged in the parks, drank cool drinks at sidewalk cafes, or indulged in ice cream from beneath big hats.

But not here. The stadium wasn't so much a stadium as a large field with wooden bleachers. There would be no soccer game today. The five of us stood at the front of four lines of twenty-five people. Indie stepped forward and explained our purpose, why they'd given up their Saturday. She'd already made the same speech in Marais and Marion. We'd be spending the next two weeks bouncing between all seven boroughs, training the humans to defend themselves from dragons.

Some people signed up willingly, the others had to be cajoled. All of them patiently listened as Indie explained the techniques we'd used so many years ago, modified for giant fire-breathing beasts. Fire to distract, air and water to protect, flora to hinder, metal to kill. The most important part was keeping the dragons in the air and away from the people and buildings on the ground. Although we had plans for that, too.

As we walked down the rows, correcting technique and offering words of encouragement, some humans tilted their head at Indie, or even made small bows.

"Are they sure there's none left?" Connery asked, while the two of us role-played the role of a dragon for a group of trainees.

"Chiara sent Egan and the other trackers to search all of Makome." The Voden had agreed to close the portals in Makome. Since they used them not only to allow wyverns back in but to supplement their food, I'd taken all of my father's cows, sheep and goats to Makome. It worked out okay. With me being gone so much with Indie, my family was running The Peregrine. Ayla took over as host, using her extensive board game strategy skills to handle the dining room floor. Keen continued to bus tables and my mom learned to mix drinks.

The Voden begrudgingly admitted that the dragons had gotten lazy with their mind shielding. Rakesh was not a dragon from court, but lived closer to the portal to Kysalt. She hadn't known he was in Lashia until I crash-landed in her amphitheater.

"You ready for Saturday?" He used a gust of wind to shoot my flames fifty feet and twelve people dived out of the way, rolling like we'd taught them so they wouldn't get injured.

"Can't wait." I made a face, and he laughed. On Saturday, I'd pull King Sandlin, Queen Mina, Halorn, Isabelle and Ian to a hotel we'd found in Chelsea. The proprietors had restored it to its extravagant former glory, but its main selling point was its distance from the more populous cities.

I swept my hand and threw up a short wall of fire. The fae worked together to send one another over it. We clapped when there were only superficial burns. A healer darted over to help before running off to another group.

"Chiwel's doing well," said Connery. He was working with a group of damaris, teaching them how to use their power sparingly in order to weaken temporarily, instead of binding completely.

The man in question gave me a thumbs up. The council had pardoned him in exchange for testimony against Arthur. Arthur, the fine upstanding citizen he was, immediately made a deal for his testimony against two of the councils' staff members whom he'd been bribing for years.

General Antonio was teaching Ayla how to interrogate Halorn without him noticing. We would not try to get him to reveal his third power. He'd be ready for that. Instead, we'd focus on his dragon knowledge. Chiara said that Koli's power over Claudius was greater the closer she was to him. Halorn wasn't with Rakesh, so he must have been controlling him from the dragons' world. Which explained why the green dragon could partially resist him.

I didn't like the idea of bringing any of them here. But Antonio was right, he'd be off his guard in Lashia. And proving my ability to jump worlds guaranteed me the marriage contract.

A whistle blew, and one hundred humans stood to attention and faced Indie.

"Thank you for all your hard work today, all of you." She tipped her head at the huddle of healers to our right. "We fought beside you once before, and are prepared to do it again. Because this place is worth it. You are worth it. Things may get very difficult, but panic creates mistakes, so focus on your objective and your training." Beside me, Connery nodded. "Never let your guard down until you are certain the threat has passed." She clasped her hand in Simon's. "And while it is admirable to sacrifice yourself in favor of another,"—she gave me and Audre a pointed look—"don't use heroics as an excuse to give up. Every person may not live through an attack, but if you decide right now to fight for *every last breath*, we, as a world, will survive."

"Can't help feeling there was a message in that speech," Audre said out of the corner of her mouth. Morgan still wasn't speaking to me. Audre was conflicted, to say the least, but grateful.

"It did seem a little heavy-handed, didn't it?" I mused loud enough for Indie and Simon to hear as they came walking over to us.

"I don't want your martyrdom rubbing off on my soldiers," Indie sniffed. "Morgantown?"

"Right away, Madame President." I bowed to her, and we jumped.

I'd half-zipped the sleek gold dress I'd bought in Trevesten when my arm refused to bend any farther.

"Let me help," Erik said, stepping behind me before unzipping the dress. It would have pooled at my feet had I not grabbed the straps at the last minute.

"That isn't helping." But it was hard to be mad while his mouth roamed over my neck and his fingers pulled my hips back against him.

He let out a disgruntled noise against my skin before stepping back and pulling the dress back up over my shoulders and zipping it.

"Are you going to behave tonight? Or do I need to send you home?" I picked up my earrings and turned to him, eyebrows raised.

He reached out and straightened the one I'd just put through my ear. "I'll be good." But sadness weighed in his voice. In order to avoid any awkwardness—the last thing I needed was Sandlin deciding Morgan was the safer option—Erik was keeping his distance tonight.

"Did some more digging on the contestants. Based on my research, and several overpriced bribes, I have five of Isabelle's powers and six of Ian's."

Putting on my shoes, I nodded at him to go on.

"Ian is an electric eel and wolf shifter. He can wield water and air, has enhanced strength, and is a luvit, like Morgan. Isabelle is a fire, flight, and air wielder. She also has invisibility and that mild glamoring we saw."

I pushed my toes into my heels and took deep, measured breaths. There was none of the excitement I was used to feeling before big jobs. No fear either, though. If Connery wasn't still in Adnatia, I'd have blamed him for this strange calm.

"Thank you," I said. "For telling me. Should make for a lively contest."

Erik's face transformed at the mention of the trials. From sadness to sharp angles, an undercurrent of indignation. He stalked toward me, pushing me back against the desk. His hands slid up, gripping my waist. I tried to speak, but he swallowed my words with his kiss. My eyes fell closed as he pressed hard against me. The edge of the desk dug into the back of my legs as wet heat gathered between my thighs. I could hear him undoing his belt as he continued to kiss me. His fingers pushed up the edge of my dress, as he bent my knee and pushed it back to give him greater access.

There was a ripping sound, and I gasped when my underwear came away in his hand. When he sank inside me, I moaned, my head tipping back.

"I want to know you're thinking about this. Whenever anyone else touches you, in this life or the next, I want you to remember how ready you are for me and how good this feels." He slammed into me. The desk crashed against the wall with each thrust, causing a thin crack to run up to the ceiling.

Feeling his frustration, I understood only too clearly how Morgan and Audre felt and why they seized every opportunity to be alone. I clenched around him and dug my nails deep into his shoulders.

Erik let forth a string of expletives before dipping his head into the crook of my neck. ", baby."

"There's only you," I panted. "There will always be only you." I barely got the words out before my release hit hard and sudden, and we both fell apart.

The hotel's private dining room was beautiful. Thick red curtains hung around each of the floor-length windows. The owners, a married couple named Stan and Sheila, were losing a lot of money on the place before their cuffs had come off. Now, with her power to change the appearance of any inanimate object, and his ability to clean, they'd started making a good living. Sheila had specifically asked what colors I'd like for the engagement party.

"Red? Aw, like the color of love," she'd cooed.

"Sure, let's say that," my father had grumbled under his breath. My parents were still very unhappy with the whole arrangement. But I promised I would be okay.

The contracts I'd be signing tonight would ensure that if I was at all unsafe in the marriage, I could walk away with a hefty penalty paid by the Boraltan crown. The Boraltans could get rid of me for the same reason, but otherwise, their last chance to change their mind ended tonight. After the first trial, if I didn't like any of the contestants still standing, I'd have one more chance to back out.

Between the first and second trial, the three losing contestants would have to agree never to raise arms or encourage their new home countries to do so. If they lived to be exiled, that is. As the de facto future queen of Boralta, it would be up to me to accept those oaths.

The chandeliers sparkled, and bouquets of red flowers decorated the long tables. My mother admitted, begrudgingly, that it was beautiful.

At the appointed time, I pulled Sabine and Connery from Adnatia, Indie and Simon from their house, and King Sandlin and Queen Mina, as well as their four guards, from the Boraltan castle. I'd sent Audre to Morgan since, for obvious reasons, she wasn't coming to this dinner. Taking my lead from Sandlin's first dinner, I didn't feel the need to invite the other contestants. When everyone else was assembled, I brought only Ian, Halorn, and Isabelle.

Other than Erik and Connery, Sabine had brought no guards, not even Antonio. It was one in a series of choices to show that this was a family affair.

"It's a pleasure to see you again, Lim." Halorn bowed to me. "This is amazing." I knew he was referring to his visit to a new world and not the room.

"You look beautiful," Isabelle smiled, but her eyes were wary as she took in the surroundings. She wore a fitted black suit. Underneath, instead of a shirt, was a series of thin gold chains that cascaded down her chest.

"Incredible." Ian's eyes were darting to the windows. I could tell he was itching to get out and explore. "And yes, so sorry, you do indeed look breathtaking." He gave me a genuine smile and even bent to kiss my hand.

"Thank you all for coming. I'd like to introduce my family, Tobias, Delia, Keen, and Ayla Revin." The contenders shook hands with everyone, including the children. King Sandlin and Queen Mina had brought gifts for them all, too. Despite her objection to the occasion, I saw Indie snag the bag of Boraltan candy.

"It's for the baby," she huffed.

Once the guests had given many hearty congratulations and well-wishes to Indie and Simon for their impending nyssar, servers began appearing, and we took our seats. To my right, was Halorn and Ayla. Isabelle sat to my left and Ian directly across from me. A blank-faced Erik stood with the other guards near the two doors to the room. As the room warmed, I really regretted not putting on another pair of underwear. His eyes slid to me like he knew what I was thinking and feeling, but his face remained impassive.

"I'm positively dying to know how you ended up here," Isabelle asked. Mina, along with Sandlin and Ian, were luvits, so she kept a foot near Isabelle's, while Sandlin handled Halorn. Sabine relied on Indie and Connery to translate.

With some additions from Simon (who I'd strategically placed across from Isabelle to give her someone new to look at) Indie, and Connery, I provided a redacted version of our trip from Trevesten to Lashia. We left out the cuffs and the fact that the humans had magic too, saying only that we'd been trapped here until I'd received my power.

"But wouldn't that make you a third life? Not a second?" Halorn asked.

"I'm sure you've noticed the drag on your power since you've been here?" Simon asked.

The others nodded their heads uncomfortably.

"Things don't work the same in Lashia. Staying here, without frequent trips to Malan, will drain you. Possibly even remove your power completely. Until Lim got this new power, we'd been living almost as humans," said Indie.

The others looked horrified, particularly Sandlin. "Like humans? Powerless?" He grimaced. "You poor things."

"Indeed." I sighed a little too dramatically and Isabelle cocked her head at me. Simon coughed to cover up his snort of laughter.

The servers removed our salads, and we moved on to lamb chops and seared cod.

"Do you really have dragons in Boralta?" Ayla directed the question to Halorn and Sandlin.

Before they could speak, I answered. "Not dragons Ayla, wyvern. They're different." Taking a sip of my wine, I bobbed my head in apology to Sandlin for interrupting, but he, having half a lamb chop in his mouth, shook his head congenially. Chiara had begrudgingly told me that Rakesh didn't see who had forced him to make the portal and whoever it was, they didn't seem to understand that Rakesh couldn't predict where he'd end up. Based on that, we had to believe Halorn didn't know the dragon had appeared in Marias.

"Dragons have four legs and two wings," Halorn explained. "Wyverns have two legs and wings that are attached to their arms, like a bat." He cocked his head. "Do you have bats here?" He was again drinking only water, but I also noticed his food was not only equal in size but also in taste, each one containing the same amount of each item.

"Yes, obviously, we have bats," my mother said in exasperation. Halorn looked chastised, and Isabelle smirked.

"And wyvern are much smaller," Sandlin added. "At least that's what we're led to believe."

"Do you have other songs like One-Eyed Clyde, then? My sister says she taught it to the Lashians." Ayla made a dubious expression to show how truthful she found my claim. I was pretty sure there was no power behind her questions yet.

My parents, expecting the reference to Clyde, laughed. "That song is very popular with children and people who have had too much to drink."

Sandlin grinned. "It's the same in Malan, I think."

"How come there's not a similar song for wyverns?" Ian asked. "Where are their fun songs?"

"Since the wyvestri see them up close and personal, along with their very sharp teeth"—Sandlin snapped his mouth playfully at my mother and Ayla—"they're less likely to romanticize them in song."

"Has a wyvern ever fallen in love with a fae? Because that would probably do it," Ayla asked, spooning a large helping of mashed potatoes on her plate.

Isabelle cackled, but Halorn tipped his head up. "I suppose that would do it. But if I think too long about Koli and Claudius, my head hurts."

"Why?" Ayla asked innocently.

Ian hid a smile while Halorn threw my mother an apologetic look as he stammered a response. "Because, uh, that part of their relationship was difficult to picture, since she wasn't a dragon."

"Yeah, why would he fall for a woman who couldn't...?" She raised her eyebrows comically. I couldn't feel her power since she wasn't using it on me, but this was how she'd rehearsed it with Antonio. My father rolled his eyes and my mother turned herself an effective shade of pink in feigned embarrassment.

"I don't know. Certainly magic... uh... makes things possible. And they loved each other very much..." Halorn was the same color as the curtains and looked desperate to change the subject.

Isabelle gave Halorn a sneering look, but came to his rescue. "When you become queen, Lim, do you have any grand plans for the country?"

Across the table, I'd shared a look with Sabine at Halorn's response. If he didn't know Koli's true nature, that didn't rule him out as someone who could control wyverns, but it made it less likely he was her heir.

"Seeing as this just happened, maybe give her a chance to catch her breath, Isabelle," Mina said.

Indie, next to Mina, said, "She's probably going to educate you all on the ridiculousness of arranged marriages."

"Indie..." I sighed.

"What? I'm not allowed to say anything?" She shoved a bread roll in her mouth and chewed insolently. My mother crossed her arms as if she too would like to join Indie in her objection.

"Think of it as more of an alliance than a marriage. It can become wonderful." Sandlin gave his wife a loving look. "But it's about stability between our two countries. Since, unlike any of the others, we share a land border."

"And," Mina added, "since Lim is obviously so close to you, it will benefit Lashia as well, to have more friends in Malan."

Indie stabbed a piece of broccoli, but didn't argue.

After dinner, Sandlin beckoned to a guard who stepped forward with the documents. He arranged them neatly on a nearby table. I'd already read my copy, but on Bastian's vehement advice, read them again to be sure nothing had changed. Behind me, the air was charged. My friends and family were holding their breath, waiting for something to stop me.

Wordlessly, I picked up the pen and signed my name. With the last letter, I felt the magic seal the agreement, and the potential consequences. Isabelle, Halorn, and Ian, along with the other contenders, had already signed.

There was a flicker of motion in the corner of my eye, but if I looked at Erik, I might have cried. And then Sabine and Connery would object. Part of me felt relieved, though. Doing this would ease the last of my guilt. And seventy-five years wasn't that long if I got at least one more life. I stole a surreptitious look at three of my potential spouses.

It would be okay. It had to be.

Putting on my most cheerful attitude, I sat back down at the table and ate a large piece of chocolate cake.

41

After the party, I wanted to send everyone straight home. But I'd promised to be a good hostess and give everyone a tour. Considering I didn't live in Chelsea, it was going to be a very short and boring tour. Nevertheless, everyone reassembled in front of the hotel the next morning. Sandlin and Mina looked excited. Halorn was staring at the buses in amazement, and even Isabelle looked curious.

"It's more advanced than I thought it would be," Ian said.

Indie crossed her arms, and Connery snorted. But the muddy-skinned shifter's face was full of good intentions, so we let it go.

I shouldn't have worried about not knowing any of the landmarks or history of the place. The others were far too interested in asking questions about the distinctly human things they saw. Simon took the lead in answering Halorn's questions about how engines and telephones worked, Indie explained germs and surgery to Isabelle, and my parents discussed farm-to-restaurant life with Sandlin and Mina.

Erik stayed within arm's distance the entire time, but we didn't speak. Instead, he and Ian entertained Ayla and Keen by shifting into their animal forms and doing tricks. Apparently, Ian was comfortable enough showing us his wolf.

Once I'd felt I'd sufficiently discharged my duty, I said goodbye to everyone and sent them all back to their respective fae courts. Erik wanted to stay, but I reminded him he still had a job. But mostly, I didn't want him to see when I broke. The whole marriage and queen thing was looking startlingly real. The entire event had drained me more than I realized, and spent the rest of the morning in bed, staring at my ceiling. Brax head-butted me before resting his head on my stomach.

"Buck up, at least you're not a dog," He said in that smooth and pompous voice of his.

That evening, I moved automatically, pouring drinks and running food without paying much attention to what was happening around me. Outside, it was a beautiful night. The moon's mournful face lit up the streets and the faces of people standing outside The Peregrine.

At one point, Audre passed me a grilled cheese and gave me a bracing look. It took me a minute of staring at it to realize it wasn't for a table but for me. She'd tried to thank me, but as was the nature and habit of our friendship, I told her it had nothing to do with her and to stop being so emotional.

But I smiled at her and gratefully stuffed the cheesy offering into my mouth. My stomach grumbled like I'd been ignoring it for days.

Just as I swallowed the last of it, the air sirens started.

Indie had them installed after the first attack. They were hand-cranked and sat at the tallest buildings in each borough. When one went off, the rest were supposed to copy and soon the air was full of discordant wailing.

I jumped outside to see not one but four dragons circling the air. These were not twisting in pain like Rakesh, but still looked like they were fighting the control. Their wings didn't pump smoothly, and they flew erratically. Halorn had chosen children this time. No doubt because they were easier to control.

"No," I whispered, fear gripping me as a familiar dark blue dragon came into view. Oyo was listing to his right, his movements stilted with none of the quick playfulness I'd seen before.

"The soldiers are already organizing." My father's voice was alarmed but strong.

"Tell everyone that we know the dark blue dragon." We'd told the soldiers that their lives were the most important, but that the dragons were not attacking us willingly. I watched in horror as Oyo sent out a deep red flame, scorching the sky and temporarily dyeing the moonlight red.

Someone smacked me on the shoulder as they rushed outside, hastily shoving on a green armband. Others poured out from nearby homes. I itched to run toward the dragons, but that wasn't my role. As the only person who could remove them, I had my orders.

Simon had identified places within each borough where I could safely pull the dragons. We'd traveled to each one, making sure I could easily jump there when necessary. The dragon, however, didn't seem interested in flying toward the other boroughs. They hovered over Marais, darting away from the air-wielders' defenses and circling the buildings.

I jumped to my parents' field. Two seconds later, Chiwel, Leo, and Simon stood before me.

"Ready?"

The three of them nodded their heads, forming a circle. I pulled Halorn from wherever he was in Malan into the center. He was shirtless and wearing pajama pants. Leo grabbed him around the shoulders. Simon braced himself for Halorn's defenses, prepared to fly at any moment. But I used my power to keep him in the circle as Chiwel reached out and grabbed his hands.

"What in the Mother is going on?" Halorn shouted as he struggled against us. His eyes widened and his face paled as Chiwel applied the blue cuffs blocking his power. We ignored him as we all looked in unison toward the sky.

Nothing changed. The dragons still flew in that stuttering way. They were still being controlled.

My eyes flashed to Halorn. "You're not controlling them, are you?"

"What are you talking about? Get these things off me!" His words died off as Oyo flew close, headed toward us before twisting back on himself, roaring in opposition.

"I'm trying, Oyo, I will get you home," I yelled, ignoring the dragon etiquette. "Fight it!"

"Help!" Oyo's voice was so small, so much like Keen's when he was younger.

"Damn it," Simon said, "if it's not him, who is it?"

"It's Isabelle," Halorn said. His face was still pale as he looked down at the glowing blue cuffs on his forearms.

"How do you know that?" I asked. One of the other dragons, a pale yellow one, got too close. Flames shot into the air as the museum roof began to burn.

"I told you, all the contestants research each other's powers. Isabelle can control the wyverns. Much better than this." He nodded to the dragons. "I had my people plant some rumors that I could do it too, to see if she'd start digging." He frowned again at his cuffs. "Apparently, it worked a little too well."

"Fine," I said, rubbing a hand down my face. "Stand over there. I'm bringing her here to us."

"I can help you, if you let me. I'm a rozko." He gestured at Chiwel in silent demand.

"He means he can manipulate size," I explained.

"What do you think?" Chiwel asked.

"Seems like a useful guy to have around," Leo said, watching the dragons swoop overhead.

I nodded. "If you betray us, I can send you *anywhere* I want. Clear?" He nodded and I swear something like respect bloomed in his eyes.

Chiwel undid his cuffs. We stood in a circle again as I pulled Isabelle to us.

Nothing happened.

I tried again with the same result.

"What's happening?" Simon looked at me with concern. "What's wrong?"

"I don't know. The power is there, I can feel it."

"Can people block you? Stop you from using your power?" Leo asked, his head cocked. We all turned as another building went up in flames.

"I don't know. I can't wait while we figure it out. Halorn, you're with me." I sent the others back to their respective homes and jumped the two of us to my assigned field. My father checked in a few minutes later and I explained the problem.

A dragon the color of a shining amethyst was roaring just outside the field. In every sound she made, I could feel her pain and fear.

"I'm trying to get you to me and I can send you home to the Voden." Her golden eyes landed on me in the field, and she twisted her body, pumping her wings to aim for me. She gained speed and roared, the fear in her expression replaced with pure determination.

"I don't think she's coming to you for help," Halorn said, his hands raised.

He was right. She was aiming for me on purpose, and this time, there was no fight in her against Isabelle's control. Isabelle wanted her to attack me.

"I knew I didn't like her," I said before explaining to Halorn what I needed to do. When the dragon was almost close enough for me to pull, Halorn's hands reached up, and she slowly but surely shrank. The closer she got, the stronger his power was.

Out of the corner of my eyes, I could see the other dragons in the distance. I pulled, my power reaching out and wrapping around her.

By the time she skidded to a stop, she was the size of a large wyvern and I leapt onto her before jumping us to Makome.

This time, I remembered to jump out of the way, saving myself from further head injuries. Chiara wasn't in the amphitheater. Only a single dragon guard stood looking out into the distance.

I screamed as loud and as shrilly as I could. That ought to have annoyed enough of them close by.

The guard roared and advanced on me, but stopped when he saw the purple dragon thrashing for control.

"Wake the Voden and subdue this dragon. A fae named Isabelle is controlling your dragons and sending them into my world. You have to stop her or the dragons she's sending may die. The humans will defend themselves."

I didn't wait. I jumped back to the field, and a very confused Halorn.

"I'm sending you to Indie. She can jump too, but not between worlds, so you'll still need to get the dragons to me. But she can get you to them to help." He opened his mouth to speak, but stopped when I held up a hand to silence him. "Use your powers to keep them as small as possible, but try not to hurt them."

Halorn blinked but said nothing more before giving me a firm nod. When he was gone, I pulled Audre to me.

"You got one, right? I just told your Dad that Oyo and the green one are fighting it better than the yellow one. We should focus on that one." Audre was sweaty, like she'd been far too close to the dragons or the fire-wielders.

"Good. But right now, I need you to get to Makome. Take Erik too."

"Okay, why?" Her fingers flew over her chest as she spoke, checking her knives and stars were secure.

"I can't pull Isabelle. She's got a lot more control now. But it would be stronger if she were in Lashia. I don't think she'd risk getting stuck here, but she needs to be close."

"So you think she's in Makome? Near the portal?" Audre's eyes squinted out over the swamps to where we'd seen the dragons first appear. "Not that close, at least."

"Yes, you need to find and stop her. Tell the dragons to only send the biggest and strongest to fight her."

"Done."

I sent her to Trevesten. Audre could jump to the portal to Kysalt, and then to Makome. It would likely use most of the power I'd given her.

The sky was alight with fire from the dragons and the wielders. Water wielders were putting out the fires as soon as the dragons started them. Smoke wafted over Marais, reminding me again how badly we needed this to end. The people of Lashia had already had enough of fire. I knew it wouldn't take much to turn their gratitude for the fire-wielders to resentment.

Taking a deep breath, I jumped close to the yellow dragon. He flew directly past me, his great long teeth on full display.

"Hey! Hey! You're looking for me!" I shouted up at him.

His head snapped back toward me, and I jumped. Every hundred yards, I stopped and beckoned him again. Over and over again, each time I felt myself tire like I was running sprints. He followed me, hissing his annoyance and streaming fire at my back. Jumping again to the middle of the field, I threw up thanks to the Allmother that the purple dragon had not reappeared.

Turning, I watched as the dragon tucked its wings and dived for me. Halorn had shrunk this one as well. When it was close enough, I pulled it toward me, aiming it so its fiery snout passed me and I could grab onto its leg.

We rolled into the amphitheater again, but this time, it was full of dragons.

Erik and Audre were already there. The guards were dragging the yellow dragon into a cave on my left.

"They're sending us with Egan and another tracker to find her. The dragons think she's using velvetleaf to stop you from portaling her to Lashia," said Erik. I didn't miss the way his eyes examined me for injury.

"Of course she is." I winced, rubbing the smoke from my eyes. Something warmed brushed my side, and I opened my eyes to find Morag holding a wet cloth out.

"Thanks, Morag. This is just soaked in water, right?" I asked, eyeing the cloth suspiciously. He nodded cheerfully, and I applied it to my face, sighing in relief.

"If we can grab her, you can pull the both of us. According to the dragons, that should be enough to get her to you," Audre said.

"How will I know when to get you?" Out of the corner of my eye, I could see Chiara watching me, but she made no move to come closer. The other dragons were rapidly talking amongst themselves or eavesdropping on our conversation.

"We'll send you a signal," Audre replied.

Erik pulled me into his arms while Audre gave Morag a curious look.

"Do you need more people? To take her?" I wasn't sure I knew any of the guards well enough to pull them to me, except for Antonio. It would distract Audre to have Morgan here. Pulling Connery seemed like asking for trouble.

"Don't worry about us. We can do it." He gave me a bracing kiss and one of those cocky smiles of his before turning to Audre. She grabbed his arm and jumped.

42

When I hit the ground in Lashia again, there was already a green dragon hurtling for the field, Oyo close on its heels. Using the same maneuver I'd used to get the last dragon, I jumped back with him to Makome.

Oyo had disappeared when I got back. The fires were mostly out and Marais was strangely quiet. The sirens had stopped.

"No. Please, no," I jumped toward the center of town, searching for the dark blue dragon. I practically ran into the group of fire-wielders who had downed Oyo. Pushing through the crowd, I yelled for them to stop. But when their faces turned toward me, there were no triumphant expressions.

Halorn came flying over to us. Both of us stared at Oyo, who was still breathing but covered in angry red lash marks.

"We weren't aiming for him. He dove into our fire instead of away from it. Like he was trying to get burnt." A young woman with blond hair said. I had the vague thought that her name was some kind of flower.

"Healers!" I yelled, pushing my own hands against Oyo's side. Me and two others pushed our power into the dragon's hide, while Halorn shrunk him even farther, until he was the size of Brax. Everything was moving too slowly. The bleeding in his beautiful scales, the bruising on his stomach, even with every last drop of my healing ability, it had barely come together when I saw a firework go off in the sky.

Now or never.

I grabbed Oyo and Halorn and jumped to Makome. It hurt to breathe. I would need to rest soon. I left Oyo in the amphitheater with Halorn, hoping the dragons could help the rest of his injuries. My power was waning, and I was exhausted. The dragons circled us as I pulled Erik and Audre to me.

Erik gripped Isabelle by the neck with one hand and twisted her arm behind her back with the other. Her nails dug into his arm, hard enough to draw blood. Audre held fast to Isabelle's other hand while Isabelle's fire burned into her skin. Aided by Simon's impervenan power, my friend's clothes burned and her skin bubbled, but it did not break. Still, the scent of melting flesh was stomach-churning. Erik's eyes watered as they held Isabelle, who looked incensed.

This close in proximity, her power was considerably stronger and the dragons surrounding us no longer felt like protection. But Chiara's eyes flashed as she eyed the first fae in millennia to control them. Two smaller gray dragons reared back, their eyes angry. They surged forward and blew a torrent of fire at us. Halorn held out his hands, and the fire shrunk to a third of its size, barely missing us. Spotting him, Isabelle laughed.

"I should have known. You and your fucking bedtime stories." She got a hand free and used her air power to push a barrage of pebbles toward him and me. Half a dozen pelted my face, no doubt leaving a pattern of ugly bruises and cuts. After all the random scrapes and injuries I'd already experienced tonight, my share of Simon's power was gone.

Erik wrested her hand back, and she dropped to her knees, Audre falling with her.

"Get them out of here!" I yelled to Chiara, and she took off. The other dragons grabbed the gray ones who were struggling against Isabelle's power. But as they lifted off, one of them broke free and dove straight for us. This time, I jumped too slowly. The talon at the end of its wing caught me in the side, and I bit back a scream of pain as I felt blood soak my apron.

"Get ready," Halorn said. He stepped to my side and put one hand on the wound. His healing power shot out from one side while he used his other hand to launch a precise blast of flame at Isabelle. I took the opening. Ignoring the dangerous way my skin ripped, I lunged for her hands. She screamed as she felt her power ripped away by the cuffs. Erik and Audre dropped her, letting her fall forward as she stared in horror at her hands.

"Damari bitch! He's not here to help you!" She pointed at Halorn, who had disappeared from my side.

Erik and Audre flanked me, weapons out.

"What is she talking about, Halorn?" I pulled my flames up, but they were weak. Where was Morag and his gross salve when you needed him? The slice I'd received from the dragon had stopped mending when Halorn took his hands off me.

But Halorn wasn't listening to me. There was an intense fervor in his gaze. It was so at odds with the measured precision I'd come to expect from him.

"He wants to marry you so he can control Boralta and Makome. He thinks you're Koli's heir." Isabelle spat blood into the stone beside her, her face full of contempt but not defeat.

"Oh, and your intentions with Lim were so honorable?" Audre asked, pulling a star from her belt and keeping it trained on Isabelle. But she, too, was watching Halorn closely. "You can come back now, Chiara. We got her," she said in a clear voice.

"I thought you were Koli's heir?" I said, confused. Halorn was really creeping me out. He'd jumped up onto the dais and was holding something out over the stone. A piece of fabric. Looking down, I realized it was a piece of my bloodied apron.

"I am distantly related to her. But Koli and Claudius died from the heartbreak of never getting to have the child they deserved. The Voden must be kin to them both. Don't you see? You can help. This world can live again. We can rule together." He gave me that too calm smile again. I was starting to suspect Halorn was some kind of psychopath. My memory flickered. He'd been the one to suggest I replace Morgan.

"That's not what happened," I said. My tone was gentle, the way I'd speak to Ayla when she was little and seconds from a tantrum. He'd been telling the truth when Ayla compelled him. But wherever he got his facts, they'd been twisted horribly. "They didn't love each other. Koli forced Claudius. She cursed Makome because she knew she'd lost."

"Don't bother. He's believed all of that nonsense forever. I thought he was just naïve. Until we found out you could portal. Clearly,"—she gestured to the dais where Halorn was muttering to himself— "you're not shit. But if anyone is ruling the dragons, it's going to be me." Isabelle flexed her fingers, concentrating. Was she strong enough to remove the cuffs? "Thank you for that ridiculous interrogation, by the way. Once I knew where my first dragon showed up, it was easy to have them track your scent."

Erik's sword was already out and pointed it at her throat as he gave her a look that said he'd enjoy ending her. Audre spun her two stars with similar enthusiasm.

Chiara's massive green body descended on the amphitheater. Before any of us could do anything, The Voden sent out a flame so hot it was blue. It rushed from her throat, lighting the sky and warming the air. Isabelle didn't even have time to scream. Only a pile of ash remained where my potential future spouse had been.

"That saves me some effort," Erik said under his breath, but his eyes were still trained on Halorn. Erik ascended the dais, getting closer to where Halorn walked the platform as if looking for something.

Chiara said nothing before taking off again.

"Wait," I called after her, but the Voden didn't even look back. Isabelle was gone. Why was she leaving? Not that I thought we'd be best friends or anything, but I didn't even get to ask if Oyo was okay.

"Why isn't it working?" Halorn said, bringing our attention back to him. He'd dropped to his hands and knees and scrubbed the stone with the bloodied fabric.

"This guy is deranged," Audre muttered beside me. "Can we just leave him here?"

Part of me wanted to agree, but he had helped us in Lashia. Believing in magical stories that didn't quite work out was something I was a little familiar with. And the dragons had closed all the portals. The only ones open were the ones Isabelle had forced the dragons to create anew, and I assumed, but couldn't be sure, they'd be in the same place.

He suddenly strode for us. "You went to Laloten. You were born of human parents. It's supposed to be you!"

Erik stepped in front of me. "You're going to stop right there," Erik's voice rang with authority. The tip of his blade was a breath from Halorn's chest.

He didn't even seem to notice Erik, but he did stop. "Koli and Claudius's child was powerless," he explained. "Claudius brought it to Laloten where its deficiencies would be normal."

"Crazy and rude," Audre said, scoffing at the insult. Her body was taut, but her arms shook with slight tremors. The fight with Isabelle had taken a lot out of her.

"And again, untrue," I added. "Athena told me the child didn't live long and Claudius disposed of it." As the words left my mouth, I realized they were not quite right, backward. Athena said Claudius disposed of the child and it didn't live long. "Wait a minute. You're saying he brought it to the human world, and that's where it died?" To a dragon, a human lifetime was nothing, barely the blink of an eye.

Erik's eyebrow rose and Audre frowned.

"The two of them vowed that Makome would not thrive until their descendant was Voden. Koli sealed it with her blood."

I doubted Claudius had anything to do with that vow. Koli must have known she was dying. Claudius may have already taken the child to Lashia, and she cursed him in a last ditch effort to control him.

Halorn was examining my body in a way that made me supremely uncomfortable. "You're the only fae that can portal, just like the dragons. And you were born in Laloten." A vein was popping out of his forehead. The revelation that I was not heir to the dragon throne was really bothering him.

"Right, well. Sorry. It's not me. So we're going home." I edged away. "Do you want my help getting to Boralta or not?"

Erik still had his sword trained on Halorn. But one minute, he was pointing at his chest, and the next, his leg, then a massive toe. Erik stumbled back and Audre ran to my side as Halorn sprouted up like a gigantic oak tree, his skin stretching to accommodate the rapid growth.

He was twenty feet tall. Then thirty. The three of us ran for the mountain. Before we could reach the opening, Halorn's hand wrapped around me, squeezing me until I thought I would pop.

"Lim!" shouted Erik.

"Put her down," Audre spun a star straight toward him, and I ducked as it landed just below his eye. He barely blinked as the smallest pinprick of blood appeared. He lunged and grabbed her as well. She changed into progressively smaller people, but he held on tight.

I needed to pull Halorn to Boralta. But wasn't sure I could do it on my own. The amount of power I'd given Audre wasn't strong enough for her to jump much more, but she could help me. If I could touch her.

"I'm not trying to hurt you, Lim. I just need you to stay here until I figure this out." Halorn adjusted his grip on me and I sucked in a breath at the momentary relief. My head spun as he reached down and wiped my blood on the stone again. Nothing happened. "Damn!" He gripped me hard again in his frustration, and I felt the tear along my side break wide open.

"Stop squeezing me!" I said as I pressed a hand to my side and pushed the last of my healing power through. The fire in my veins rallied, and I burned the skin surrounding me until Halorn loosened his grip. But now I was in a cocoon of acrid, peeling flesh. My stomach clenched as my last meal threatened to make an appearance.

Halorn was limited by holding on to the two of us, but he still sent waves of fire at Erik as he flew high above us, circling Halorn's enormous head.

Stars popped in my eyes. He had tightened his grip, distracted by Erik's attack, and I was losing circulation. Just as Erik dove for Halorn's eye, I sent every drop of fire I had into the blackened flesh. Flecks of blood and blackened skin coated my clothes. Erik transformed back in time to drive his sword directly into Halorn's eye. There was a squelching noise as it dragged down his iris, Erik weighing it down from the other end.

Halorn bellowed in anger. "That's totally uncalled for. I'm trying to help you, Lim." Every dragon in Makome must have heard him, but still, they did not come. He dropped me, slapping his charred hand against his bleeding eye.

Before I hit the ground, I jumped to Audre. I didn't even blink before jumping all three of us into a cave. Breathless and dizzy, I grabbed onto Erik and he held me upright.

"We can't risk him coming to Lashia," Audre said.

"Agreed." I looked at Erik. From this close, the flecks of deep gold were visible in his eyes.

"Give me your orders, baby." He gave me a twisted smile, and I felt it in my chest.

"I might be able to pull him to Boralta if Audre and I work together. I'll come back for you once my strength returns. Who knows, maybe,"—I made my voice annoyingly shrill—"one of the dragons we just helped could give you a ride! Or," I said in a softer voice," you can find Isabelle's portal and fly through."

Audre snarled, casting her eyes outside where the dragons should have been helping us. "Seriously. What the fuck kind of thanks is this?"

But Erik just pulled me in for a kiss, his hair brushing against my face. "Good luck."

Not wanting to waste a moment of magic, we ran to Halorn, leaping onto his foot, my hand clasped in Audre's.

The Boraltans screamed as we crashed into the stone pavilion outside the castle. Halorn tripped, his foot coming down hard on Audre's leg. There was a sickening double crack, and she screamed. He stumbled, and I dove out of the way, my body crying out in pain as I slammed into and over a low wall. I grabbed my side, shocked at the emptiness I found there. The hole was far too deep, my skin held together only by the tight strings of my apron. Blood soaked my right side from stomach to thigh.

The wyvestri shouted, but they stopped, no doubt confused at the sight of Halorn and unsure of the threat. The rocks dug into my back as I watched a normal-sized Halorn fly off above me, straight toward the castle.

On the other side of the wall, there were rising sounds of curiosity but less panic.

It wasn't the same. This time, there were no shadows at the edge of my vision. Instead, the glittering jewels of the Boraltan castle winked at me like stars. Those orange glass orbs hung from the endless balconies and the smell of sugary pastries filled the air.

Grabbing the wall, I hauled myself up and opened my mouth to shout. Audre's eyes found mine, and she smiled in relief. Another healer noticed me and began running forward.

"Too slow. At least I'll be on my feet this time." My voice was nothing more than a slurred whisper. Audre's eyes widened, and she tried to get up, throwing off her healer in her attempt to get to me.

Did Erik make it back? Would any of the dragons help him? Was Oyo okay?

Looking up, I thought I could see them flying toward me. But then, all at once, as if swept away by the same cool wind that washed over me, the jeweled stars winked out.

43

ERIK

BORALTA, 7727

It was a sprawling country estate. It had six buildings, not including the stables, and walls of windows, all of which were lit by the glowing glass orbs so favored by the Boraltans. Erik flew up to her balcony to perch on the ledge.

He'd been inside, once or twice, while the family was out. Only to check that it was enough. The furnishings were rich, the place warm and welcoming. Her family knew what she was, what she meant. When her power developed enough for them to be sure, they'd alerted King Sandlin. He'd immediately notified Sabine.

Sabine sent mapmakers to get her picture. Erik hadn't looked. Audre had confirmed it was her. Both Trevesten and Boraltan law forbid them from contacting her. Not that they would have. She wouldn't recognize any of them, and from experience, he knew that shit could hurt. The family was out right now, so Erik allowed himself a glance into her room. Stuffed wyverns, a fireproof bed, and building blocks.

Not his Lim. A child and a stranger.

He ruffled his feathers. He'd considered going with her. But Morgan and Sabine wouldn't hear of it and his power, unlike Lim's, wasn't unique enough for any of them to be able to find him without a royal tattoo.

So, instead, he mourned her as if she were truly gone. He'd done some catastrophically stupid things in his grief. More than once, Connery and Audre pulled him out of a fight he definitely would've lost. He'd even tried to learn to cook, with some atrocious results. The palace chefs barred him from the kitchens after the last time.

The dragons agreed to leave the portals to Lashia and Boralta open. Even after Audre refused to lower her voice as she told the dragons quite extensively what she thought of their failure to help. At least the Revins wouldn't have to watch an empty fish tank, not knowing what had happened.

And she had Brax.

The chimera had appeared at the gate to Adnatia palace six months after her funeral. The guards had let him in and he'd headed straight to Erik's room to find him neck-deep in depression. He couldn't speak to Brax, but he was pretty sure the beast had called him a pathetic loser.

He could have been projecting.

Brax disappeared a month later when Erik was finally dragging himself back into the world. Somehow, she'd brought the animal to her. Or perhaps he'd tracked her all the way to this home beyond the Gyemain mountains. There were little strands of dark red hair on her bed, along with patches on several of the stuffed wyverns where needle-like teeth had chewed on them.

Four years down, twenty-one to go.

The bedroom door opened, and he stilled. But instead of a strange child, it was Brax. The chimera entered as if he already knew Erik was there and gave him that same chastising look.

"I'm going, I'm going," Erik grumbled as he took off into the night. He left her alone to enjoy her childhood again, ignorant that three of their seven worlds were anxiously waiting for her to grow up.

Soon we'll find out how good Erik is at waiting!

The last book in the trilogy, All the Hidden Things, is available now for pre-order!

If you'd like a bonus heist scene and other magical content, head on over to my website to sign up for the newsletter (or scan the QR code below). The newsletter is the best way to find out about bonus content, new releases, and other fun stuff!

ACKNOWLEDGEMENTS

Endless appreciation to my beta readers, Whitney Weatherly and Tessy Dockery, every single ARC reader, my editor Amanda Oraha, my husband for your constant patience with me as I navigate this weird new chapter, and every person from whom I demanded adjectives and synonyms completely without context. Here is the context. Thank you to all the new readers who have reached out, especially my newsletter subscribers. It makes me feel warm and fuzzy every time. Writing is equal parts terrifying and fantastic and I'm having *such* a good time.